to fans of Debbie Macomber and other contemporary Americana authors."

"Winning and humorous . . . [in the] manner the ever-popular Michaels always employs in her believable and highly entertaining tales."

#1 *New York Times* bestseller!
THE NOSY NEIGHBOR

"A humorous, rollicking tale of adventure and intrigue."

"A tense thriller. . . . Fern Michaels provides an interesting paranormal romantic suspense thriller that never slows down."

"An exciting read with lots of witty banter between the characters."

CROWN JEWEL

"A wonderfully heartwarming, compelling story about families and the lock the past can have on the future, *Crown Jewel* is a grand drama of discovery and love."

"Long-buried secrets cause tension and emotion to run high."

"A story of forgiveness and personal redemption . . . [from] the prolific Michaels."

NO PLACE LIKE HOME

"Uniquely charming . . . bursting with humor . . . this warm-hearted confection is as soothing as a cup of hot cocoa."

THE REAL DEAL

"Exciting contemporary romantic suspense. . . . The exhilarating suspense plot is filled with twists. . . . Will appeal to fans of Nora Roberts and Jayne Ann Krentz."

"If you are seeking a story of passion, suspense, and intrigue . . . *The Real Deal* is the perfect choice."

LATE BLOOMER

"Michaels does what she does best [in *Late Bloomer*]. . . . Entertaining, action-packed . . . fun to read . . . engaging romantic suspense."

"Heartwarming . . . *Late Bloomer* is nothing short of wonderful. You won't want to put it down."

FERN MICHAELS

THE
DELTA LADIES

POCKET BOOKS
New York   London   Toronto   Sydney

Pocket Books
A Division of Simon & Schuster, Inc.
1230 Avenue of the Americas
New York, NY 10020

This book is a work of fiction. Names characters, places, and incidents either are products of the author's imagination or are used ficticiously. Any resemblance to actual events or locales or persons, living or dead, is entirely coincidental.

This Pocket Books paperback edition September 2008

POCKET and colophon are registered trademarks of Simon & Schuster, Inc.

For information about special discounts for bulk purchases, please contact Simon & Schuster Special Sales at 1-800-456-6798 or business@simonandschuster.com.

Cover design by Lisa Litwack.
Cover illustration by Alan Ayers.

Manufactured in the United States of America

17 16 15 14 13 12 11

ISBN-13: 978-0-671-79917-5
ISBN-10:   0-671-79917-7

Chapter 1

At an altitude of five hundred feet, a pilot could expect to experience occasional patches of scudding clouds misting against the windshield and ruffling like hazy feathers as they were chewed in voracious bites by the twin-engine Beechcraft. But the day was cloudless, the sky a vibrant blue. The early morning sun had scorched away the sporadic tufts of cloud and blazed through the cockpit, giving off a steady, baking heat that even the direct flow from the air vents could not dispel. It was a glorious day, the kind of day Cader Harris associated with dropping a baited hook from the fertile banks along the river and snagging a pike, or, with extraordinary luck, a meal-sized catfish. It was a good day for returning to his hometown of Hayden, Louisiana.

By squinting his eyes and looking off to the west, Cader could see the long stretch of hard-packed clay leading to the black-topped strip of the local small-plane airport. A glance at his fuel gauge assured him he had another fifteen minutes of flight time before the spiky needle pointed to empty. On a sudden whim, he banked to the left twenty degrees, heading east now, away from the airstrip. He hadn't called in to the flight tower for permission to land as yet, and he allowed his impulses to take him on a long, slow circle of the town. From his increased altitude of seven hundred feet, he imagined he would experience a new perspective on the place of his beginnings.

There, on the Louisiana Delta, on a lazy spur of the Mississippi flowing into the greater waters of the Gulf of Mexico, rested the town of Hayden. The white-spired steeple of the Baptist Church, circled by an expanse of new, lushly green lawn and dotted at its rear by neatly tended tombstones, was easily discernible. A peaceful town, populated by some fifteen thousand upright, law-abiding citizens, it was named for Jatha Hayden, its founding father, and had carried his name proudly for nearly one hundred seventy-five years.

Cader smiled to himself. Seen from up here it could be any small town in the country. The myriad styles of architecture from the Greek Revival to the New England saltbox represented a kaleidoscope of life styles. Even seen from the ground Hayden could have been anywhere in the continental United States, with its street names like Magnolia Drive and Chinaberry Circle, and Sunday dinners of fried chicken and pecan pie. But Cader knew it was the people, their values and prejudices, the highs and

lows of their humanity that made Hayden what it was—
just another town.

Cader's sharp eye caught sight of the narrow strip of
railroad tracks that divided the town. Deliberately, he
veered his Beechcraft again, preferring to remain on the
north side of Hayden, away from the overgrown tracts and
rows of ramshackle hovels where he had been born. Instead, he concentrated his attentions on the more favored
side of Hayden, the scrupulously tended lawns and neat
rows of houses.

Cader remembered the markers the Junior Women's
League had erected amid the tree-lined streets that de-
noted the supposed, rather than the exact, location of such
historic and memorable events as: Jatha Hayden House,
first established homesite, or the Jatha Hayden Library,
founded by Jatha and Cloris Hayden, nestled in among
other interesting and necessary tidbits of the town's history.
Cader's back teeth clenched and he grimaced in a way
that passed for a smile. In new-found, mature understanding he realized the only thing "historically accurate" about
these markers was that the ladies agreed on where they
should be placed.

The blacktopped roof of the Jatha Hayden High School
tipped into view. Cader had attended the school for four of
the most important years of his life: four years of fame and
glory on the football field that eventually led him to college and ultimately into the flamboyant world of pro ball.

While a young student at Hayden High, Cader's ability
for football had come into prominence. In spite of his poor

beginnings, coming from the wrong side of the tracks as he did, he drew the notice of Foster Doyle Hayden, the last living descendant of the founding father to carry on the Hayden name. Football had always been Hayden's obsession, and when Cader had come into the limelight during his high-school career, Foster Doyle noticed him, taking vicarious pleasure in the young man's success. Rumor had it that Cader had been offered a scholarship to Tulane University and had accepted it.

Cader's mouth tightened to a grim line. Some might call what he'd done "selling out." Cader preferred to call it cutting his losses. And when Cader cut his losses, he cut everything, including Irene Hayden, Foster Doyle's white-skinned, golden-haired daughter. Irene, the original golden girl, with the autocratic temperament of a thoroughbred racehorse and the lusty appetites of a high-class whore. When Foster Doyle told Cader that Irene was pregnant with his child, Cader saw all his ambitions going down the drain.

Expecting Hayden to ride his back and demand he marry Irene, Cader visualized a future with himself under Foster Doyle's imperious thumb, running the bases at the man's whim. Instead, Hayden floored Cader by offering him an escape—leave town . . . never see Irene again . . . and Cader would be rewarded with enrollment at Tulane University, tuition and all expenses paid, not to mention a very healthy allowance paid to a bank once a month.

Escape . . . a way out . . . a path with which Cader Harris was very familiar. More than an escape . . . a dream . . . something he'd wanted all his life and always believed was beyond his reach.

Tulane . . . the gem of the Southern universities . . . money for clothes, a car, enough left over to see to his drunken father's support. All he had to do was agree to Hayden's bargain.

Still, there was Irene to consider. Hayden had sneered at Cader's hesitation. Irene had a position to maintain and the family name to consider. Irene's problem could be solved.

Cader hadn't been able to reach an immediate decision. He loved Irene, but the lure of escaping his humble beginnings to the upper echelons of Tulane, paid for and supported by Hayden, was impossible to resist. He would have everything going for him. He already had the magazine looks, the physique to wear the magazine clothes and the athletic and sexual prowess to bring it all together. He would be a star! A football hero! Pursued by the girls, envied by the guys.

To Cader's own amazement, breaking ties with the hometown had proved to be difficult. While in attendance at prep school to gain the necessary credits to enter the university in the fall, he had subscribed to the town paper. It was there he learned of the surprising marriage of Irene Hayden and Arthur Thomas. The news depressed him. Despite the enthusiastic female attention surrounding him, his thoughts still clung to Irene. He admitted a sense of loss, a heartfelt regret, yet upon reflection he was relieved to have made his escape with so few scars.

One evening, after football practice with the Tulane

team, he happened to read the Hayden paper. In the social column was the announcement that Irene Hayden Thomas had given birth to a son, Kevin Hayden Thomas. A quick count on his fingers gave him his answer. A son. His son.

When Foster Doyle had proclaimed he would "take care of everything," Cader had assumed he meant an abortion for Irene.

Looking out of the cockpit down on the town of Hayden, Cader brought himself back to the present. Somewhere, down in that green patchwork, was his son. A boy known as Kevin Thomas. And Cader would see him, find him.

He had merely cut his losses, Cader justified; he hadn't really traded Irene and his son for a chance to cross the tracks into acceptable society. And he'd kept his bargain, until now. Not even when his father had died had Cader returned to Hayden. Not that he would have been so inclined anyway. But he had kept his bargain, and if in a weak moment his conscience pricked him, he knew with supreme arrogance and utter confidence that with a snap of his fingers he could cancel it all out and Irene would come running. So far, he hadn't had to draw on his one last reserve; he'd never snapped his fingers.

Having flown beyond the limits of town, the landscape below had become low, flat plains; he was over the truck farms that skirted Hayden. Six or seven miles to the south the tall stacks of the catcrackers belonging to the Delta Oil Company were visible and the eternal flame of the flare-tower smoked hotly into the noonday sun like an angry, fire-breathing sentry. In a natural progression of thought,

Cader smiled, squinting against the glare bouncing off his windshield as he accelerated his Beechcraft toward the offensive sight of gray steel and blackened machinery and sterile girders that were the Delta Oil Company. One thought just naturally seemed to follow the other these days; old man Hayden, the granddaddy of us all, and good ol' Delta oil.

Long before he approached the blackened Erector-Set construction of the oil refinery, Cader glanced down and was able to pick out the wide, three-mile strip of beach and the hundreds of acres of pampas grass behind it that were the bone of contention between the magnates of Delta Oil and the citizens of Hayden. It was there, on what had always been referred to as Jatha Beach, that Delta wanted to erect those ominous-looking and lethal-sounding, liquid natural gas holding tanks.

Although the title and deed for the innocent playground of the young people of Hayden rested in the town's hands, Foster Doyle Hayden, last living descendant of the original founding father to carry on the name, was bitterly opposed to the plan. His opinion weighed heavily in the small, sleepy town.

Foster Doyle Hayden was pleased when he heard himself referred to as the genteel, soft-spoken, white-haired town father. He was a paternal figure, upheld for his civic responsibility and generous endowments to *his* town. He was a paragon, a model of virtue. Secretly, he likened himself to Teddy Roosevelt, speaking softly and carrying a big stick.

On more than one occasion the members of the town

council, on which he served as president, had seen Foster Doyle's big stick. And on the matter of Delta Oil's infiltration into the town, they had felt it.

Foster Doyle was a reactionary of the first order. All argument proclaiming the economic advantages Delta Oil would bring was lost on him. He liked the town as it was, sleeping and submerged, untouched by progress. Delta Oil's intrusion would mean a change. Any commercial growth would involve an influx of trade and people into *his* town. If Delta Oil meant growth, and growth meant change, Foster Doyle would have none of it. He didn't want to lose control of Hayden to a pack of upstarts with revolutionary ideas and possibly more money than he had to see those ideas to fruition.

Foster Doyle was confident of his control as it now stood. The council understood his thinly veiled threats, just as they were meant to. They comprehended his stated concern that the new medical center could be delayed indefinitely; that financial contributions for the library's new wing and various and sundry other pet projects of the council would never see the light of day without his financial support.

The town of Hayden rested in Foster Doyle's gnarled hand, a hand that could close like a vise if and when he chose. Delta Oil needed someone to combat Foster Doyle's influence. Who was better for the job of turning opinion in favor of the LNG (Liquid Natural Gas) than Cader Harris? A native-born son of Hayden, retired from a football career in which he became a national hero and pride of his hometown, Cader filled Delta Oil's bill. He was a handsome, vital man of thirty-six, irresistibly attractive to women, while at the same time considered a "man's man." Delta considered their problem practically solved.

The title of Public Relations Advisor was dreamed up by Cader himself. It was meant to salve his conscience, while in truth Harris needed no second urging, trumped-up title or no. He had too much to gain to be concerned with scruples, even if the least of these advantages was the easing of the life-long grudge he'd carried around with him against the town of Hayden and its democracy-loving citizens. Cader saw his position with Delta as an ideal opportunity to retaliate for the hurts and slights he had suffered at their hands while he was growing up among them. He'd make them accept those natural gas tanks, accept them and love them even. And then he'd take the money and run and never look backward to see if those great gray giants ever blew up in their faces.

Revenge wasn't the only reason Cader jumped at this chance. The success or failure he brought about for Delta was tied in with his own personal success or failure. He knew what it meant to be a "has-been." The popularity Delta Oil insisted Cader enjoyed in Hayden was not indicative of the status he experienced beyond the town's limits. The high salary and financial rewards he'd earned as an athlete had been lost to extravagance and poor management. All that remained was several thousand in the bank, this twin-engined Beechcraft given to him by the enamored daughter of a manufacturing scion who expected love in return for her generosity, and a rapidly crumbling identity. Cader knew there was no middle of the road. You were either a "somebody" or you were a "nobody." Money went a long way in ensuring you the former status.

A quarter-of-a-million-dollar commission and a contract for commercials and advertising endorsing Delta Oil would have been inducement enough for Harris to set fire to the whole damn town, let alone *persuade* them that the LNGs would be *good* for them.

Just thinking about it caused a fine beading of perspiration to moisten his upper lip. Taking his powerful, sun-gilded hand from the stick, he wiped it away. He knew this was do or die. The end of the road. He knew he couldn't make that uphill swing from nobody to somebody again, no matter what. This was his last chance and he had to make the best of it. A sinking, gut-churning feeling, like a steel rod stirring his insides around, hit him full force. The way things had been running these last few years he'd need everything Lady Luck could blow his way. It was almost as though he had grease on his sneakers and he was on a downhill slide. This was it, everything, and he *had* to make a good job of it. Delta Oil was his salvation; indeed, it had become his redeemer.

The faint cough from the right engine caught Cader's attention. Immediately, his eyes flew to the fuel gauge. Empty. Just enough reserve to land. Christ! Just when he almost had it all, it would be just his luck to daydream his way into a tailspin and finish his life where he started it—in the rubble outside the limits of Hayden. He reached for the headset and adjusted it, tuning for the air control, requesting permission to land.

*   *   *

Sunday Waters brushed her long, honey-blond hair out of her eyes and concentrated on guiding her blue Mustang down the quiet, tree-lined street. She gently pressed the clutch with her neat, white-sandaled foot as she glided to a stop at the corner light at Jatha Hayden Boulevard and Leland Avenue. A quick look at the gold circle on her wrist and she sighed with relief. She was early for her appointment with Marc Baldwin, the gynecologist.

With her slender hand on the gearshift as she waited for the line of traffic to move on Hayden Boulevard, she caught sight of a low-flying plane circling over the high school. Narrowing her light blue eyes against the glare of the sun, Sunday leaned forward and peered up at the craft. She supposed it was one of the crop dusters who earned extra pocket money by taking on aspiring students who were bent on earning their pilot's license. However, on closer examination, the plane didn't appear to be one of the patched and repatched disasters the pilots around Hayden used to spread their insecticides on the crops.

A pinch of memory nearly caused her to stall out the '72 Mustang. A memory of Cader Harris and herself stretched out in the tall grass skirting the airport, watching the planes take off and land on the steaming, sticky blacktop in the midday heat of summer. Cader had always been crazy for anything connected with flying, and he had dragged her out to that landing strip more times than she could count to watch the fragile machines soar into the air and to listen to their engines sputter and finally roar to life as they wound up for takeoff.

The tall, scratchy grass would whisper all around them, concealing them from passers-by. The millions of insects hiding there with them would often sting them in buzzing protest at this invasion. But Sunday would have cheerfully walked into a snake pit with Cader Harris if she could lie there beside him and watch the excitement mount in his dancing dark eyes and know that soon, when he had had his fill of watching the aluminum birds sweep the sky, he would turn to her, take her in his arms and teach her to fly even though her bare little ass never left the dry, sunbaked ground.

Sunday was lifted from her reverie by the sight of a young boy and two girls approaching the boulevard. How young they were, as young as Cader and herself all those many summers ago. God, was she ever that young? Of course she was, but she had never looked like the young-sters approaching the crosswalk. They were Ivy League, spit and polish, Ivory soap and Crest toothpaste. She had spent her teen-aged years wearing made-over dresses from her aunt who lived in New Orleans. New clothes and even decent meals took second place to Bud Waters's daily con-sumption of liquor.

She recognized the young people as they neared the curb. Kevin and Bethany Thomas, Arthur's children, and Judy Evans. Sunday blinked when she saw Kevin throw back his head and laugh at something his sister had said. A knot of nostalgia tightened in her chest. She remem-bered being carefree and smart and having someone look at her that way. Cader Harris had when Sunday had been his girl—his blond and bouncy and wonderfully happy girl. Until he tried to make that leap across the tracks into Hayden's inner circle via Irene Hayden who could open those doors for him. Sunday sighed; one way or another, even without Irene, Cader had opened those doors. And the result was the same; Sunday had been left behind.

The Mustang bucked slightly with the pressure of her foot, and as the children passed the car, Sunday noticed the proprietary look in Judy Evans's eyes. Young romance, she mused to herself, as she eased the car onto Jatha Hayden Boulevard. And what was that glimmer of hostility on Bethany's face? Sunday frowned. If she hadn't known they were brother and sister, she would have marked it down to jealousy. Now what the hell did that mean? Whatever, it was none of her business. Sooner or later their father, Arthur Thomas, would tell her every niggling little problem riddling his family. It was impossible to have an affair with a man and not be aware of his problems. If they were problems. And somehow, in her gut, she knew the Thomas kids were a problem. With Irene Thomas for their mother, how could it be otherwise?

Stopping for yet another traffic light, Sunday let her eyes travel the length of the boulevard with its patriarchal sycamore trees. Everything looked normal and tranquil. Yet she fully expected that at any moment the world would turn upside down. Cader Harris was coming back to Hayden. To open a sporting goods store, rumor had it. She had been serving the usual Scotch and water to Gene McDermott in the Lemon Drop Inn where she worked as a cocktail waitress when Neil Hollister broke the news. It was a miracle her hand remained steady when she placed Gene's double Scotch in front of him. Neil had said he was writing up a feature story on Cader, and he knew the wire services would pick it up. Then he had winked at her and grinned. "Stud Harris," he had laughed. "Every woman in town will either run for cover or else they'll become overnight sports buffs." Sunday had remained silent, smiling vaguely, trying to hide the fact that her heart was leaping up her windpipe.

Why was he coming back to Hayden now? After all this time? Oh, she'd heard that tale about the sporting goods shop, but Cader wasn't a merchant type. Unless he had changed drastically over the years, he'd never make a go of it. A business took time, effort and money. Money was something Cader had always been short of, saying it was something to be spent and enjoyed; let someone else take care of the rainy days. Still, after a career like his, money should be the least of his worries. Maybe he had changed now that he was older and settled. But somehow she didn't believe Cader Harris had changed one bit.

Behind her a horn sounded, and she pushed the clutch to the floor and moved with the traffic. She still had ten minutes to make it to Dr. Baldwin's office for her monthly Pap test. Now, there was a man, she thought. Marc Baldwin. Attractive and virile, and no doubt a master of a woman's psyche. She shook her head to clear her thoughts and pulled into his parking lot, obeying the sign that said to park "head on." *A Freudian slip, doctor?* She laughed to herself. It was funny, but she had never thought of Marc as making known his sexual preferences. She had always thought of him in the context of complying with a woman's preferences. Lucky Julia, Marc's wife.

Sunday stepped from the car and smoothed her cornflower-blue dress over her hips. She knew it matched her eyes perfectly and did wonderful things for her complexion and honey-colored hair. Squaring her shoulders, she headed for the Medical Building, which housed an ophthalmologist, two dentists, an optician and, of course, Marc Baldwin's ob-gyn offices.

When Sunday stepped into the cool of the air conditioning, she frowned slightly when she noted Marsha Evans sitting at the reception desk. She chastised herself for making her appointment on Marion's day off. Sunday didn't care much for Marsha. She couldn't say why, exactly; Marsha had always been very pleasant and never looked down her patrician nose at Sunday for being a mere cocktail waitress. Still, it was hard to read Marsha. All the signals got crossed somehow.

"Hi, Sunday. Marc will be ready for you in a bit." Marsha smiled, her voice soft and friendly. "Have a seat. It must be getting really hot out there."

Sunday forced herself to answer politely. She found herself actually clenching her back teeth to keep from spitting out the replies. Why did Marsha Evans have this effect on her? Going one step further to hide her hostility, Sunday volunteered, "I just saw Judy crossing the boulevard with the Thomas kids. She looked so pretty, all smiles and giggles."

"I'd guess she had a lot to giggle about," Marsha

answered, looking at Sunday levelly, her dark green eyes holding a soft, maternal humor. "The last day of school. Remember how that felt, Sunday? Three long months out of jail to play and swim and have a good time?"

"Yeah, I remember," Sunday answered, reaching impatiently for a dog-eared magazine and pretending to see something of profound interest in its pages. She supposed Marsha hadn't meant anything in her remark about fun and swimming and good times. Maybe that's what *her* summers were like, but there was nothing in what Marsha said that even faintly resembled Sunday's summers. Hers had been an endless chore of taking in ironing with her mother and slaving away in the tobacco fields while the sun burned half her brain to a crisp, and forgetting what it felt like to stand up straight until someone came along and cracked her back so she could hobble over to the truck that would take her back to town.

Sunday was suddenly nervous. Even the quiet beige tones of the waiting room couldn't quell the jittery feeling creeping over her. Cader was coming back to town.

A buzzer sounded on Marsha's desk, and she closed her appointment book. She fixed a crisp, professional smile on her face and walked into the examining room, her hips swaying seductively in the white uniform.

Sunday sighed as she looked around the office. Besides her, the only other patient was an older woman whose name eluded her at the moment. Discarding her hastily chosen magazine, she reached for one with a new-looking glossy cover, relieved to note it bore the latest date. Leafing through the silky pages, something caught her eye. The caption read, "Is it possible—the multiple orgasm?" She suppressed a smile. You betcha! Her smile widened to a grin. Once, when she was in high school, she had had a triple with Cader who almost went out of his mind as he matched her, O. for O. So much for novices who claimed it was merely a myth, she thought smugly, closing the magazine and tossing it onto the glass-topped table.

Was it warm in here or was it her? She noticed the soft hum of the air conditioner. No, it was her. Gently, she brought her fingers to her cheek, careful not to smudge the rosy blush on her high cheekbones. She felt flushed. Even as she thought of the word, she had an instant vision of herself disappearing down the bottom of a filthy toilet and Cader Harris pushing the handle again and again as he laughed down at her. *Flushed, all right, right down the old john.* Well, that's what he had done, wasn't it? When he'd gotten that "too good to turn down" offer to attend Tulane. She wondered vaguely if she were running a temperature. God, she couldn't get sick now, not with Cader coming back to town. *And,* she reminded herself, *I have to stop by Arthur's funeral home.* "Damn!" she muttered, why had she promised she would stop by today? For the hundred dollars, she admitted with rare honesty. Pap tests every month were expensive, not to mention the douches when you used them as often as she did. Besides, the extra money would come in handy just about now. There was a stunner of a dress in the Monde Boutique that would knock Cader's eyes right out of his head.

She shrugged. As fly-blown as she felt today, she would

keep her promise to Arthur. He needed her and in some small way she was able to make him happy, temporarily, until he went home to face his wife, Irene Hayden Thomas. Well, there was nothing she could do about his home life. Everyone had problems. It seemed enough for Arthur that Sunday offered him her friendship and a quick piece of ass in the casket display room. Funny thing about that though, Arthur had become a special friend to her. It had nothing to do with the money he pressed on her and she readily took, it was much more. He had become someone who was really interested in her, in what she was feeling. Sunday had shared some of her most personal secrets and fears with stodgy old Arthur Thomas and, most important of all, he seemed to care. At least he never laughed at her, not to her face anyway. She was bursting to tell him that Cader was coming back to town, but somehow she knew she wouldn't. How could she admit, even to herself, that even after nearly twenty years she could still get herself into a flap at just the mention of his name. Eighteen long, frustrating years since she last saw the tail end of Cader Harris. What would Hayden's wonder boy think when he saw her now that she lived on the right side of the tracks and wore the right clothes and makeup?

"Sunday, Dr. Baldwin will see you now," Marsha Evans said in her most professional tone as she stepped aside to allow Sunday to pass into the examining room. "You know the procedure; you can hang your clothes there on the rack. There's a fresh gown on the shelf. The doctor will be with you shortly."

Sunday's eyes narrowed and she shot Marsha a quizzical

glance. Was that some kind of crack, that bit about, "you know the procedure"? You could never tell with Marsha. Sometimes butter would melt in her mouth, and other times she could be as caustic as the lye vat Granny used for making soap. Stepping into the cool, almost cold, examining room with its austere stainless steel fittings, Sunday reached behind her and shut the door with emphasis. As she struggled with the long zipper on the back of her dress, she wondered why Marsha's remark should rub her the wrong way. So what if she was a fanatic about these Pap smears? Wasn't it a known fact that her own mother had died of pelvic cancer that was discovered long after there could be any help for her?

And Ma had been a good woman, she thought as she wrestled with her panty hose, not like . . . me! She finished her thought with determination. Admit it. Ma always said only women who lived sordid lives got diseases in their female organs. Ma's shame about the cancer had almost been greater than her pain and fear of death.

Marsha Evans stepped back into the confining cubicle just as Sunday was folding her panties and placing them neatly on the little swivel stool. She handed her the pale blue paper gown and tied it at the neck after Sunday pushed her arms through the arm holes.

"It'll be a few minutes yet before Marc is ready to see you," Marsha explained. "Have a seat. Would you like a magazine while you're waiting?"

Sunday shook her head. "I'll be fine."

Marsha heard the phone on her desk buzz and made a quick, smooth exit.

Sunday lowered herself onto the stool and crossed her elegantly long legs. She wanted a cigarette but knew Marc wouldn't approve.

Being naked under the tissue gown made her vaguely uneasy. Being here in this sterile atmosphere was different from being naked in her apartment or being naked with a man. Here, she felt exposed.

She could hear Marsha's voice speaking to a patient on the phone. Her voice was softly modulated, quite unlike the harsh scream Sunday knew she was capable of. During their high school years Marsha was a member of the cheerleading squad. Sunday laughed to herself. This was the fourth time in a single hour that she had paused to reflect on those long ago days. She supposed hearing about Cader's return to town had everything to do with her turn of thoughts.

As she listened to Marsha's voice, her thoughts spun back again to when she was a freshman in Jatha Hayden High School.

The day had been warm for the end of September, even by Louisiana standards. Notice had been posted on the bulletin board that tryouts for the cheerleading squad would be held on the athletic field immediately after school. In honor of the occasion Sunday had changed to her least faded pair of shorts and had carefully whitened her broken-down sneakers with shoe polish the night before. More than anything, she wanted to make the squad. She knew she was good. Her slim, graceful body was agile and when she made her jumps and splits her thick, honey-blond hair would bounce appealingly.

Sunday knew looks counted and was optimistic about making it, but she had certain apprehensions concerning Irene Hayden, the stuck-up captain of the cheerleading team, and her covey of cohorts, which included Marsha Taylor and Julia Wilson. But they had always been nice to her, even if there was a distinct flavor of condescension in their attitudes. Sunday wasn't in their league and she knew it. More important, they knew it too. Girls from the wrong side of the tracks just didn't find a welcome in the ranks of Hayden's leading families' darling daughters.

At the far end of the football field the Jatha Hayden High School Band marched through its paces, the sound of the snare drums setting the beat, the blare of the trumpets reverberating through the air. On the bare clay patch near the bleachers the contenders gathered, observed and measured by Mrs. Hurley, the girls' gym teacher, and the existing cheerleading squad. Sunday saw Irene Hayden watch her arrival on the field. Sunday lifted her chin and smiled a greeting that was ignored by the modishly dressed Miss Hayden. Marsha Taylor and Julia Wilson sat on either side of the squad's captain, and both of them gestured a greeting. But Irene's eyes were hard and cold and appraising.

A commotion of masculine voices startled Sunday and, turning to her right, she could see several members of the football team gathering to feast their eyes on the bare legs and sweatered bosoms of the contenders for the two open positions on the squad. A bright golden head caught her attention, and she knew without looking that it belonged to Cader Harris, Jatha Hayden's star player. She heard Rudy Barnett's jeering comments as the first girl went through her routine of cheers. Sunday flushed pink. Why did Rudy Barnett have to be here now? Rudy, with his leering eyes and coarse comments and groping hands. He played fullback for the team, and his influence over the guys was second only to Cader's. Sunday hated Rudy. He was a pig. Only last week he had followed her home, trailing behind her in spite of her determination to ignore him. Long ago, Sunday had learned that boys like Rudy Barnett thought she was an easy lay. And what infuriated her more than anything was that their opinion was derived more from where she lived than from what kind of girl she was. Girls born and bred in the row of shacks lining the tobacco fields always had a rough time of it, and Sunday was no exception.

When Sunday was next in line to go up, she glanced into the bleachers and saw Irene Hayden whispering to Marsha and Julia. Their giggles and stares told her that she was the subject of their laughter. Sunday wanted to run off the field, but then her eyes fell on Cader. He smiled at her encouragingly, his eyes squinting against the sun, his strong teeth flashing. In spite of her self-consciousness, Sunday smiled back. Cader Harris had always been one of her favorite people. Even though she came from the row of shacks on the other side of town, he ignored her reputation. The few times he had even spoken to her she had gotten the feeling that he liked her.

Mrs. Hurley was calling her name. She was up. After

a quick glance into the bleachers and seeing the expression on Irene's face, Sunday knew she wasn't going to be picked. She had seen Irene's curious glance move to Cader and then back to Sunday. It was as simple as that. Sunday Waters was a loser again.

She went through the cheers mechanically. Her voice cracked as she yelled the familiar cheer, and she shrank from the puzzled frown on Mrs. Hurley's face, a frown that said Mrs. Hurley knew Sunday was capable of a much better performance.

A titter of excitement trilled through the other contenders as they waited for the results to be called. Sunday sat alone, her heart sinking lower and lower. She hadn't made it. Of that she was certain. She hadn't done her best. She had been put off by Irene's glaring looks and Rudy's lewd comments.

The two girls were picked and called amid a clapping of hands and hoots from the boys. As she had predicted, she was not named. Not even as a substitute. Sunday slunk off the field, heading for the locker room and the showers.

The locker room was empty, as she had anticipated. She kicked off her sneakers, now smudged with dirt and clay from the field and, with a true aim, they landed with a rumble in the bottom of her locker. Impatient fingers tore at the button at the waist of her shorts and pulled them down over her slim, curving hips. As she sat on the long bench to tear off her socks, her emotions welled. *It isn't fair! It isn't fair!* The injustice of it all overwhelmed her. *If* she had been born a Hayden, not a single boy in town would have had a word to say about her, even if she were the biggest put-out in the school. *If* she had nice clothes and lived in a nice house like the rest of the girls, she would have been accepted. *If* Irene Hayden wasn't such a snot, she would have had a better chance of making the squad. *If* Cader Harris hadn't looked at her and *if* Irene hadn't seen him, she wouldn't have been the object of ridicule, and she could have done her best. *If! If! If!*

Furious with herself, she slipped the light sweater over her head and fumbled with the clasp of her bra. Impatiently, she slipped her arms through the straps and twisted the garment around so the hooks were at the front. She stepped out of her panties and grabbed the thin, frayed towel she kept in her locker.

The showers were empty and would most likely remain so. All the other girls had nice houses with nice bathrooms and indoor plumbing. The best thing about school was being able to take a shower, even in the winter, when the water from the pump at home would freeze to a thin layer of ice in the dishpan unless it was left heating on the stove.

The needle-sharp spray stung her shoulders and the steam rose near her feet. She wouldn't think about the cheerleading squad. She'd been dumb to think she could have made it anyway. Besides, if you were a cheerleader, you were expected to look nice all the time. Her two outgrown dresses and three skirts and four blouses didn't exactly compose a wardrobe. And then there were the homecoming dances and the Varsity Hops. . . .

A sound echoed through the hiss of water. Turning to the

doorway, she almost fainted when she saw Rudy Barnett and his cronies leering at her.

"Get out of here, Rudy Barnett," she screamed, "and take your trash with you!" She turned to face the wall, conscious of her bare behind exposed to their gaping stares.

"We didn't know you were in here, Sunday. Honest! Right guys?" His voice betrayed him as a liar. "We just heard the water runnin' and we came in to shut it off. Right guys?"

"I don't care what you're here for. . . . Get out!" She was crying, humiliated.

They knew she was alone in here. They had come after her. Silently, she prayed.

"Now, Sunday," Rudy mocked, "why don't you shut that water off and bring your lil ol' ass over here? We only want to see if that's all you. We got a little bet ridin' on it. Some of the guys don't believe that's all you under those tight sweaters. . . ."

"Get out!" There was hysteria in her voice.

"I told them that was all Sunny Waters in those sweaters. I told 'em how I ought to know, only they don't believe me." Rudy spoke smoothly, sneeringly, threateningly.

"You don't know anything, you pig. Now get out of here!"

"Come on, Sunny, don't make a fool out of me in front of my friends. All we want is a little fun, right guys?" She heard his step on the tile floor and pressed herself closer against the wall. "All we want is a little of what you're givin' to everybody else. It's for the good of the team, ain't it guys?" There was a low rumble of voices and jeers and taunts.

"Let's see it, Sunday, c'mon. Just let us see it, we won't touch you, right guys?"

"Please, leave me alone," Sunday pleaded through her tears and the rushing water. "Please, leave me be. . . ."

"You heard the little lady," a voice strong with purpose, in contrast with Rudy's wheedling, echoed in the shower room and contracted the muscles in Sunday's back. "Now get your asses out of here and make sure I don't hear of you pulling another stunt like this. Leave her alone and that goes for now as well as later."

"Christ, Cade, we didn't mean nothin'; we was only havin' a little fun," Rudy whined.

"I don't give a shit what you thought you were doing. Now get out of here!" His voice rang with authority.

Vaguely, through her terror, Sunday recognized the shuffle of feet leaving the shower room. She crumpled to the floor, her face hidden in her hands. Her whole body was in flames of humiliation.

She heard Cader moving through the shower room and realized he had turned off the water. Her towel fell over her. "Sunny, Sunny, I'm sorry this happened to you." His voice was soft with compassion and closer than she would have imagined. She took her shaking hand away from her eyes and looked up into his. He had dropped to one knee beside her. "I'd give anything if those animals hadn't done this. If I'd known what they were up to, I would have stopped it long before this. Better not come into the locker room alone for a while. Okay?"

Her head nodded automatically.

"Now get yourself dressed. I'll be waiting for you out-side the door. I'll walk you home so those guys don't get any funny ideas. You gonna be all right? Should I get Mrs. Hurley in here to help you? I wouldn't want to get the guys in any trouble, but you could say you were feeling sick. . . ."

Sunday shook her head. Her voice became unstuck and sounded feeble. "I'll . . . I'll be all right."

"You sure?" His hands closed over her shoulders, helping her up. When she looked up into his eyes again, she saw that he held her gaze, being certain not to allow his eyes to wander.

When she heard him close the door behind him she set about dressing. She wanted to get out of the shower room, out of the lonely locker room. She wanted to be out of the school. Out of Hayden itself. If she let herself think about what had happened, she knew she would die. *Not here, get home. Just get home.* The thought of the dark little shack on the other side of town became her target. *Just get home.* Never before had she realized how comforting that word could be. Home.

Cader held true to his word. When she stepped out into the hallway, he was waiting for her. "You don't have to walk me home; I'll be all right." Her voice was shaky.

"I'm going that way; it's no problem." His tone was still soft, compassionate.

She fell into step beside him, her eyes fixed on her old loafers with the now-dull pennies in the slots over the instep.

If the sun was still warm, she didn't feel it. She only felt the warmth of the friendship Cader was offering her. And if there were sounds in the street, she didn't hear them. She was only conscious of the sound of his voice.

"Feeling better?" Cader asked when they were almost to the lane that turned down toward her house.

"No," she answered flatly, candidly. "I'll never feel better again."

"That's no way to be, Sunny. Those jerks can't get you down; you're made of better stuff than that."

"But they *saw* me! They *saw* me!" Her tone rose to a pitch, just below hysteria; her face flushed scarlet. "They think I'm a whore and that I'd put out for anybody. And the truth is I never . . . never . . ." She broke off into sobs.

"Hey, don't you think I know that?" Cader placed his arms around her and soothed, "I know what kind of a girl you are, Sunny. Look, I can't let you go home like this, c'mon." He took her hand and led her onto the dirt road through the tobacco crop. Still crying, Sunday followed, unmindful of the crusty black dirt beneath her feet and the breezes bending the yellow-green tobacco plants that stood sentinel as they awaited a late harvest.

Cader led her to a grassy oasis on the far side of the field over which one lone oak provided shade. Leaning against the trunk of the gnarled tree, he took her in his arms. "Cry, Sunny. Cry it all out."

"I can't cry like that, Cader. It won't come out like that. I'm too mad. Too humiliated."

"Aw, why are you humiliated? You've got nothing to be ashamed about. Don't you know that? You're beautiful, Sunny. The most beautiful girl I've ever seen. You're too good for those jerks and they know it. You watch, they won't be able to look you in the eye, not the other way 'round. You just hold up your head 'cause you know you're too good, too beautiful for the likes of them."

Sunny lifted her head, blue-gray eyes swimming with tears, a look of wonder on her face. She could hardly believe this was Cader Harris, *the* Cader Harris, talking to her this way. She had always liked him because, while he was brash with the other boys, he had always been nice to her. But she hadn't known how kind he could be, how sweet and gentle. Cader Harris was the only boy in school who never frightened her, who had never looked at her as though she were a piece of meat. She had always supposed he had never noticed her, but now, here he was telling her that she was beautiful.

Softly, his lips brushed her cheek. Lighter than the wings of a butterfly, softer than the touch of the sun and gentler than the caress of her mother's hand. Cader kissed her.

He told her she was good, that she was beautiful, and she knew he was sincere. As she leaned her head against his chest, she could hear the thumping of his heart. In that instant she knew that she wanted to belong to Cader Harris. For ever and ever. And with a knowledge beyond her experience, she knew she would give herself to Cader Harris. Soon. Soon. And that would be the happiest day of her life.

Sunday Waters smiled to herself when she remembered that hot afternoon in a tobacco field. Cader had been warm and understanding and caring. He had shown her the person inside the football hero, the gentleness behind the rough exterior, the generosity beneath the selfish facade. Sunday knew intuitively that whatever else Cader Harris displayed to the world, she had seen the real man that day in the tobacco field. Beneath the hot Louisiana sun, shaded by the outspread arms of a lone oak, Sunday Waters had given her heart to Cader Harris.

Marc Baldwin knocked perfunctorily before admitting himself into the examination room. Sunday had seen him only two nights ago at the Lemon Drop Inn; now, somehow, he seemed different, taller, leaner in his white coat with his stethoscope hanging casually from his neck. His dark hair was trimmed to exactly the correct length and his face was still smooth from his morning shave. She could even pick up the faint aroma of his Aramis cologne.

"How are you today, Miss Waters? Any problem or just the Pap smear?" Marc always referred to her as Sunday whenever she met him socially, but in the office it was always "Miss Waters." And it was nice the way he always said, "How are *you* today," rather than using that cutesy medical lingo of "How are *we* today?" He knew how to treat people, especially women, as individuals. He was never patronizing.

"The Pap smear . . ." Sunday said softly, grateful for the fact that he didn't lecture her about the ridiculousness of these frequent tests. He had long ago explained to her that if these checkups gave Sunday peace of mind then she was entitled to his time and patience. She adored Marc Baldwin, just as all the other women who comprised his practice loved him. He was the answer to a woman's prayers. A progressive thinker with a true appreciation for the female species. Women's Lib had invaded Hayden, and Marc's office was littered with appropriate reading material, such as *Ms.* magazine and *Viva*. Even *Playgirl* made its appearance among the copies of *Cosmopolitan*. Not for Marc Baldwin's office were the ragged copies of *Good Housekeeping* or *House Beautiful*. His approach to his patients was friendly and capable and he made them feel comfortable discussing their most intimate problems as he lent an interested ear. And consideration! Marc Baldwin was the leader in his profession as far as consideration was concerned. Didn't he actually warm his instruments under hot water before inserting them into the tensed vaginas of his patients? This alone, the ladies of Hayden agreed, proved that Marc Baldwin was an understanding friend and physician.

Attaching the blood-pressure cuff around Sunday's arm, Marc instructed Marsha to prepare the slide for the Pap test. While the scratchy sleeve swelled on her arm, Sunday watched through narrowed eyes as Marsha took her place behind the stool where the doctor would sit.

"Blood pressure's normal. Now, for your heart." A moment later, "Everything sounds just fine." Stepping closer, the fragrance of his Aramis wafting across the small space between them, his long, gentle fingers probed the neck of the paper gown, exposing her breasts. He lifted her left arm. Tension. Quickly and expertly, his slender fingers probed and prodded. A silent sigh. "Fine, Miss Waters. Now for the Pap test and then you can take advantage of what's left of this beautiful day. It's really getting a head start on summer, wouldn't you say?" he asked, smiling warmly, waiting for her answer, giving every impression that he was interested in her opinion. In truth, Marc Baldwin was prolonging the moment before he began the examination.

"I would say," Sunday answered, her voice tight as she slid down on the paper-covered table and hooked her bare feet into the icy stirrups.

Dr. Baldwin motioned for Marsha to hand him the speculum that had been warming in the pan of warm water in the sink. He lowered himself onto the stool at the foot of the table, his eyes level with the tender pink between Sunday's spread legs. Another examination to get through. Whenever he conducted pelvic examinations on any except pregnant women, he dreaded the ordeal. It was like looking into a bird's vacated nest. Damp and dark, void of all life. During pregnancy, it was suffused with color, a nesting place, a nurturing place, a place of miracles.

Half listening, he heard Sunday say something. "Hmmm," he murmured. *Goddamn it!* Why did all women think they were duty bound to keep up a running conversation while he probed their vaginas.

Marc let his breath out slowly as he inserted the instrument. Deftly, his hand steady, he scraped her cervix and wiped the swab across the glass Marsha held out for him.

Sunday felt the machinations connected with her examination, aware of the slightest touch, even of Marc's breath feathering against the inside of her thigh. There was no shame here, no feeling of being immodest or clinically explored beneath the indecent light which cast its warmth between her spread legs. When Marc Baldwin was at the helm, even the awkward position necessitated by the examination was like a sensuous pose for a girlie magazine. Marc wasn't the kind of doctor who hurried through the exam, tittering nervously and barely touching his patient with his sterile, rubber gloves. When Marc touched you, you knew it. His grip was firm and personal. His attitude confident and unembarrassed. God! Lucky Julia. Here was a man with a true appreciation for the female body, inside as well as out.

"Everything looks fine, really fine," Marc assured her in a deep voice. Inside the dark depths of her own vagina was the one place a woman could never look. It wasn't as if it were her liver or kidneys. No one else could look there either without the help of machines. This was a private place, her own place, where others could look only with compliance on her part and a good strong light. It was the place where she gave and received pleasure during the sex act, the place from which she bore her children. And yet, lovers, husbands, strangers even, could look into the depths of a woman's vagina and see what she herself could never see.

"No sign of irritation," Marc continued. "Good color, a healthy pink. No sign of blood or swelling. Everything looks better than normal."

That was another of the phrases Dr. Baldwin used to make Sunday, as well as his other patients, feel special. "Better than normal." Somehow those words put a woman above all others.

Unceremoniously, he removed the speculum. Sunday

Waters, Marc thought to himself, was the only one of his patients who didn't flinch when the clamp was inserted and who didn't squeal, "Oh, what a relief!" when it was removed. Marc could feel the tension leaving his jaw as he saw out of the corner of his eye Sunday unhooking her feet from the stirrups and sliding backward on the high table to a more dignified position. Jesus, he thought for the millionth time since he began his career in gynecology, why, when he peered into the dim, rosy depths of a woman's vagina, did he always expect to see teeth? Christ! What was it that Sunday was saying about multiple orgasms? He nodded to show her he had heard and made a pretense of studying her words. "Anything is possible, Miss Waters. So many women, unfortunately so, consider discussion about orgasms . . . embarrassing," he managed to choke out before returning to his chart.

Sunday rearranged her paper gown. "On the contrary. I find it very interesting," she bubbled delightedly. "I once had a friend who had a triple orgasm." A sigh from Marsha. "It must be one hell of an experience, don't you think, Doctor?"

Marc Baldwin swallowed hard, his head bent over the chart. Jesus, sweet Jesus. He looked up from the chart, a smile warming his lips, his expression conveying little else besides a physician's concern. "An unforgettable experience, in my opinion." Then, changing the subject, "There's no need for you to come into my consultation office. Everything looks fine. That is, unless you have something you'd like to discuss with me."

Sunday returned his smile. "No, everything is fine in every other department too."

"In that case, have a nice day, Miss Waters."

Back in his office Marc Baldwin sat down on his swivel chair behind his massive desk and turned till he faced the blank wall behind him. *Jumping Jesus!* He got them all. Multiple orgasms, triple orgasms! He wondered if Sunday herself was the one with the triple. No doubt. He swallowed again as he rubbed his temples. This time her vagina had smelled like tangerines. Last month it had been Listerine and the month before that, lilacs. He turned on his chair and wished fervently that the hospital would call, telling him that Sara Stone had gone into labor. Anything to avoid Mrs. Gallagher's pelvic examination. He hated to see the wrinkly, leathery skin of her thighs and the sparse, white hair between her legs. And she always smelled of dry urine. Not to mention that she was the worst squealer of the lot. "Oooh, Doctor! That hurts!" she would cackle and he knew damn well she loved every minute of it. He also knew the day some woman had an orgasm on the examination table was the day he would end his practice.

Marsha Evans opened the door and spoke quietly. "Mrs. Gallagher is ready in room three and your wife called. She said for you to call her back when you have a free moment. I made an appointment for Sunday Waters for next month, and she paid by check."

"Thanks, Marsha. Tell Mrs. Gallagher I'll be right in. Did her report come back from the lab?"

"I enclosed it in her file. It's on your door shelf."

"Marsha, if you'd like to leave a little early today, Mrs. Gallagher is our last patient, and there's no need for you to straighten up. The cleaning woman comes in at five. By the way, Marsha, I really appreciate your filling in for Marion."

"Love doing it, Marc. But I will take you up on your offer to leave early. Today was Judy's last day of school, and I promised we'd go out for dinner."

Sunday exited the doctor's office, her mood lightened now that the examination was over. She knew she was paranoid about uterine cancer, but she couldn't help it.

She backed her Mustang out of the parking space, narrowly missing Mrs. Gallagher's Mercedes. That's what her name was. Gallagher. God, she was old. Imagine having to examine a pussy like hers. Poor Marc Baldwin. She wondered if Mrs. Gallagher would be as uncomfortable in Marsha Evans's presence as she had been. She shivered in the warm closeness of her car and flipped on the air conditioning and headed for Arthur Thomas's funeral home.

First, she would park in the lot and walk toward the drugstore, and, if no one was about, she would go in the back door of the mortuary. She looked at her watch. Four forty-five. A quick one, home for a shower and then on duty at the Lemon Drop at five-thirty. It would be cutting it close, but she had promised Arthur, and she wouldn't go back on her word.

Just as she climbed from her car she noticed Kevin and Beth round the corner and enter the mortuary. *Damn! How long would they stay? At least fifteen minutes,* she told herself. She looked around again and climbed back behind the wheel. She would call Arthur from home and make other arrangements. Later in the week, Friday or possibly Saturday afternoon. This way, when she went to the bank on Monday, she could deposit her pay and Arthur's contribution at the same time.

Once again, she backed her Mustang from its parking place and this time headed for home. She would try to make it Friday.

That way she could feel secure with his hundred dollars in her purse.

Chapter Two

The well-oiled hinges of the mortuary door opened and closed silently. Arthur Thomas looked up from the magazine he was reading and was surprised to see his children standing there. Furtively, he glanced at his watch and prayed Sunday would be late. Of all days for the kids to stop by, why today? "What brings you down here?" he asked heartily.

"It was the last day of school. Did you forget, Daddy?" Beth asked, bouncing over to plant a kiss on her father's fleshy cheek.

"Yes, I guess I did. Still, what are you doing down here? You know your mother . . . I know, you need an advance on your allowances, right?"

Beth laughed, her long, strawberry blond braids bouncing. "No, Daddy, we still have our allowances. Kevin wants to talk to you about something. Tell him, Kev," she said, digging her elbow into her brother's side.

"Dad," the young man said respectfully, his dark eyes grave and glowing beneath his shock of sun-streaked blond hair, "would you mind if I applied for a job at the new sporting goods store that's going to open on Leland Avenue? I saw a sign on the window this morning on the way to school. I asked the real estate agent who rented the store, and she said she had put the sign in the window at Cader Harris's request. It's going to be his store, Dad."

Arthur felt an unreasonable jealousy rise in his chest. It was the way Kevin's eyes sparkled and the way his voice became so animated that caused the cold stab in his chest. The whole town was talking about the returning hero. A sports hero. Just the kind of man a boy like Kevin could look up to, unlike himself who was fighting the battle of the bulge and losing and who didn't know one end of a golf club from another.

When Kevin didn't receive an immediate reply from Arthur, his strong, indomitable chin rose in the air, just like Irene's, Arthur thought. "Southern aristocratic supremacy," Irene would chide whenever he pointed it out to her.

"Look, Dad, I can do the job; I know I can. I've helped out here with the bookkeeping and running errands. And I know I can handle sports equipment."

"Say yes, Daddy, please say yes," Beth pleaded.

Kevin put his arm protectively around his sister's shoulders. "What d'you say, Dad?"

Arthur Thomas knew from the moment Kevin mentioned working in Harris's store that he would have to put a stop to the idea. Irene wouldn't like it one bit. *Her*

children working like common folk? She would find
the idea appalling. But when Kevin put his arm around
Beth, Arthur knew that, for the children's sake, he must
answer yes. They needed to get out of the house, away
from Irene's smothering. Since they had been born, she
had coddled them, kept them apart from other children,
saying they would catch unholy childhood diseases. Finally, after the threat of chickenpox and scarlet fever was
over, Irene admitted the true nature of her obsession concerning the children. According to Irene, Kevin and Beth
were not *ordinary*. They were descendants of a long line
of Haydens; they were a part of her own late, great family of southern aristocracy and should only socialize with
children from similar backgrounds. Arthur's protests were
feeble. He had been so involved in making a success of the
funeral home he had left the child-rearing to Irene. His
children had grown up with only their mother for company,
having outside friends only in carefully controlled doses
and an overbearing, autocratic grandfather, Foster Doyle
Hayden himself. Naturally, Beth and Kevin were close, he
told himself, closer than most brothers and sisters. They
needed each other. But soon Kevin would be going off to
college, and it was time to break him from this mutual dependency. Likewise for Beth. There had been times when
the two of them complemented each other so completely
that one seemed to know what the other was thinking. It
was incidents like these that planted a distinct uneasiness
in Arthur. Sometimes, it even gave him the creeps.

"Please say yes, Daddy," Beth pleaded, her green eyes

sparkling, and the lamp from the foyer making a red-gold nimbus of her long, silky hair.

Looking around the waiting room as he tried to decide upon his answer, Arthur thought of how he hated the hushed quiet and the odor of embalming fluid which always surrounded him. The wire flower stands and the thickly padded carpet all seemed to stand in silent rebuke. The courtesies and gentle ministrations to the bereaved families were painfully dull. This business, this funeral home, had been chosen *for* him, not *by* him. His dreams had been to become a first-rate medical examiner in a bustling city. Noise, confusion, drama: those were the elements missing from his staid, well-ordered life. He had been intent on embarking upon that exciting career when Irene telephoned him at medical school and told him she was pregnant. Pressure and conscience pointed Arthur's short, fat feet in the honorable direction. Gone was the dreamed-of career as medical examiner; in its stead was the humdrum life of the undertaker.

Looking up at Kevin, seeing the excitement and anticipation in his dark eyes, Arthur decided he would give the boy the answer he most wanted to hear. He would do all he could, even confront Irene head on, to save his son from discarding his dreams and missing opportunities. Arthur's fate would never be Kevin's. "I think it's a fine idea, son. It would be good for you. A good way to spend your summer," he added, keeping his eyes away from Beth, thinking that what he really meant was that it was a good way to get Kevin away from Beth and Irene.

"That means I can apply for a job there too, right, Daddy?" Beth chirped, her eyes meeting her father's levelly. "I can work in the ladies' sportswear," she added confidently.

"Now, wait a minute, little girl, there was nothing in this deal concerning your working for Mr. Harris."

Beth's eyes turned to chips of ice. "If Kevin can, so can I," she argued unreasonably. "Why don't we ask Destry what he thinks."

Arthur Thomas turned to see his black associate, Destry Davidson, standing in the doorway.

A wide grin appeared on Destry's face. "Little miss, I never mess in other people's business, especially white folks' business. Your Papa will give you sound advice. There's only two things in this life that I could offer advice on—dead bodies and . . ."

And Aunt Cledie's house of ill repute, Arthur added silently. "Can I help you, Destry?"

"Mrs. Marlowe passed on; the family just called."

"Is she one of yours or one . . ."

Destry's grin tightened and then vanished, leaving his almond-colored face devoid of all expression. "Mrs. Marlowe was the cook and housekeeper at Aunt Cledie's," he said softly.

Arthur couldn't help it; the words were out even before he stopped to think. "That should slow down business for about thirty minutes."

Destry's face remained impassive, but his eyes were mocking when he spoke. "Give or take a few minutes either way."

Arthur cringed. Life did go on. Aunt Cledie wouldn't let

a little thing like death interfere with her thriving brothel— service with a smile, twenty-four hours a day. Jesus, would she close up shop for the viewing and funeral? He knew he should say something, anything. Destry was waiting. "Take care of it, Destry. If you need my help . . ."

"I'll call you," Destry replied coolly as he walked from the room. Why in the Goddamn hell did white people always think a black color would rub off? His gut rumbled as he remembered the first time Arthur Thomas had seen him drain the blood from what he called "one of his own." He had looked shocked when he saw that the blood ran as red as his own! That was a long time ago, and Arthur Thomas had come a long way with regard to the black populace of Hayden. Now, he merely considered them second-class citizens deserving of Destry Davidson.

Arthur blinked, knowing he had somehow offended Destry without meaning to. He was uptight, he told himself. He would apologize later.

"Daddeeee," Beth said through clenched teeth. "Are you listening to me?"

"Of course, I'm listening. Now what were you saying?"

"If Kevin can work, so can I."

"What would your mother think, Beth? You know how she is; she would never agree to your working in a shop this summer." Something had gone wrong here, Arthur thought; he was being conned and he couldn't give one goddamned good reason for telling Beth he didn't want her hanging around Kevin's neck.

"Mama has no choice. I've decided I'm going to work

for Mr. Harris right along with Kevin. Just let her try to stop me!" The girl's lower lip jutted out and her chin rose in defiance.

"Dad's right, Beth," Kevin tried to soothe. "Besides, you've already signed up for tennis and water skiing. You can't back out now."

"Kevin!" Beth whined. "I don't want to spend my summer with a bunch of kids. I want to have fun like you! Please, Daddy," she turned back to Arthur, "don't say no!"

"Beth, honey, there's no assurance either one of you will get the job. Perhaps Mr. Harris wants more mature sales help. And you wouldn't want to narrow your brother's odds of landing the job, would you?" he appealed.

"Kevin won't take the job if I'm not hired too, will you, Kev?" she said with stubborn certainty. Kevin looked at her blankly, and Arthur read the boy's thoughts. Poor kid, he was being torn in two between his sister and wanting the job.

"Now look, Beth," Arthur said sternly, "that's an unfair position to place Kevin in. And it doesn't show much maturity on your part." This wasn't going the way he had intended. The only reason he had decided to confront Irene head on was to get Kevin away from his mutual dependency with Beth. Now she was going to get herself a job working right alongside him!

"I don't care how mature it seems to you, Daddy. I'm going to apply right along with Kevin. And if I'm hired, neither you nor Mama can stop me!" she said hotly. Beth had Irene's angry determination in getting her own way. Arthur knew argument was useless. Sighing, he nodded his head.

"Provided you don't make it a stipulation that both of you are hired. Understand? Beth," he said again, "do you understand? The whole matter rests with Cader Harris." Arthur frowned at the change in his daughter. Her sparkling green eyes were murky, and there was a strong set to her jaw.

"Well then, go to it and good luck. Both of you," he added reluctantly. "I'll see you at dinner, okay? Don't be late. Your mother's going to resist this idea, and we don't want to add more fuel to her fire." He clapped Kevin heartily on the back and lowered his cheek for Beth's kiss, but not before he looked into her bright eyes. He was stunned by the calculating, manipulating look that met his gaze. A chill washed over him as she backed off, her eyes unwavering, almost defying him to say something.

Beth had always been manipulative. From the time she was able to talk she had managed her mother and thought she managed him. It amused him at first to give in to petty little demands. Why was it only he who saw through her shallowness and not Irene or Kevin and, least of all, her grandfather? Another chill washed over him as he stared at his daughter. It was one thing when only he had been aware of her deviousness, but now that Beth was aware of his knowledge, he felt frightened. Frightened somehow for Kevin and for himself. God, didn't he have enough problems? He would deal with it later. Later when he could force himself to take a good long look at what Beth was becoming.

When the door closed behind their excited chatter, Arthur Thomas's shoulders slumped. It was ten minutes after five and Sunday wouldn't show up today. Not if she had to be on duty at the Lemon Drop at five-thirty as was her custom. He would stop by the Inn on his way home and set up another date. He needed to tell someone about these uneasy feelings he got about Kevin and Bethany, and Sunday was always a good listener.

Pastor Damion Conway shifted his long, lean body behind the desk in the rectory of the First Baptist Church. His cobalt-blue eyes focused on the blank sheet of paper before him. He had to concentrate and come up with a soul-stirring sermon for next Sunday's services.

Don't desert me now, he pleaded silently as he raised his eyes heavenward. Lately, it was becoming more and more difficult for him to gather his thoughts together and put them on paper.

He cleared his throat several times, forcing himself to cough. Then he brought his long, slender, artistic hands together, making a steeple of his fingers. *Get on with it,* he scolded himself. *Pick up the pencil and make notes. Anything. Just get your mind rolling.* Viciously, he tossed the yellow pencil across the quiet, masculinely paneled study and rose to his feet. Perhaps a walk to clear his thoughts.

Hands jammed into the pockets of his faded jeans, he straightened his stiff back and gazed out the mullioned window toward Jatha Hayden Boulevard. Damion saw Keli McDermott before she raised her eyes to the rectory window. He frowned as he watched her hand go to her throat. She paused a moment, indecisive, her blue-black hair glinting in the bright sunlight. She closed her door quietly and hitched her arm through the strap of her handbag. She didn't walk, Damion observed as he watched her cross the parking lot, she floated.

When she had left his line of vision, he walked back to his desk and scribbled a few words. "Testing the emotional winds," he wrote. Next Sunday's sermon. Now, all he needed was another nine hundred ninety-six words and he had his sermon.

Unlike the other times Keli McDermott came to his office to deliver the prepared sermons she had volunteered to type for him, he was anticipating her soft knock on his study door. Everything Keli did was soft. She looked soft; she moved softly. Delicate and soft, like a moonbeam on the water. Soft hair, skin silky and the color of a summer peach.

Damion Conway had long since come to terms with the emotional response Keli McDermott evoked in him. A minister was also a man, and a man couldn't help but be moved in some way by the sight of Keli. She was the incarnation of all that was feminine. Even the western clothes she had adopted in place of her native Oriental costumes looked soft and crushable.

She entered his study, an expression of childlike bewilderment on her features. The look was a part of her; she wore it the way other women wore makeup. Damion made no move toward her. He smiled and motioned for her to sit down. Her features became the epitome of Oriental inscrutability as she sank down into the leather chair opposite his desk.

He waited. At times she just sat, saying nothing. When some indeterminate span of time elapsed, she would rise and leave, never uttering a word. At other times she would talk about everything and nothing. Keli had been coming to the rectory off and on for the past six months, and Damion still didn't know what her problem was. Or even if she had a problem. Yet, she presented a picture of pain, willing him with her dark, oblique gaze to make it go away. For the past three months, since she had volunteered to do his typing, she had been coming regularly twice a week. Each time it was the same; yet each visit was different.

He spoke quietly, gently, so as not to frighten her. Gradually, she relaxed and leaned back in the chair, her hands folded primly in her lap and her small, narrow feet planted firmly on the floor.

"You wonder why I come here like this," she said quietly. "It would be simple to leave the typing downstairs with your housekeeper." Her voice was husky, femininely throaty, with just a touch of accent to enhance her sometimes awkward choice of words and phrases. "I don't know why, Damion. It is so peaceful here. Sometimes, when I rise from sleep in the morning, I know I must come and sit. Perhaps talk."

When she spoke his name, she made it sound like two words, enunciating each syllable with gravity. Dami-on, she called him, giving his name an Oriental flavor, making him one of her own. Although her English was nearly perfect, her speech had a cadence that was undeniably foreign, almost exotic. He waited for her to say more. Suddenly, without any outward sign of movement, she withdrew from his presence. Her long sloe eyes closed; her hands gripped each other a bit more tightly. There would be no further words between them, and the silence would become a special kind of communication. Like an oasis in the desert the silence was a balm giving peace and respite from a world where words could become meaningless sounds masking the emotions and abrading the senses. These silences were uplifting; a type of intimacy without touching.

When Damion's eyes went to Keli again, she was staring at him. She had beautiful eyes and the thickest, longest lashes he had ever seen on a woman. He smiled at her. He was here, ready to talk, ready to listen. He said nothing. He knew by some finely-honed instinct that Keli was afraid of words.

She stood, moving away from his desk, away from him and, for the first time since entering his office that day, Keli smiled. Her dark sloe eyes became lit from within and a feeling of sunshine filled the room. Because of him Keli had smiled.

There had been rumblings of racial discrimination against Keli in the beginning, but the "power of the pulpit" had quickly squelched it in one fire-and-brimstone sermon from Damion. When she was gone, he tried to remember what she had been wearing. Something soft. Even the colors eluded him. All he could see was the utter bewilderment and the picture of pain that was Keli McDermott here in the inner sanctum of the rectory office. Someday, he would sit down and write that book, and he knew that his hero would love a girl just like Keli.

The sermon. He must get it done. His mind wandered

again. Was Gene McDermott Keli's problem? Perhaps
Keli was homesick for her family in Thailand, Damion
speculated. No, she would share those feelings. He decided, as he had in the past, that it was retired Colonel
Gene McDermott, USAF, who was Keli's problem.

Hastily picking up the yellow pad and opening the
desk drawer where he intended to stow it, hiding the visible proof that he couldn't concentrate today, he saw the
daily paper he had put there earlier that morning. He
had shoved the news out of his sight, irritated that Cader
Harris was coming back to Hayden. Why not admit it to
himself? Cader Harris's return threatened him in some
way. Cader Harris meant trouble. As if there wasn't dis-
sension enough already with the town's opinion divided
because of those liquid natural gas holding tanks Delta Oil
wanted to install on the beach strip. It was growing into a
heated problem fraught with all the furies of another civil
war. Brother against brother, only this time all the brothers
lived right here in Hayden. As their pastor, Damion felt
his congregation looked to him for unity and guidance. A
fantasy of self-importance, he chided himself, yet in every
fantasy was a grain of truth. So far, he had managed to
remain neutral on the subject, but that state of cowardice
wouldn't continue for long. The Junior Women's League
and the Masons were already clamoring for him to speak
at their meetings, and it had been hinted at that his opinion would be asked concerning Delta Oil.

*What this town doesn't need right now, if ever, is good old
jock Cader Harris.* He was a wise ass even when they had

been in college together. The "punting parson," Cader would tease in the locker room after the games. The nickname had caught on and even the media sportscasters had picked it up and used it over the air.

Use and abuse, that's Cade's policy, Damion thought uncharitably. As long as Cader Harris was *número uno*, all was right with the world. Always *número uno*.

There was no putting it off; Damion gritted his teeth. He supposed he could find Cader at the sporting goods shop. Cader would show those square white teeth and clap him on the back and make him feel like some local yokel while he pinned up photos of all the celebrities he had hobnobbed with during his fantastic career on the gridiron.

The ride to the new sporting goods store belonging to Cader Harris was a short one. The air conditioner really hadn't had a chance to change the temperature inside the black, somber-looking Dodge. All it had done was blast him with the odor of stale cigarette air. Beneath the shade of the striped awning Damion found the door locked and the storefront dark. But deep in the dim recesses he had seen a burgeoning of daylight and decided to walk around the block to the store's loading dock. He stepped over cartons and skirted a stack of baseball bats that were wired together. As he inched his way around a crate of tennis rackets, his eye caught movement in the corner of the back room. "Cade, is that you?"

"Yo! Over here," came the jocular reply. "Damion, you son of a gun, what brings you down here?" Cader Harris said, stretching out his hand in greeting.

"Would you believe to welcome you to the flock?" Damn, now why had he said that? He wanted to steer things away from his ministry; he didn't want to give Cade an easy opening for his jokes. "Don't believe it, huh? How about downright curiosity on my part?"

"You got it," Cader grinned, his square white teeth gleaming in the dark tan of his face.

Damion flinched at the show of teeth. Nobody had that many teeth! It was hot in here despite the dimness. The aroma of leather and new wood, along with excelsior packing, stung his nostrils. Cader muttered something about fresh air, but he made no effort to move toward the door and outside. Damion felt as though he were once again in the locker room; all that was missing was the sweet-sour smell of manly sweat. It was obvious that Cader Harris was once again in his own element. "What say we go outside?" he offered, moving toward the door. He'd get Harris outside beneath God's blue sky, Damion Conway's element.

"You son of a gun!" Cader slapped him on the back. "It's good to see you. Ever get yourself hitched? I didn't think so," he said at Damion's negative nod. "Listen, Damion, Catholic priests are supposed to remain celibate, but not Baptist ministers. Whatever happened to the old 'punting parson'? Nobody around here in Hayden got your blood moving?"

"Don't you ever think about anything besides sex?" Damion snapped, knowing that Cader was thinking his own thoughts. The sportscasters had picked up the polite form of Cader's nickname for Damion. The original version was "cunting parson" after word got out about a particular drunken orgy where Damion was discovered in a back bedroom with two girls from a nearby sorority house.

"How do you handle the celibacy, Damion? Or do you go into New Orleans every once in a while?"

"How do you handle your thing, Cade?"

"Gently, very gently. But I do think about other things. Money and football. What else is left?"

"Believe it or not, there are a few other things."

"For Christ's sake, Damion, you aren't going to give me a lecture like back in the old days. Don't you think we're a little old for that crap? You live your life and I'll live mine. You know you rode pretty hard on me when we were in college. I guess we rode pretty hard on each other."

"Yeah, only your mouth was bigger than mine. What I considered private, you considered public. I still haven't forgotten that little handle you pinned on me."

"We were boys then, Damion; we're men now. Forget it, will you? Don't start preaching fire and brimstone to me like your old man did. You go about your business and I'll go about mine."

"Which is?"

"Hell, man, did all that religion go to your head? My sporting goods store!" Cader Harris smiled winningly, the same smile he used on women when he was cajoling to get his own way.

Conway's guts were churning and his instincts were fully aroused. "There's something else, Cade. I know it in here," he said bitterly, pushing his fist against his chest. "There's something you're not telling. This isn't the right town to open a sporting goods store in, or any other kind of store, for that matter. The town's dying. It's all the established merchants can do to keep Hayden's business from floating down the highway to New Orleans. It's fine for incidental stuff, a drugstore and that kind of business. But sporting goods? That's expensive equipment you've got stashed there," he said, kicking at one of the cartons with the Adidas trademark stamped on its face. Damion noted the grim set to Cader's jaw and his tightly clenched fists. Everything concerning Cader Harris was physical. Super jock, macho hero.

"I don't know what you're talking about, Conway. What you see is what you get."

"Yeah!" Damion scowled. "But this has got to be the quickest operation I've ever seen. Word only leaked about you coming back last week, but from the looks of all this," he gestured toward the merchandise, "it's been in the planning for months."

Harris shrugged. "All it takes is a connection, a phone call and a show of credit cards, and it's delivery the next day."

Damion's scowl deepened as he watched Cader with a speculative eye. "How many football jerseys can you sell? How many tennis rackets? Once the school athletic teams pass through, what's left? Why did you come back here, Cade?"

Cader Harris's dark eyes looked straight into Damion's. "To open a sporting goods store," he said slowly and distinctly. Damion turned away in disgust.

"Of all the things I know you to be, Cade, I know you're

no shopkeeper. Two months and this little enterprise will go down the drain."

"Why did you come here, Conway? To tell me I'm not your usual merchant type?"

"I don't really know. Or at least I didn't until I walked in and saw that you'd actually come back to Hayden. Now, I realize it was to tell you that I know in my gut you're here for another reason entirely and to tell you that I'll be watching you. These are my people here in Hayden, and I'll stand between you and them."

Harris threw back his head and laughed. "Now you sound just like your old man, Damion. I guess his preaching got to you more than I thought. He used to lecture me, too, whenever he lowered himself for the good of the souls on the wrong side of the tracks. Funny thing is, I never thought you liked your father well enough to follow in his footsteps. I was always of the opinion you agreed to enter the ministry more out of fear of him than anything else."

Damion Conway blanched. Cader had hit closer to the truth than he cared to admit even to himself. How many times had he asked himself what he was doing wearing a clerical collar? Recovering quickly, he said gravely, "You know where the church is. If you ever want to talk to someone, that's where you'll find me. Just call," he said, swinging his leg over the low iron rail on the side of the steps.

"Hold it, Damion. Listen," Cade said, leaping the railing, landing next to Damion. "What's this I hear about Delta Oil? If they set up shop, why, man, this town will boom. And," he said, whacking Damion on the back, "you told me this was a dying town." He eyed the minister, watching for reaction. Was his alliance with Delta Oil still secret? Damion would know.

"It is, dying that is," Damion said seriously. "Delta will never make it. The people are up in arms." He shook his head, watching Cader carefully. "Don't count on Delta to make your business boom. It's too dangerous," he repeated ominously.

"Why?" Cader asked, seeing nothing in Conway's demeanor that revealed any knowledge of his undercover assignment for Delta.

"I know you don't give a damn, but I'll tell you anyway. Pollution, the possibility of an explosion. Human life, Cade. Any environmentalist will tell you liquefied natural gas is a hazard. Even though Delta will store it in tanks, they have to get it here; it has to be transferred from ship to terminal. Cade, stored liquefied natural gas or LNG, as it's called, has the energy potential of several atomic bombs if it's ignited. Now, do you understand? I care; the people of this town care. Delta will never get into Hayden."

"Pity," Cader said airily.

"Yeah, a real pity," Damion repeated coolly. "If you need me, call."

Cader laughed again. "And you'll give aid and comfort as is your calling, right? I'll try to remember that. Thanks for stopping by and wishing me luck. Hey, Damion," he called out, "d'you play racquetball?"

"No!" Damion yelled, not bothering to turn around.

As always, when he was distressed, Damion tugged at

his earlobe, mashing the plump flesh between his thumb and finger. He climbed behind the wheel of his car and turned the key in the ignition.

Damion pulled into the flow of moving traffic, his mind occupied with thoughts of the effort it would take to monitor Cader Harris's activities. Pulling to a halt at the red light on the corner, Damion's thoughts indexed over his relationship with Cader Harris like a two-million-dollar computer. "Harris" was a synonym for "humiliation" as far as Damion was concerned, and one little file from out of the past stood out from the rest and demanded review.

Methodical and orderly, his thoughts brought him back to senior year at Jatha Hayden High School and the debating team, the one area where the talents of Damion Conway could shine. He had been surprised to discover that Cader Harris, already the school favorite because of his prowess on the gridiron, was a fellow member of the debating team. This had puzzled Damion and, upon questioning, Cade had answered, "Look, man, I've got to get myself into a good college if I'm going to make anything of myself. You've got your old man and your Honor Society to get you where you're going. I've got to get there by the hair on my balls and scholastic achievement. What better way than the debating team? I know that college admissions boards are interested in things like that." He grinned at Damion, an ingenuous, dazzling grin that suggested a more serious attitude than Cader admitted.

"As captain of the team," Damion said, extending his hand, "we're glad to have you. It takes a lot of work, Cader, let me warn you." Damion tried to keep his voice easy, which was the opposite of the way he was feeling. He felt intruded upon. This was *his* territory, something he excelled in, and he didn't like Cader Harris interloping on his domain. Why couldn't Harris stay in athletics where the limelight was certainly brighter?

As the weeks rolled by and Cader continued making extraordinary plays on the field, Damion was watchful and wary. A captain was responsible for the performance of his debating team, and he was ever mindful of the fact that Cader seemed to lead a very busy life. Training for football, other studies and the arrival on the scene of Sunday Waters, Cader's new girl. Yet, each week, when the debating team met, Cader's material was prepared and his theories held water. They had already participated in two or three debates when they were informed that admissions officers from four separate colleges were to be present at the next competition. Damion's team had achieved a "no loss" status. This debate was an important one.

The subject was social security and the pros and cons had been meticulously explored. On either side, each member of the four-man team knew his arguments, and Damion himself was to be the last speaker, sending their arguments home with a punch. Cader was to speak just before him, and his theories were presented in such a manner as to establish Damion's arguments. They had it in the bag; they couldn't lose.

In Jatha Hayden auditorium, the debating team waited in the wings. Cader was peering out from behind the curtain when he turned to Damion. "Which ones do you think they are? Those college admissions officers."

Damion shrugged. "We only know they're out there, Cade." He had warmed to Cader over the weeks, seeing he had a real zeal for winning, the same zeal he displayed on the gridiron each Saturday. Cader knew where to stress a point, where to emphasize a phrase.

Cader glanced hastily at his notes, and Damion noticed his apprehension. "Not scared, are you? Don't freeze up on me now. We're a team, Cader, and none of us can win this on our own. It's not like out on the football field."

"Yeah, yeah," Cader answered impatiently. "I know."

Damion walked away feeling confident. His team was going to win. More important, he would send the winning argument home. Pro or con, whichever the toss of the coin said was the side they would take, they were going to win. He imagined this was the adrenaline flow Cader got when he ran out onto the field every Saturday. Sure, the football team won, but everybody knew they only won because of Cader Harris. Same thing here, the debating team would win, and everyone would know it was because of Damion Conway. He prided himself on his quickness of thought and his agile maneuverings during debate. He knew his voice had a clear, masculine ring over the loudspeakers, and he was confident of the tone of sincerity he could bring out in his delivery and the haunting look of zealousness which shone in his indigo eyes. Damion Conway was impressive; everyone said so, and he would stand second to none on the pulpit when he became a minister.

Halfway through the debate, the time clock buzzed before the second man on the opposing team could finish his argument. More points for Damion's team. Cader would speak next. Damion sat at attention, listening to every word the moderator spoke. The palms of his hands tingled. Soon, he would have his chance, and he would bring the victory home. He, Damion Conway, would be a hero.

Cader began his argument. Damion was so familiar with the material as they had programmed it that he allowed his mind to wander, dwelling on the impression he would make on the college admissions officers. Suddenly, something Cader said caught his attention, and he realized that Harris had skipped over some very important points of argument and was plunging into the end of his speech. Damion's thoughts clamored. This was terrible. Cader would be left with time on the clock and nothing to say. Their team would lose its point advantage!

Cader drew to the end of his argument. His eyes flew to the clock. Only for an instant, for a syllable, did his voice falter. Cader continued.

Damion's mouth opened in shock. Instead of backtracking to the section of the argument he eliminated, as Damion had expected, Cader Harris bounded on, presenting the argument that should have been Damion's. Unbelieving, Damion listened. He wouldn't! He couldn't! He had. Cader Harris had stolen Damion's argument! He brought the final statements home to a rousing finale, his voice clear and vibrant, emotion rising, just as he had seen Damion practice it.

The clock buzzed for time. The audience applauded, something unheard of in the middle of a debate. Applause was saved for the end.

Aghast, Damion realized the last man on the opposing team was struggling with his point of view. Cader's argument, no, *Damion's* argument, had unnerved him. Damion watched the clock with terror. There was nothing to say. Cader had said it all, using Damion's words! Anything at this point would be anticlimactic. Open-mouthed and staring, Damion willed the clock to stop. He couldn't think! He had had it all wrapped up, and Cader had made a fool of him. It was his turn. The moderator's eyes were on him; the audience's eyes were on him. He groped for theory, for argument, for his voice. Nothing came. Dumbstruck, Damion stood up abruptly, knocking over his chair, and ran from the stage, humiliation burning the backs of his ears, hatred for Cader Harris choking off all reason.

The night was black, protective, covering his shame, hiding his hatred. Footsteps.

"Damion? That you?" Cader Harris asked.

Damion stood tall, willing the night to conceal him, furious that Cader had followed him and found him.

"Christ, Damion! I don't know what made me do it! I forgot the whole middle of my argument. Must have tightened up knowing those officers were in the audience. Christ, I'm sorry, Damion. I couldn't think of a thing to say. Only those closing statements of yours came to my mind. I guess I was pretty impressed with them to remember them. . . . Hey, Damion, you believe me, don't you?"

"Get away from me, Cade." His voice was flat, belying the roiling emotions he was experiencing. Cader Harris had stolen his thunder. There he was, everything any guy in school would give his back teeth to be, and he had to go and steal from a nonentity, Damion Conway.

"You've gotta believe me, Damion. I didn't realize what I was doing until the words were out of my mouth. . . ."

"Shit, you didn't know! Don't give me that crap! You took from me, Cade. Just as if you'd put your hand in my pocket, you stole from me!"

"I deserve that, I know it. But I didn't mean to. It just happened, believe me; it wasn't as though I'd planned it."

"I might believe anyone else, Cader, but never you! Now, get away from me before I kill you." Damion's hands closed into fists.

Now, honking horns broke through Damion's thoughts. The light had changed, God knew how many times, and he was holding up traffic. His foot tromped the gas pedal, and the car burned rubber as it sped across the intersection. Damion's hands were clenched on the steering wheel, and with mental effort he loosened his grasp. He could feel the backs of his ears burning as though he had suffered the humiliation only yesterday.

His reverie had reinforced his position. Cader Harris would bear watching. Cader Harris was a man without virtues. He was arrogant and self-serving. Cader Harris could turn his back on honor and obligation. Cader Harris was without conscience.

*   *   *

Cader was busy storing cartons when he heard a sharp knocking at the locked front door of the shop. He reached for a football and tucked it into the crook of his arm. Now, he felt dressed. *Never meet your public without feeling dressed*, he grinned to himself. He decided he would saunter to the front of the store. *Showmanship. Always give the public what they want.* Stepping into the dimness of the shop, he saw two young girls and a tall, well-built young man staring in through the glass at him. He immediately surmised they had come to apply for jobs. Hayden, being what it was, offered limited employment for young people. He expected to be swamped with applications.

Cade fixed a lopsided grin on his face, the grin he was known for, and sprinted to the door and undid the latch. The football was held loosely in his suntanned, brawny fist. His nut-brown eyes quickly took in the youngster, and he tossed the ball to the tall blond young man. "Great catch! You handle the pigskin like you know what to do with it," he praised, clapping the boy on the back. He held out his hand. "Cader Harris."

"Kevin Thomas." He handed back the football and waited a moment. "I played first-string quarterback for the school team."

Cader felt the wind knocked out of him. His hand gripped the boy's involuntarily. His son. Recovering, he purposefully released Kevin's hand and forced his voice to work. Even as he spoke, he eyed the boy's handsome features and measured his physique. His son. His son. The thought reverberated in his head.

"Yo! That's what I played when I went to that school. Hey, gang," he addressed himself to the others in the small group that had followed the Thomas boy and the two girls into the store, "is he any good?"

"The best. And he's my brother," Beth Thomas said quietly. "The coaches compared him to you all season. They said his arm was every bit as good as yours, and he could run faster than you."

"Did they now? Is that what they said, Kevin?" he asked, a speculative look in his eye, squelching an earthquake of paternal pride.

Embarrassed, Kevin said, "More or less."

"If business gets slow, we can take a run out to the field and toss a few. Been awhile since I had a workout. Okay, let's get down to business," he said, remembering the crowd of job applicants. There would be time for these alien emotions later. "The applications and pencils are on that packing case. Just fill them out, and I'll give you a call so a schedule can be set up. I only need part-time clerks and one full time," he said, eyeing Judy Evans who, much to Beth's rancor, had found her way to Harris's store at the same time as Kevin.

Casually, Cader draped his arm around Judy's shoulder and grinned down at her. Christ, no kid this age had a right to have that kind of expression in her eyes. "What's your name, honey?"

"Judy Evans. My mother's name used to be Marsha Taylor. She says you went to school together." Judy's shoulder pressed tighter against Cader's arm. All the while her eyes were on Kevin to see if he noticed or cared that Cader Harris had chosen her over his fairy princess sister.

Cader laughed and tweaked her cheek. "I thought you reminded me of someone." His dark eyes watched her as she strained to see the others filling out their application forms. A smile formed on her full lips when she saw Kevin Thomas straighten and glance around. Beth hastily scribbled her name on the bottom line of the application and inched her way toward her brother. Both of them walked toward Cader. Simultaneously, they handed him their applications and waited while he scanned them quickly.

Cader was most interested in Kevin's application; there was no question that the job was his. Beth was something else. If there was one thing he didn't need, it was a brother-sister act. "Beth, is it? I'm sorry, honey, but I don't think you're what I'm looking for. I need someone more aggressive, someone who knows how to sell, like this little chicken." He waved the application toward Judy. "You've got the job. Kevin, that is, if you want it, and I assume you do. Every day from one to six P.M., and ten to six on Saturday. You can start tomorrow. I want everything in shape for Saturday's opening. We have a lot of stocking to do, and there's more merchandise coming in every day."

Judy narrowed her eyes at Kevin and waited expectantly. Would he take the job without Beth? Poor, poor Bethie, look at the tears. Kevin saw them too and inched a little closer to his sister. "Mr. Harris, I know my sister hasn't had any experience but she can learn. Couldn't you give her a chance?"

"'Fraid not, son. Once I start with a kid I like to keep in step with him. What would be the point in hiring her for just a few days and letting her go? Are you telling me, by some chance, you don't want the job unless I take on your sister?" Cade asked harshly, dreading the answer. He wanted to get to know his son but not under the overly possessive eye of his half-sister, Beth.

"No, sir, Mr. Harris. I'll be here tomorrow at one." He moved another step until he was directly behind Beth. Lightly, he placed a hand on her shoulder. The fierce protectiveness and the alliance between the two was disconcerting.

The moment Kevin's hand touched Beth's shoulder, Cader felt Judy stiffen beside him, and he could see the tight set to her full lips. *What have we here*, he wondered. He wasn't surprised to see tears gather in Beth's light green eyes. Just like her mother. Irene had also resorted to tears when something didn't go her way. "You're Irene Hayden's kids, aren't you? I'd heard she married Arthur Thomas while I was away at college. Tell me, are you off to college in the fall?" he asked pointedly, wanting to know everything there was to know about Kevin. When Cader knew he was returning to Hayden, he had supposed that sooner or later he would run into Irene's son. He had never imagined the tidal wave of emotion that would engulf him when he came face to face with his own flesh and blood.

"Yes, sir, it's right there on the application, Mr. Harris. Tulane. I leave on the twenty-second of August."

Jesus! His own alma mater. It was almost like coming full circle. Soaring emotions plummeted when he realized that Kevin would never know he was walking in his father's footsteps.

Cader was aware of the hostility that surrounded the three young people. Judy was suddenly relaxed and young Beth was strung as tight as a clothesline. There was more here than met the eye. "Good school. I'll keep my eye open for a replacement at the end of the summer. Who knows? You may find your way back to Hayden next summer to rest up from all the attention you'll get from the girls at school. If everything works out, you can depend on a job for next year." He smiled enthusiastically, catching the slight narrowing of Beth Thomas's eyes when he had mentioned girls at school. "The job's yours, Kevin. I'm sorry, little lady," he said to Beth, "try me next year when you're a little older." Beth ignored him, her hazel-green eyes full of disdain. It had to be disdain, Cader thought. Denying her the job wasn't cause for murder, and that was the only other word that came to mind when he felt her eyes finally turn to look at him.

Cader watched the Thomas kids hold open the door for a woman to enter as they left the shop.

"Hi, Mom," Judy called.

"Hi, honey. Cade, it's good to see you. Remember me? Marsha Taylor. How are you?" she said, stretching out her hand to meet his.

"How could I forget the prettiest girl in Hayden? How are you, Marsha? Heard your husband died. Sorry about that. He was a real talented guy." He saw Marsha's eyes go to Judy, then back to him. "What have you been doing with yourself, Marsha? It's been a long time. I met your girl here. You should be proud. She's as pretty as her mother at the same age."

"Prettier." Marsha laughed. "As for what I've been doing, it's just a little of this and a little of that, I'm afraid. Actually, it's a whole lot of nothing. Today was my day to help out in Marc Baldwin's office."

Cader looked at the white Qiana uniform with the mandarin collar and long sleeves. It was all under there; everything in its tidy, sexy little place. "How about this bachelor and this bachelorette having dinner? How's Tuesday of next week? We'll go out to the Lemon Drop."

Marsha smiled. "Why not? Pick me up around seven. Listen, honey," she addressed Judy, "do you think you could walk home? Keli McDermott is having car trouble, and I said I would pick her up and drive her home. She's at the garage."

"Okay, Mom. Mr. Harris, I didn't fill out an application and I really want the job. You weren't kidding when you told Beth you were going to hire me, were you?"

"Me? Kid a nice little girl like you? You've got the job, Judy. Same hours as Kevin." Now, why the hell had he said that? He didn't need two full-time clerks. He shrugged. It wasn't his money, so what difference did it make? Besides, it might give the boys at Delta Oil something else to squawk about, something other than when and how he was going to start putting pressure in the right places to get those tanks into Hayden.

Chapter Three

Kevin's stomach churned as he walked beside Beth down tree-lined Mimosa Lane. He should say something, anything, to wipe away the hurt look in her eyes. It wasn't his fault that Mr. Harris didn't want to hire her. He had intervened on her behalf, hadn't he? Damn, why did she have to make him feel this way?

His dark eyes lightened as he laid a hand on her arm and stopped at the crosswalk. "I'm sorry, Beth." Damn! There he went apologizing to her again. He held his breath, waiting to hear what her answer would be. *Say anything*, he pleaded silently, *just don't keep looking at me that way!*

Beth imperceptibly shook off his hand and raised her eyes. Stunned by what he saw there, Kevin could only stare at her. Where was the hurt, the wounded look he had expected to see? Instead, a pair of glazed hazel eyes glared through him as she spoke in a carefully controlled voice:

"If only one of us could have the job, I'm glad it was you. Mama said she was giving you a limited allowance this summer, so the money will come in handy for you."

Say it, Beth, his mind shouted. *Say I want the money for college in the fall. Say it! Don't pretend I'm not going and that I want this money to blow on good times this summer. Say it!* He walked along beside her as they crossed Mimosa Lane toward their house. Taking a deep breath, he blurted, "The money will come in handy when I leave for Tulane at the end of August. I can manage for the summer with what Mother gives me; it's September that'll put me in a bind." Kevin swallowed hard and looked down at Beth. She raised tear-filled eyes and sprinted ahead of him down the street to the white neo-Grecian house that was home.

Kevin remained on the curb, his eyes narrowed against the late afternoon sun. Should he race after her? Should he apologize to her? It wasn't his fault he got the job and he was going off to college.

Leaning back against a gnarled sycamore trunk, he scuffed at the moss near the base of the old tree with the toe of his sneaker. The older you got, the more complicated life became, he told himself sagely. He knew in his gut that as of today his life was going to change. Meeting Cader Harris, graduating from high school tomorrow night, working at a bona fide job were only the first of many changes. He could feel the presence of change in the air.

Telling his mother that he'd taken a job would bring about another change. Getting Beth to come around and cheering her out of her sulk would be another. Judy. Beth hated Judy for her good looks and free, easy spirit. Tacky was the word Beth used for Judy. He grinned. There was a lot to be said for tacky. He blinked and his ears felt warm when he imagined what Judy's round, full breasts would feel like cupped in his hands. Guilt and disloyalty erased the fantasy. Beth hated Judy, had hated her since grammar school. The same animosity still raged between the two girls, even after all this time. Beth was just entering her senior year, and Judy was graduating in his class.

Kevin lowered his eyes to the destruction he had created at his feet. Emerald-green moss lay in clumps, and specks of rich, brown earth dotted his white sneakers. He hunkered down and carefully fitted the clods back into place. Satisfied that no outward sign of damage showed, he rose to his feet, dusting off his hands. He squared his shoulders and jogged home. To home and Beth.

Keli McDermott watched Kevin jog down the street and smiled to herself. She turned slightly in the car seat and spoke to Marsha. "Kevin Thomas is such a nice boy. Irene must be very proud of him. Gene . . . Gene told me the boy was going to Tulane in the autumn. It must be wonderful to have children. Children to make one proud."

Marsha turned slightly and looked at Keli. She frowned when she spoke. "What you say is true, Keli, but sometimes a mother and a father, too, take children for granted. We want so much for them, and when they fall short of the measure, we feel cheated. Somehow, I can't imagine

Kevin Thomas ever falling short. Irene wouldn't stand for it."

Keli said softly, "I would like to know how it feels to be a mother."

Again, a quick, light glance and then back to the road. "One day soon, you'll know. Then you won't wonder any longer."

"Marsha, are you wondering why I asked you to drive me home?"

"Glad to do it. Is Gene out of town that he couldn't pick you up at the garage?"

Warily, "I . . . I called him and there was no answer."

"But doesn't Gene always work on his book from nine in the morning till five? He made a point of saying that, boasting about it, at Julia's dinner party last week. He said it was all a matter of discipline," Marsha said, risking another quick glance at Keli. How beautiful and defenseless she was. Like a butterfly perched on the edge of a blossom, tentative, with a kind of trembling sense of her own beauty. God would only know how, with the protective cocoon Gene wrapped around his wife, this beautiful little butterfly managed to emerge, she thought sourly.

Shyly, Keli said, "He may have been walking in the garden; he does that to clear his head when things don't go right for him at the typewriter."

"I'm sure that's what it is. I don't mind giving you a lift. Keli, will you pick us up tomorrow as planned? Remember, we all have to be at the school at noon."

"I would be most happy," Keli breathed softly. Keli's

natural graciousness always made Marsha feel as though she had the tact of a buzz saw. "If Gene will permit me to use his car, I will pick you up first and then Irene and Julia. Thank you for the ride, Marsha," Keli said, opening the door almost the moment Marsha braked in front of her house. "See, Gene is home and waiting for me." She pointed a slender finger at a burly man walking down the flagstone path toward the car.

Marsha's jaw tightened as she saw Gene McDermott peer intently into the car, trying to recognize the driver. She slipped the car into gear, but not before she saw the colonel's arm go around Keli.

Marsha drove furiously, her mind whirling. She could have a hand in teaching Keli to speak English and to dress stylishly, but she couldn't protect her from her own husband, retired USAF Colonel Gene McDermott. *Christ!* Any woman living under his roof, let alone soft, uncomplaining Keli, would have a tough time keeping her spirit from being buried under his bush. Gene McDermott was reducing Keli's identity to a thin shadow. She had never met such an overbearing, self-righteous man in her entire life. He was a bull. He was just the type to marry an Oriental girl, thinking that they, above all other women, would be acquiescent and obliging to his demands. Hating Gene McDermott, she jammed her foot to the floor and rounded the corner onto Mimosa Lane on two wheels.

Arthur Thomas climbed from his car and stood watching Marsha as she careened around the corner, her tires screeching. If she didn't watch it, she would soon be availing herself of his services at the funeral home.

He was tired. God, he was tired, he thought as he wiped at his wide brow. If he had his way, he would slip out to the garden and lie down in the hammock and sleep for a week. Oh, no, he had to shower and change for dinner so Irene wouldn't be able to complain that he smelled of embalming fluid. And he would have to shave. "I hate shaving at six in the evening," he muttered to himself as he let himself in the front door.

"Irene," he called without enthusiasm, "I'm home."

"You have ten minutes until dinner is ready. You're late, Arthur," she said, walking into the dining room to place a silver bowl of yellow tea roses precisely in the center of the lace cloth. She walked over to her husband in a cloud of White Shoulders and dutifully presented her cheek for his light peck. "Oooh, you positively reek, Arthur! You are one man who always brings his work home with him." She frowned.

Arthur ignored her. "What's for dinner?" He wrinkled his nose to see if he could get a clue to her culinary masterpiece of the day.

"Great-Aunt Matilda Hayden's famous meat loaf," she answered quietly, her eyes daring him to reproach her.

Again, Arthur ignored her. "Must we go through this Cecil B. DeMille production for meat loaf?" he asked, waving his hands toward the lace cloth, the bone china and the sterling silver cutlery. "Why can't we have dinner on the patio?"

Irene sucked in her cheeks and issued her favorite retort to Arthur's comments on her elaborate dinners. "Daddy always said you can't make a silk purse out of a sow's ear. If you want dinner on the patio, I'll have Dulcie serve you out there—alone. The children and I will dine in the manner to which we are accustomed, the manner in which all civilized people dine."

"One of these days, Irene, I will do just that, and," he said ominously, "I will wear the suit I wore at the funeral home, my *work clothes*, as you call them, and I will enjoy eating on the patio." Turning on his heel, he left her standing, her mouth agape at his sharp tone. "And spare me another of your daddy's homespun philosophies."

Dressed in what Irene called his "at home dinner suit" of light blue seersucker, he paused and looked at his reflection in the cathedral mirror. "I am sick to death of the Haydens. I am sick of Daddy Hayden, and I am even sicker of Great Granddaddy Hayden. As a matter of fact, Irene, I'm getting pretty sick of you!" Enraged by the close-fitting tie that was an essential part of his dinner outfit, Arthur struggled with the knot and ripped it from beneath his collar. He stared at himself in the mirror and didn't like what he saw there. There, in his place, was a middle aged, running-to-fat man with a receding hairline, who had somehow managed to snag the heiress to the Hayden money.

Arthur never understood why *the* Irene Hayden noticed him in the first place. She was from the finest family in town and had never given him any indication she was, or could ever be, interested in a simple country boy from a middle-income family. It had been when he had come home from college on spring vacation that she had all but thrown herself at him. To this day, when he thought of that night in his old '53 Chevy, he couldn't believe that the girl who had wrapped herself around him and welcomed him to her with soft moans of delight was the same Irene he had married. A hasty, whispered phone call placed to his fraternity house announced she was pregnant and he had to marry her.

When Kevin was born, eighteen years ago, Arthur imagined himself to be the luckiest man in the world, and all thoughts of abandoned ambition and becoming a medical examiner were banished from his mind. A year later, when Bethany came along, Arthur knew he had the world on a string. It was then his relationship with Irene changed. From an eager young girl who sought his arms and his lovemaking whenever possible, she had become a nag, fighting off his advances, at last resigning herself to her "wifely duty." There was no joy left, no anticipation, no anything. Screwing Irene was like screwing one of the corpses in his preparation room.

Resignedly, Arthur once again wrapped the tie around his neck and began knotting it. In spite of it all, in spite of everything, he still loved Irene. Regardless of his thwarted career, regardless of hearing over and over again how he owed his prospering business to his father-in-law, in spite of her unresponsiveness in the bedroom, Arthur Thomas loved his wife, and he knew he always would. He was in awe of her, and although she dressed in staid, matronly clothes and allowed her hair to darken to its present mousy color, Irene was the most beautiful woman who had ever come into his life. Even Sunday Waters, lovely as she was, could not compare with Irene's inborn class and charm.

A sound from above reminded Arthur that the kids had applied for work at Cader Harris's. Dinner was going to be unpleasant at best, he thought morbidly. Once Irene was told about their applying for work, that was. His face brightened momentarily when he thought that for once Irene was going to get her tail feathers singed a little and ol' Daddy Hayden and Great Granddaddy Hayden, deceased, couldn't do anything about it. He was still smiling when he entered the dining room in time to see Irene seat herself and pick up the small silver bell which rested near her place. "Try for a dirge tonight, Irene. Great-Aunt Matilda's meat loaf could use a little mood music."

"It must be your obnoxious profession, Arthur, which makes you behave in such an uncivilized manner. I wouldn't be surprised if rigor mortis hadn't settled in your brain." The silver bell tinkled and she announced in a musical tone, "Dinner is served."

Beth and Kevin came into the dining room and seated themselves at their mother's graciously appointed table. Beth's eyes were downcast. She toyed with her fork and the thin slice of meat loaf on her plate. Kevin helped himself generously and then, looking at his sulky sister, resisted the impulse to begin eating.

Arthur's eyes scanned the members of his family,

concentrating on the faces of his children. He sighed and spoke. "Irene, Kevin applied for a job this afternoon. How did it go, son?"

Before the meaning of her husband's words settled in her consciousness, Irene heard her son say, "I was hired, Dad. I start work tomorrow."

"Fine, son, I'm proud of you." Turning to Irene, he said, "Kevin will be working for Cader Harris in his new sporting goods store."

"A job! Kevin, what in the world are you thinking of?" Irene hissed, her fork poised in midair. "Haydens never seek employment until after college. A job! Never! You just call . . ." Her words were cut off in midstream. It had suddenly dawned on her that Arthur said Kevin would be working for Cader Harris. Her heart began a mad thumping in her breast. Irene knew Cader had returned to Hayden. How could she help knowing when the whole town was buzzing with the news? She had even been formulating a plan which would throw her into contact with him again. But to have Kevin working for him! Never! She didn't want Kevin anywhere near Cader Harris. She leaned against the high-backed chair, her gaze challenging Kevin, a war of emotions erupting within her.

"Look, Mother, you know as well as I do that I could use the money." Kevin chanced a sidelong glance at his sister and saw her chewing through her salad, a smug expression on her face.

"You have your inheritance from Granddaddy Hayden, Kevin," Irene protested. "And Haydens never . . ."

"Kevin is a Thomas, Irene," Arthur said curtly, jumping to the defense, "and we Thomases have been known to work for a living. The money isn't the only consideration here; it's a question of independence. Finding a job like this is commendable. Commendable!" he emphasized as he cut into the dirt-colored meat loaf.

"Mama, I happen to agree with you," Beth said pertly, her eyes sparkling. "Kev doesn't need the money, and why should he take the job from some poor person who really needs it?"

His daughter's statement caught Arthur's attention. Apparently, Beth had applied for the job and was turned down. Arthur loved his daughter, but, as a man, he sympathized with his son. So, Kevin would be free of his sister around his neck, and Beth didn't like that idea at all. Now, more than ever, he supported the idea of Kevin working for Cader Harris. "Kevin needs the experience of responsibility. This will be a good way for him to gain a knowledge of the working world, and it will prove profitable."

Irene swallowed hard and forced her hands to be still in her lap. "Kevin can learn responsibility by looking after Beth this summer."

A flurry of rage rose in Arthur. "That's what he's been doing since Beth was born, Irene, and it's time things changed. Beth will have to learn to get along without him. Kevin's graduation will mark the beginning of his adult life. He can't stay with Beth for the rest of his life, and Beth might as well begin knowing that now!" He pounded his fist on the table.

"Be reasonable, Arthur." Irene gulped. It had been years

since she had seen Arthur work himself up over the children this way. Usually, he acquiesced to her wishes. Not since Kevin came home telling them he had tried out for the football team and was accepted had Arthur interfered this way. She was going to lose this battle, she knew it, and there wouldn't be a thing she could do about it. "I still say the answer is no!" she said with all the imperiousness of generations of Haydens.

"No one was asking you, Irene," Arthur said quietly. "Therefore, your answer is not required. Kevin has landed the job at the sporting goods store, and I'm proud of him."

"Mama is right, Daddy. You always take Kevin's side," Beth accused.

"It's not a question of taking sides, Bethany. Find friends of your own and leave Kevin to do as he wants. The two of you spend too much time together as it is." He glanced at Irene accusingly.

"Arthur!" Irene shrilled. "The answer is no! For one thing, think of what it will do to our dinners together. You know as well as I what a task it was to convince Dulcie to come back in the afternoons to serve dinner," she whispered, looking toward the kitchen door for signs of the black housekeeper. "I do declare, she's getting more and more independent. This civil rights thing has destroyed genteel Southern living. . . ."

"Irene! We are not talking about your house-help," Arthur said forcefully, familiar with Irene's ploys to change the subject. "We are talking about Kevin's job. What time do you quit every day, son? Six, did you say? Good. See there,

Irene, surely you won't be too inconvenienced by holding dinner another fifteen minutes. If not, I'd be happy to eat out on the patio with Kevin."

"Arthur . . ."

"Mother, I'm taking the job. I gave my word, and I told Mr. Harris I'd report for work tomorrow. I'm going to," Kevin said in a hard, cold voice. He purposely avoided Beth's eyes when he made his declaration.

Irene sputtered, "How . . . how will it look? Think of how it will look! I forbid it!" Her hands were trembling; tears formed in the corners of her eyes. *Cader. Cader.*

"I've got the job, Mother, and I'm going to take it. Excuse me, Dad, I'm not hungry," he said, rising from the table and making a hasty exit.

Beth jumped to her feet, tipping her water glass onto the lace cloth in the process. Tears glistened in her eyes as she ran up the stairs behind Kevin.

"Now, what am I going to do with this meat loaf?" Irene asked nervously. Cader Harris was back in town. *Cader Harris,* her mind repeated over and over.

"Do what you always do with your great-aunt Matilda's meat loaf. Give it to the cat," Arthur said callously.

Irene sat at the table long after the others had left, her mind churning at what Arthur had said. Kevin was going to work for Cader Harris. Kevin was going to work for his father. Wearily, she massaged her throbbing temples. What had Cade thought when Kevin appeared in his store? More important, what did he feel when he looked at the boy? Surely, he recognized his own features in Kevin. She had to be careful and not say too much in front of either Kevin or Arthur. She couldn't give it away, not now after all these years. Kevin was Arthur's son, that's what the child's birth certificate read, Kevin Hayden Thomas. Panic coursed through her for a split second. Cade wouldn't claim parentage now, would he? Oh, God, what had the boy thought when he saw Cader Harris? Was he impressed with him? Did he like him? Did he notice any resemblance to his own clean-cut good looks? She had to do something, make some kind of plan. Plead, beg with Cade not to divulge their secret. Daddy! Oh, no, not this time. Cade, she would go to Cade and straighten out everything.

Irene stared at the lace tablecloth and then down at the severe dress she wore. The sensible walking shoes and less-than-sheer hose. Dowdy. How had she allowed herself to become dowdy? Arthur, that was how. Arthur was dowdy—a balding, pudgy old man at forty-two. If she sprinkled em-balming fluid over herself and fluffed up her hair, he would be in seventh heaven. And for what? His hands were always so cold. All those customers of his made his hands cold. Cade's hands had always been warm, hot and searching and then conquering.

Defiantly, Irene reached behind her to the sideboard and pulled a package of crumpled cigarettes from the drawer. She puffed steadily, drawing the smoke deep into her lungs.

Nineteen years since she last saw Cader Harris. Almost an eternity by some people's standards. Where had the years gone; what had she done with them? *Existed*, she told herself, crushing out the cigarette and immediately lighting another. Just existed, knowing that Cade would come back and they would live happily ever after. In her fantasies she had imagined Cade looking at Kevin and then rushing to her and taking her in his arms. First, he would thank her for giving him such a wonderful son and then he would tell her he loved her, had always loved her and that was why he had come back, because he knew now he couldn't live another day without her and his son. Arthur. Arthur would always manage to weave his way into her fantasies at this point and spoil everything. Arthur always spoiled everything. Still, she could really hurt him by telling him Kevin was Cade's son. Arthur genuinely loved Kevin and the boy returned that love. Arthur was Kevin's father and that was all there was to it. When you really stopped to think about it, Arthur had everything. He had the love of his son, a sweet daughter, a perfect wife, and all those bodies to while away his days. And what did she have? She had a respectful son, a whiny daughter, a less-than-perfect husband who smelled, and meetings. It wasn't enough. "I want more. I deserve more." She grimaced as she let ashes drop into her coffee cup. "Tsk, tsk," she muttered, "ashes in the old Hayden china. Who in the goddamn hell gives a good roaring fuck," she said viciously. She lit another cigarette and blew a perfect smoke ring and then she laughed. That was what she needed, a good fuck, frontwards, backwards, sideways and hanging upside down, dangling from the window, on the beach, in a pile of leaves. Anywhere, anytime, anyplace. It had been a long time since she had had a big O. and here she was just thinking of Cader Harris and getting it off.

Nineteen years ago she had felt like this, but then she didn't have to depend on fantasies or memories. Cade was real and always ready. A smile tugged at the corner of her mouth. How well she remembered the first time she had been physically aware of Cader Harris. It was in her senior year in the lunchroom at school. Sunny Waters had walked in and sat down at a table, and Cader Harris, who was carrying his tray, noticed Sunny just as he passed Irene. Because she was sitting down and at eye level with his crotch, she had seen the immediate swell in his pants as soon as he set eyes on Sunny. She had made up her mind right then that she wanted to cause the same response in him.

Irene Hayden leaned back in the cane-backed chair, the cigarette dangling from her fingers, as she became the eighteen-year-old cheerleader who had cheered Cader Harris to victory on the emerald field.

"You're edgy today, Irene," Marsha Taylor said irritably, "your cheers are off beat. Can't you stay in tune with the rest of us?"

"Five minutes to halftime," Irene said, twirling her pom-pom under Marsha's nose. Her eyes sparkled with what she intended to do. Before the night was over she would have superstar Harris eating out of her hand.

"I don't like that look in your eye, Irene. What are you up to?" Marsha demanded, her eyes glued to the battling figures on the grassy carpet.

"I've decided that I want Cader Harris, and I'm going to get him, tonight after the game," Irene said loftily.

"Ha! You and every other girl in this school. Besides,

Cader Harris already has a steady girl, Sunday Waters, or hadn't you noticed?" Marsha snapped.

"Of course, I noticed. Everyone has noticed. He's only taking her out for one thing and you know it. I know it and so does everybody in school. Why, I could get him just like that!" Irene said, snapping her fingers.

Marsha Taylor stared at Irene Hayden and knew she meant every word she said. Poor Sunny, she wouldn't have a chance with the likes of Irene Hayden. "And when you get him, what are you going to do with him?" Marsha demanded.

"Do with him?"

"Yes, do with him. Cade Harris is physical. By that, Irene, I mean he is going to want to do more than hold that lily-white hand of yours."

"Well," Irene sniffed delicately, "he is almost acceptable now that he's been nominated for All State. I don't see any harm in kissing him."

Marsha laughed at the vague look on Irene's face. She wanted to shock her, drive her out of that gilt and ivory tower she lived in. "Are we talking about kissing your mouth or your pussy? Somehow, Irene, I can't picture you opening your legs, and it's always been a mystery to me how you put your bloomers on."

"Marsha Taylor, for shame!" God, was that what Cader Harris would expect? Did that tacky Sunny Waters let him do . . . Oh, God!

"Well, which is it?" Marsha demanded in a laughing voice. "Boys like pussy, face it. You shower with the rest of us after gym and you've heard the girls talk just as I have. Cade

Harris only wants one thing from you or any other girl."

"Oh pooh, Marsha. He'll respect me just the way all the boys do. If he doesn't, then I'll tell Daddy and have him booted off the team. I'm no slut like Sunny Waters."

"You don't know Sunny Waters is a slut, so just watch it, Irene. I happen to like her and so does Julia. The only reason you don't like her is because she has Cade wrapped around her finger."

"She puts out," Irene said huffily.

"So will you if you go out with Cade," Marsha giggled, "and then what is Daddy going to say?"

"You hush, Marsha. I'd never go all the way. Have you?" she asked curiously. Marsha and Julia Wilson locked stares and then scampered away to Irene's acute discomfort. She couldn't . . . she wouldn't . . . !

The opportunity to speak with Cade came during half time when she tossed her pompom into the air and purposely shot wide, knowing exactly where it would fall. Giggling, her cheeks flushed, she raced to the fallen pompom and scooped it up, but not before she winked at Cade and whispered. "You're playing a great game. If you make another touchdown, I'll let you take me to the Shrimp Boat after the game."

Cader Harris blinked and did a double take. Old man Hayden's kid asking him for a date. There certainly was a lot to be said for football. Here was his chance to see how the other half lived. Irene Hayden asking him, Cader Harris, for a date! Why in the hell was she licking her lips like that, he wondered uncomfortably. He couldn't be too eager and he didn't really have enough money to take her to the Shrimp Boat, and, besides, he had promised to take Sunny to a late movie. He raised his head and narrowed his eyes. "It depends on how tired I am."

"Tired! Somehow, I never thought of you ever getting tired," Irene cooed. If she didn't pull this off and make him promise now, Marsha would have it all over school that Cade Harris turned Irene Hayden down in favor of that slut, Sunny Waters. "Sorry, football man," Irene said coolly, "you have to let me know now, because there are other guys who asked me out and I thought I would give you first choice since you are the star and all."

"Okay," he grinned. "Did you say one touchdown?"

"I'd like two, but one will do." Irene preened.

"You got it and I'll meet you at the gate after I shower."

Irene danced her way to the other cheerleaders and smirked. "Cader Harris is taking me to the Shrimp Boat after the game. I told you I could get him to ditch that slut. From this point on Cader Harris belongs to me. Pass the word along so that all the girls stay out of his way. He's mine!"

"Now that you got him, what are you going to do with him? I know I asked you that before, but at the time it was just in the talking stage, but now that he's definitely yours, I'd like to know what you're going to do with a big, virile, he-man like Cade Harris. You're just an itsy bitsy lil ol' Southern gal with a starched petticoat and you're a Hayden to boot."

Irene stared at Marsha, hating her for what she was saying. "I'm going to play with him until I get tired, that's what

I'm going to do, and when I'm tired of him, I'll still be a virgin, not like you and all those others. Haydens don't mess around, so there, Marsha Taylor."

"That's only because they never met up with a Cader Harris, and don't be so damned pompous. My mother told me your father is Cledie's best customer, so don't get snotty with me."

"I'm talking about Hayden women. Cader promised to get me two touchdowns, what do you think of that?" Irene said, trying to change the subject.

"I think he's just as crazy as you are." Marsha grimaced.

Cade was as good as his word; he scored a touchdown in the first ten minutes of the third quarter and a second one in the final five minutes. Each time he tossed the pigskin onto the turf, he looked toward the row of squealing, bouncing cheerleaders and grinned.

Irene was beside herself with the second touchdown, preening and giggling for the other cheerleaders, knowing they envied her and would have given their own virginity, if still intact, for the evening ahead of her.

Marsha had to literally restrain Julia from strangling Irene when she pranced her way to the bleachers and looked straight at Sunny while she spoke to a friend sitting two seats away. "I'm going to the Shrimp Boat with Cader Harris after the game, so don't wait for me." Marsha watched Sunny's knuckles go white and her face drain of all color. It was to Sunny's credit that she sat out the remaining minutes of the game before she left, her slim shoulders in their faded sweater slumped for all to see. "I hope you get a good dose of the clap, Irene Hayden," Marsha hissed.

Irene ignored Marsha, her eyes on the field and Number Fourteen who was standing staring at her. Cader Harris was hers. She won him just like he was winning the game for Jatha Hayden High. He was hers. As far as she could tell, her only problem at this point was her father, and when she tried, she could wrap him around her finger. Still, she would have to sneak around, but that would only add to the excitement. A date with Cader Harris and two touchdowns, what more could any girl ask for? By tomorrow every girl in town would know she had staked out Cader Harris and Sunny Waters had gone down the drain. Irene giggled as she waved her pompoms.

Irene waited in her brief cheerleading costume near the gate for Cader, knowing she should have changed her clothes, but she wanted Cade to see how her legs looked up close. Boys always admired girls' legs and she had good legs, might as well put them to good use. "Oweeee, Cader, over here," Irene squealed. She watched his loose-limbed stride as he approached her. He didn't look as though he was in any hurry to make his way to the gate, stopping to talk to first one boy and then a girl and then a parent. He wore a wide grin, accepting the admiration of his fellow students with ease.

Irene liked the way he stood before her and stared at the short red skirt and her tan legs. His voice was low and husky, sending shivers up her arm. "I kept my promise, now what are you going to promise me?"

"Why, Cade, to go to the Shrimp Boat with you. That's

what I promised, all that I promised," Irene said nervously.

Cader Harris leaned against the fence post, his muscular arms folded across his chest. "Maybe," he drawled, "we better get something straight before we take off for the Shrimp Boat and I go blowing my money on you. The coach has all the players on a ten o'clock curfew. Tonight, because of the game the ban is lifted till eleven-thirty." He looked at his watch pointedly. "It's nine-twenty and I sure as hell hope you eat fast because I have other things in mind. Make up your mind now before we leave because I don't spend money on any girl unless I get some kind of a return."

Irene pretended not to understand. If she backed off now, she'd be the laughingstock of Jatha Hayden High in the morning. She stared at Cader and suddenly didn't care what she had to do. She wanted to walk into the Shrimp Boat with Cader Harris and have all the girls sigh in envy, especially Julia and Marsha. So what if he stuck his hand down her sweater and felt her breasts, and so what if he stuck his tongue in her mouth? Who would know? Her heart thumped wildly when she remembered all the stories she heard about Sunny Waters. Sunny certainly didn't spread them so it must have been Cader. He must have bragged to the other boys and . . . oh, God, would he say those things about her? She would make him promise with the threat of Daddy booting him off the team. "Cader Harris," she said arrogantly, "I didn't ask you to pay for me at the Shrimp Boat. All I did was say I would let you take me. I intended to pay my own way. Heaven's sake, what kind of girl do you think I am?" She had a quarter tucked into her saddle shoe and would order a cherry phosphate and that would be it. She would pretend she had an upset stomach from all the excitement.

Cader was silent for a minute. "I know exactly what kind of girl you are, and you know exactly what kind of guy I am. You want to be seen with me so you can brag to your friends, and it won't hurt my image to be seen with you. You want something from me and I want something from you. Simple. Now, are you going to put out or not?" he grinned, moving closer to her and touching her cheek with his thumb.

Irene swallowed the lump in her throat and knew in that second that she would do whatever Cader Harris asked of her. He knew it too. "All right, Irene Hayden, you're my girl. I'll give you my football sweater and you give me your class ring." Irene had the ring off her finger before he stopped speaking and could barely wait for him to slip off the bright red sweater. He really was hers. The sweater said so. Now, she could order the shrimp platter and forget about the cherry phosphate. When you were going steady, the guy paid, and all she had done was sell herself to the number-one guy in Hayden.

Irene's entrance into the Shrimp Boat was everything she hoped it would be. The girls all stared at her with envy and the boys looked at her differently, and it wasn't just her imagination.

Irene watched Cader as he wolfed down his shrimp while she toyed with hers, pushing the succulent morsels from one side of her plate to the other. God, it looked like he wasn't chewing the shrimp but swallowing it whole. The sooner he finished, the sooner he would want to leave. "Eat mine, Cader, I don't think I can finish it," Irene said hastily.

"I have a better idea," Cader grinned, "let's take it with us and I'll eat it in the car. We are taking your convertible, aren't we?" Cader asked, a hint of envy in his voice as he eyed the gleaming, customized Ford Fairlane with the rolled and pleated interior.

"If you want. Do you want to drive it? Daddy gave it to me for my birthday and it only has fifteen hundred miles on it," Irene babbled.

"Sure, get in," Cader replied, taking the offered keys. Irene was left to open the door herself.

"Where are we going, Cade?" Irene asked, watching the wild and reckless set of his features as he tooled the convertible onto the open highway.

"How about Jatha Beach? We can watch the submarine races," Cade shouted to be heard above an eighteen-wheeler whizzing by.

"Why don't you take me some place you haven't taken another girl. Some place that will be just ours, yours and mine," Irene said, a tinge of hysteria creeping into her voice.

Cader slowed the convertible and glanced at her. "On your side of the tracks or mine?"

"I think we should stay on this side of town because my car might be noticed. . . . What I mean is . . . over there you people don't . . . I don't care," she said suddenly, "you're driving, let's just drive till we find some place you like."

Cader laughed and pressed his foot to the floor, the yellow car shot forward and sailed down the highway as though on wings. Irene's hair whipped about her head, and she felt exhilarated beyond belief. She couldn't wait for the car to slow down and come to a stop. She wanted Cader Harris. She realized she no longer felt frightened or apprehensive.

When Cader maneuvered the car into a rutted road that was dark as ebony, she let her breath out in a long sigh. Before he turned off the lights, Cader looked at his watch and said, "We have exactly sixty-two minutes." The moment the engine died he had her in his arms and was crushing her mouth to his while his busy hands searched and probed her soft flesh

In the darkness Irene felt herself being crushed against Cader's chest. There was a faint aroma of deodorant and aftershave, and, although his grip was tight and rough, his lips were soft, caressing her mouth, teasing it and persuading it to open to his.

His hands were in her hair, on the back of her neck, on her throat. This wasn't like the fumbling of some of the other boys who had tried to seduce her. This was the expert handling of a man, the man of the hour, Cader Harris.

She had been determined to charm him into obedience, flirt with his ego and eventually have her way with him by leaving him panting with desire yet respecting her virginity. But the touch of his mouth on hers, the caress of his tongue searching for hers, the unhurried exploration of his hands on her breasts seemed to beat the will out of her.

She had never felt this way before. She had sometimes allowed a boy to kiss her and even to slip his tongue into her mouth. And if he were very nice, she might let him go so far as to touch her breasts, but never, ever, had she wanted a boy to open her blouse, undo her bra and run his tongue over her nipples. Now, here with Cader Harris, she wanted this more than she wanted breath.

Her own fingers fumbled with the buttons on her blouse. Unashamed, she impatiently worked the hooks on her bra and tore it free from her body.

He acceded to her demands, allowing her to lead the pace and set the limits. She heard her own gasp when his hand touched her flesh, heard his moan of passion as he bent his head to touch his lips to the rosy crests, felt a curling heat build within her and ignite between her thighs.

With the same impatience she had displayed with blouse and bra, Irene removed her skirt and panties. She didn't dare to stop to think what she was doing. She only knew she wanted to be naked with Cader Harris. She wanted him to touch her all over in that same teasing and feathery way that he touched her breasts.

There, on the front seat of her Ford Fairlane, Irene Hayden gave herself to Cader Harris. And when she felt him tremble as he entered her, she was unaware of the sharp momentary pain. She was only aware that Cader was saying her name over and over.

They stayed out long past Cader's curfew. Loving and kissing and exploring one another. They were both naked now, the chill of the early October air making their bodies smooth and silky against each other. Irene forgot all about her decision to save herself for marriage; she forgot entirely about the fact that she was a Hayden, one of the privileged, and that

Cader was from the wrong side of town; she even forgot that she had met his challenge and lost. The only thing she could think of was Cader, his mouth, his hands, the way he whispered her name. Irene Hayden, for the first time in her life, loved someone else more than she loved herself.

Her inexperience was no deterrent to her inventiveness. When the passions flared between them again, she moved him into a sitting position and straddled his lap. His hands played with the firm flesh of her bottom as she lowered herself onto him, greedily taking him inside her. Her long, tapered thighs were strong and her body agile as she moved her hips in slow, undulating circles. And when she pushed herself against him and his mouth found her breast, she cried out his name and the wind carried it above the treetops. Irene Hayden had found passion and fulfillment and love. Irene Hayden had found Cader Harris.

Dulcie entered the dining room and had to repeat her question before Irene could break herself from the memory of that night. Even as she responded to Dulcie's question of "Will that be all for the day? Can I go home now?" she was aware of the wetness between her legs.

Cader Harris was back in town. Had he come back for her? Did he still love her? Or had he come back for Kevin? A dull heaviness weighed on her chest as she looked at Kevin's place at the table. She swallowed hard, choking back her dread. Irene Hayden knew from experience that Cader Harris always got what he wanted.

*   *   *

Hours after Dulcie had cleared away the half-eaten meal, Bethany paced the ruffled confines of her room. She wrung her hands together to keep them from trembling with anger. How could Kevin do this to her? How could he take a job with that awful Cader Harris? *How could he work with Judy Evans every day?*

Judy Evans. She'd had her eye on Kevin since kindergarten. She wanted Kevin for herself! Well, she couldn't have him. Kevin belonged to her, Beth, his sister, and nobody, nobody in this whole world could take him from her. Not Judy, not Cader Harris, not Tulane, not anyone or anything!

She paused before the pier glass and studied her reflection. Slowly, as though afraid to look, she pulled her robe apart and saw her nakedness reflected in the mirror. She scrutinized her slimness, curling her lip in distaste at the whiteness of her skin and the smattering of freckles left over from last summer's sunburn. Why couldn't she tan like the other girls, like Judy Evans? She was always as white as a fish's belly except for the patch of bright red hair at the V of her thighs. Even that looked pale and washed out to her eyes. She had seen Judy many times showering after gym, and her pubic hair was thick and glossy and black against her skin.

Her hands cupped her small, symmetrical breasts and she bemoaned the fact that they weren't full and ripe like Judy's. With a jerk she pulled the flaps of her robe tightly around her nakedness, blocking it from her view in the pier glass. Well, she was herself and not like Judy at all. Judy was a different type altogether. There were lots of beautiful women in the world whose breasts were small and whose skin was white, she reasoned. *Just think of all those women Kevin and I used to look at in Daddy's girlie magazines.* The ones he had kept hidden in the bottom drawer of his bureau. Lots of the girls in there had been milk-skinned and slim. Once Kevin had even pointed one out, saying that Beth would grow up to look just like her. She remembered studying the glossy page, noting with satisfaction the way the girl's legs had a long, sensuous curve to the slim hips and the way her breasts were high and firm, not like some of the others whose breasts hung halfway to their waists.

Beth had asked Kevin if he thought the girl in the picture was beautiful.

"Gee, yeah, Beth! If she weren't beautiful, do you think she'd have her picture in the book?"

That had been years ago, Beth thought, pulling herself back to the present. A lot of magazines and rainy afternoons when they had been left alone had gone by since that day, and each time they had experimented and explored each other's bodies with the offhanded innocence of children.

One day, shortly after Kevin's thirteenth birthday, Beth had suggested they take a peek in Daddy's bottom bureau drawer. It had been months since the two of them had gone into Mama's room together. Kevin had glanced at Beth uneasily and then quickly looked back to the book he was reading. "Aw, c'mon, Beth. That stuff's for kids. It's better to forget all about it." He was embarrassed; Beth could sense it and it puzzled her.

"Have you forgotten about it, Kevin?" she sulked.

"Yeah, Sis, all about it." He closed off any further

discussion by immersing himself in his book, but Beth knew he was aware of her standing there, looking down at him with tears smarting her eyes. Kevin could tell her he'd forgotten about those times in Mama's room till the cows came home and she'd never believe him. She sensed she would make him angry if she continued to push in that direction, and she decided she would never make an issue of it again. But she'd never forget. Never. How could she forget her very own brother? Her own, very own, beautiful brother, Kevin.

Beth heard a sound from the room next to hers. Before she realized what she was doing, she was out in the hall and quietly knocking on Kevin's door. He murmured something and came to open the door. She heard the snick of the lock. When had Kevin started locking his door? Was he locking himself in or locking her out?

He stood there facing her, a book in his hand. He was forever studying and restudying, trying to get a jump on the courses at Tulane. "Beth, if you've come to argue with me again or to pull another of your sulks, forget it. I'm taking the job with Mr. Harris and that's final."

"That's not why I'm here," Beth began, her mind racing to find another reason. She didn't want him to expel her from his room and to widen the breach that existed between them. "I just wanted you to know that Luther Guthrie asked me out. Do you think Mama will let me go?"

The shocked expression on Kevin's face amused her. "Boomer? Boomer Guthrie wants to take you out? You've got to be kidding!"

"And what if I'm not, Mr. Bigshot? What's wrong with me anyway that you don't think a boy would ask me out?" she shot back in annoyance.

"Don't get me wrong, Sis. It's not that I don't think Boomer wouldn't want to take you out. That's easy enough to believe, you're so pretty and all. What gets me is you'd actually consider dating him. Boomer?"

Hotly, "Darn right I would, Kevin Thomas! Luther is one of the best looking boys in the graduating class!"

"Yeah, and one of the horniest! You're not going out with him, Beth. That guy's a menace to the flower of Southern womanhood."

"Luther is not! He's a perfectly nice boy and there's not a thing you could do to stop me from seeing him!" Beth enjoyed seeing Kevin react this way. Groping for a reason for coming to his room, even though it was a lie, she had hit on just the right mark.

"Beth, listen to me, I've heard girls complain that Boomer has more hands than an octopus and he's got a very nasty temper when he's turned down. Be serious now, find some okay guy to date."

"I don't know what you're talking about, Kevin Thomas. Luther is nice and he wants to take me out!" she lied again.

"Look, Beth, they don't call him Boomer for nothing. And that's not a name he got on the football team either. He's been called Boomer ever since sixth grade when some of the guys caught him playing with himself in the boys' room going, 'Boom! Boom! Boom!' at the top of his voice. That's all he could think about then and that's all he still thinks about, and no sister of mine is going out with him!" Kevin's rage flushed his face and his ears were burning.

"I won't be dictated to, Kevin. Why should I listen to you? You don't care what I think! You're going to work for Mr. Harris and be with that tacky Judy Evans every day."

"Just where did Boomer ask you to go with him?" Kevin asked, trying to get the subject away from Cader Harris and Judy Evans.

Beth's mind raced for a reply. "Just to that movie over in Dunstan that I wanted to see. The one with Barbra Streisand," she pouted.

"Tell you what, Beth. I'll take you. Would you like that?" Kevin asked, his eyes pleading with her.

Suddenly, "Oh, Kev, you're the best brother ever! Would you really take me? When?" She threw herself at him, hugging him tightly around the neck, waiting for his arms to go around her.

"How about this Friday? I'll get the car from Dad. Okay?"

"You betcha!" she exclaimed, giving him a final squeeze, pressing close to him, very aware of her own nudity beneath the thin robe.

"Okay, get yourself out of here for now," he pushed her toward the door, "I've still got some studying to do and then I want to hit the hay early."

Chapter Four

Cader Harris sat quietly atop a packing crate and made no effort to answer the shrilling phone. When a phone rang at the ungodly hour of 7:30 in the morning, it could only mean one thing; anyone who wanted to reach him didn't have one damned good thing to say to him. He stretched his thick, muscular neck and wiped at the perspiration on his brow. He had just arrived at the store a few minutes ago and the air conditioning hadn't had time to cool off the stale air hanging like a shroud in the topsy-turvy shop.

The thin madras shirt he wore was open to his waist, revealing a wide expanse of chest dewy with sweat. He flexed his shoulders and felt the moisture trickle down his sides. Christ! Was this the way he was going to start every day here in Hayden? Fear and uneasiness gnawed at him. Sooner or later he would have to answer the fucking phone, and he damn well better do it before his new sales help came in for the first day on the job. But not now. Now he just wanted to drink the coffee he'd picked up at the carry-out sandwich shop and savor the wet, cardboard taste.

The shrilling phone cut off in mid-ring, causing Cader to flinch as though he'd been struck a blow. It would ring again, and soon. It would ring and ring until he picked it up and said what he was supposed to say. What he was getting paid to say. *They're really going to bust my balls till they hear for the hundredth time what I've already agreed to do. What the hell happened to a man's word and a handshake?* Everything had to be done yesterday and the day before that. "When you stick a poker up someone's ass, make sure it's red hot!" he said aloud. "Sixty lousy days to whip this town into shape," he muttered. It was just like the gridiron, you could either run with the ball or stick around with your finger up your ass and wait to get clobbered. Just stick with the game plan and then take the money and run.

The phone shrilled again; this time he picked it up. "Cader Harris," he bellowed into the receiver.

"Mornin'. How's our man?"

"Mornin', Mr. Fairfax, how's things at Delta Oil?"

"Now remember, Cade, we agreed no names, right?"

"Right."

"How's things going?"

"It's too soon to tell."

"We know we can depend on you, boy. You'll have it all sewed up in a week's time."

"I wouldn't be too sure of that, Mr. . . ." He stopped himself just in time.

"No names," he was reminded. "What do you mean, 'don't be too sure'?"

"It's just that it will take awhile. This town isn't going to be easy to convince that they want, even need, those storage tanks."

"We've all got a lot riding on you, Cade. You know that. There's even something in it for you, or did you forget?"

Forget a quarter of a million dollars? he thought to himself. He said, "No, sir, I haven't forgotten." Harris knew Delta Oil had sixty days to bid on a huge shipment from Algeria. It was imperative to have a firm decision on Hayden accepting the erection of the holding tanks. Failure to have the okay for the tanks could cost Delta millions of dollars.

"Good then. As we arranged, we'll be in contact daily. If there's anything I can do . . ."

"Yes, sir."

"Good. One of us will talk to you tomorrow. Till then." The receiver on the other end of the line clicked quietly, leaving Cader's half-said goodbye to fall on a dead line.

Christ, he thought to himself. It was going to be hard enough to convince the right people that the storage tanks should come into Hayden, let alone have a time limit on it. That sixty days bit had been something they had thrown in at the last minute. The bastards. He could see it now. He'd do all the ground work and then his time would be up. Then some sharpshooter would come into town or they'd put a few healthy bribes in the right places and he, Cader, would be out in the cold. When he had suggested a payoff to them in the first place, he was met with strong opposition. Delta Oil wouldn't risk the possibility of a scandal. It would be better, much better, if the town opted for the LNGs on their own. No, it would be better, much better, if Cader would go back to Hayden as a merchant. That way it would appear that he'd have a natural interest in seeing the industry come into town.

"Sure, sure," he kicked out at a carton of tennis balls, "you'll come in when everything else is done and grease a few palms and I'll be out in the cold. Well, I won't let it happen. I've got too much riding on this deal. My whole future. I'll squeeze the quarter mil out of Delta Oil before the ink even has a chance to dry!"

In his mind Cader began reviewing the tactic he would take to inveigle himself into the town's confidence. Sure, he was already their returning hero, but that didn't count for much when there was so much at stake. He had, at one time, thought of befriending the men on the town council. That was until he began studying the town newspaper and noticing that the Junior Women's League of Hayden had among its rolls all the wives of the men on the council. Marvin Guthrie, Hayden's own mayor, was married to the Women's League president, Alma. That's where he would begin, he smiled to himself confidently, aware of his past successes with women. Hell, if he could get them to pull down their pants, it would be easy to get them to endorse the LNGs. A good-looking jock tells a woman the marvelous things Blass and Halston could do for her and bingo . . . she wants her husband to provide them. And this jerkwater town would need a healthy boost in commerce that only Delta Oil could provide.

He went down the list of members in his mind, finding the names familiar and recalling the way most of them had looked in high school. Some ladies' names he didn't recognize, but he recognized their husbands' names, remembering jocks he'd played ball with and which ones had sat in the bleachers wishing they were Cader Harris. One name that didn't make any connection at all was Keli McDermott. Must be new in town. Her old man too. His dinner date with Marsha Evans would help break him into the right circles. Marsha, he knew from studying the back issues of the paper, was secretary of the Junior Women's League as well as being a real fine-looking piece of ass. He thought of Marsha and how she looked in that clingy white uniform, but his mind kept turning to the name of Keli McDermott, and he wondered if she were a blonde or a brunette.

Colonel Gene McDermott (ret.) added the coffee to the percolator and plugged it in. At the sound of the first plop of the bubbling water, he cracked eggs into a bowl and stirred them carefully. Just as he was about to add them to the hot butter, the phone rang. "McDermott here," he said briskly.

"Dr. Baldwin's office calling. May I speak to Mrs. McDermott?"

"Mrs. McDermott can't come to the phone right now, would you care to leave a message?" A worm of concern began biting into Gene's flat, drum-tight stomach, making him sound raspy and unsure of himself.

"Well, tell Mrs. McDermott Doctor Baldwin will see

her tomorrow at one o'clock. I've had a cancellation and this is the earliest I can fit her in," the clinical voice at the other end of the receiver explained.

"Is this her regular checkup?" the Colonel asked, licking dry lips.

"Goodness, no. Checkups are made a month in advance. This visit is for a consultation concerning the lump in her breast. The doctor knows and understands how worried you both must be, that's why I scheduled her as soon as possible. We'll see her tomorrow at one."

"Yes, yes, I'll give her the message. Matter of fact, I'll bring her myself."

Gene McDermott listened to the last plop-plop-plop of the coffee pot and looked at the eggs in the bowl. Suddenly, he felt sick. Sick and beaten. The one beautiful thing in his entire life and they were going to mutilate her. Never. Gene knew all about lumps and breasts and doctors. Hadn't he seen his own mother undergo a mastectomy and hadn't she died an excruciating death?

He'd never let them get their hands on Keli, mutilate her and scar her body. He'd seen what a woman looked like after her breast was removed, and nobody was going to hack away at his beautiful wife and mar her perfection. When something was perfect, you didn't tamper with it. He wouldn't let them touch her. Asshole doctors, what did they know? Put an M.D. after their names and you might as well smear the word "God" across their foreheads. And that Baldwin was the asshole of the lot. "Like hell you'll take a knife to my Keli!" he shouted hoarsely.

A towel wrapped around her body, Keli walked into the kitchen and was shocked at the hateful look on her husband's face. Her doe eyes fearfully raked the room for some sign, some clue to his apparent outrage. "What is it, Gene, did you burn yourself? What is making you angry?"

At the sight of the slim woman standing before him, his outrage cooled immediately. "Honey, why didn't you tell me you had an appointment with Dr. Baldwin?"

Keli sucked in her breath and reached out an arm in entreaty only to remember she needed both hands to hold the towel around her nakedness. "I didn't tell you because I didn't have an appointment. The office said they would call me when there was an opening. I don't want to upset and worry you, Gene."

"Honey, honey," he said gruffly, "what do you think I'm here for? I'll always take care of you. As long as I'm alive, you have nothing to worry about. I'll never let anything happen to you. I love you, don't you know that?" Tenderly, he cupped her face in his hands and looked into the velvety depths of his wife's eyes. "You should have told me," he chided gently. "There's no need for concern. I'll take you to see Doc Baldwin and I'll set him straight. No one is going to touch you. I give you my word."

"But, Gene, I am not a child. I am a woman. I know that sometimes surgery is needed. Ever since I discovered the little lump I have done some reading. At times they take a little piece of it and make the necessary, what they call biopsy."

"It's only necessary if I say it is necessary." He spoke distinctly as though she were a backward child. "You're my wife and I swore to take care of you and that's what I'm going to do. Scoot now and get dressed. I'll make eggs Benedict as a special treat. You just put this whole thing out of your mind, and we won't mention it again. Go on, now, get dressed," he prodded sternly.

Tears glistened in her velvety eyes as Keli turned to leave the copper and brick kitchen. What was the use? No matter what she did, no matter what she said, Gene would have his way. If he said she wouldn't have an operation, then she wouldn't have an operation. She would have to endure the pain and try to ignore it. A fatalist by nature, she fully and completely believed that her life was predestined. She knew the lump was cancerous, and she knew she would eventually have her breast removed or she would die. She had learned to live with other things and she would live with this. Gene would take care of her. Gene would always take care of her.

While she dressed, she let her mind wander to Julia and Marsha and how they would have reacted to her situation. Would they, with their Western ways, be better able to handle what she was going through? Julia would, of course, she was married to Doctor Baldwin; Marsha would bite her lower lip and see it through to the end. And then there was Irene. Irene had a philosophy and a solution for everything. Besides, no cancerous lump would have the audacity to inflict itself on Irene's body. A small smile tugged at the corners of Keli's mouth. After all, some time or another, Irene's Daddy Haydon must have come across the same problem and would have handed down to his daughter some sage advice.

Her bra secure, Keli flinched when she tugged it into place and felt it dig into the soft flesh under her arm. Now it was swollen, she noticed and once more tried to adjust the soft silk cupping her breasts. Perhaps she could go without the bra today if she wore a dark blouse. Quickly, she removed the offending garment and let her breath out in relief. Gently, she worked her arm up and down and shrugged her slim shoulders. It was definitely easier to bear the nagging soreness once the bra was removed.

Her eyes fell to the neatly typed pages resting on her dressing table. Damion's sermon for next week. It had taken all her concentration to overcome the pain in her breast and under her arm last evening when she had drummed out the sermon on the typewriter. She didn't think she'd be able to type for him again. At least not until something was done to alleviate this almost constant discomfort. How was she going to tell him? She frowned. She liked to think he depended on her. That someone depended on her and thought of her as a capable adult. It was terribly confining to be the kind of individual who aroused the protective instinct in everyone around her.

Colonel McDermott downed the bitter liquid at the bottom of his coffee cup and slammed it down into its saucer. The phone call from Dr. Baldwin's office had unnerved him, and he was aware of a creeping fear swelling in the pit of his stomach. He could hear Keli's movements from down the hall as she dressed and was aware of the faint scent of her perfume. His beautiful Keli.

Gene rubbed his heavy-knuckled hand over his short-cropped hair, feeling the hard bones of his skull beneath his fingers. Though his hair was mostly silver now, his physique and unlined features were those of a man considerably younger than his fifty-eight years. Out of those fifty-eight years thirty had been spent crawling up the ranks of the Air Corps until he reached the rank of colonel. It had been a tough struggle at times, but he had known that a life amid a world of men suited him perfectly.

It had been during his last campaign, while he was serving in Vietnam, that he had discovered Keli. While on assignment with Thailand's forces, he had been attracted by a local religious ceremony being conducted in a public square. Kneeling before a shrine, dressed in traditional costume, was the most beautiful creature he had ever seen. Her black hair was wound atop her head and fresh exotic blossoms were arranged between the strands. Her face had been a study of innocence and virtue as she knelt with her offering to the strange god. She represented something that Gene had always suspected was absent from life: goodness and purity.

Gene McDermott's experience with women had always been of the basest nature. Women were available for men's use; they were the providers of necessary sexual release. The Air Corps provided everything else in the realm of comfort. Meals were prepared and laundry done with none of the hysterics or messy emotional reparations he had noticed his married colleagues being forced to endure. Everything in the Corps was done cleanly, efficiently, unemotionally. A man could take his meals in the mess and not feel obliged to make small talk with the cook. He felt no indebtedness to the person who washed his Jockey shorts and who pressed the creases in his uniform slacks. Life was clean, without involvement.

It was when a man became involved with a woman that his values were upset, and the orderly life that was natural to the male species became emotional and peppered with havoc. Fights erupted in the bars among friends who had their eye on the same prostitute; married men were obliged to leave the officers' club early, even during a winning streak in an endless poker game, muttering some vagary about the "little woman." Even on a battlefield women impaired a man's judgment, even if that instant appraisal of a situation was necessary to self-preservation. He'd seen it over and over again. That instant of hesitation, that error of judgment, that irrevocable choice. "Come back to me, darling," they would write in their voluminous letters to husband or lover, imposing on a man the determination to survive the war not for the sake of his own life but for some higher, more noble reason which surpassed even the will to live: that of return-ing to the woman who had assured him she could not live without him. That was until he received his "Dear John" letter and then was so demoralized, so confused about his own value, that he would walk into the line of fire, leaving his chances of survival to a much higher authority.

Some lived and some died, and according to Gene's observations, it was always because of some woman.

Being an astute individual, Gene had decided never to be entrapped by a woman. He would take what they had to offer, use it or turn away from it, as was a man's inalienable right. It didn't seem strange to him that he equated all women with the prostitutes with whom he traded money for sexual release and irrevocable proof that he wasn't a queer. He didn't hold with the theory he had heard expounded at great length that prostitutes were products of their circumstances, that their entire economy was simply a matter of supply and demand, a demand created by men, an economy created by society. There was only one theory which seemed plausible to Gene McDermott: there were "good" women and there were "bad," and the worst of the lot were the prostitutes who frequented the watering holes of the United States Air Corps.

Being a man committed to his conviction, many times after paying a prostitute for her services, Gene would give her a sound beating in the bargain. Bad women had to be punished. Bad women spread diseases. They passed their corruption and infections onto men, smiling as they did so, distracting the unwary male with sighs of passion and hungry lips. In his rage and hostility directed at women in general, Gene never stopped to wonder where the women became infected in the first place. To him, disease and corruption were synonymous with the name "woman," and it was bred and festered within their bodies, in the dark regions between their thighs.

When Gene McDermott saw Keli, he recognized the difference between her and other women immediately. Keli was pure where other women were sullied. She was guileless and beyond reproach.

Having made subtle inquiries, he discovered she was from a fine, if impoverished, family, and she was, in fact, as pure and unworldly as his every instinct told him she was. He made arrangements with her family to marry her, see to her family's safety and make financial arrangements to provide for Keli. His tour of duty separated him from her for nearly four years, and the only contact he had with her was through stiffly interpreted letters.

Throughout their separation, Keli studied English and learned to read and write until she finally produced her first letter to Gene in his own language. It was formal and held her own quality of innocence. Gene treasured it.

Finally, political upheaval and red tape cleared, he retired from the Air Corps and brought his beautiful wife home to the States, settling with his young bride of twenty-two in the town of Hayden.

With a successful military career behind him, financial independence, a nice home in a nice town, friends at the country club and a beautiful wife, Gene McDermott should have had the world by the tail. Yet, somehow, it was all disconnected and he knew himself to be unfulfilled. It never occurred to him that his discontent stemmed from his unfortunate and twisted view of what his wife should be. Somehow, the shrine where he first saw Keli had become an altar for her purity. In the two and half years of living with her and sleeping in the same bed with her, he had never been able to achieve a sexual relationship with his lovely, sloe-eyed bride. Each attempt ended in failure, leaving Keli with quiet tears shining in her dark eyes, and leaving Gene with a profound feeling of inadequacy.

Since the first time he had seen Keli praying in the pageant and making contact with her family, Gene had abstained from sexual encounters, telling himself that a girl as chaste as Keli deserved a man of moral fortitude. He would make himself as worthy of her purity as possible.

Somehow, it had all backfired. Gene had become totally incapable of having a sexual relationship. He glossed over this fact by telling himself that it was because he couldn't bear to take from Keli that one quality which set her apart from and above all other women: her virginity.

He had seen Keli's eyes following the children in the playground. He had heard her sweet bubble of laughter when a particularly precocious child appeared in a television commercial. He knew she wanted a child. But a pregnancy would be a violation of her body, robbing her of her innocence, submitting her to a life growing within her, a life that would share an experience with her that he could never share. He wanted to protect her from that violation, from the indignity of childbirth, from the acknowledgment that she was like all other women.

This is what he told himself. He was informed about the practices of contraception and could have put any number of them to use. He never bothered. He knew, even without admitting to himself that he knew, that everything else was a lie. His adoration of his wife, of her purity, of her beauty was all a lie. They were excuses and he knew it. What Gene McDermott couldn't and wouldn't admit to himself was that he was impotent.

Chapter Five

"Judy! I'll be leaving in a few minutes!" Marsha Evans called, her voice carrying up the stairwell to the second floor bedroom where her daughter primped with pimple cream before her bedroom mirror. Determined, she tried to soften the strident tone which habitually crept into her voice when she dealt with Judy. If there was anything she didn't want this morning, it was an emotional scene with a petulant sixteen-year-old whose face was dotted with chalky, flesh-colored acne ointment for a skin disorder that didn't exist.

Ever since Rod and Marsha had been divorced three years ago, Judy had become more and more difficult to handle and the situation had worsened since his death in an automobile accident the summer before.

It didn't take a fancy, high-priced psychiatrist to conclude that Judy accused Marsha of Rod's death and found her guilty. With the inimitable logic of a teenager Judy had reasoned:

"*You* were the reason my father left us. *You* were inadequate and he went away and divorced *you* and me, too! If *you* were the kind of wife he needed, he never would have left *me!* He never would have been in that car when it crashed!"

"Judy, did you hear me? I said I'll be leaving in a few minutes!"

No answer.

Taking a deep breath to steel her nerves, Marsha waited for a response. Receiving none, she called again, hearing that dreaded, strident tone rise upward to her daughter. "I said I'll soon be leaving! I would like to talk to you before I go. Now, please come down here!"

Still no answer. Instead the sound of footsteps scuffing along the upstairs hall. Judy appeared at the top of the stairs enveloped in a pink wrapper, her face predictably disguised with pimple cream and her hair wrapped around lethal-looking electric curlers.

"I can't talk to you while you're up there and I'm down here. If you would please."

Judy stomped down the stairs. "I didn't hear you, Mom."

Near exasperation, Marsha took another breath and purposely softened her tone. "Judy, I'm going out this morning. Mrs. McDermott will be picking me up any minute now. But I'll be back later this afternoon. Before you leave for the day, I expect you to pick up your room and straighten the bathroom. It's beyond me how you manage to create such a mess. . . . A new client will be coming by this afternoon to discuss my redecorating her home. You know I like to take prospective clients through our house to show them some of my ideas. It would help a lot if your room and the bathroom were in order. Okay?"

Judy lifted her eyes heavenward in a display of boredom. "I've heard it all before, Mother. Yes, I'll pick up my room. And the bathroom. But I think you should consider that I'm working now, too, and I don't have all that much time."

"You've still more time than I do, young lady, and your working for Mr. Harris doesn't excuse your responsibilities around the house."

"Mr. Harris, Mother? I thought you called him Cader. The two of you seemed awfully chummy when he hired me for his new store." Judy grinned.

"What are you getting at? Cader and I went to school together, we're old friends." Marsha laughed, relieved to hear the light note in her daughter's voice. Their relationship had improved in the past few weeks and Marsha suspected that reason for improvement was Kevin Thomas. The accusations concerning Rod's death had ceased, and Judy seemed content with judging her mother merely inadequate.

"I'm not getting at anything. I was just wondering how you got to be 'Johnny on the spot' and managed to connive a dinner date with him, that's all," Judy teased.

"You were right there. You know how it came about!"

"Yeah, you're right, Mom. I saw that little maneuver and I don't blame you. I believe in going after what you want."

"Is that how you feel about Kevin?" Marsha asked conversationally.

"That's right. I want him. I went after him and I've almost got him. And I'm not going to let him get away."

The answer was curt and truthful and Marsha knew Judy compared herself to her.

Keli settled herself behind the wheel of Gene's Camaro, a look of dismay marking her exquisite features. Stick shift. She didn't know if her arm could hold out, and she didn't want the others to know she was in pain. Mentally she counted how many stops she would have to make and how many corners there would be before she arrived at the high school. Weakly, she leaned back in the bucket seat and toyed with the idea of staying home or calling one of the others and asking them to drive.

Rejecting the idea, her foot eased the clutch down as she slipped the car into first gear and then into second. A fine beading of perspiration glistened on her smooth brow and alabaster teeth dug sharply into her lower lip. Third and fourth, cruising speed. When she stopped for Marsha, she would slip it into neutral, as she glided to a stop, and then into first. That way, she told herself, there would be less of a jolt on her arm.

Keli rounded the corner and Marsha recognized Gene's Camaro. Marsha smoothed her pearl-gray silk shirtwaist over her hips and wished she'd waited inside in the air conditioning. The day was humid and the sun baked the dew off the lawn into sticky vaporous waves. The cream-colored sports car came to a jolting halt at the curb and Marsha strode down the path, the strap of her bag slapping against her leg. Tucking her knees below the dashboard and fastening her seatbelt, she turned to Keli. "Hi," she said huskily.

"Good morning, Marsha. I'm sorry I'm late but sometimes I am not used to this car and my hands and feet don't work at the same time," Keli apologized softly.

"You're here and that's all that matters." Marsha smiled. "Are you picking up Irene or Julia first?"

Keli let her mind wander to the various stops along the way and finally decided Julia would be her first stop. "Julia, I think."

Out of the corner of her eye, Marsha watched Keli's trembling hand close over the gear shift and was momentarily alarmed by the tense grip the slim girl applied to it. Keli's whole body was ramrod stiff and her jaw clenched tightly. Something was wrong. "Would you like me to drive? You look like you're upset about something. Do you want to talk about it?" Thoughts of her problems with Judy flew out of her mind as she waited for Keli's response. She had never seen her this way, so tense, so frightened.

Tears gathered in Keli's eyes. The kind offer had disarmed her and she suddenly felt very much as though she wanted to tell her best friend. "Marsha, there is something I wish to ask you. No. That is wrong. There is something I want to tell you; something I want you to keep in confidence."

Alarmed by Keli's soft, urgent words, Marsha could only nod.

"I . . . I have a lump here," Keli began, touching her long, slim fingers to her breast. "Tomorrow, I am to see Doctor Baldwin. Gene . . . he insists on taking me himself. He answered the phone this morning about my appointment." Her voice broke and Marsha cursed Marc's bumbling, busybody nurse for not asking to speak to Keli instead of blurting everything out to Gene.

"Gene has already decided he will never allow me to have an operation if it is called for."

"Oh, my God!" Marsha breathed, thoughts whirling around in her head.

Keli heard Marsha's intake of breath and continued. "Once, when Gene was telling me about his family, he told me how his mother died. It began with a lump in her breast. . . ." She fought to gain composure. "He said he would never let anyone scar my body. . . ." It was impossible to continue. Impossible to talk about it without condemning Gene for his attitude.

"I understand, Keli. You don't have to talk about it if you don't want. Poor baby." She reached for Keli and gathered her into her arms in an embrace. Gently, she stroked the silken head and crooned soft words of comfort. "Poor baby, I'll stand by you. I'll speak to Marc. He's the most understanding man I know. I'll explain about Gene. Don't worry, Keli, I'll make it right for you." Squeezing her eyes shut against the torrent of tears gathering there, Marsha silently prayed for the wisdom to say the right words to comfort Keli.

Finally finding her voice, Marsha crooned, "Keli, honey, it may not be what you're thinking." Somehow she could not utter the word "cancer," yet it stood between them like the shadow of a carrion bird circling for the kill. It carried with it every fear common to all women. Disfigurement and death. "Lots of women get lumps and bumps and most of them turn out to be nothing. Don't go thinking the worst, honey," she murmured, still cradling Keli's head against her shoulder.

Swallowing hard, Keli moved away from Marsha and spoke hesitantly. "If you would not mind, Marsha, take me to the parsonage and go on to the high school with Irene and Julia. I think today is not a good time for me to be with other people. I promised Damion I would deliver his sermon today, and if I do it now, perhaps I can help him with something before . . . tomorrow." In spite of her determination, she couldn't help the slight hesitation. "Tomorrow," a word meaning "the future," yet it sounded like the end of the present.

"The hell with the rest of them, Keli, you shouldn't be alone. I'll just run in and call the girls. . . ."

"No, please. I would like a little time to myself. Gene . . . he doesn't understand that I sometimes need time to be alone. . . ."

"I understand, honey. I'll pick you up when we finish the uniforms," Marsha said, climbing from the car.

"I have thought again; I will walk to the parsonage. I'll find my own way home. Thank you anyway. Drop the car off at the house and Gene will give you a ride home. Today I feel the need to walk and be alone."

Bewildered, Marsha could only agree. Sadly, she climbed behind the wheel and looked up into Keli's face. "Keli—," she began, then cut off her words. What could she say? What could she possibly say to lessen the fear, the pain? "If you need me, you know where I'll be. I'd rather not go and listen to those gossipy . . ."

"No! You must go, Marsha!" A note of hysteria tinged Keli's voice. "I won't need you, Marsha."

Keli turned in the direction of the parsonage, her head bowed, her jet hair falling over her face and forming a curtain between herself and the world. Instinctively, she knew she had hurt Marsha by telling her she wasn't needed. Just as she knew she had hurt Gene by not telling him of the lump in her breast, by having him find out about it through a casual phone call. Marsha and Gene had little use for one another, yet in some ways they were remarkably alike. She pushed the thought from her mind. *She* was the one who needed help. She needed someone, and she knew she could find that help, that strength, in Damion Conway.

Her thoughts still centered on Keli, Marsha pulled the car over to the curb in front of Julia Baldwin's sprawling ranch-style home. Looking as though she stepped out of the pages of *Vogue*, Julia smoothed her gleaming cap of auburn hair and adjusted the collar of her pink silk blouse.

"Marsha! Isn't this Gene McDermott's car? Where's Keli?"

"Something came up and I dropped her off to see Damion Conway. Maybe she'll join us later, although we can manage without her for the day. Irene told me there were only nine band uniforms that still needed new braid and one that needs repairs on a sewing machine. Christ! The way she goes on about sending the band to Disney World you'd think it was for a command performance at Buckingham Palace!"

Julia laughed. "Irene takes on about everything. It's her style. I only asked about Keli because she doesn't seem to have her normal vitality lately. She's withdrawn. Have you noticed? I'm concerned about her."

Marsha swallowed and tried to keep her voice from quaking. What was she doing here prattling about this and that with Julia when Keli, her best friend, was sick and troubled and needed someone? "I'm sure it's nothing," Marsha answered. "I know she wanted to get a job and Gene won't stand for it. It has something to do with not feeling useful," Marsha lied.

"I can understand it. We all need something to get us through the days. There was supposed to be a meeting at the school auditorium last night about Delta Oil. Marc had a delivery so he didn't go. I was wondering how it all came out."

"Want me to turn on the radio? We might catch the news."

"No. I've got a miserable headache this morning. I hope Irene doesn't keep us waiting. I'm not in the mood for sewing today. And to tell you the truth, I'm absolutely not in the mood to listen to any more tales of Great-Granddaddy Hayden and how Arthur always smells like embalming fluid, however that smells. I'm sorry, Marsha, I didn't mean to bite. It's this ghastly headache, and, for God's sake, don't mention headache to Irene or she'll be expounding all day about how only really intelligent people get migraines and the rest of us have to suffer with plain old aches in the head!"

Marsha laughed and felt some of the tension leave her

shoulders. "I'm kind of in a funk myself today. Let's just get the job over with as soon as possible. Relax," she said, guiding the Camaro to the curb. "Irene is ready and waiting. That is Irene, isn't it?" she asked, pointing through the windshield.

Julia narrowed her eyes behind the polished glasses. "She's gone and got herself a new hairdo and she's lightened it! Christ! She must have dragged her hairdresser out of bed at the crack of dawn!"

"I like it," Marsha added. "It makes her look more feminine. Younger. She was getting awfully dowdy there."

Julia smiled, "I wonder what Daddy Hayden thinks of his little magnolia now. The word 'chic' almost comes to mind."

"Girls," Irene greeted them as she climbed into the back seat. "Hot, isn't it?" Her hand patted her new hairstyle which hung loose to her shoulders in place of the tight, heavy, drab knot she'd worn at the back of her head for longer than anyone could remember.

Almost by tacit, mutual consent, Marsha and Julia murmured something about the heat and said nothing about Irene's coiffure.

"Where's Keli?" Irene added, almost as an afterthought, chagrined that neither Marsha nor Julia mentioned her hair. She'd choke before she brought it to their attention and fished for a compliment. Her mirror told her all she had to know. Now, if she could only lose those eleven pounds before meeting up with Cader Harris.

"Keli couldn't make it today, but she was good enough to lend me Gene's car. That should make you happy, Irene.

We all know how you just 'love' Keli," Marsha said nastily.

"Marsha, I refuse to allow you to bait me today. You know I just adore Keli."

"My ass you adore Keli," Marsha all but sputtered. "You were the one who said, 'Oh, dear, those slanted eyes will never go over in this town,' and if you had had your way, you would have run her out of town on a rail. Admit it, Irene!"

"I'll admit to no such thing. You're a terrible person, Marsha, to even . . . to even think I didn't like that child."

"Keli is not a child!" Marsha shouted. "And I don't want to hear any more from you about her."

Always a gracious loser, Irene said, "Well, what's wrong with your car, Marsha? Why did you have to borrow Gene's?"

Changing the subject, Marsha said snidely, "I like your new hairdo. Don't tell me the morticians' union is having a dinner dance!"

Irene ignored her caustic words and plunged ahead. "I'm tired. I thought a change would do me good. As a matter of fact, I'm off to New Orleans tomorrow to do some shopping. I've been thinking of going to Elizabeth Arden and getting the works."

"That's a wonderful idea," Julia said, leaning over the back of the seat to look at Irene. "I've been thinking about going to New York for a week or so. It never hurts to improve the outer shell a little."

"New York is frightfully expensive," Irene offered.

"Irene, dear, the Haydens aren't the only people in the world who have money. Marc's income is more than substantial and I can afford to go to New York if I please," Julia said testily.

"For heaven's sake, Julia, you are touchy this morning. I didn't mean to infer he didn't make enough money. Gracious, his practice is certainly successful. It's possible he has almost as much money as Daddy."

Julia gagged and turned around in the seat. If Irene said another word, she would leap over the seat and strangle her, new hairdo or not.

"I'm just so tired this morning. Arthur had a late viewing and was called for a removal before he got home. My daddy always says you should never lock up before the man of the house is snug in his bed."

"Was that with or without his wife?" Julia snapped.

"Did someone singe your tail feathers last night, Julia?" Irene asked, her claws showing in the tone of her voice.

Marsha jumped into the verbal exchange and blurted, "Cader Harris invited me to dinner on Tuesday. Have either of you seen him since he came back to town?"

At the mention of Cader Harris, Irene stiffened. Her eyes pierced the back of Marsha's head as she pushed down her jealousy and felt herself almost choke on it.

"Really? You're not joking are you?" Julia asked.

"Would I joke about something like that? Of course he asked me and I'm going shopping for a new outfit tomorrow."

"Marsha, did you say Tuesday? Listen, how would it be if I gave a dinner party and invited all of Cader's old friends? We'll give him a rousing welcome." Julia's face brightened and for the first time she removed her sunglasses.

"Julia!" Irene complained. "That's really not fair. After all, it is Marsha's date!"

"Not at all, Irene," Marsha said, "I think Julia has a wonderful idea."

"In that case, we can have the party at my house," Irene insisted. "Let's do it up right."

"Meaning I don't?" Julia challenged.

"No . . ." Irene hastened to amend her words. "It's just that I have all the Hayden china and silver, not to mention the stemware. It can be a formal affair. . . ."

"Not on your life, Irene," Julia interrupted. "I refuse to eat another of your old Aunt Matilda's meat loaves. Shrimp Creole, my grandmother's recipe from the bayous. What do you think, Marsha?"

"Fantastic."

Irene pouted. This had nothing to do with jealousy over Cader Harris. This was something nearer the point of honor. *She* had always been the one elected to have important dinners. Like the time the Governor visited the Delta Oil refinery and had stayed in Hayden. The dinner had been a marvelous success and from that time on she had more or less become Hayden's official hostess. There had been a little write-up in the town's paper. . . .

"Shrimp Creole, a crisp green salad, what kind of wine do you think?" Julia asked Marsha.

"Hrmmph! And on what do you intend to serve this provincial masterpiece, Julia? Paper plates?" Irene grumbled nastily.

"How about my Wedgewood? Would that suit you?"

"Nobody, absolutely *nobody* eats on Wedgewood!" Irene stormed, oblivious to Julia's sarcasm.

"Then bring your own plate," Julia said callously. "I can't wait. As soon as I get home, I'll make all the calls. Ten people should round it out quite nicely."

"Why not just eight. Eight is so much more intimate," Irene pleaded.

"Irene Hayden Thomas . . . shut up. This is my dinner party and not yours. This town isn't ready for another of your Cecil B. DeMille productions. But I won't embarrass myself, I promise you. I'll even use a tablecloth!"

"Are you going to invite Keli and Gene McDermott?" Irene demanded. "I don't like Gene. He's a foreigner."

Marsha smiled. It was just like Irene to refer to Gene as the "foreigner" and pretend to accept his Oriental wife as one of her own.

"Irene," Julia said, exasperated, "just because Gene came from Connecticut doesn't mean he's a foreigner."

Irene defended herself. "Well, I wouldn't be surprised if he starts dinner off by singing the 'Battle Hymn of the Republic.' Great-Granddaddy Hayden was in the military, and he never behaved like Gene McDermott."

"Do I have to remind you the South *lost*, Irene?"

Irene was about to retort when she saw that Marsha was pulling into the parking lot behind the school and she clamped her mouth shut.

Chapter Six

Damion Conway closed the Bible with a loud snap and impatiently raked his hands through his hair. The Bible wasn't going to help him cope with Cader Harris. In order to cope with Cade, you always had to be one step ahead of the arrogant bastard. He could just hear Cade call him the "punting parson" in front of the town's leading citizens. He sighed. Everyone had his cross to bear, and Cade Harris and the title he had bestowed on Damion in college was his. He knew in his gut that sooner or later old Cade would spill the beans and then he would be in for it. Discretion was not one of Cade's virtues. Come to think of it, Cade had no virtues.

Damion pushed back the old-fashioned, wooden swivel chair and started to pace the floor. Cade meant trouble. He knew it as surely as he knew he had to take a next breath. He wasn't opening a store for the reasons he said.

Cade never did anything without a reason and whatever that reason was Cade always came out *número uno*. What could he possibly be up to and why? For days he had been torturing himself with these questions and what he could do if he found out.

"Damn!" Damion exclaimed just as Keli walked in the door, his sermon clasped in her hand. Something was wrong. It was in the set of the slim shoulders, in the trembling hands. Why was there a look of pain in her eyes?

Shyly, arm extended and hand trembling, she handed him the folder with Sunday's sermon. "Damion, I must talk with you. I will not be able to type your sermons anymore."

Damion waited. When he realized there was to be no further explanation, he smiled and motioned for her to sit down. "I understand, Keli, and it's all right. I'm surprised that you put up with my chicken scratching as long as you have. I'll throw myself on the mercy of one of the good ladies of the town. I wish I could have paid you more, Keli, but that's all that was allowed in the clerical budget."

Her dark eyes were filled with tears. "No, Damion, that is not the reason. I . . . I have a small problem and until it is . . . resolved, I cannot help you. It is not that your writing is bad or that the money is not sufficient. It is a personal matter," she said, lowering her eyes to stare at her folded hands.

"Keli, do you want to talk to me about it? If I can, I want to help you. Sometimes, not all the time, but sometimes it helps to talk out a problem. If I'm not the one you want to talk to, then perhaps you should talk it over with a relative or someone close to you. You did say you had a cousin in Los Angeles, didn't you?"

Her face showed overwhelming relief. "I feel very disloyal," Keli said, letting her breath out in a whisper. "It is not easy for me to talk of this . . . this problem with you or with anyone."

"Sit down, Keli, and let me get you a cup of coffee. Tell me," he said, his voice purposely light, "what did you think of this week's sermon? Will I reach the good people of Hayden and will they understand what I'm trying to tell them?"

Keli's sapling spine straightened imperceptibly. She felt rather than saw Damion leave the room. She would take a deep breath and say what she had to say and then it would be over. Damion would understand why she had come to him.

She saw the tray.

It wasn't just a tray, Damion was holding it. The silver winked and glittered in the sunlit room, making her blink.

And Damion. Quiet. Still. His presence reassured her. Offered her strength . . . an escape from the fear. He watched her, his eyes riveted to hers. Still. Quiet. Only her own people were that quiet. That still. She knew an overwhelming relief. A sense of coming home.

Unhurried, Damion set the tray on the corner of his desk and then took his place in the swivel chair. He wasn't too close, that was good, Keli told herself. He had a quiet, almost serene, face. A serenity that added to his handsome features and gave him a quality of maturity beyond his years. There was nothing to cause fear in Damion

Conway's face. There was a certainty about him, a touch of infallibility. Then his expression changed. The lines around his mouth tightened and she read there concern. Concern for her, she knew. He made no sign. No overture. Yet, when their eyes met, she felt free to speak.

Confident now, she spoke slowly and distinctly, her almond eyes staring straight into Damion's. "My marriage to Gene has never been consummated." She waited, her gaze unwavering.

Damion's thoughts lingered on the way she had pronounced "consummated." As though she had never heard the word before but had read it in a book and wasn't quite certain of where the inflection should be placed.

When Damion said nothing and his expression remained unchanged, she continued. "Why is not important. But it will never be what other people . . . it will never be a marriage."

Strangely, he felt relief at Keli's words. Relief because, although he had refused to face it until now, he had always turned away from the thought of Keii belonging to Gene. "The 'why' is important, Keli," he said softly. "Is it because of his age?"

Keli lowered her eyes, refusing to answer.

"Look at me, Keli. I can't help you unless you tell me."

She looked at him, her eyes liquid and shining, willing him to understand, reluctant to answer his direct question. "Gene is . . . is impotent," she whispered, "and it's my fault. He tries . . . so hard . . . but he can never . . . never . . ."

"I understand," Damion said, seeing the relief in her face. "But why? Is it physical?"

"No," Keli blurted. "There is no physical reason. Gene doesn't want a wife; he wants an idol, a goddess, not a flesh and blood woman."

The heaviness in Damion's chest lightened. He understood. Gene was reluctant to mar Keli's perfection, her purity. He wanted her always to be a virginal maiden. Damion remained motionless. He hadn't known what to expect, but this wasn't it. Saliva swirled in his mouth, and he found it difficult to swallow. If he swallowed, Keli would see his throat working and know that she had shocked him. He could feel Keli was about to say more. He felt it in the way she braced herself in the chair. Swallow, damn you, he cursed himself. Swallow and wait.

Momentarily, Keli's dark eyes shifted and Damion swallowed, his stomach muscles relaxing. He felt cold, chiseled, like the figure on the cross hanging from wires in the center of the church.

"I will never know what it is to give birth and feel the warmth of a child against my breast." It was a statement. Her oblique, dark eyes widened and filled with tears. "How true," she whispered, "I never realized . . ."

Her spine stiffened and Keli rose to her feet. She advanced a step and then another. When she was a foot from Damion, she dropped to her knees and held out her hand. He reached for her slim fingers and clasped them in his two hands. Again, he waited. Instinctively, he knew he could not speak, could not move or frighten her in any way.

"I have a . . . there is . . . I know . . ." She gulped. "Damion, I have a lump in my breast. I know it is cancerous. I need strength. Gene will not . . . Gene will not permit me to have it removed. I know I am going to die, and I have come to you for strength." Her eyes brimmed with unshed tears and she lowered her lids.

His voice, when he spoke, was almost a gurgle. "How do you know it's cancerous? Have you seen your doctor?" First things first . . . get to Gene later . . . the marriage was something else. No child to her breast. . . . Help me, God, he prayed silently.

"I know," she said simply. He believed her implicitly.

Damion's eyes narrowed slightly as he watched her tears well and remain in her eyes. How could that be, he thought incongruously. Tears always had to fall. He was suddenly aware that her hands were not trembling. Where were the words he should say? Why weren't they bubbling from his mouth? Why wasn't he being the good minister he was? There were words. He only had to search for them. Words. Gentle words of comfort, of strength. Soft words. Soft like Keli. Slow words, safe words. They wouldn't come. Keli didn't want words. There were none. Keli knew it and Damion knew it.

Softly, she said, "I have upset you and for that I am sorry."

"Keli," he whispered, finding his voice. "You say Gene will not permit you to have it removed. I can't pretend to understand why, not now, at least. I only question your sense of responsibility to yourself. It is your body, your life." He tried to keep the tone of urgency out of his voice.

Keli sank back against her heels, shoulders slumped, head bowed, long, jet hair shielding her face from his view.

She spoke so softly he strained to hear her. His gaze was centered on her hands which had fallen to her knees, palms up, fingers curved. Slowly, she began to tell him of the circumstances under which Gene had first seen her. She told him of the political danger her whole family had been in and how Gene's contracting to marry her had saved them. Because of Gene they had been able to relocate and place themselves under the protection of the American forces in Thailand. Gene was a powerful man. He was a generous man. He deserved her total respect and obedience.

As she spoke, Damion began to understand. Gene had been placed in the position of an honored ancestor. To Keli and her family and because of their culture, he was venerated, nearly deified. Respected without reservation. Revered. "I cannot, I will not, disobey Gene. I am grateful I see no questions in your eyes. I could not bear that, Damion."

She was wrong. His mind was filled with questions. Yet, he made no comment. Then at last he murmured, "Your answers will come from within you, Keli." He spoke gently, with great difficulty, aware of the pain his words could inflict. "I can listen to you, Keli; I can at least do that. You have a choice; you haven't denied that. I only ask that you not make it quickly. Consider, Keli."

"Gene . . ."

"Not Gene, Keli. Choice. Gene's an intelligent man; he'll reconsider his decision." He saw in her eyes that she knew Gene would not. Damion winced when Keli reached out to grasp the corner of his desk to pull herself to her feet. He saw the pain reflected in her eyes. Where had the tears gone? He wanted to know, he needed to know. He wanted to know everything about Keli McDermott, where she drew her strength, her serenity, where her tears went instead of falling on her cheeks.

"Thank you, Damion," she whispered. "I will try to remember what you have told me."

She was gone and Damion was left standing in the center of his study, the saliva gathering in his mouth again. He reached for the white linen handkerchief he always carried in his pocket and never used. She had thanked him. For what? What had he said to her? He couldn't even remember. Words, meaningless words. What good had he done her? What comfort had he brought her? Instead of doing the human thing, taking her in his arms and letting her cry it out, he had done what his father had always done. Lecture. Only he wasn't as proficient with gracious phrases and calling down the Lord's blessing as his father had been.

Damion's white clerical collar felt tight around his neck; his skin felt chafed. The Reverend Ephram Conway, Damion's father, had been Hayden's evangelist for nearly thirty years while Damion was growing up. He, Damion, had suffered all the pains of being the minister's son, and Ephram had fulfilled all the clichés of the tyrannical father with a calling for the Lord's work. Because of a stroke retirement was forced on Ephram by the bishopric. As a last favor, Damion had been granted a position in his father's former congregation. The people seemed to accept him as an extension of old Ephram and to all outward appearances everyone was happy. Everyone except Damion.

All his life Damion had done exactly what was expected of him. It was expected, as the minister's son, that he be exemplary in his behavior. It was expected that his grades be the highest, that his morals be beyond reproach. It was expected that he follow in his father's footsteps. It seemed to Damion that everyone knew what to expect from him except himself. Countless times he had asked himself why he had allowed himself to be pushed into the ministry. The closest he could come to an answer was that, perhaps, he would at last have something in common with his father. A common ground that would open communication between them. But it hadn't. If anything, the sparring and conflicts now ran deeper than ever. Each week at least, he could expect a phone call from old Ephram, asking about how the congregation was getting along. Never how are *you*, Damion. Always how are *things*. As though he had no identity apart from that of the spiritual leader of the people of Hayden.

And mother Rachael Conway. A whirlwind of activity. Visiting the sick, leading the choir, teaching Bible school. On and on, her list of Christian duty read. She was a veritable knight pitted against the forces of evil. A perfect mate for Ephram and together they shared and enjoyed their lives and interests. Mother's light never hid behind the proverbial bush. She was right up there, up front. She had father, and father had his church, and together they were happy. Damion grew to manhood feeling like the little urchin with his nose pressed to the bakery window, always feeling outside of things, yet never wanting for anything. Rachael's family was well founded in land

and transportation. That alone eased their lives, providing them with a generous living, never reducing them to the generosity and the stipend that the congregation bestowed.

Damion sighed. This was old hash. He had come to terms with this ages ago. Keli was his main concern right now. He could almost hear his father chastise, "A good minister never involves himself *personally* in the lives of his congregation. You are called upon to give spiritual counsel. You mustn't become emotionally involved, Damion. That can be a minister's downfall."

Goddamn it! He was involved. Keli had involved him. Everyone who came to him for guidance or advice involved him. Involved him and drained him. Perhaps he hadn't inherited his father's glibness of speech, but he had developed it, been cursed with it sometimes it seemed, out of a responsibility to his congregation. And practically the whole town was his congregation. The only other church was nearly fifteen miles away, aside from the small church attended by the blacks on the other side of town.

Damion reached for the manila envelope Keli had left on his desk. He saw how his hand trembled and knew why. He knew why his body was shaking, and he also knew there wasn't a thing in this world he could do about it. Keli. Dear God, not Keli. One of the truly beautiful people he had ever known. Brave, tranquil, with an inner beauty which just happened to coincide with her outer appearance. Tender, gentle, good. Honorable and loving. Keli. His fist slammed down on the desk, the pain shooting into his wrist and forearm a companion to the weary dread he was experiencing. Keli.

He rose from his desk. He had to do something and do it now. He had to get out of this office and away from his thoughts. Thoughts and feelings he couldn't afford if he was to be any help at all to Keli. Walk. He'd walk. Go to the library and get something heavy to read. Something to force his concentration. Don't think about anything, he warned himself. Don't admit anything to yourself, he cautioned. Slow and easy. Walk. Don't think.

As always, the library represented comfortable, happy times. Hours spent among books researching one project after another. He loved the sight of the spines in muted colors stacked on the shelves. The smell of books, slightly moldy with the dry, almost antiseptic odor of paste.

Suddenly, a laugh bubbled from his throat and he stopped in midstride—seeking solace and comfort in the library when he had his own church. He was a minister, a preacher, and he was seeking peace in a small, ivy-cloaked library. The tension eased and he took the steps two at a time and thrust open the screen door that squeaked on rusty, protesting hinges. He made his way through the anteroom to the laden, tiered shelves.

As his eyes explored titles and authors, he decided he wanted something not quite as heavy as he originally intended.

Dodsworth, Dostoevsky, Dumas. He wasn't in the mood for Dostoevsky and the way he explored the souls of his characters. He knew Dumas and *The Three Musketeers* the way he knew his Bible, and there was no way he was going to get into Dodsworth and his Nobel Prize literature, not today. He finally settled on Hemingway's *A Farewell to Arms*. As an afterthought, he picked up Oscar Wilde's *Lady Windermere's Fan*. Perhaps his witty, funny dialogue would lift his spirits, and, in his opinion, Wilde was better than Shaw any day of the week, although he knew he would get strong arguments from some of Shaw's fans. "Why not?" he muttered to himself as he laid the books down on the scarred oak table and settled himself comfortably.

Before he opened his book, he looked around and was surprised to see Beth Thomas seated down the table and across from him. He drew his brow into what his mother always called the "numeral eleven" and stared at her. Engrossed in her book, she did not notice his close scrutiny. School was out, so what was she doing in the library?

From time to time Damion lifted his eyes, but the young girl made no move except to turn the pages of her book. What could she possibly be reading that was so engrossing on such a beautiful summer day? He had to know.

Quietly, he laid the book on the table and stood up. He breathed a sigh of relief when the chair made no sound on the slick floor. He felt like a sneak when he walked up behind her and leaned over. Jesus! Eustace Chessar's *Love Without Fear*.

Beth Thomas lifted her head and stared at Damion while making no move to close or hide the book she was reading. He was shocked at her clear, level-eyed look that almost dared him to make a comment.

Damion forced a smile and spoke lightly. "I could say something like 'What's a nice girl like you doing in a place like this on such a beautiful day?' but I won't."

Beth smiled with her mouth, but the clear, sharp eyes were piercing and still level. "And I could say something like 'I don't like people peering over my shoulder!' but I won't."

"Touché," Damion said softly.

Damion backed away from her chair and was not surprised when she lowered her eyes and was again totally engrossed in the book. He picked up the two books he had selected and took them to the librarian to be checked out. While he waited for the card to be stamped, his eyes traveled again to Beth. She had treated him almost with defiance. It bothered him. Everything was bothering him lately, he realized. Everything and everybody.

Beth Thomas closed the book the moment she heard the screen door close. A smile tugged at the corners of her mouth. *And that, Reverend, should give you something to think about all day.* She glanced at the watch on her wrist. A few minutes before closing should be a good time to stop in the sporting goods store to see what was going on. The tennis racket at her feet needed restringing and what better place to take it than the shop where Kevin worked. By now, he was probably bored to tears and would welcome a chance to take a break and talk to her. And if he were busy, although she doubted it, she would wait out on the loading platform till he was free.

Covertly, she looked around the library and deftly slid the book into her tote. When she got home, she would put a book cover on it and no one would be the wiser.

Chapter Seven

Foster Doyle Hayden looked around his musty office and felt as dry and dusty as the contents of the room. This was his private domain, an office he had kept long after retiring from his professional life—a place to come and think and to smoke the forbidden cigar which he allowed himself along with a double shot of Wild Kentucky Bourbon. He liked the aroma of the cracked leather and the stale cigar smoke; it reminded him of his middle years when he abandoned his law practice for a seat on the bench in the county courthouse.

Gently, he touched the peeling leather on the humidor that rested in a prominent position on his desk—the last gift from his wife before she died. Now, why was he thinking about her at a time like this? Because, he answered himself, Irene was coming to the office. If there was ever a time that he longed for the company of his wife, this was it. He was going to tell Irene that he would not tolerate any shenanigans with Cader Harris now that the bastard was back in town.

Why had Cader come back? It couldn't be because of Kevin! Even if Cader recognized Kevin, there wasn't a damn thing he could do, was there? Cader had been gone so long no one ever gave Kevin's resemblance to him another thought. But with Cader back, the resemblance was going to be there for all the world to see.

In a way it was good that Cader had fathered a Hayden child. The old blood had been in need of a little rejuvenation, and Kevin was the proof that it worked. Hayden blood was good for girls like Bethany, but no matter how Foster Doyle tried to fool himself, he had to admit that Harris's bloodline was what made Kevin what he was. Christ! He loved that boy and nothing was ever going to change that.

Foster Doyle was becoming agitated with such thoughts; he could feel it in the wild flutterings of his heart. Or was it the forbidden cigar he was chomping? Cader Harris could spoil everything. Irene, if she wasn't controlled, could spoil everything. Even Arthur, milquetoast Arthur, could spoil things if he ever got downwind of the fact that Kevin was Cader Harris's son. Kevin and Cader had to be kept apart. That was all there was to it. It could be easily done. Kevin was leaving for Tulane at the end of August, and if Foster Doyle knew anything at all about Cader Harris, it was that he wouldn't last in this town. Irene was the only stumbling block, and surely, she wasn't so stupid that she couldn't see what would happen if she so much as glanced in Harris's direction.

A tight ache that was closer to a pain ripped across his chest, and he sat down, forcing himself to a calmness he didn't feel. He stubbed out the cigar with regret, knowing full well that the tobacco wasn't what was giving him the pain. It was fear. Fear of Cader Harris. Fear of what Irene would do. She wasn't a giggling teenager any longer. She was a grown woman with a grown woman's passions. Cader Harris would be like the forbidden fruit. And Irene would reach for that fruit like a drowning man clutches at straws. Foster Doyle rubbed his hand over his eyes. If Irene should ever discover that Cader Harris had been bought off, she would never, never forgive Foster. She would accuse him of meddling, and he would be the object of her tearful outrage. She would never once stop to judge the man who had left her alone with a child in her belly for a paid college tuition. He could never allow Irene to find out that her own father had paid Harris off; Irene was all Foster Doyle had left. Irene and Kevin, Cader Harris's son. And, of course, Bethany, he reminded himself as an afterthought. For some reason he always forgot about Bethany, possibly because she was so much like Irene, spoiled and whiny and always demanding.

Why did Harris have to come back to Hayden now, when Delta Oil was threatening intrusion into his beloved town of Hayden, named for his own great-grandfather?

Irene Hayden Thomas stood in the doorway, observing her father. Her emotions were mixed. She loved him, and yet there were times when she almost hated him, such as now. He had summoned her to his office, demanded she be here to discuss Cader Harris's return. She had ignored the first summons, pleading one thing and then another, but she knew she couldn't avoid a second demand. Foster Doyle looked so vulnerable sitting there behind his desk with his eyes closed. Vulnerable and yet formidable. She continued to stare at him, hardly believing he was approaching seventy years of age. The steel gray hair and the piercing blue of his eyes belied those years. His flesh was firm and more than one person had commented on the square cut of his jaw and his masculine form. Momentarily, she was proud of him until she remembered why she was here. Apprehensively, she said, "Daddy, are you sleeping?" as she walked into the room.

"Good heavens, no. Sit down, Irene, I want to talk to you. It's apparent to me that you've been avoiding me, and I know it's because of Cader Harris's return. There's no reason for you to fear discussing this with me. After all, I am your father and the grandfather of your children. . . ." Foster Doyle's words drifted off into space. He was looking at his daughter, actually looking at her. She had done something with her hair; it was lighter, younger looking. Makeup, jewelry. . . . Foster Doyle almost moaned aloud. It was too late, Irene had already determined that she would throw herself into Cader Harris's company. Why else this overhaul that had turned a dowdy matron into a smartly dressed, attractive woman?

"I'm not afraid of you, Daddy, I just haven't been able to get over here before now. I've just been over at the school working on the band uniforms. Honestly, you can't imagine the wear and tear those uniforms . . ." Foster Doyle displayed his contempt for the turn in her conversation, and Irene halted abruptly. "What is it you want to talk about?" she asked testily.

"Cader Harris," Foster Doyle boomed, angered by his observations of the change in Irene. "I want your solemn word you will do everything in your power to keep Kevin away from him. Everything in your power, Irene," he repeated forcefully. "I won't settle for anything less than your word."

Irene blanched. "It's too late, Daddy. Kevin applied for a job in Cader's sporting goods shop and was hired. Arthur insisted he keep the job. There was nothing I could do."

"Nothing you could do!" Foster Doyle Hayden shouted. "You're a Hayden and you sit there and tell me there was nothing you could do. Are you telling me that . . . that . . . keeper of dead bodies tells you, a Hayden, what to do? May all the Haydens that walk the heavens have mercy on you."

"Daddy, you don't understand. Kevin already had the job. Arthur is the boy's father and he insisted. For me to nag and nag would have made him suspicious. There was nothing I could do! I tried! You have to believe me. Daddy, say you believe me."

"I'll give the boy whatever sum he's earning in the shop if you can keep him home. The Haydens don't work, Irene. I can't believe you allowed this to happen," Foster continued to shout, thumping the shiny surface of his desk with his clenched hand. "And I want to know why Cader

Harris is back in town. Have you been in touch with him over the years? Don't lie to me, girl," Foster said, leaning over the desk, his blue eyes staring into Irene's. "That business was settled eighteen years ago, and it's over and done with," he said, not waiting for her denial.

Irene flushed and lowered her eyes. "No, I haven't been in touch with him, and I have no idea why he's here in town. Oh, Daddy, do you think he wants to take Kevin from me?"

"That's the kind of thinking that got you into this mess in the first place. I don't know why he's here, but I intend to find out. I want you to send Kevin to me tomorrow. If necessary, I'll force the boy to quit the job. I'll carry it one step further. I'll tell the boy I'll cut him *and* you out of my will. Bethany too. He'll come around when he realizes I mean what I say. If you have a mind to, Irene, you can reinforce my . . . request . . . with cutting off his funds for Tulane. You did tell me that you were paying for his education because business was bad and Arthur had to . . . what is it those keepers of the dead have to do?"

Irene was stunned. "Daddy, you wouldn't! You can't do that to Kevin! He would hate you."

"Better he should hate me than come to like that . . . that football jock."

"Oh, God," Irene mewed. "We have to discuss this calmly, Daddy, and not do anything any of us will regret later. Daddeee, are you listening to me?"

"Irene, you will do as I say or I will indeed remove your and your children's names from my will. I will leave everything to the Jatha Hayden Foundation for the elderly," Foster Doyle said slowly and distinctly to be sure his daughter understood.

Irene's eyes took on a dangerous glitter as she matched her father's cold stare. Her shoulders squared imperceptibly and the gesture of defiance was not lost on Foster Doyle Hayden. "Your days of threatening me are over, Father. You almost ruined my life once, but you won't do it a second time. It's time you and I had a father-daughter talk. I'll do the talking and you do the listening. I know that you had something to do with Cader leaving here, but I can't prove it. You've maneuvered and manipulated all your life, and sometimes you're so smug I almost believe you put the squeeze on Cader because you thought it would get you what you wanted. Eighteen years ago I was a gullible, frightened young girl. I'm not that girl any longer. The biggest mistake of my life was in telling you I was pregnant with Cader's child."

"Irene, there's no need to go through all this," Foster Doyle said testily, not liking the determined look on his daughter's face.

"Well, I think there is every reason. I'm just a little too old to be threatened. I won't tolerate it. Now is as good a time as any for me to tell you that I only *seemed* to go along with your plans to send me away to have the baby and then bring him back as a distant relative who was conveniently orphaned. I never had any intention of following through. I knew that once you got your hands on my child, mine and Cader's, that you would raise him your way. And if you think for one minute that this town would have bought that story of some long-lost relative suddenly bestowing a baby on you for safekeeping, you're wrong. I just want you to know that I saw through all that. I might not have said anything at the time because I feared your wrath, but this is today. I had made up my mind to have Cader's baby one way or another."

"Irene," Foster Doyle interjected, "you're overwrought and you're upsetting me. I don't want to hear any more of this nonsense."

"Well, I'm not finished yet, and you're going to hear it whether you like it or not. I loved Cader Harris. I loved the idea of bearing his child. When he left here so suddenly, I wanted to die. He left not knowing I was going to have a baby. How in the name of God do you think that made me feel? Part of me died then and now that part of me is alive again. Cader's back."

"Yes, Harris is back," Foster Doyle said coldly. "Have you given any thought at all to what will happen to you if he decides he wants Kevin? If you haven't, I suggest you think about it."

"Kevin is not a football to be tossed back and forth. He's my son. Mine and mine alone. For the public, Arthur is his father, but he's mine, all mine, and I intend, for the time being, to keep it that way. And speaking of Arthur, it's time for you to know that I maneuvered and manipulated him just the way I've watched you do over the years. When Cader left town, I moved in on Arthur so fast, he didn't know what hit him. I opened my legs and prostituted myself so that I could keep my baby. To this day, Arthur thinks Kevin is his son. What do you have to say to all this, Daddy? Defend yourself," Irene said bitterly.

Foster Doyle felt himself shrink beneath his daughter's penetrating stare. He never in his life had to defend himself, and the feeling was so alien, he felt the need to gag. "It wasn't the child I objected to, Irene, it was Harris himself. He wasn't the man for you; he still isn't. He may be Kevin's biological father, but that's all he is. And I knew all along what you were doing. After all, you are my daughter. It's not doing either one of us any good to rehash all this and open old wounds. You can't do anything foolish now that will jeopardize Kevin's well-being and future."

"I told you to stop telling me what to do. If I want to see Cader, I will. If I, and I said *if I*, decide to tell him about Kevin, it will be my decision and mine alone. And last, but not least, your threats about the children's and my inheritance don't scare me at all. I have Mother's money and I control the children's trusts," Irene said stonily.

Foster Doyle snorted. "Only on paper, Irene. I'm the one who drew up the papers, and I know exactly what they say. I control everything. If I wanted, by noon tomorrow, you would be penniless. Am I making myself clear?"

"You're threatening me again, Father, and I told you not to do it. You do what you have to do, and I'll do what I have to do. Do you understand that?"

Foster Doyle winced. She was his daughter all right. "Yes, I understand that you're turning against me, your own father."

"If that's the way you see it, there's nothing I can do about it. I will do what I think is best, and I'll do it without any interference from you or anyone else. Kevin is my first concern. Arthur can take care of himself just as you can take care of yourself. Neither of you needs me, but my son does. I will be the one to handle matters from now on."

Foster Doyle's heart started its mad fluttering as he stared at his daughter. Did he dare to pull his fainting trick on her or was it better to sigh and leave it all in the hands of God. God and Cader Harris? The moment he sighed, Irene knew she had won. She too sighed. It was so nice to have a father to depend on. A father who always saw things the way she saw them . . . in the end.

As Cader Harris sat in the comfortable leather chair behind the impressive-looking desk, his eye wandered to the main part of the shop. Kevin was a good worker; he had been hustling his butt for the past three hours without a break. And that was saying something, with that sexy kitten hot on his tail. He grinned. Another hour and either Judy would have him cornered in the back room or he was a backwoods country boy who didn't know where to put his peter. You could bang a girl leaning against a wall just as easily as you could in bed. He had lost count of the number of times he had banged Sunday Waters in the janitor's basement of the school, and it had been good, damn good. Maybe he should offer the kid some advice; he looked like he needed it. Just a little good old Harris philosophy.

His grin widened and he hoped Judy's old lady was as

good as the kid was. Marsha had class while her daughter had . . . an "earthy" approach to getting what she wanted. The word surprised him and he laughed aloud. If he could get Marsha to mix a little earth with her class, he would be doing just fine.

Kevin Thomas hefted a case of Spalding gloves onto a work table and prepared to slit open the top. He turned to get his knife and bumped into Judy. She was so close he could feel her warm breath on his neck. His heart pounding, he stared at her. He had to say something. "If you would do a little more work and less following, we might get home by six. I don't wanna stay here past closing."

"I wouldn't mind if you were here with me . . . and we were alone," Judy said, moving still closer. "Perhaps I can arrange it . . . we could do all sorts of things." Her voice became husky, her eyes searching.

"Like what?" Kevin challenged, reading the answer in her flashing eyes, feeling the curl of heat in his loins.

"Like unpacking the rest of this junk. Or we could neck," she cooed, leaning closer till he felt the round fullness of her breasts against his chest. "You name it, Kevin. I'm game."

"You're crazy for talking like that, Judy. Some guy might take you up on it."

"I wouldn't mind, Kevin, as long as you're that guy." She pressed closer, her voice a murmur, her gaze direct, defiant.

"If Mr. Harris heard you, he could take it into his mind to fire both of us. I don't know about you, but I need this job, so knock it off."

"Kevin, are you afraid of me?" Judy persisted. "I bet you never made it with a girl, did you? Of course not, how could you with your fairy princess sister hanging around your neck every minute of the day," she snorted.

"Drop it, will you, Judy? What are you doing back here anyway?" Kevin said gruffly.

"I came back to use the dressing room. Mr. Harris wanted to know what I thought of these new tennis outfits. I thought I'd try a few on." Judy looked up at him from beneath lowered lids. She smiled, sweetly, but Kevin saw the challenge glittering in her smoky gaze.

Beth pressed her face against the plate glass window and peered into the depths of the sporting goods store. Kevin was nowhere in evidence. Her heart skipped a beat as she pondered her next move. Fifteen minutes till the store closed. Kev must be either on the loading dock or in the back storeroom. If he were in the storeroom, then Judy was with him. The tennis racket in its plastic mitten banged against the brick wall as she swiveled and raced for the side driveway that led to the loading dock.

Quiet was the name of the game, she thought viciously. She would creep up the stairs and watch and see what dear old Judy was doing. After all, she had a perfect right to be here; her tennis racket needed restringing. She took the concrete steps two at a time and once again squinted into the dimness of the storeroom. No one. Voices. Carefully, she inched her way into the vast storeroom with its leather smells and wide assortment of athletic equipment. Laughter.

"How do you like it, Kevin? These Chrissie Evert outfits should go over big," Judy said, laughing as she twirled and preened for his benefit. She had deliberately left off her bra, knowing the taut pink crests of her breasts would strain against the thin nylon outfit. Kevin too, she could see, was aware of the straining fabric. "Let's play mixed doubles next weekend, and I'll talk my mother into buying this outfit for me."

Kevin felt his face flush and grinned, enjoying Judy's modeling. "If you wear that outfit, you'll win hands down. No thanks. I have to keep my mind on the game."

"Oh, Kevin, I knew if you were away from that snotty little sister of yours, you would open up and be human. Why do you let her tag around after you like that? All the kids in school call her your albatross."

Kevin's mood changed abruptly. "Leave Beth out of this. She's no concern of yours and I don't care what anyone says about the way she 'hangs around me,' as you put it. She's my sister."

Judy swung her arms out and then thrust them behind her, clasping her hands, making her full breasts jut out even further. "So okay, she's your sister. Are you taking her to Jackie's party on Saturday?"

"I didn't know Jackie was having a party and, no, I'm not taking her," Kevin said, hefting a carton of footballs onto a shelf.

"Will you go with me?"

"What makes you think I'll be invited?" Kevin hedged.

"Because Jackie came into the store today and told me

she was sending out the invitations this afternoon. Her parents are going out and won't be home till after eleven." She giggled.

Kevin stared at Judy, his mind racing. Why not? Judy was a tease, a flirt, but he liked the way she played up to him. It had been awhile since he went anywhere without Beth and really enjoyed himself. Did the gang really think of Beth as an albatross around his neck?

"Well?"

Kevin grinned. "Okay, you got yourself a date."

Judy squealed in delight, throwing herself into Kevin's arms.

"We'll have such a good time, you'll see. Boomer said he was going to sneak some beer into the party, and he promised there would be enough for everyone. Did you ever drink beer before, Kevin?"

Kevin reached up to loosen Judy's grip around his neck and felt his breathing quicken. She smelled warm and sweet, like a wildflower in the meadow. Even her hair smelled nice. Suddenly, he felt reckless and daring. "Sure," he lied.

Judy moved and let her hands drop to her sides. "Great! Then I know I'll be in safe hands," she said softly, never taking her eyes from him.

"You'd better get out of that outfit and put it back before Mr. Harris sees you." He felt hot, feverish. "Hurry up, Judy. All we have to do is stack these T-shirts and we can leave."

"Will you walk me home, Kevin?" Judy called from behind the dressing room door.

"Sure, if you get a move on."

"Kev? Are you back here?" Beth called as she moved into sight from behind a loaded dolly.

Kevin felt like a kid with his hand in the cookie jar as he swung around to see his sister advance further into the storeroom. How long had she been standing there? How much did she hear? What was she doing here in the first place? Irritated, his eyes swept over her. She carried her tennis racket, the one that needed restringing. One look into her bright, accusing eyes and he knew, without a doubt, she had heard and seen enough. She had heard him agree to take Judy to Jackie's party and to walk her home. She had seen Judy in the skimpy tennis outfit and she was angry. He wondered what Cader Harris would do in a similar situation. In his gut he knew Cader Harris would never allow himself to be placed in a situation like this.

"Here I am," Kevin called out in a tightly controlled voice.

Beth's eyes were furious when she stared at her brother, but her voice was calm and sweet when she spoke. "I brought my racket to be restrung. Take care of it for me, will you? I hope you don't mind stopping by the drugstore. I need some shampoo. Then Daddy can give us a ride home."

Her accusing glance dared Kevin to defy her. "Sure, if that's what you want," he heard himself answer.

Judy emerged from behind the cartons and laughed openly. "Thanks for the offer, Beth. Your father won't mind dropping me off too, will he? And I have to get some toothpaste at the drugstore myself. You're a sweet . . . kid, for reminding me of that. I'll just tell Mr. Harris we're going and, Kevin, don't worry, I'll tell him I'll come in a half-hour early tomorrow to fix the shelves. As a matter of fact," she smiled brightly, "I'll ask Mom for the car and pick you up." With a lofty wave of her hand she sauntered into Cader Harris's office and closed the door behind her.

Beth watched Judy weave her way among the boxes and cartons and felt bile rise in her throat. Her mind sought a word for Judy and the only thing she was able to come up with was one of Irene's favorites—Jezebel.

While Kevin tidied up his work area, her mind raced. She had to find a way to get to the party—with or without Kevin. Boomer. Boomer would take her. Boomer would love to take her. He'd been puffing and panting after her all year. If Kevin could take that . . . that Jezebel, then she could take Boomer. Only she would pretend that it was Boomer who invited her. Why not? Why not anything? Kevin was changing right before her eyes. Any other time he would have been glad she dropped by to go home with him, but now, today, he actually seemed to resent her.

Tears gathered in her eyes as she watched him place her racket in a box marked for restringing and come back to her, a wary look in his eye.

"I'm ready when you are," she said lightly, a forgiving note in her voice. Her heavily fringed eyes were still furious and now openly calculating as she linked her arm through Kevin's.

Judy and Cader Harris emerged from Cader's office and approached the pair. Harris smiled a welcome to Beth and boldly removed her arm from Kevin's. He turned and began leading her toward the front door. "Little lady, where I come from, actions like that are suspect." His grip was tight and unrelenting as he led her from the store, Judy and Kevin trailing behind.

Cader Harris didn't like her, Beth knew. She had seen it that first day when she and Kevin had applied for the jobs. She didn't care; she hated him. It was all because of *him* that Judy was getting her claws into Kevin.

"Didn't anyone ever tell you, little missy, that big brothers aren't supposed to be sissies? What are you trying to do to Kevin? Don't you think you're a little old to be hanging onto his shirttails?" Not bothering to wait for a reply, undaunted by the venomous look she was giving him, he continued in a conspiratorial tone, "Can't you see that little temptress next to him is trying to make out and you're standing in their way? You know what I'm talkin' about, don't you? Right?"

"Wrong, Mr. Harris. Kevin has a mind of his own and can do whatever he pleases." With a quick, almost violent gesture Beth was free of his grip. Her voice was choked when she turned to Kevin and said, "I just remembered that Mother bought shampoo this morning, and I promised Boomer I'd stop by his house late this afternoon. Why don't you walk Judy home?" Without another word she sprinted down the street.

Cader narrowed his eyes at the stricken look on Kevin's face and then at the grateful expression on Judy's. He winked, as if to say, "All in a day's work."

Kevin's mouth tightened as he looked from Cader

Harris to Judy. He knew he'd just been manipulated. "You can pick me up in the morning, Judy. I'll see you, Mr. Harris." Before either of them could say another word, he was loping after Beth, his young face set into lines of anger and frustration. Frustration for himself for running after Beth and anger with Cader Harris for involving himself in what was none of his affair.

When something went wrong, it really went wrong, Judy thought angrily as she walked home alone. She'd been after Kevin ever since junior high and now, just when she almost had him, Beth screwed it up. She brightened momentarily when she realized that Beth wouldn't be in the way come fall. So far, it was her secret, hers and her mother's, that she had only last week been accepted to Tulane. If she played her cards right, she could arrive at the same time as Kevin. Wouldn't he be surprised! A whole year without drippy Beth to contend with. Kevin liked her, she knew he did. She could see it in the way his eyes followed her when he thought she wasn't looking. Mom liked Kevin; she'd be happy that he was taking her to Jackie's party.

Judy wondered why she was sometimes so rude to the only person she had left in this whole, entire world. She loved her mom, but sometimes. . . . If Dad were still alive, she wouldn't be having these troubles. Dad had always been so easy to talk to. He would have listened to her when she wanted to talk about Kevin, and he wouldn't ever have ruffled her hair and smiled indulgently as though it were just kid stuff the way Mom did. She would have been able to tell him about Beth and how she was always trying to keep Kevin to herself. If only he hadn't been in that car when he had that heart attack. Even the doctors said it was the crash that killed him, not his heart.

It was all Mom's fault. Stress and strain killed people, everyone knew that. It was the stress of fighting with Marsha, the bitter quarrels they didn't know Judy was aware of that killed him. Especially that last night when they had argued over custody of Judy. Dad wanted her with him and Mom said absolutely not.

It had all been Mom's fault. Dad had had the heart attack almost immediately after that last bitter quarrel. It had happened as he was driving from Hayden. Mom had driven him away because she was somehow inadequate. Daddy had died because he loved his daughter, and Mom wouldn't let them be together.

Judy opened her change purse and counted her money. Three dollars in change and a wilted one-dollar bill. She sprinted down the street and around the corner, skidding to a stop outside the florist shop. With any luck Mr. Carpenter would have some kind of arrangement for four dollars.

Breathing heavily, she swung open the door, apologizing to the stoop-shouldered old florist. "I'm so glad I got here before you closed, Mr. Carpenter. Do you have something already made up for four dollars? I want to take a run out to the cemetery and put them on Dad's grave."

Adam Carpenter looked at the young, breathless girl and saw the grief in her eyes. She was the only kid he ever knew who saved her pennies and bought a single Shasta daisy to take to the cemetery. So many times he wanted to add extra flowers or a sprig of fern but she would decline his generous offer. She paid for whatever she bought, even if it was just a single flower. "Nothing made up, Judy, but it will take only a minute to wire a bouquet of Shastas for you. Would you like colors or white?"

"Make them all different colors. Dad always liked colors. If I have enough money, would you add a little fern? Wait, I have an extra quarter in my jeans that I forgot about."

"Judy, how many times do I have to tell you there's no charge for the fern?"

"You're just being nice, Mr. Carpenter. You have to pay for the fern. I want to pay for it, really I do."

Adam Carpenter's pale gray eyes lightened and he smiled crookedly. "You always were too smart for me, Judy. A quarter it is," he said, twisting the wire around the stems of the daisies, careful not to damage the leaves. "That will be four twenty-five." Judy handed over the money and accepted the flowers. Judy sure was different from her mother, he thought sourly. Not once in all the time Judy's father had been laid to rest did Marsha ever come into the store to order flowers. Come to think of it, she hadn't even sent a spray to the mortuary, and he knew that for a fact because Arthur Thomas had made a point of mentioning it. It was the least she could have done. After all, she was married to him for a long time and he was Judy's father. There's just no accounting for some people's actions, he told himself as he locked up for the night. Just no accounting at all, he continued to mutter as he walked out to his car.

* * *

Beth looked over her shoulder, and when she saw no sign of Kevin, her eyes burned furiously.

Deftly, she skirted the corner and headed for the driveway that led to the mortuary. She'd show him and Judy too. She'd go into Daddy's office and call Boomer. "I'll show them," she muttered as she brushed impatiently at the tears burning her eyes.

Kevin sprinted along, his mind whirling. Lately, it seemed all he did was run after Beth. Girls! Mother! Beth! Judy! Why couldn't they just leave him alone? Everything was a problem lately. Damn!

He slowed at the corner of Jatha Hayden Boulevard and Mimosa Avenue and looked both ways. Beth was nowhere in sight. A grin tugged at the corners of his mouth when he realized he had stopped and when he also realized that even though he'd been doing a lot of running after Beth, for some reason he never caught up to her. Was he doing it unconsciously or . . . no point in wasting his energy now. He could take his time and walk home and appreciate the warm day and the thought of taking Judy to the party. Guys were supposed to think about girls on days like this, so why shouldn't he? Judy was okay. A little different but still okay. Too bad Beth didn't like her. Beth didn't like anyone. Maybe Dad was right and they had been spending too much time together. Now was as good a time as any to wean Beth away. The end of August would arrive all too soon and then what would Beth do? The question bothered him and the muscles in his shoulders constricted. He was worried about Beth and he didn't know why.

Kevin brightened momentarily when he thought of the active life at college and all the new friends he would make. He would be alone and on his own for the first time in his life. The end of August couldn't come soon enough for him.

As Kevin's mood brightened, Beth dialed Boomer's number. She wasn't surprised when she heard his voice on the other end of the line. "Boomer? This is Beth. Beth Thomas. Are you surprised?" she asked in what she hoped was a coy voice.

"Oh, yeah, sure Beth." His voice sounded distracted and she babbled on anxiously.

"I just thought I'd see what you were doing with yourself. Being summer an' all, I haven't seen you around." Beth bit into her lower lip to keep it from trembling. Boomer Guthrie had always terrified her, ever since grade school when he would find every opportunity to corner her alone and say dirty words. Once, he'd even pushed her down in the playground and she could still feel his eyes on her when her dress flew up, exposing her panties. Even this last year he seemed to take delight in eyeing her hotly and making lewd gestures until she blushed in embarrassment.

"Yeah. Well, that's how it is. I've been busy," he answered indifferently.

"Yeah, I know how it is," she plunged on, trying to seem casual. "I was just wondering if you were going to Jackie's party." She held her breath.

"Who? Oh, yeah, I am. What of it?" Suddenly, there was a ring of interest in his question.

"Oh, nothing, I was just wondering if you'd asked anyone to go with you." Beth heard her heart thumping madly. He couldn't have, he just couldn't have asked anyone.

"Yeah. Well, as a matter of fact, I didn't get a chance yet. I thought I just might go stag to this one," he lied. He'd been trying Judy Evans's number all day and there'd been no answer.

As though reading his thoughts, Beth said breathlessly, "Judy is going with Kevin. If you're going stag, maybe you'd like to come along with us instead."

"Yeah?" She could almost see his face pinch up the way it did when he became thoughtful. "You asking me to take you to the party, Beth?"

"Well, I thought, I mean, if you weren't going to take anyone, you could go with us and not have to go alone."

"Alone? Me? You know better than that, li'l Bethy."

"Yeah," she said tonelessly. This wasn't going the way she had intended. What was wrong with him? He'd been after her all year and now he was acting as though he didn't know what she wanted. He couldn't be that dumb, could he? She held her breath, listening to the silence on the other end of the line.

"You wanna go with me, Beth?"

"How nice of you to ask me, Boomer!" She hoped her voice sounded convincing.

"I said, you wanna go with me? You asking me to take you?"

Beth recognized that tone of voice. That sly, baiting tone he used when he whispered dirty words to her. She wanted to hang up on him before it went any further. But she couldn't. This was so important. She couldn't let Judy get her hooks into Kevin.

"Yeah, Boomer, I'm asking you to take me," she managed to choke out.

"Yeah? No kiddin'? Sure, I'll take ya, li'l Bethy, but first you gotta tell me what you're gonna gimme if'n I do."

God, she hated him; he was a slime. "Wh-what do you want, Boomer?" She squeezed her eyes shut, dreading to hear his answer.

"Me? What could a guy like me want?" She could hear the sneer in his voice.

"Oh, I don't know." She tried to keep her voice level as she glanced quickly around to be certain she was alone. "Look, Boomer, I'll give you anything you want. I've just gotta go to that party," she blurted, covering her mouth with her hand, not believing what she had just said.

"Yeah. Well, what d'you know? Li'l Bethy's finally come around. You plannin' on wearin' a bra?"

Beth felt scared. "What difference does that make?"

"Well, it makes a difference. I always had a yen for your nice little titties." He lowered his voice but Beth heard him loud and clear. Again, she glanced over her shoulder.

"Boomer, I don't wear a bra," she gulped.

"That's nice, Beth, real nice."

"Well?"

"Well what?"

"Do we have a . . . a date or not?"

"Yeah. Sure, why not?"

"We . . . we'll double with Kevin and Judy. Okay?"

"Does good ol' Kev know about this?"

"Of course. He's one of your best friends, isn't he?" She held her breath, daring him to deny it. She had to get off the phone with him before she lost her nerve. "Pick me up around eight, okay?"

"Yeah. Maybe I'll call you tonight, around nine. Be home. You and me can talk some more. I like to hear you talk, Bethy."

Perspiration broke out on Beth's brow and she felt damp under her arms. She knew the kind of talk Boomer wanted to have and she felt sick thinking about it. She should hang up on him right now. She should tell him it was all a joke, a dare. She should make a fool out of him. Instead, she steadied her voice and answered, "That would be nice, Boomer. I always like to hear from you." To her own amazement, she actually had pulled it off. Her voice dripped syrup.

"So there, Kevin," she muttered as she replaced the receiver in its cradle with a trembling hand. "So there!"

Chapter Eight

Kevin knew something was amiss when he woke to find his grandfather having breakfast in the kitchen with his mother. Kevin eyed the two of them carefully as he withdrew a container of orange juice from the refrigerator. "Good morning, Grandfather," he said respectfully as he bent down to peck his mother on the cheek.

Foster Doyle rose from the chair and clapped the boy on the back. "Fine morning, so I decided to go for a walk and decided at the last minute to stop by. I understand Dulcie left some of her famous cinnamon buns, and you know I can't resist those."

They were conspiring against him, he could sense it, almost smell it. Where was Dad? For that matter, where was Beth? He knew he needed an ally—desperately.

"Your mother tells me you have a job for the summer at the new sporting goods store," Foster Doyle said affably.

Kevin grimaced. Well, he might as well get it over with now. Dad was on his side and that was all he needed. "Yes, Mr. Harris hired me on the spot. He gave me good hours and is depending on me. I shook hands with him and gave him my word that I would do a good job," Kevin said tightly. "And, Grandfather, I mean to do just that."

"Commendable idea, boy, commendable, but the Hayden young never work till they're through college. What are the townspeople going to think of you? You surely don't need the money, and by accepting the job you're taking it from some poor, deserving youth. Tell me what Harris is paying you and I'll ante up the same and you'll have your summer free to do what you want."

Kevin's eyes narrowed. "I appreciate what you're saying, Grandfather, but I want to work; I think I'm going to like working in the store and I like Mr. Harris. He's an okay guy. I've already taken the job; Dad gave his approval."

"I agree with your grandfather, Kevin, let some other deserving boy have the job and you can spend your summer with Beth. After all, you're going to be going away at the end of August and she's going to miss you terribly. A little consideration is all we're asking, Kevin," Irene pleaded.

Kevin stared at his mother and then at his grandfather. They were doing it to him again. They took sides against him and against his father. He'd always given in to his mother's pleas, but not this time. This time he was going to do what he wanted. Dad was on his side.

"If you're such an independent fellow, then how would

you like to work your way through Tulane?" Foster Doyle snapped irritably.

"I've given that some thought, too," Kevin replied, watching Foster Doyle carefully. "I applied for a job in the cafeteria for the dinner hour. My meals would be free."

"Kevin," Irene screeched. "What's happened to you? Where are you getting these ideas?"

"I've always had them, you just never bothered to listen. Dad thinks it's a good idea. Look, I have to go now or I'll be late. It was nice seeing you, Grandfather. Mother, I'll be home at dinnertime. If I'm late, don't hold it for me. I'll eat with Dad."

Foster Doyle unclenched his hands when the screen door closed and stared at Irene. "Is that what you call taking care of things?" he said harshly.

"I told you his mind was made up. Arthur is on his side, and now that I've had time to think more on the subject, I don't think it's such a bad idea at all. If Cader suspects anything, I'm sure he won't say anything. After all, Kevin is his flesh and blood and he wouldn't deliberately hurt the boy, and Kevin would be hurt. Cader is no fool, Daddy."

"We've lost this battle, but the rest of the war is still not finished," Foster Doyle said thoughtfully. At that moment he made up his mind to see Cader Harris and set things straight. And the sooner the better.

Irene was dabbing at her eyes and wishing she had a cigarette. "I'll take care of matters, daughter. Wipe your eyes and go out shopping. Buy yourself a new hat, one with lots of feathers, the kind I like. I'll take care of Kevin, that asinine husband of yours and Cader Harris."

Irene's stomach churned. Why couldn't he let her handle her own affairs? Kevin was her son, and Cader's. She and Cader should be the ones to settle things. At that moment Irene Hayden Thomas hated her father with an all-consuming passion. The intensity of her feeling frightened her, so she left her father standing with his mouth hanging open. She ran to her room and searched wildly for one of her menthol cigarettes. She fumbled with the crumpled package and succeeded in mutilating four of the slender cylinders before she finally managed to bring the cigarette to her mouth and light it. A sob caught in her throat.

Arthur Thomas tugged at the vest of his somber, blue-striped, three-piece suit before walking into the viewing room near the back of the mortuary. The room was reserved for the black wakes and was appointed in dark, turkey reds and bright gilt which catered to their taste for the flamboyant. Arthur always flinched slightly whenever he came into this room. He had long ago reasoned that it was because it was the scene of unbridled grief. Unlike the formal, carefully controlled funerals and wakes common to whites, blacks were far less repressed, more prone to outbursts and wailings. He supposed that after all these years he would have become used to the wailings and public weepings, but he had not. It still embarrassed him. He much preferred the quiet, solemn ceremonies of his own people. With his own people it was only necessary to be considerate of their grief, to be polite and carry out his duties in the most efficient way possible. Grief among the blacks was a more personal emotion and weighed heavily upon anyone who came in contact with it. Their prayers, their hallelujahs, their gospel songs required an emotional response, something that was too easily aroused in Arthur Thomas.

It was because of his discomfort in dealing with black funerals that he had hired Destry Davidson, his black associate. Arthur's eyes sought out Destry and signaled him to come out into the foyer.

Destry Davidson was tall and immaculately groomed. He carried his height with dignity and he never seemed to hurry, although Arthur knew him to be a man with economy of motion. The word "conservative" always came to Arthur's mind when he looked at Destry. Even his woolly hair was tailored, cut and shaped to his head so that no stray hair was visible. His shirt was niveous white against his almond-colored neck. Irene said Destry was spit-and-polish but more spit than polish if Arthur knew what she meant.

"Will you be coming back this evening, Mistah Thomas?" Destry asked in his serious, somber tone.

"Not tonight, Destry. You've been here alone . . . with your people before tonight; you don't need me. As a matter of fact, I've been meaning to talk to you about me being here when one of your own is laid out. Somehow, I think it would be better if you managed alone."

Destry folded his long arms over his muscular chest and stared at Arthur Thomas, the man he had called "Mistah Thomas" for the past ten years. "Does that mean you don't want me in attendance when one of . . . your own is laid out?"

"No, that's not what it means, Destry. You know I couldn't run this place without your help. All I'm saying is I think your people feel more comfortable when I'm not around."

Destry's licorice eyes were inscrutable as he stared at Arthur. "How did the council meeting go today? Did anyone make any firm decisions?"

"A lot of bickering and fighting but that was what I expected. You're in favor of the tanks, aren't you, Destry?"

"Yes, Mistah Thomas, I am, as we have discussed many times. This town needs a black mortuary and one day I hope to open it. If the tanks come to Hayden, then black people will come too. Personally, I don't think the pollution and danger is what the people of this town say it is. This town is going to stagnate soon enough, so why not get ahead on some kind of industry? If not the tanks, then something else. We need new blood and new ideas. I speak for my people and myself, of course."

"I think it's too early to tell what's going to happen. The Town Council meeting is just a few days away and then we'll see which way the wind is blowing. I haven't made up my mind either way. My wife now, she has very definite opinions about this whole thing, but I have no intention of letting her influence me one way or the other. I want what's best for this town and everyone in it."

Destry looked pointedly at his watch and then at Arthur Thomas. "Miss Bethany is waiting for you in your office,

Mistah Thomas, and if you don't leave now, you'll miss your dinner."

"What time is your viewing?"

"In fifteen minutes. I made a special concession this evening for the immediate family. It's going to be . . . er . . . emotional," Destry explained, aware of Arthur's abhorrence of unbridled grief. "When a black child dies, it's not something that's easy to handle."

"Good night, Destry," Arthur said, heading for his office.

"G'night, Mistah Thomas. Enjoy your dinner," Destry said softly.

When Arthur sat down at the carefully appointed dinner table, he fully expected to enjoy his meal. He had noticed Irene's new hair style and that she had had it lightened almost to the color it was when they were first married. He had been generous with his compliments and for the first time in years Irene had blushed beneath his appreciative gaze.

Only a few minutes after Dulcie served the ham, Arthur knew that Irene's new hair-do wasn't going to defuse the charged atmosphere. Beth picked at her food and Kevin jabbed at his ham with his fork, never bringing the succulent meat to his mouth. Arthur looked from his children to his wife and back to Kevin. Pretending to eat, he watched Beth's covert glances toward Irene, and he knew something was in the wind, and whatever it was, it wouldn't do Kevin any good. Sooner or later, Irene would get around to whatever it was Beth wanted from her. He was proved right when Dulcie served the pecan pie and whipped cream.

"Kevin, Beth tells me you're going to Jacklyn's party with Judy Evans. Beth has been invited to the same party by Luther Guthrie and I think, as it's her first more or less grown-up party, that you should double date and keep an eye on her. I'll feel more comfortable if you're together."

"Irene!" Arthur almost shouted. "Why do you insist on pairing these children off together? In the first place Luther is too old for Beth to date, and in the second place Kevin doesn't need to look after his sister. Stop arranging their affairs for them. How do you know Kevin isn't doubling with another couple? The least you could do is give him the courtesy of asking before you make these arrangements."

"Arthur, children are a mother's responsibility, and I think Beth has every right to go to the party, and Luther is such a nice boy. Don't you remember how adorable he looked when he was the ring-bearer at Anna Delphine's wedding?"

"Irene, that was ten years ago. If you're so worried about Beth needing someone to look after her, then she's too young to go. Kevin will not double with Beth and that's final!" Arthur said, standing up from the table, his eyes fierce and cold.

"It's okay, Dad, really it is. I don't mind," Kevin mumbled.

"There, you see, Arthur, even Kevin says it is all right."

"The boy knows that's what you want. I mean it, Irene, Kevin will not take Beth to the party. It's time she did things on her own!"

Beth jumped up from the table, her eyes tear-filled. "You hate me, Daddy! You always side with Kevin. My very first party and you spoil it for me. Now I don't want to go; you ruined everything!" she wailed.

Arthur stood his ground, puzzled by the strange look in his daughter's eyes. She really expected him to back down, he could see it. When she saw that he had no intention of rescinding his order, Beth flounced from the room and raced up the stairs to her room.

"Now, see what you've done," Irene cried.

"I've done nothing and you know it, Irene. Kevin has a right to a life of his own, and it's time he started living it. He's done everything you asked of him for the past seventeen and a half years. Enough is enough!" Arthur roared, banging his fist so hard on the lace-topped table that Irene almost fell from her chair.

"Very well," Irene said coldly, "but if anything happens to Beth, it will be your fault. You just remember that, Arthur Thomas. And you, young man," Irene said, poking a finger under Kevin's nose, "you remember that you, by your very actions, if not words, made it clear that you don't want your sister to go with you to this party."

"Mother . . ." Kevin entreated.

"I'm not interested in hearing any more excuses from you, and you're excused from the table, Kevin. Leave my sight. I never thought I would live to see the day when my very own husband and my very own son would turn against their sister and daughter like this. Haydens," she said imperiously, "do not do things like this. Why, I can almost see Granddaddy Hayden turn over in his grave over such goings on."

"Irene, Granddaddy Hayden was the biggest rake going, so stop pretending he was some sort of saint. I hardly think he would turn over in his grave because his grandson wanted to go to a party without his sister. As a matter of fact, he would probably cheer Kevin on. This is the end of the matter, Irene, and I don't want to hear another word about it again, do you understand me?"

Irene ignored him as she rose from the table. She would ignore Arthur the way she always did. When she really concentrated, she could pretend he didn't exist.

Cader finished his solitary cardboard sandwich and tossed the remnants in the trashcan next to him. He leaned back, his feet propped on the scarred desk. His eyes were glued to the parking lot and the long, sleek Lincoln Continental that was maneuvering its way between the white lines. *A whole damn parking lot, and he has to worry about the white lines.* Cader grimaced. He waited.

Foster Doyle Hayden came in through the storage room and then through the shop before he noticed Cader sitting in what passed for his office. Cader let his eyes lock with those of the old man and deliberately remained seated. Since there was no other chair, the old man was at a distinct disadvantage and Cader wanted it that way. He was in control and Foster Doyle Hayden knew it.

"Why are you here? Is it the boy?" he asked bluntly. Cader said nothing. Strategy. Let the old geezer talk and, hopefully, he would get so rattled something worthwhile would come of the confrontation. "Surely, it can't be Irene;

she's married. This town doesn't need a sporting goods store any more than it needs you. This town never needed the likes of you. What do you want? How much, Harris, to pack up and get out?"

Cader lit a cigarette and tossed the match on the floor. What a wonderful thing power was. Now he knew why the old man thrived the way he did. *Jump, you old bastard,* he thought bitterly.

"Well? How much?"

Cader eased the chair down softly and leaned across the desk. "You bought me once and you owned me for four years. We played by your rules, crooked rules. But I played because that was the bargain we made. You told me Irene was getting an abortion, and I halfway believed you. Right now, you son of a bitch, we're playing by my rules and those rules say I don't have to tell you anything. My debt has been paid."

"I'll have you thrown out of town," Hayden blustered.

Cader laughed. "And all the while you're having me escorted through the main street, I'll be playing pied piper. Irene and Kevin will be right behind me. In case you don't understand, you wise-assed bastard, I'm holding all the cards."

"Surely, you wouldn't hurt Kevin, your own son. If you tell him now, it could do only harm. The boy is happy, content, with Arthur Thomas as his father. I'll pay you whatever you want, give you whatever you want, if you'll just give me your word," Hayden pleaded.

"Right now, my word is just about as good as yours

was eighteen years ago. And, Mist-tah Hayden, there isn't enough money in the world to buy me off a second time. I'm not for sale. I rarely give advice, but this time is an exception. Get your skinny ass in that hearse you're driving and get the hell off my property. And don't come back. I've developed a deep sensitivity over the years, and you're offending me. What that means, Mist-tah Foster Doyle Hayden, is you're being dismissed by one football jock named Cader Harris."

Foster Doyle's face reddened and then turned a deep shade of blue. He gasped and placed his hand over his heart and then groped in his pocket for a small vial. With shaking hands, he popped the pill in his mouth and waited, his white knuckled hands clutched on the rim of the desk. Cader's eyes narrowed but he made no move to help or hinder the old man. Blind hatred surged through him.

"You would have let me die, wouldn't you?" Foster Doyle asked in stunned shock as his breathing and color returned to normal.

"I don't know," Cader said honestly.

The old man's slumped shoulders straightened. Cader Harris would never know what that effort cost him.

Cader Harris locked the store and stood a moment looking up and down the quiet street. All the merchants were gone for the day and the storefronts stood sentinel.

Deftly, he backed the rental car from the parking area and at the last minute decided to go to the Lemon Drop for dinner. Food was the least of his interests right now, so it made no difference if he ate his dinner or if he drank it. A couple of short ones and a trip to the other side of the tracks to Aunt Cledie's and a little poontang was what he needed. A little dark meat went a long way and was always better after a long abstinence. He grinned to himself at the thought and then sobered. He bit into his lower lip as he wondered how the council meeting went. Perhaps someone at the Lemon Drop would know.

While he drove, Cader let his eyes pick out sites he had long ago forgotten. Damn town never changed. He grimaced. Christ, if he had to live forever in this jerk-water burg, he would go out of his mind. Bright lights and firm flesh were what he wanted. And, by God, he was going to make damn sure he got it . . . one way or another. Hayden was the end of the rainbow for him, and his pot of gold was going to be filled to overflowing. He would invest a little and spend a lot. Let the twilight years take care of themselves.

Sunday Waters, a tray in her hand with a double Scotch on it, spotted him immediately when he entered the room. It was all she could do not to drop the tray and run over to him and throw her arms around his neck. Damn it to hell, no man should be able to do this to a woman after eighteen long years. In a split second the years were erased and he was the Cader of high-school days. He couldn't see her as yet, she thought, since coming from the outside into the dimness of the supper club would momentarily blind him. Give the customer his drink and then walk nonchalantly over to the bar where he would be sitting and say something cool and mocking. Something with class.

Her hand shook slightly when she placed the drink in front of the waiting customer. "Would you care for some nuts or pretzels?" she asked softly. "Enjoy your drink, sir."

Thank God she had taken pains with her makeup and dress tonight. She'd had her hair done this afternoon. She looked good. She knew she looked good; the man with the double Scotch had looked at her with more than approval, and if she had cared to make a small overture, she could have had him eating out of her hand in a minute.

Deep breath. No subterfuge for Sunday. Straight from the hip. Why bother with small talk? What was wrong with showing Cade she was glad to see him and just winging it from there? "Hello, Cade," she said, smiling as she perched on the stool next to his.

Cade's eyes widened as he let his eyes drink in the sight of the attractive woman sitting next to him. "Yo, what have we here?" He grinned. "Don't tell me; it can't be, but it is . . . Sunny!" The bar stool swiveled and he had her wrapped in his arms in a hard embrace. "Damn if you aren't a sight for these eyes. Jesus, you're all grown up."

"How do you like it?" Sunday grinned. "You don't look so bad to these eyes either," she said softly. So what if her lips trembled; so what if he saw. He could stop them; he knew how. "I've thought of you often, Cade. More often than is decent. Tell me a lie, Cade, tell me you thought of me too."

"Baby, it wouldn't be a lie. I thought about you more than I thought about any woman. Before . . . that was a long time ago. I had things to do and places to go. What we had . . . well, it was fine, but we both knew it couldn't last . . . we both knew that, Sunny."

"You're wrong, Cade. I never knew that. I wanted it to last. I loved you, don't you remember? Tell me another lie and say you remember."

"Eighteen years is a long time," Cade said, his throat constricting at the open, hungry look on her face. Who said people change? Whoever said change affected Sunday Waters? She might be wearing her hair differently and she might smell different, but she was still the same. There was that ever-present vulnerability in her glance and the sexy pout of her full, shapely mouth that just bordered on trembling. She was still that young girl who had clung to him out of shame and fear. People who were born on the wrong side of the tracks like Sunday Waters and Cader Harris never changed. Times changed, circumstances changed, but never the people.

Cader leaned his elbows on the polished bar, his drink sitting in front of him. The Lemon Drop Inn was new in town. At least it had been established during his absence. It was nice, in a New York style, polished and plush with a separate dining area. He had seen better and he'd seen worse. For a town like Hayden, this was definitely better.

In the wide, frosted mirror behind the bartender, Cader's eyes followed Sunday as she went about her duties. He could hear her soft, husky laugh. Her figure was better than ever—fuller, more womanly, although it hadn't lost the girlish firmness and smooth curves. Men looked admiringly at Sunday, openly appraising her.

Cader realized he was frowning because of something someone said that made her laugh. He recognized the expression in the man's eyes as he looked at Sunday and it annoyed him. No, things hadn't changed that much. The boys had become men, and now, instead of leering at Sunday Waters, they lusted.

Taking a swallow of his drink, Cader suppressed the old, dredged-up feelings of possessiveness and protectiveness. Sunday didn't need him anymore. She had learned to handle herself. Regret made his drink taste bitter. Then he caught a glimpse of Sunday's face as she turned away from the table to take the order to the kitchen. There, buried behind the glossy facade of sophistication, was still that scared little-girl expression. Somehow, his drink tasted sweeter.

When Sunny Waters left the Lemon Drop Inn, she was only slightly surprised to find Cader Harris parked beside her in the lot. She walked over to him as he leaned out the window, the lamppost light falling on his blond hair and making it silver. His dark eyes bordered by those incredibly long lashes looked up at her and she felt her knees go weak. "Shall I follow you home or do you want me to drive you?" It was a statement more than a question. Just like Cader, bypassing all the amenities and getting right to the heart.

"Follow me," she heard herself say. As she was driving down Main Street to her apartment over the boutique, she went over all the games she might have played with him. She might have played hard to get, but that wasn't her style and no one knew that better than Cader. It had been so long, so damn long, and yet here she was getting wet between her legs. *Pavlov's dogs!* She grimaced. *One look at Cader and a bell goes off in my head and my pussy starts to lather.*

Sunny fumbled with the key in the lock, distracted by Cader's presence pressed against her back. Finally, the door opened and her hand reached for the light switch. He gripped her wrist, pulling her hand to his mouth and pressing his lips to her palm. "Don't touch the lights, Sunny, we don't need them, do we? Don't we remember each other as though it were only yesterday?" His voice was husky, sweet. His mouth had come so close to her ear that she could feel his breath against her neck.

Somehow, the door closed behind them. Without ceremony he pulled her against him. She could feel the length of him, the hardness of his body, the quivering jump of the muscles in his back through his light sport jacket. Her mouth met his hungrily, washing away the years they had been apart, kindling all the excitement just being near him could bring.

He followed her into her bedroom and inhaled the fragrance of her perfume that had permeated the draperies and bedspread and mingled with the spicy aroma of hair spray and talcum powder. "I wanted you to see my apartment," she said softly. "I wanted you to see how far I've come since we lived on the wrong side of the tracks."

"Ssh," he murmured, "I'll see it all later. Right now, I just want to look at you." He reached down to the bedside table and flicked on the night lamp; it glowed dimly, illuminating the room in a pale pinkish glow. "Let me see you, Sunny."

Sunny gasped, was it possible he remembered the first time they were together like this, in the run-down shack he lived in with his father? They had been alone that night too. His father had been out at Aunt Cledie's on a binge, and Cade had assured her they wouldn't be disturbed. That night too, after he had kissed her and petted her and told her that he wanted her, loved her, he had whispered, "Let me see you, Sunny," as he reached down to undo the zipper on her skirt.

It was like being in a whirlpool, in water that was blood warm. The past and present were becoming confused in her mind. She was sixteen again and she loved Cader Harris, and she was on the brink of her first sexual experience. There was no right or wrong; there was only Cader and the fulfillment that he promised by the touch of his fingers caressing her breasts and touching her tenderly between her legs. He made her feel beautiful; he made her feel desirable. He made her want to give to him. Give, give, give, wholeheartedly, without reservation.

Slowly he undressed her, tenderly he touched her, pressing his mouth lovingly against her soft flesh. She heard herself moaning with pleasure. His lips ignited tiny flames of fire that she had thought were long dead. At the very last he unpinned her hair, running his fingers through it and pulling it down around her shoulders.

"You're so beautiful, Sunny. So beautiful," he whispered before he sat down on the edge of the bed and pressed his head against her flat stomach.

She wanted to be beautiful for him. She wanted to make him happy, bring him pleasure. In Cader's pleasure she would find her own, just as he had taught her to do when she was fourteen. He laid her down on the bed, leaning over her, caressing her mouth with his own, licking at her lips, probing deeper with his tongue. She offered her mouth to him, answering his kisses, touching his lips with the tip of her tongue in the way she knew he liked.

His mouth left hers and pressed against the fragrant column of her neck while his hands explored her gently, tentatively, softly. Over her breasts and down the flat of her stomach to her haunches. Silkily gliding over her flesh, arousing in her a fever that came down to her from the past to make the present sweeter. No longer was she that shy little girl, afraid of her own responses, needing to be gentled like a wild colt. She opened herself to him willingly, expectantly, waiting for his remembered caress, feeling his mouth travel the length of her until he found her center. A shudder went through her as her thighs yielded to him and the bed sank beneath his weight. He fell to his knees and stroked and explored her with his lips.

She watched him as he undressed and carelessly dropped his clothes into a heap on the floor. He was beautiful. The promise of his slenderness as a boy had come to fruition in the hard-muscled flesh of the man. His chest was broad, his arms powerful, his hips narrow. The golden hair on his chest threaded over his taut stomach to bloom again in a darker grove between his thighs. His legs were long and well-muscled, but it was to the darkness between his legs that her eyes returned.

She reached out her hand to touch him, her fingers lovingly grazing his maleness and falling between his thighs. She propped herself on her elbow, drawing him closer with her hand, her mouth finding him and taking pleasure from the sound of his indrawn breath.

"God, Sunny. Your mouth, your beautiful mouth . . ." he whispered so quietly she thought she was imagining it. His hands touched her head, her neck, her shoulders. ". . . Oh, Sunny, your mouth." She brought him closer still, holding him, her palms on the smooth roundness of his haunches. "Love me, Sunny. I need you to love me. . . ."

He pulled away from her, slipping himself from between her lips and pushing her back against the bed, following her, pressing against the length of her. When he kissed her, she could taste herself on his mouth, knew he could taste himself on hers and the thought excited her.

His mouth tasted her, relished her, devoured her as it covered her breasts, her midriff, her haunches. His hands stroked her, loved her, took possession of her as he moved between her thighs.

Sunny's eyes closed, her lips parted, her body undulated against his exploring, tantalizing fingers. She reached down and grasped him in her palm and held his throbbing virility in her hand and began to rub it against her wet, yearning body, murmuring over and over, "Love me, Cade . . . love me."

She felt him rise and envelop her in his powerful arms,

kissing her, his tongue coming into her open mouth. She opened herself to him so that he might come into her and fill the pulsating emptiness and yearning inside her. He entered her, the velvet tip entering slowly, ever so slowly and gently, pausing, waiting, demanding that she reach out for him and take him into her warm moistness.

He watched her, his eyes studying her face. Eyes heavy with desire, he saw the same emotion reflected in her smoky, glazed depths. She was beautiful, so beautiful, and never more beautiful than now. Time had not changed her; there was still that sweet innocence about her full mouth and the same honesty in her eyes. Even now, on the brink of orgasm, her eyes widened in surprise, as though this were a totally new experience, as though this were her first time. A smile broke on her lips, she gazed up at him, eyes shining, as though he had given her a wonderful gift.

Cader began to move within her, thrusting gently, becoming more insistent. Thrusting and withdrawing, taking his pleasure from her, immersing himself in the soft, honeyed flesh she offered. She offered and he took, pushing against her, burying himself within her, filling her with a savage, insatiable hunger that demanded more . . . more!

She welcomed him, met each thrust with one of her own. Taking him, holding him, wanting him deeper, deeper and deeper. Undulating her hips in a slow, swaying circle to his insistent rhythm.

Together they reached remembered heights. Ecstasy became heaving, curling waves of indescribable rapture.

Sunny lay with her head on Cader's shoulder. His arm

around her offered comfort and tears threatened to spill from her eyes. How long she had wanted this, prayed he'd come back for her. And now he was here. "Cader, why did you come back to Hayden?" she asked softly, wanting to hear him say he'd come back to be with her.

"Hmmmn?"

"I asked you why you'd come back to Hayden. You've always hated this town. What made you come back?"

"You know, Sunny. Why do I have to tell you?" His voice was sleepy, but he couldn't fool her. Cader Harris never went to sleep on a woman, not even in his callous youth.

She propped herself on her elbow and looked down at him. "I don't know, Cade. I want you to tell me."

He looked up at her in a pretense of nonchalance. "I came back to open the sporting goods store." He could see in her frank appraisal that she didn't believe him. Suddenly, it wasn't necessary to lie. Sunny knew the score and he'd always been able to be honest with her. No matter what he did, no matter how he had betrayed her with other girls, she had always taken him back. Sunny never played games. She had come from the same side of the tracks as he had and she knew what a hard climb it was to get to the other side. If there was one person in this whole fucking world who would understand what he was doing in Hayden and why, that person was Sunday Waters.

"I'm here doing a job for Delta Oil," he told her, expecting to see surprise in her frank gaze. Instead, she nestled back against his shoulder.

"I thought it must be something like that. I knew you

couldn't have changed that much. Being a merchant just isn't your style. Tell me about it. Maybe I can help."

Cader told her. "So, if I can change the town's opinion by a little careful persuasion, there's quite a bit in it for me, Sunny. I don't have much to show for my career on the gridiron. My plane, a little in the bank and some big plans. This time I won't be so foolish."

"How much is in it for you, Cade?" she asked, nuzzling her lips against his neck.

"A quarter of a mil and a contract as public relations spokesman. It'll mean commercials and advertising. There's a lot of money in that, babe, and I mean to cash in. And the contract is open; I'd be free to endorse other products. Once it gets around that a big outfit like Delta is using me in advertising, the offers will come rolling in." She heard the satisfaction in his tone.

"And then what, Cader? After you cash in, I mean."

"Then I'm going to have to blow this town. There's no way I can stay here, not after people realize that I was just feathering my own nest with *their* feathers."

"And then what?" she asked hopefully, waiting to hear him say that he meant to take her with him.

Cader was silent as his hand moved possessively over her face, bringing her mouth to his once again. In the urgency of her renewed need for him she forgot that he'd never answered her question.

Chapter Nine

Keli McDermott transferred the contents of her shoulder bag to a flat clutch. Now the heavier bag wouldn't be weighing her down. Sometimes, she would almost forget the dull ache in the left side and hang the shoulder bag there, wincing with pain every time the leather swung against her body.

A last, cautious look around the room and she knew she couldn't postpone the inevitable a moment longer. If she dallied now, she would be late and Gene would be annoyed with her. It was time to go, time to put all thoughts from her mind, time to think of nothing else save the visit to Marc Baldwin's office.

The beige sheath blended with her tawny skin, and her rope sandals and clutch bag made her seem all of a piece, she noted as she walked toward the door with its long, narrow mirror. Was that beige person her? Where was her life and color? Would she slowly fade away to nothingness, this slim, beige person who was closing the door now and walking into the kitchen?

Gene rinsed and placed his coffee cup in the dishwasher, his eyes on Keli, making his movements awkward and clumsy. How beautiful she was. He would make certain nothing happened to her even if it meant making a punching bag out of Marc Baldwin. No one was going to hurt her or mar her.

"I'm ready, Gene. Do you have the checkbook?" she asked quietly.

"No problem, honey. Now there's nothing for you to worry about. Nothing is going to happen to you; no one is going to hurt you. Trust me, honey," he said, putting his arm around her shoulder comfortingly. "You don't even have to go there if you don't want to," he coaxed, hoping she would take his suggestion. "It's a simple matter of a phone call."

"Gene, please, I must know what is wrong with me. . . ."

"All right, honey," he sighed.

Tears gathered in Keli's dark chocolate eyes as Gene led her toward the waiting car that would take her to Marc Baldwin's office.

The waiting room was empty, the air conditioner whirring softly as bright afternoon sunshine spilled through the separation in the drapes. Keli walked over to the receptionist's desk, glad that Marsha wasn't working here today. She didn't want Marsha to take her under her wing the way Gene was doing. They were so alike in so many ways, she thought wearily. Her husband and her best friend imposed themselves on her. This was *her* business, *her* body. She should be allowed to do this for herself.

The middle-aged woman at the desk looked up, her skin ruddy against the stark white of her uniform. "Your name please?"

"Mrs. Keli McDermott."

"If there's one thing I appreciate, it's a patient who arrives on time." The receptionist smiled, striving to put this lovely woman before her at ease. A quick look at her notes beside each name on the appointment book told her why Keli had come to see the doctor. A shame, a tragedy, her eyes said.

Keli's oblique glance narrowed slightly as she correctly interpreted the look the receptionist was bestowing on her. "Mrs. McDermott," she heard the receptionist say, "is this your first visit with Dr. Baldwin?"

Keli nodded.

"In that case you wouldn't mind filling out this information sheet, would you?" She slipped a long, yellow sheet of paper out of the desk drawer and handed it to Keli.

"Do you have a pen? Never mind, here, use this one." The woman smiled, suddenly made uneasy by Keli's quiet manner. "You can sit over there with your husband."

Keli took her place beside Gene on the soft, apple-green bench that rested against a matching wall. She was glad Gene hadn't picked the beige chairs next to the beige wall covered in heavy burlap. She couldn't bear to be part of the office even if it was only for a few moments. She needed color . . . she needed life. She needed . . . God, how she needed.

Gene helped her fill out the information sheet. She was surprised that she was able to hold the pen — her insides were quaking. Yet her hand was steady, her handwriting smooth. When she had finished, Gene took it back to the receptionist.

"Thank you," she murmured, giving the paper a cursory glance. "Mrs. McDermott, if you'll please come with me. You can get ready while the doctor is on the phone."

Keli stood, her knees feeling as though they would buckle beneath her. She followed the white uniform into an examining room, Gene close behind.

It wasn't until the receptionist turned to close the door behind Keli that she noticed Gene. Her expression showed her surprise. "Er . . . Mr. McDermott, why don't you wait outside? Mrs. McDermott is in good hands, I assure you. . . ."

Gene pushed his way into the small cubicle. "I'm staying with my wife," he said gruffly, daring the woman to contradict him. "She needs me."

"This is quite unusual. . . ."

"I don't give a damn, I'm staying!" His voice rose in anger, his tone commanding.

The receptionist glanced at Keli who was slowly unbuttoning the front of her dress. "If Mrs. McDermott has no objections . . ."

"Why the hell should she? I'm her husband."

The woman hastily handed Keli a paper gown and quickly retreated from the room. The doctor wasn't going to like this, not at all. She closed the door behind her, leaving Gene and Keli alone.

"Here, let me help you with that," Gene murmured

solicitously as he helped Keli out of her dress. He was about to unfold the paper gown and slip it over her when he saw Keli lifting the hem of her slip.

"What are you doing?"

"I can't be examined with my clothes on, Gene," she said softly.

"Here, let me help you then," he offered, deciding not to argue. His hands gently grazed her skin as he pulled the lace-edged garment over her head and dropped it onto the circular stool. He unhooked her bra and removed it, his eyes traveling to her breasts, searching for a change in their symmetry. Keli stepped out of her panties and took the paper gown from the examining table and poked her arms through the slits. She climbed up onto the table, her feet hanging over the sides. Gene bent to undo the buckles of her sandals. She almost told him it wouldn't be necessary, then decided it didn't make any difference. Besides, it gave him something to do. His hands touched her slim ankles as he removed her shoes. Tentatively, she felt him caress her leg, sliding his fingers over her smooth, honey-colored skin. Keli squeezed her eyes shut. It had been so long since Gene had touched her this way. She didn't want him to touch her, to caress her, to explore her. It was too indicative of what their whole marriage had been based on. Gene, touching her, caressing her, as he would a fine piece of art. Then he would hold her against him and lie down beside her, his arms wrapped possessively around her. And then, nothing. How ashamed she had been those times when his gentle hands had elicited a response in her, when her body cried out to be loved, loved as a woman wanted to be loved. Poor Gene, she thought, a tear forming in the corner of her eye. He knew, he had felt her need for her husband to love her, to make love to her, to give her children. Sometimes he would cry, great heaving sobs, and she would hold him and comfort him. They never spoke of it; words were meaningless and wouldn't change anything.

Marc Baldwin knocked on the door before entering. Keli could see he wasn't surprised to find Gene with her. The receptionist had warned him. "Hello, Keli. Gene."

They both nodded perfunctorily.

"Gene, why don't you wait outside? This can't be very pleasant for you, and sometimes a husband can make things more difficult for the patient. . . ."

"I'm staying. I'm Keli's husband and I'm staying." Gene glared at him defiantly.

Marc's eyes flew to Keli. "It means so much to him, doctor," she said resignedly.

"All right, then. Look, Gene, sit over there and try to keep out of my way."

Gene picked Keli's clothes off the stool and held them on his lap, obediently following Marc's directions.

Marc unhurriedly began his examination procedure. Blood pressure. Temperature. Reflexes. "All right, Keli, now if you'll just lie back."

Gene watched as Keli lay back on the table, the crisp paper beneath her slim body rustling. He watched as Marc Baldwin lowered the paper gown to Keli's waist and placed his hands on her right breast.

"Lift your arm over your head, Keli. That's right." His fingers probed, touched, massaging her breast, squeezing the coral nipple gently. "Now the left," he murmured tonelessly.

Gene's eyes followed Marc's fingers as he began the examination of Keli's left breast. Then back to the right, back to the left. There was something wrong. Keli flinched each time Marc touched the soft flesh on the outer side of her left breast. Time and again Marc's fingers returned to that spot.

"Okay, Keli. Now just slide down on the table and I'll help you put your feet in the stirrups. . . ."

"The hell you will!" Gene burst out, standing suddenly, Keli's clothes dropping to the floor. "Get away from her!"

"What the hell's the matter with you, man?" Marc challenged.

"You're not going to touch her down there! She came in because of something in her breast."

"Now, look! This is routine." Marc was beginning to perspire. The grape-sized nodule in Keli's left breast was highly suspect and filled him with the same sense of dread he experienced whenever the possibility of cancer reared its ugly head.

"Routine or not, get away from her!"

"Gene . . . please . . ." Keli's voice was almost a whimper.

"No! He's not going to touch you!"

Keli turned her face to the wall.

"I thought you came here for help," Marc persisted. Keli was in trouble and he needed to complete the examination. Often abnormalities in the breasts were reflected in the reproductive organs. "Don't make this any harder on Keli than it already is," Marc said authoritatively.

Gene seemed to acquiesce. Marc persisted. "Now, sit down over there and be quiet!" To his amazement, Gene obeyed, his squarish head lowered in resignation.

Marc quickly positioned Keli and began the examination. He was relieved not to find any swelling or growth. Skillfully, he took a smear from her cervix and dropped the prepared slide into an envelope with her name on it. He couldn't find any signs of abnormality but what he did find was just as puzzling. Keli's hymen was still intact! Keli was still a virgin. Marc's eyes fell on Gene who was still sitting there with his head hanging. Now he understood his reluctance to have Keli examined. Marc shook his head. Christ, you just never knew! Here was Gene McDermott, all man, all Air Corps, and he probably couldn't get it up. Marc helped Keli up to a sitting position, determined not to add to her discomfort by showing any sign that he had discovered their secret.

"You can get dressed now, Keli," Marc said as he turned quickly to avoid looking into her frightened eyes. "We'll talk in my office. Why don't you wait for Keli in the waiting room, Gene . . . ?"

"I'll wait right here," the colonel interrupted fiercely, his face reddening with fury. His arms crossed threateningly over his massive chest.

"Have it your way," Marc answered shortly as he closed the door behind him.

"Get dressed, honey," Gene said softly as he wrapped the crisp white sheet around her shoulders to cover her nakedness. "Remember what I told you. No one is going to hurt you or do anything to you."

"Yes, Gene, I remember," Keli sighed as she slipped from the cold table and picked up her clothing. Before she turned her back on her husband to begin dressing, she gave Gene a last little-girl-lost look.

The colonel sensed Keli's terror and his heart sank. He knew Marc Baldwin had found something, otherwise he would have set their fears to rest immediately.

In his quiet, booklined office Marc Baldwin sat solemnly in his swivel chair, his gaze fixed on the partially open door. He licked at dry lips and breathed deeply when he saw Gene McDermott hold the door open for Keli and usher her solicitously to a deep leather chair.

Marc cleared his throat and began talking. His eyes were warm and compassionate as he addressed Keli. "It is suspect, the lump. I want to arrange a mammography for you, at once. But I'm certain of the results. It will have to come out, the sooner the better. I'll make an appointment for you with Doctor Adam Clayton in New Orleans. He'll want to examine you, and, of course, run the mammography test. For now, I can give you some literature to look over. I don't want you to be frightened, Keli. Clayton is a good man, some say he's the best."

"No operations, Baldwin!" Gene McDermott snapped, jumping to his feet. "No one is cutting into Keli! And there won't be any other appointments either! Did you hear me? No one is cutting into Keli!"

Astounded, Marc Baldwin stared at the man who was

daring to take responsibility for his wife's life. Her very life! He turned away from Gene, ignoring him. His gaze was directed at Keli who was huddled down in the deep chair, fear distorting her lovely features. "This is not your husband's decision, Keli," he said softly, hoping his words were getting through to her. "You must decide for yourself. From a medical point of view, you have no other choice."

There it was again. That word. *Choice.* Decision. Choice. "I understand, Marc," she whispered, not daring to raise her eyes to meet Gene's.

"I'm waiting, Keli." Marc pierced her with a questioning look. "I'm waiting for you to tell me to go ahead and make the appointment for you with Dr. Clayton in New Orleans. No, no, don't look to Gene, this is *your life, your decision.*" Behind him he could feel the colonel was about to explode. He imagined it was the feeling a matador gets when the bull was charging for his back.

Keli's head bowed, her long silky hair forming a curtain between herself and the rest of the world. Gene sniffed loudly and Marc anticipated another outburst. But Keli raised her head, her eyes tearless, her mouth set in a grim line and a look of hopelessness on her face that quelled her husband's outburst.

Softly, she said, "You do not understand, Marc. You have no idea of the kindness my husband has shown me . . . me and my family. Without him, his love for me, we would have all perished in the war." She said this without an excess of emotion, but her eyes fell on Gene and delivered a message of gratitude and respect. She looked back at Marc Baldwin, her gaze level and direct. "I will not disobey my husband."

Marc understood. But she was so young, so lovely to be bound by such loyalty and with so much at stake. "Keli, I understand, believe me, I do." He leaned forward, over his desk, his hands clasped in front of him. "I am your doctor."

Keli knew he was referring to the examination just a few minutes before. He was aware she was still a virgin. He knew that Gene had never claimed her as his wife.

Suddenly, Marc slammed his fist down on the desk, papers ruffling. "Damn it, Keli! It's your life we're talking about here, not some cultural belief! Gene is your husband. He's only a man! Don't, I beg you, don't allow *his* fears, *his* terrors to stop you from preserving your own life!"

Gene had had more than enough of this. He stood abruptly, his bulk seeming to fill the room, his rage seeming to suck all the air. "C'mon, honey, we're getting out of here." Roughly, he pulled her up from the chair, causing her to wince with pain.

Keli stood, pulled to her feet by Gene's force. She leveled him a calm, unblinking stare and extricated her arm from his fingers. She turned and left the office without another glance at the doctor or her husband.

Out in the parking lot she raised her eyes to see a swoop of starlings circling in the sky. Even birds made decisions. To fly or not to fly. She had to decide between life or death. Even then there would be no guarantees. If she disobeyed Gene, she could die anyway and she would have disgraced her family, her husband. If she disobeyed Gene and lived, she would be in disgrace.

Keli stumbled once on her way to the car. She threw her hands out in front of her and balanced herself. She smiled. Of course she wanted to live. Just the way she had caught herself from falling and doing herself possible harm. She wanted to live. Life was her choice. Somehow, she had to make Gene understand.

Marc Baldwin felt his insides churn. He'd handled Gene and Keli all wrong. He should have disregarded the fact that they were personal acquaintances; he should have been more professional. He shouldn't have allowed the colonel to get under his skin; he shouldn't have involved himself at all, he finally decided. *That's right*, he thought, disgusted with himself, *always take the coward's way out*.

"Nothing personal, Keli, but if you have cancer, I don't want to know it. You may be calm and serene and believe in destiny and all that stuff, but, you see, I have trouble holding onto my breakfast when I'm confronted with a life-and-death situation." The sound of his own voice brought a taste of bitter gall into his mouth. What the hell was wrong with him? What kind of doctor was he? "I should have been a dermatologist. No house calls, no worries, no life-and-death decisions. If a rash doesn't clear up in two weeks, it will in a month. No need to get involved."

Suddenly, before he could change his mind, he picked up the phone near his left arm and told his receptionist-secretary to get hold of Adam Clayton in New Orleans. He'd at least inform Adam of Keli's case and ask, as a personal favor, for him to see her without delay when and if she decided to seek consultation.

While he was waiting for Dr. Clayton's return phone call, Marc busied himself with two pregnant patients and happily announced that everything was progressing normally with each of them. Later, while going over his case files, the phone on his desk rang.

"Doctor Clayton returning your call, Doctor Baldwin," Marion announced in her most professional tone.

"Put him through."

"Marc? How are ya? How's your golf game?" Adam Clayton, surgeon, asked in his congenial, Southern accent.

"Just up to par," Marc answered tonelessly. "Look, I'm not calling you to wrangle an invitation to play on that fancy golf course you've got down there in N' Orleans. I'm after another favor."

"What's up, Doc?" Clayton joked.

"Cut the shit, will ya? I'm not in the mood."

"Sorry, Marc. What can I do for you?" Clayton leveled his tone and asked somberly. His physician's antennae snapped to attention and signaled an alert. It would be about a patient, he knew. How often had he heard that same note in his own voice when a situation was critical?

"I've got this patient, name's Keli McDermott," Marc began without ceremony as he went on to describe Keli's condition.

"How's she handling the pain?" Adam Clayton asked while penciling notes as Marc spoke.

"So far, so good."

"It can get worse, a lot worse," Clayton said flatly.

"Yeah, I know."

"Sounds to me as though you've made an accurate diagnosis from what you tell me. Of course, you'll need tests to back you up."

"Yes, and that's where the problem arises." Succinctly, he told his colleague of the problem between Gene and Keli, omitting his findings when he had examined Keli internally, telling him only that there didn't seem to be any involvement of the reproductive organs.

"Tell me what I can do for you, Marc. You know there's nothing you can do unless this woman seeks medical attention. You sound as though you're pretty much involved with her. It's hard, I know it is, but . . ." Marc could envision Adam shrugging his burly shoulders when he didn't complete his statement.

"I want you to see her. That is, *if* she decides to . . . Shit, Adam! When the pain gets bad enough, they'll come to me for the answers. What I want is for you to handle it when they're ready. I only hope it's soon enough to save her. Take down her name and have your secretary keep on the alert. If she calls, give her an immediate appointment. Okay?"

"You've got it! Listen, is there anything I can do in the meantime? You say you and Julia see the McDermotts socially. Perhaps you can talk to the man, try to make him understand."

"Adam, that bastard doesn't want to understand. He's afraid his beautiful wife will be mutilated and he can't handle that."

"Look, that's what I'm getting at. Hold out some hope for the guy. You say this girl is an Oriental, right? Small breasts, right? Did you say anything about breast reconstruction? It can be done within a year after surgery."

"I'm not up on these new techniques, Adam. I've heard about it, read about it, but I didn't know it was in widespread use."

"It's not. At least it wasn't until women discovered there was such a thing and began demanding it. There was a gal up in New York who brought her plastic surgeon into the operating room during her mastectomy. We've had several cases right here in N' Orleans. The results are spectacular! Some of the old relics in the surgery service are against it but not me. Hell! If a little bag of silicone can give a woman back her self-confidence, I'm all for it!"

"No kidding! What about the nipple?"

"The surgeon takes it off and grafts it onto the woman's thigh or groin area. When she's ready for reconstruction, he grafts it back into place. In the cases where the mastectomy was performed without preparation for reconstruction, a small circle of vaginal tissue substitutes. The results are fantastic. Tell you what, I'll send you some literature and the best of the photos. You can show them to this McDermott guy and let him see for himself. If it is cancer, it may just give his wife something to live for. Christ, can you imagine being married to someone who's only interested in your physical attributes and doesn't give a shit whether the person you are lives or dies? Christ! Someone should do a frontal lobotomy on that guy."

Chapter Ten

Julia Baldwin cast a critical eye over her dinner table and was satisfied that even Irene would not be able to find fault. A quick glance at the sunburst clock on the wall of the dining room told her she had a little over an hour till the first guests started to arrive. Where was Marc? Surely, he wouldn't be late, not tonight, when he knew she was having a dinner party. Her mind raced—was anyone due to deliver? No, only Sara Dunlap and she still had a month to go. Where was he?

Halfway up the polished stairway, she heard his key in the lock. Finally. Not bothering to turn around, she called over her shoulder for him to hurry. She would lay out his clothes while he showered, since he didn't like it when she steamed up the bathroom.

Marc tossed his medical bag on the foyer table and didn't bother to answer Julia. What good would it do if he told her he needed a drink—a drink to wash out the taste and thoughts of Gene McDermott. Ever since the consultation in his office he couldn't think about anything but Keli and Gene. "Damn!" he muttered to himself as he climbed the stairs. Tonight he would have to keep his mind on dinner table conversation. Dinner table conversation that would all be about Delta Oil. Everyone would voice an opinion and then they would all talk it to death. Irene Thomas could talk the hide off a buffalo if she got the chance. Christ, how was he going to keep his mind on what was going on if Keli and Gene sat within eye range of him? How would the obnoxious colonel behave? He knew how Keli would act, quiet and serene like she always was. "Damn it to hell," he mumbled as he stripped down and entered the shower.

Marsha Evans removed her ruffled apron and stood looking at her sullen daughter. "You barely touched your dinner, Judy. Is something wrong? Is something bothering you?"

Marsha felt her brows knit into a frown as she watched Judy toy with the food on her plate. "Why don't you have a few of your friends over for a little television or to play some records? Are you just going to mope around all night?"

"I'm in the mood to mope tonight; is that all right with you? You mope when you feel like it; why can't I? Is that dress new? You never bought new dresses when Daddy took you out to dinner," she accused.

"Judy, that was a long time ago. When are you going to understand that the divorce was not *all* my fault? It takes two people to make a marriage or a divorce. You can't go on blaming me the rest of your life. You're old enough to understand that being miserable is no way to live."

"And now Daddy's dead," Judy said, jumping up from the table and running from the room.

Marsha sat down at the wrought-iron table and nestled her face in her cupped hands. Patience, she warned herself. Judy would come around. She had already taken long strides since the accident. This was no time to cry, she told herself. If she cried, she would have to redo her eye makeup, and she wouldn't be ready when Cader Harris arrived. She could always cry later, when she was in bed with the lights out and no one was around.

Cader Harris stretched his neck and straightened his tie before he rang Marsha's doorbell. He wished he'd worn his white sport jacket and slacks, with his copper silk shirt which he always left unbuttoned halfway down his chest. Women liked skin and masculine gold chains. Instead, he had worn his dark blue suit with shirt and tie. Hell, if you wanted to do business with people it was always a good idea to at least try and look like them. His lip curled in distaste. He *never* wanted to look like the local yokels in Hayden.

The door opened, revealing Marsha standing there in some kind of green thing that hugged her curves. "Hello, Cader. What's so funny? You look like the cat that swallowed the canary."

"I was just thinking about a cat," he answered, widening his grin.

From the way his eyes flicked approvingly over her,

Marsha figured *she* was the cat. "How about a drink before we go," she said warmly.

"Why not?" Cade grinned. "Double Scotch will be fine. Nice place you've got here," he added, roaming through the living room and pretending interest. When she handed him the squat glass containing the amber liquor, he took a long pull from his drink and sized up the woman before him. She was beautiful in a sultry kind of way. The dark of her hair whitened her skin, lending it a luminescent glow. He liked the way her brows winged upward toward her temples and the way her full mouth lent itself easily to a smile. And her figure was excellent, long limbed and full breasted. It always had been, ever since he could remember.

But even in school Marsha had been a "hands off, eyes only" kind of girl. And there was no reason to assume her attitudes had changed.

Uncomfortable because of Cader's scrutiny, Marsha stammered, "We'd better be going; we don't want to be late."

"Who's going to be at Julia's tonight?" he asked as he led her out the door and to his car.

"Same old crowd. Julia and Marc, of course. And there's a new couple in town, Gene and Keli McDermott. I suppose the Guthries will be there, they always are somehow. Oh, you wouldn't know, but Marvin Guthrie is Hayden's mayor now. Do you remember him?"

"Little fat guy, isn't he?" Cader climbed behind the wheel and inserted the key into the ignition.

"That's him," Marsha laughed. "And I think Damion

Conway will be there. And of course, Arthur and Irene Thomas." She eyed him covertly to see how the mention of Irene's name would affect him. Seeing no response, Marsha settled down in her seat.

"Somehow, I never figured you for a vulture, Marsha." His statement was offered matter-of-factly but it had the required results.

"Cader?"

"Don't pretend ignorance. You know perfectly well what I mean. You wanted to see if you could get a rise out of me by mentioning Irene. Well, even if it didn't show, you did. I've been wondering when I would run into her. Tonight's as good a time as any."

"Cader, I'm sorry, I didn't mean . . . Yes, I guess I did mean," Marsha sighed. "No one ever understood why you left for college the way you did and why Irene married Arthur Thomas when she'd never shown the slightest interest in him. Guess I was just feeding my curiosity."

"That's okay," he excused her, patting her hand. "Friends, right?"

"Friends."

"Okay, old buddy, I'll tell you. Sure, I want to see Irene, I don't suppose I've ever really gotten over her. We really had something going for a while. But, you know, it was the old bit about the right boy from the wrong side of the tracks and the little princess. I just wasn't good enough for her; old man Hayden made that pretty clear."

"This is where we turn," Marsha instructed, sorry that Julia's house wasn't further away. She had the distinct impression that Cader would have gone on talking, telling her, after all these years, what exactly had come between himself and Princess Irene Hayden Thomas.

Irene sat beside her father as he wove the long Lincoln through the narrow streets. Her nerves were taut and she kept glancing at Foster Doyle. Nothing in life seemed fair somehow. When she had learned earlier that evening that Arthur had unexpected commitments at the funeral home, which would prevent him from accompanying her to Julia's party, she had bubbled with secret delight. If only Foster Doyle hadn't been there when Arthur called and insisted that he would take Arthur's place as her escort. Foster Doyle might be a crafty old fox, but he wasn't going to outfox his own daughter. He knew as well as Irene that Cader Harris would be at Julia's tonight, and he intended to make sure Irene's emotions didn't lead her astray.

Foster Doyle maneuvered the car toward the curb and threw the gear shift into park. Irene waited for him to come around to the passenger side and open the door for her. She would have been quite willing to open it for herself and was annoyed that she forced herself to sit there, as her father expected, while he played the gentleman.

Irene drew in her breath and felt her heart pounding in her chest as Foster Doyle held the door open and she saw Cader Harris in the flesh for the first time in more than eighteen years. He was the same. Tall and brawny, blond and handsome, with still a hint of the boy about him. Were her eyes playing tricks on her? Time was the ancient ravager, why should Cader have escaped it? Suddenly, she was nervous and unsure of herself. She wished she had had more notice that he was coming back to town. She could have prepared better. Started on that diet sooner, taken more time for facials. What would he see when he looked at her? What would she read in his eyes? She had had opportunities to see Cader before this, Kevin working for him being the most plausible one. But she hadn't availed herself of the right to visit her son at the sporting goods store. She had been too frightened, more so of what she wouldn't see in Cader's eyes than of what response she would find there. And now she drank in the sight of him and reveled in the sensuous pull of his magnetism.

Irene was simultaneously aware of her father's controlled astonishment when he fastened his eyes on the tall bulk of Cader Harris, Cader's wry smile and the static shock waves charging through her. It was Irene who spoke to Cader and Marsha as they advanced toward the house. She held out her hand and Cader took it in his. "Welcome back to Hayden, Cader."

Harris's eyes widened as he held Irene's hand. Jesus. Was this Irene Hayden? This regal, soft-spoken woman who had enough class and good looks to depose Princess Grace? He grinned, showing perfect white teeth. "It's good to be back," he answered, a surge of long-remembered tenderness softening his voice.

Irene was surprised her hand was steady. How could she be so outwardly calm and be in such a turmoil on the inside? "It's nice to see you again, Cade."

"It really is true what they say on the commercials, isn't it?" Harris continued to grin, looking down into Irene's upturned face.

"What's that?" she asked coyly, almost knowing what he was going to answer.

"That you don't get older, just better."

"How nice of you," Irene rejoined demurely, to Marsha's astonishment. This wasn't the same simpering, flighty Irene. This was an attractive woman, no, a beautiful woman, looking up into the eyes of a man whom she found irresistibly attractive. There was no pose of the spoiled Southern belle in Irene's demeanor. Her gaze was frank and open and perhaps speculative, but certainly not simpering or self-indulgent. This was an Irene Marsha had never seen.

"I think we should be getting inside; we don't want to be late for Julia's 'happy hour.' After all, Cade, you are the guest of honor," Marsha said, taking him by the arm and tearing him away from Irene. She was the only woman in Hayden who could clutch with her eyes, Marsha thought nastily. Irene Hayden Thomas clutched with her eyes because she didn't have the guts to clutch with her hands.

Julia opened the door and smiled warmly at Cader Harris as she ushered the guests into the long, formal living room with a light, airy, "You know everyone, so why don't we just have our drinks and settle down to some cocktail chatter?"

Foster Doyle crossed the room, his back tall and straight, his distinguished gray hair smoothed close to his head, and seated himself in a high-backed Queen Anne chair near the fireplace. He lowered himself onto the chair and sat stiffly, hands placed firmly on knees, and seemed to preside over the room. By his posture and appearance he commanded attention and respect, like a Supreme Court judge deliberating his verdict.

As always, people were drawn to him. Marc Baldwin, Mayor and Mrs. Guthrie, Marsha Evans hovered near him, seeming to hang on his every word and basking in the attention the old man paid them.

Cader watched, sneering inwardly, half expecting to see them all kowtow in obeisance. Turning his scrutiny away from the silver-haired gentleman, he accepted his drink and smiled at Julia's guests, making each feel special under his gaze.

Julia settled herself in a low, comfortable chair—her eyes never leaving the muscular figure of Cader Harris. Her mind whirled and refused to focus on the conversation floating around her. God . . . he was good looking. Virile and . . . God . . . he was virile! Every woman in the room was looking at him. Was this the way it happened? Was this the way women decided to have affairs? Did they lock eyes with a man and know instinctively that sooner or later, preferably sooner, they would end up in bed together? She felt the beginnings of a flush on her cheeks. She let her eyes travel to her husband, Marc, who was saying something about the weather. He looked bored to death and mechanical. There was certainly no animal magnetism there. She turned her head to look at Cader Harris who was leaning against the mantel in the relaxed pose of a man about town. It never occurred to her that the pose was studied, and, if he had a pipe in his hand, he could have come right out of the pages of *Town and Country*. He was talking to Marvin Guthrie about the cost of freight, but his eyes were talking to every woman in the room.

Irene rose from her chair and moved across the room. She could feel Cader's eyes follow her as she moved past him. The silky fabric of her white jersey sheath hugged her hips and restrained the movement of her legs. Now, instead of feeling confining and restricting, it felt good against her limbs, brushing against her skin, sending a flush of pleasure through her. The back was draped in a long cowl, baring her superbly tanned skin to the waist and outlining the high swell of her buttocks. She knew it set her figure off to an advantage. An advantage, she knew from experience, Cader Harris would notice and appreciate.

Cader Harris took Irene's hand in his and smiled down at her. "I want you to sit here and tell me everything you've been doing since we last saw each other."

Irene felt deliciously wicked in this crowded room, aware of Foster Doyle's disapproval. For the first time in her life Irene didn't care what Daddy thought. She was all grown up now and she didn't need Daddy's blessing. She knew she was a full-grown woman; the proof was there in Cader's enveloping gaze.

She smiled up at him, her heart beating a rapid tempo. She should hate him. She should want to scratch his eyes

out. He didn't even remember when they'd seen each
other last, when they'd last spoken to each other. What
they had meant to each other. But *she* couldn't forget. Did
not want to. She only wanted to have him smile down at
her the way he was doing and to listen to his voice, which
still held a soft edge of a Southern accent. He liked her.
She could see it in the way he looked at her. The years
hadn't changed her that much. Out of the corner of her
eye she saw Foster Doyle give her a forbidding look. It was
a good thing he couldn't read her mind.

Irene listened to Cader as he spoke of inconsequential
things, reminiscing on the past. Her thoughts were blown
from her like leaves before a wind. She watched his hands,
felt them as they reached for hers. They were gentle,
warm . . . just as she had remembered, just as she had
dreamed all those nights. All those years. Where did they
go? How could you suddenly see someone you hadn't seen
in so many years and have that time wiped away? You just
couldn't erase eighteen years. Or could you, she asked herself. From the look in Cader's eyes, *he* thought you could.

While Cader and Irene were reminiscing, the doorbell
rang and Colonel and Mrs. McDermott arrived. Keli
McDermott accepted a drink from Gene, her face soft
and serene as she gazed about Julia's graciously appointed
living room.

Keli glanced over the rim of her glass to see Marsha
staring at her. Quickly, Keli glanced away, swallowing
hard, feeling the cold liquid burning her throat. She didn't
want to talk to Marsha, didn't want to answer her questions

and defend herself against a barrage of demands for explanations of why she wasn't taking Marc Baldwin's advice. Marsha would never understand, not the way Damion understood. She would harass Keli, saying things such as "It's your *life!* You've got to get another opinion. Why? Why? Why?"

Keli centered her attention on Cader Harris, the guest of honor. He was a forceful man, she decided. Even from here she could feel his presence, and he hadn't even spoken to her as yet. He reminded her of an animal prowling the confines of his cage, stopping every so often to peer between the bars, gauging his chances of luring some unsuspecting soul close enough to devour. She decided it was his eyes—sleepy eyes, strange eyes. Calculating eyes.

"Keli, Gene! How nice to see you," Damion Conway said, smiling down into Keli's lovely face.

"Reverend," Gene said curtly, acknowledging the minister.

"You look lovely tonight, Keli," Damion complimented. The slim-fitting slacks topped by a narrowly cut dress that came only to her knees and was slashed from the hem to the hip line on each side was reminiscent of the garments worn in her native Thailand. Even though the high neckline was opened to the top of her breasts, and the simple white dress was sleeveless in a compromise to Western apparel, the association was unmistakable. She was wearing her long silky hair twisted into a coronet on the top of her head, giving her unexpected height and revealing the graceful length of her slim neck. She was lovely, Damion thought, but it was in her eyes that her real beauty was to be found.

"Have you met our 'guest of honor'? No, stay here and I'll bring him over and introduce you. Cade Harris and I go back a long time. Kids through school and then fraternity brothers at the university," Damion explained to Gene.

As Damion crossed the room to where Cader was talking to Irene, Keli's eyes followed him. If it weren't for the clerical collar, one would have thought Damion was a musician or an artist, or even a dancer. He was tall and lithe and his dark hair that always seemed to be a week past needing a haircut tumbled over his forehead in a casual, unruly manner, softening his slightly craggy, yet unmistakably handsome features. But it was his hands that revealed his sensitive, creative nature to Keli. Long and agile, fingers with slightly splayed tips, gentle hands, soothing hands.

Damion clapped Cade on the back, a smile pasted on his face. "Come over here; there's someone I want you to meet. You are the guest of honor at this shindig, aren't you?"

"Well, if it isn't the 'pun—' the local minister." Cader grinned, noticing the warning in Damion's eyes. He spread his arms loftily and grinned again, white teeth flashing. "You got it old buddy, the guest of honor. Be happy to meet your friends. You should have gone into public relations, Damion. I never did think this preaching business was for you. What the hell do you get out of it? And don't give me any of that shit about inner satisfaction," Cade murmured as he walked beside Damion to the bar.

"Then I won't give you any. Actually, I'm going to

devote my life to saving your soul. You *do* have one, don't you?"

"Hell, no! But I do have a cock which I use regularly. Can you say the same?"

"It might surprise you to know I have one too, but it wouldn't get the workout yours gets if I lived to be a hundred," Damion rejoined coldly.

"You shot your load back in college, is that it?"

"One of these days someone is going to put the screws to you, Harris, and I hope I'm around to see it. You have the balls of a Saint Bernard."

"At least I got 'em."

"You're up to something, Cade. I don't believe you'd ever come back to Hayden unless there's something in it for you. I'm going to watch you carefully, Cade. I mean it. These are my people and you're not going to do anything to hurt them."

"Fuck it, Damion. Watch me all you want. Just remember that the hand is quicker than the eye."

"Smile pretty, Cade, and try not to act like the animal you are." Coming up to Keli and Gene, Damion made the introductions. Damion's eyes were cloudy as he watched the handshakes and Cader turn on his charm.

"Well, if you aren't the prettiest thing these old eyes have ever seen," Cader said, grinning down at Keli, "and Colonel, I've heard about that book you're writing. I always wanted to be in the military, but I didn't have the guts. You guys are rough and tough; I knew I could never hack it."

Gene McDermott fastened his eyes on the athlete.

"With a little training and discipline you would have made a good soldier. I have an eye for a good man when I see one. Shame, damn shame, you didn't join the service."

"I'm sorry myself," Cader lied. "Hell, man, you got it all. Retirement as a colonel, a beautiful wife and you're still young enough to enjoy life. Yes, sir, you've got it all. Makes a man sit back and wonder where he went wrong. Sure would like to read that book you're working on."

"Stop by the house and I'll let you take a squint at the outline. Any time this week would be fine. I'm just researching for the next few days so you won't be interrupting any writing."

"I'll just do that." Cader grinned.

Damion grimaced. The only thing Cade Harris read was *Hustler* and *Screw*, and then he only looked at the pictures. *Bastard*, he seethed. His eyes went to Keli who was sipping at her drink, her eyes traveling around the room. "How are you, Keli?"

"Just fine, Damion. It's a lovely party, isn't it? Julia and Irene always have such . . . exquisite parties."

Damion smiled. "A party is a party. It's the people who make it a success." His voice was gentle, almost paternal.

Her soft doe eyes questioned his tone, not the words. "Yes, I agree." Short, clipped words that merely agreed with something he said. Well, what the hell did he expect her to say?

"Doesn't Irene look lovely this evening?"

Damion turned and stared at Irene Hayden Thomas. "I really hadn't noticed till you mentioned it, but, yes, she does look nice. I don't think I've seen Irene that dressed up since Marsha's clambake last year."

Keli giggled and Damion was shocked. He had never seen her do anything but smile. She looked so young and . . . vulnerable. Keli giggled. *Amazing,* he told himself. *Absolutely amazing!* Did Cade Harris have anything to do with it, he wondered. Perhaps it was some kind of inside joke that only women understood. He shrugged.

When Cade turned to include Keli in the conversation, Damion backed away on the pretense of getting another drink.

Marsha Evans's voice was low as she conversed with Julia about her dinner and how stunning everyone looked, including Irene.

"I think your dinner parties bring out the best in everyone, Julia. Of course, I'm the first to admit that Cader Harris just might have something to do with it. I've never seen Irene look so animated, not since her father's appointment to the bench. And, Julia," she said, lowering her voice to a whisper, "when have you ever seen any of the men in this room so . . . so spruced up or standing so straight? Look at Mayor Guthrie; he looks like he's in mortal agony holding in his stomach."

"Cader certainly is a virile-looking man," Julia agreed. "You must feel pretty flattered that you're the one he brought tonight."

Marsha's eyes darkened momentarily. "I'm not interested in Cader Harris or any man right now. I've had enough of men to last me the rest of my life. A dinner here, a movie or a concert, that's something else as long as there are no ties and no strings. I'm not looking for a relationship, Julia."

"And why not? Relationships are what makes the world go 'round," Damion Conway said, coming up to the two women.

"Damion, I do wish you had brought a date for the evening," Julia chided the reverend. "You threw off my seating arrangement, I want you to know."

"I'm sorry, but there just wasn't anyone I wanted to bring this evening. I know you'll forgive me. I've read somewhere that hostesses adore single men at parties."

"Only if there are single ladies and you have one strike against you by being a minister." Julia smiled.

Damion slouched against the mantel. "It looks like your party is a success. Cade is having the time of his life."

"That's what it's all about," Julia retorted. "The party is for Cader, to welcome him back to town. Do you think he'll make a success of the sporting goods store, Damion?"

"It's too early to tell. If charm was the only thing he needed, then yes, it would be a roaring success. He seems to have an adequate supply of money, so, off the top of my head, I'd say he has an excellent chance of succeeding. I just heard him tell Gene he was thinking of hiring a tennis pro and expanding his tennis line. It's a good idea if I do say so myself."

"Yes, tennis is the *in* game," Marsha agreed. "I've been thinking of taking it a little more seriously myself. I could use a little help with perfecting my backhand."

"I hope he can get Marc interested in some kind of sport," Julia said through tight lips.

"Leave it to Cade, Julia. Before you know it Marc will be out there with a racket or running or something. I have a feeling that every man in town will be taking up some kind of sport, and soon," Damion said coolly.

"You don't like Cader, do you?" Marsha asked bluntly.

"Does it show that much?" Damion retorted just as bluntly.

"Yes."

"Let's just say he's not one of my favorite people and let it go at that."

"We're going to have to; dinner is now being served," Julia said as she acknowledged the cook's silent signal that all was in readiness.

As Julia's guests milled around the dining room looking for their place cards, Marc encountered Keli and Gene McDermott just as they were placing their half-finished drinks on the bar. Gene stiffened his spine and purposely avoided Marc's glance. Realizing that a strain would be placed upon dinner, Marc attempted to bridge the gap. "Gene, you came to me for medical advice and I gave it to you. My opinion hasn't changed and I'm trying to understand your feelings on this matter. Let's not have it affect our friendship."

Gene puffed up, his squarish head thrust forward on his bullish neck. "Look here, Baldwin, I only came to your wife's dinner because it seemed to matter so much to Keli. I can well imagine what you think of me and I don't give a damn. Just stay out of our lives!" His voice was guttural and he seemed to hiss between clenched teeth.

Keli placed her hand on Gene's arm, her cheeks reddening with embarrassment. "Gene . . . please . . . Marc didn't mean anything. . . ."

"Don't you go defending him, Keli. I didn't want to come here in the first place. . . ." He turned to Marc. "Now just stay out of it, Baldwin, and leave us alone! I'm warning you. One more word and I'll drag Keli out of here."

Marc's eyes narrowed and his gaze centered on the throbbing pulse evident just above Gene's too-tight collar. "Don't get your pressure up; I only wanted to say I will stay out of it, for tonight, at least. Come on, Keli, everyone's being seated." He placed her arm through his. "Coming, Gene?" He glanced backward to see the colonel pouring himself another finger of Scotch and downing it. The man is scared, Marc thought in surprise. It's not just stupidity or stubbornness, it's fear. He sighed heavily. It would seem that before Keli found help Gene would have to overcome his fear and ignorance. He only hoped the intractable Gene McDermott came to his senses while there was still time for Keli.

Keli found herself seated beside Damion Conway, and throughout the dinner she was aware of his silent understanding. She was conscious of Marsha's eyes constantly searching hers and of the close attention of Marc and Gene. Why couldn't they leave her alone? Why did they have to keep watching her as though she were suddenly going to explode all over the dinner table? Only Damion understood. He was the only one who saw beyond the body to the woman she was. He offered her a quiet consolation. Unlike Gene who denied her the right to make decisions concerning herself, her own body. Unlike Marsha, who watched her with puzzled eyes, wanting to help in some way, yet wanting to take control in much the same way as Gene. Only Damion understood, not forcing his will upon her, telling her she had a choice, even if that choice was not to his liking. Damion saw the woman, the person within.

Her thoughts were interrupted by Marvin Guthrie's loud guffaw. "Now, Cade," he was saying, "we like our town just the way it is, don't we, honey?" He turned to his rotund wife, Alma, who automatically nodded while pushing another shrimp into her mouth. Actually, his words were for Foster Doyle's benefit. Next year was an election year and old man Hayden's support was important.

"And I like the town just the way it is too, Mayor," Cader answered jocularly. "It's refreshing. I've lived in cities where you couldn't turn your back and you needed three locks on the door. No, Hayden may be just the way I left it, but I like it that way."

"We're glad you do, Cader," the Mayor said in his gravelly voice between bits of crisp lettuce. "Hayden is a fine place to live and rear children. Some say we haven't progressed beyond the year 1945, but that's all right with us, isn't it, honey?" Again he looked to his wife for confirmation, and again she nodded automatically just as the perfect politician's wife should do.

"I know just what you mean," Harris bantered. "Some

may say it's a dying town, but we know better, don't we?" His words had the required, calculated effect. Mayor Guthrie nearly choked.

"Dying! Who says Hayden is a dying town?" He challenged with all the furor of a town politician.

"For one thing, the merchants of Hayden are having a rough go of it. I know. I had to look into it before I opened my sporting goods store here."

"Why did you open it here if, as you say, the merchants are having a rough go?" Foster Doyle interjected, his cold gray eyes piercing Harris suspiciously.

Harris shot him a glaring look. "Because I felt a loyalty to my hometown. Because it was time to settle down a bit, and I'd rather be here in Hayden than anywhere. This may not be a boom town but there's enough here to warrant my investment."

"That's admirable of you, boy. Your loyalty, I mean." Foster Doyle smiled to himself. Keep talking, Harris, I'll find out why you're here and then I'll blow it for you.

Cader Harris seemed to read Foster's intent and fell suddenly silent. But the mayor had uncovered a political bone and would not leave it alone.

"See here, Harris, you wouldn't be referring to Delta Oil, would you?"

"Actually, I don't know enough about it to come to a decision. It certainly would appear to be just the boost Hayden is looking for."

"Well, I can tell you about it!" Marc offered seriously. "Of course everyone understands I'm speaking strictly from a medical point of view, but I believe installing those holding tanks would be the worst thing possible to come into our town." Marc saw he had the attention of everyone at the table, and he unconsciously squared his shoulders and lowered his voice. "My concern is with the health and safety of Hayden's citizens. It is well-agreed that the Mississippi area is already saturated with nearly thirty percent of the entire United States petrochemical industry. It is second only to the New York–New Jersey metropolitan area which boasts over forty percent. I'm concerned with the children who attend schools here, not only in Hayden but also in surrounding towns. The pollution. The hazard of explosion. The possible adverse effects on our air and our water supply. My concern is with human life. Once Delta Oil gets a foothold here there's no telling how far it will go. Other towns will follow our example and allow similar installations to be built. I'm totally against it."

"I can understand that, Marc," Cader said, "and I certainly sympathize with your reasons. Only your livelihood doesn't depend upon commerce. You're a doctor. You can relocate. I'm thinking of the small businessman. If there's no work, people can't help the economy of Hayden. How long before they sell out . . . leave town? What of the teachers? Struggling towns can't afford top salaries. Our children will suffer educationally. Only second-rate teachers will be attracted to Hayden. That's where I'm at and a lot of other people here in town are thinking the same thing. Otherwise, why this split, this division? If you ask me, this town is on the brink of another Civil War."

"Nobody's asking you, Harris," Gene said quietly, "or haven't you noticed? However, I'm for progress and I've made the unpopular decision that Delta Oil should come into Hayden. What's the sense of trying to save the environment when no one will be living here anyway?"

The mayor coughed and cleared his throat in preparation for his speech. "I've looked into this matter, and I must admit I've every guarantee from the state environmental agencies that if Hayden decided to allow Delta Oil's holding tanks in here, they would be on top of the issue every step of the way. That's not to say that I'm in favor of the tanks, understand." Marvin Guthrie looked around the table making certain everyone did understand, especially the president of the town council, Foster Doyle Hayden.

Cader Harris smiled to himself. The pompous jackass. He knew for a fact that the mayor straddled the fence where Delta Oil was concerned. In no way, shape, matter or form did he want to offend potential political supporters. Reelection was coming up next year and Cader knew that Mayor Guthrie's stand was quite different when he was talking to the Chamber of Commerce and the Rotary. Nothing that could be quoted, of course, nothing that would offend the opposing faction, but it was obvious that if Mayor Guthrie could be convinced he wouldn't be drummed out of office because of this issue, he'd push for the installation of the tanks.

"As far as danger of explosion, Baldwin," Gene McDermott was saying, "the odds are strictly against it."

"Then you admit it's a gamble," Marc retorted.

"Life is a gamble. However, I've been studying this situation, and I even have letters from the federal environmental agencies. The problem in Hayden is that so many people are uninformed."

"Then inform us, please," Cader interjected. He could tell by the vibes that Colonel McDermott wasn't a popular man in the community, and he probably skimmed along on the strength of his wife's charm. But he was pro-Delta and what he had to say could be important.

"For one thing, the liquefied natural gas, or LNG, is proposed to be stored in two huge tanks. Environmentalists contend that the gas in its liquefied state presents a serious safety hazard if not handled correctly. In this I bow to Dr. Baldwin. Handled irresponsibly, it would be a serious hazard to area residents. LNG is actually frozen to two hundred sixty degrees below zero and is thus condensed six hundred times to a liquid state."

"We all know that, Gene," Marc said impatiently. "And we also know that stored LNG, as proposed by Delta Oil, has the energy potential, if ignited all at once, of several atomic bombs."

"True," Gene continued. "However, the real risks involve not so much the storage of LNG but its transfer from ship to terminal."

"Yes," Marc leaned forward, his face drawn into grim lines, "and a spill, according to many experts, could result in a vaporized plume that if ignited could result in a flash fire engulfing several miles, depending on wind direction."

"The state of Louisiana has approved proposed by Delta Oil," Cader interjected. "Ce meets all safety standards."

"That's only because a terminal here would ensure the state's energy supply for years to come," Marc said hotly.

"Gentlemen, if the real danger is in the transfer of the liquefied gas, surely Delta's proposal should be considered. A pipeline, extending miles out from Hayden into the Gulf . . ."

Foster Doyle, who had sat quietly throughout the discussion, suddenly cleared his throat. The effect was instantaneous and predictable. The room was immediately silent. All eyes focused on the gray-haired gentleman, waiting for him to speak. It was almost as if he had slammed his fist on the table. "Delta Oil will *never* come into Hayden," he said, looking pointedly at the mayor, knowing how Guthrie straddled the fence. "I will never allow it. This discussion is pointless. There will be no threat to health or environment because there will be no tanks. There will be no increase in business for the same reason. Hayden will remain as it is."

Cader focused on Foster Doyle, his expression a combination of humor and grudging respect. "*Never* is a long time, Foster." He purposely used the old gentleman's first name, reminding him that he was no longer the boy from the wrong side of the tracks; now he was an equal. "I remember when you said 'never' to me. As you can see, it's only a word and doesn't mean a thing."

Foster Doyle nearly choked. How dare Harris say that

... ow were scrutinizing ... , his gaze fell on Irene ... nowed perplexity rather than

... ood up abruptly, the muted scrape of his ... st the carpet a nerve-grating shriek in the hushe ... om. He tossed his napkin onto the table. "I will be leaving now," he stated in a barely controlled voice. Always the gentleman, showing his fine breeding, he expressed his thanks to his flabbergasted hostess.

Irene ignored her father's penetrating, silent command. She was staying!

Several moments after Foster Doyle's dramatic departure, the conversation buzzed with inconsequential subjects. Cader Harris looked speculatively at each of his dinner partners, mentally assessing their stand on the possibility of Delta Oil coming into Hayden. Only Gene McDermott was pro-LNG and he was not well-liked. It may have looked like a Mexican standoff to anyone other than Cader Harris. He had now made a foothold in society and had been included in the discussion of Delta Oil. Now it wouldn't seem strange or unusual if he should discuss it with any of the merchants or be seen in the company of anyone who approved the proposal. It wasn't going to be easy; he had known that before returning to Hayden. But a quarter of a million dollars was a lot of money, and it was imperative that he wrap things up here before Delta Oil became impatient and sent in a few of their own men with nice fat bribes to put in the right places. Damn! He

wished he had more working ca
route himself in spite of Delta Oil's obje
was only a last resort. And it would be done by
people, men who weren't working for them for a pron.
of an enormous sum of money or a contract as their public
relations advisor.

D E L T A   L A D I E S   231

...ital. He'd have gone that ... tions that their own ...actery ...ise

Eleven

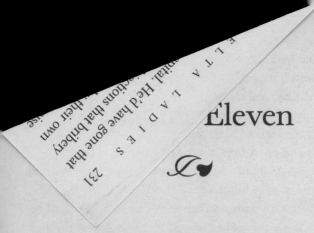

Irene Thomas stood on the patio gazing up at the clear blue sky. God, it was hot and humid! Or was it she who was hot and humid? She felt drained, empty.

She sat down on a colorful webbed chair and continued to stare at the scrubbed blue sky. She looked at her Bloody Mary and winced slightly. This was new, this drinking in the afternoon. She admitted that the afternoons were the worst time of day to get through. Was this her second or third? Who gave a good rat's ass, anyway? What if it were five or six? Who cared what she did, how much she drank? No one, she answered bitterly as she drained her glass and poured another.

Glancing at her watch, she grimaced. She had expected Cader to call before now. Why hadn't he called? Last night at Julia's house hadn't his eyes told her she would be hearing from him? Soon? Very soon? It was now twelve

hours since the pa...
from him by now.

Idly, she dipped her inde...
stirred. At first the movements ...
watched, her finger moved faster and ...
toey drink slopped over the sides of the g...
onto her white tennis outfit. She stared at the...
stain on the stark whiteness and flinched slightly.

It suddenly occurred to her that before Cader had re...
turned to town she would sit and secretly browse through
Viva and *Playgirl* magazines and make endless checks in
the boxes of the self-revelation tests in *Family Circle* and
Woman's Day, all the while wallowing in self-pity. But
she didn't need a slick magazine article to tell her that the
multiple orgasm was not a myth. It was Cader Harris who
had taught her that and who now filled her thoughts while
she filled her afternoon with Bloody Marys.

Cader's failure to call her was linked in her mind to the
way he skipped out on her eighteen years ago. She wasn't
fooling herself; he had done just that—skipped out, leaving her with a full belly that turned out to be Kevin. Bitter
that Cader had failed to call, Irene smiled smugly. She
wondered what Cader would say if he knew that Kevin was
his own son, his own flesh and blood. Perhaps if he knew,
it would strengthen the ties between them. Irene gulped,
shoving back the thought that was very close to being a
temptation. Cader must never know. What if he took it
into his mind to take Kevin away from her? It was unthink-
able. Kevin was Arthur's son. No! Kevin was *her* son! Her

No one,

...er. She was ...of masculine ..., powerful, self-...en. He had always ...her. And Cader, he'd ...n't he? Even Arthur, in ...ld the high cards over her. ...vin's love for Arthur to know ...erkss. If keeping Kevin to herself meant she ...let Cader know he was the boy's father, then so be it. It would be the only trump card she could hold against him. And Irene needed something to hold onto. God help her, in spite of everything, she still wanted Cader Harris. Wanted him more than she'd ever wanted anything. And by Jesus, she'd have him. She'd gone after him before and she would do it again. And this time, it would be on her own terms.

Squaring her shoulders and slamming her glass down on the table, Irene bristled. She chortled quietly, remembering that time-worn axiom, "Hell hath no fury . . ."

Tears welled in her eyes at the horrible injustice of it all. She had nothing without Cader and now that she had seen him again, this realization shook her foundations. A single tear slid down her cheek and she felt the taste of salt on her lip. There was an answer. She just had to find it. She had to think of something! Do something!

Irene's eyes lowered to the crimson stain on the short

white skirt. The outfit was ruined, and it was her favorite. Even if she didn't play tennis, she felt good wearing it. It was a pretend thing. Like her life. *Let's all pretend everything is all right and it will go away.* Pretend. There was nothing left to do but go out and buy another tennis outfit. She needed a tennis outfit to pretend while she drank her Bloody Marys.

She got up from the deck chair and reeled slightly. Yep, guess it was five instead of three. Laughing, she trotted into the house and up the stairs to her bedroom. Let's see, she mused, what did you wear when you went to buy a tennis outfit? A golfing outfit, of course. She giggled as she pulled up the zipper. This was another of her pretend outfits. It had been years since she'd been on the golf course.

The moment she pulled her car into the empty lot of Cader Harris's new store, she realized her mistake. Today was Wednesday and all the stores were closed after one o'clock. Maybe Cader was still in the shop and would open it for her. She really needed that outfit. She opened her bag and popped a Chiclet into her mouth, and it wasn't till she started chewing that she realized it was a Feenamint. *Shit!* A fit of laughing overtook her as she pounded on the frosty glass of the shop. "Cader, are you in there? It's Irene."

"Yo, I sure am. I was just getting ready to leave," Cader said, opening the door for her to enter. "Come in, pretty lady. What can I do for you?" He caught the glitter in Irene's eyes at the same moment he got a whiff of her breath. He could feel his adrenaline begin to surge as feelings of revenge, danger and scorn bounced around within him. Was Irene a secret drinker or had she been drinking because she needed the courage to finally confront him for leaving her the way he had eighteen years before? *Play it cool, Cade*, he warned himself. He put his brain into gear and pasted his number-six smile across his lips, the one he had used for the new toothpaste he had endorsed.

"I need a tennis outfit and I need it right away. You can't play tennis if you don't have an outfit." Irene giggled.

A tennis buff and from the looks of the outfit she was wearing she must be into golf too. Strong legs. "Good thinking, Harris," he muttered to himself. Jesus! He had never seen such hot eyes. "They're hanging up over there; take your pick," he said, pointing to a rack at the far end of the store. He continued to wear the number-six smile as he contemplated her next move.

"I'll take six, just wrap them up. Size nine. Why is it so hot in here?" Irene asked, looking around.

"Beats the hell out of me." Cader grinned, shifting into smile number-seven that held a trace of a leer and showed off his porcelain to the best advantage.

Irene frowned. "I don't remember you having all those teeth. I like them," she said, throwing back her head and laughing with delight. "Makes you look like a super jock. Are you a super jock, Cade?" she teased lightly.

"Depends on who's doing the asking." She wanted to play games from the sound of things. He liked games as long as he won. Irene would be a good loser.

"Ma-cho stud. Super jock. It fits you, Cade. God, I

can't get over all those teeth. I bet you made some dentist real happy."

Cader laughed, enjoying the conversation. "I heard he took off for Aruba for a month's vacation after I paid the bill."

Irene purposely widened her eyes, drinking in the sight of him. She wanted him, needed him. Eighteen years was too long a time to wait for anything, and she had no intention of waiting another minute. She wasn't Irene Hayden Thomas, she was an eighteen-year-old again, bent on getting the one thing she wanted most. Her eyes narrowed slightly. No, if she was going to be honest, she wasn't just an eighteen-year-old again; she was a bitch in heat. "That figures. Pull the blinds and take off your clothes," she commanded.

"I thought you came in here for a tennis outfit." Cader laughed as he closed the Venetian blind on the front door.

"I did."

"It would appear to me you have something else on your mind. It goes without saying that I've been wrong on occasion. . . . Christ, you have hot eyes. Exactly what do you have in mind?" Cader demanded, knowing full well what Irene wanted and experiencing a response that displayed itself in his nether regions.

"Whatever goes after you take off your clothes. I thought you would have figured it out by now. Sit on that chair. I'll do the rest."

"Will you now?" By God, she was something. He'd had women come on to him before, but this time there was something different. He stared at her and suddenly understood her need. What was so astounding was that he never, ever thought Irene would reach out and take it. He shrugged inwardly. Hell, he'd always been a giver. "I was never one to drag my feet," he said, taking off his shoes. By the time he had his socks off Irene was down to the buff, her feet slightly parted, her face serious, her eyes smoldering. And he thought Sunday Waters had it down for speed. This was faster than the Indy 500.

A smile played around the corner of Irene's mouth. "Sit. I'll get on top." Cader Harris sat. He knew how to obey orders. Irene straddled him, her long, muscular legs hanging over the sides of the chair. It was over almost before it started. Twice more she repeated her frantic gyrations. Finished, she slid off him and stood looking down at him, a dreamy, faraway look on her face.

"If you want an explanation, you aren't getting one," Irene said, picking up her clothes.

"Hey, Irene, this is me, Cade. If that's your style, you don't owe me an explanation. But," he said, wagging a finger, "why do I have this feeling that I've been used?"

Irene laughed. "Let's just say I wanted you to see what you've been missing for the past eighteen years." She tilted her head to one side. "As fucks go, you were all right." The sound of the zipper being pulled up on the golf shorts seemed unusually loud to Cader.

"Jesus H. Christ, is that what you call it? I was all right?" He grimaced in pretended outrage. "You fucked me, lady. I just came along for the ride. Don't stand there and tell me *I* was all right. If you want to get fucked, I'll fuck you, but we'll do it *my* way. Then you can tell me if it's all right. And I am well aware of what I've been missing."

She was Irene Hayden Thomas again. "Are you saying I hurt your manly pride? You got it off. What more do you want?" she asked, stuffing her bra into her handbag. She buttoned her shirt and continued to stare at the naked man sitting in the chair. Suddenly, she felt very powerful, like that time at the football game when she snared him away from Sunny Waters. Cade Harris was hers; he always had been.

"You used me!" Cade said in a miffed tone. "Goddamn, you came into my store to buy a tennis outfit and you used my cock for your revenge." When the full enormity of the situation hit him, he doubled over laughing. "You used my cock to . . ." Unable to continue, he lunged for Irene.

Irene stepped neatly to the side, her eyes laughing merrily. "Come off it, Cade. How many times have you used a woman? We both know you're a taker. You know that old saying; there are givers and takers. Are you going to hold it against me because I took a little?" She smiled. "See you around, Cade. You better get dressed; it's awfully cold in here."

"The next time, we do it my way, agreed?" Cader called to her retreating figure.

Irene stopped in midstride. Her tone was serious and all the merriment was gone from her eyes. "I'd like that. I'd like that very much."

"Son of a bitch!" Cader cursed as he watched the door close behind her. He had one leg in his pants when the door opened and Irene stuck her head in and grinned.

"Thanks, Cade."

One leg in his pants, the chair wiggling beneath his grasp, Cade teetered and went down. He was just too tired to get up. Jesus, how could he have forgotten how much of a woman she was? She had drained him and she was still as perky as a frisky pup.

Irene stepped from the shower and wrapped a bright lemon bath sheet around her just as the phone rang.

Suddenly, the day was different, the phone was a rare pearl in her hand, Cader's voice was a symphony in her ear, and the bright sun shining through the window making dappled patterns on the carpet, the rarest of fine laces. It was a moment before she could trust herself to speak. "Hello, Cader," she whispered. It was going to be a perfect day, she could feel it, sense it, almost taste it.

"I'm calling to ask you to have lunch with me. Can you make it?"

Could she make it? Could she breathe? Of course, she could make it. She'd die before she declined. "I think so," she breathed heavily. "Where shall I meet you?"

"I was thinking about the Cottage Inn on Westover Drive. It's far enough off the beaten track that I think you'll be safe meeting me there. I should be able to clear things away here at the shop and be there by one. Is that convenient for you?"

Of course, it was convenient for her. She'd have dropped the bath sheet and started this minute if he said so. "One will be fine, Cade. I'm looking forward to it," Irene said softly.

"Irene, do you remember the time . . ."

"That you took me there after the Thanksgiving game? Of course, I remember. I'm a little surprised that you remember, though."

"I could never forget that day. I'll see you at one then."

"Goodbye, Cade," Irene said, replacing the receiver in its cradle.

A pot and a half of coffee and a pack of cigarettes later, Irene was ready to leave. God, she hoped she didn't have an accident on the way.

A heavyset hostess led Irene to the back of the inn and settled her in a black leather and knotty pine booth. Irene ordered a vodka gimlet and settled back to wait for Cader.

As she sipped at the tart drink, she looked around. She hadn't been here since that day she had come with Cader after the Thanksgiving game eighteen years ago. It looked the same, with its rustic atmosphere. The heavy ferns in their copper baskets gleamed brightly from the dimly lit wall sconces. The worn red brick and the rough-hewn beams made her think of times of old. It was pleasant; quiet and pleasant. She knew that she and Cader could sit here in the booth the entire afternoon, and no one would bother them or even notice them in the semidarkness.

"I'm glad you chose this place," she said to Cader as he slid into the booth and immediately reached for her hand.

"I'm glad that you're glad." Cader grinned. "Yesterday we didn't have much of a chance to talk." He was still grinning, and Irene flushed but said nothing. There was no way she was going to apologize to him for her actions yesterday. "How are you?"

"I've never been better."

Irene Hayden Thomas squirmed on her seat and wished there was something she could do about the wetness between her legs. Sitting across from Cader Harris in the dimly lit cocktail lounge at high noon was something that didn't occur every day of the week. She had to try to concentrate on what Cader was saying.

"Hmmmn," she murmured as she sipped at her vodka gimlet. "Hmmmmn," she repeated. God, what had he said? Whatever it was, her murmured response must have been right.

"And so you see, Irene, if Delta Oil doesn't get into Hayden, I'll have to pack it in," Cader confided. "You just don't know how hard that would be for me to do."

"Hard, yes, very hard," Irene choked as she squeezed her thighs together.

"You of all people understand what it means to belong." His voice was lowered to a whisper. "What Hayden needs is a place on the map. You know, some new life, the shot in the arm, economically, that Delta Oil could give it." His voice dropped another octave. "Can I tell you a secret? Actually, it isn't a secret, but I want to confide in you."

Irene's heart pounded in her chest so loudly she was certain he could hear it from across the table. She couldn't speak. She was dumbfounded. Just being here with Cader, looking at him, listening to him, watching his hands play with the cocktail stirrer and trying not to think about the wetness between her legs required almost more control than she could muster. She nodded, her eyes glazed and filmy as she sipped again at her third gimlet.

"I'm almost broke, Irene," Cader whispered. His breath fell with gentle caresses on her cheek as he leaned closer to her. "I need your help, Irene." He leaned closer, taking her hand in his. "Look, I'm not going to con you into anything. I'm leveling. I've had women, Irene, lots of women. But, Irene, none of them were half the woman you are. I can't count the times I've thought about you and being here with you this way. You're the best," he said huskily.

When Irene raised her eyes from the table where their hands were touching, she stared at him in open-eyed wonder. Cader swallowed hard. He grasped her hands and looked into her tear-bright eyes. "You've got to use your influence to get Delta Oil into Hayden. You've got to make it clear that you want Delta Oil, that it would be good for the town." His voice was gruff, but it was sensually husky to Irene's ears.

"Is that all? It won't be easy," she warned. "I'll have to go against Daddy and I don't know if I want to do that. I'd . . . have to think about it. I know if I went against Daddy it would kill him."

"Foster Doyle is from a past generation, Irene. This is today, the here and now. Think of the present generation; they're all leaving Hayden. Face it, it's a dying town. Aside from my own interests in the project, you have to admit Delta Oil would be good for this town. Besides," he whispered closer to her ear, "if things work in my favor financially, it would be that much sooner that I could leave Hayden and take you with me."

Irene looked up into his eyes, hoping he wouldn't notice how she ignored his statement about leaving Hayden. "Someday, Cade, I'm going to tell you a secret. A secret that will make you forget all about leaving Hayden and me."

A sinking feeling descended in Cader's gut. He knew he had asked for too much too soon. Irene would never willingly leave Hayden. She liked being a big fish in a little pond. He would have to convince her; he must.

Cader reached for Irene's hands and with his elbow slid her drink away. "I like my women to have their wits about them," he murmured.

"I do, I do!" Irene whispered in return. "Oh, I do, Cade."

"Come on, baby, I'm taking you to the best damn motel I know. We have a lot of lost time to make up for."

Cader looked down at Irene. Her blond hair was strewn across the pillow and tangled around her white throat. He kissed the hollow beneath her ear and blazed a trail to the fullness of her breasts. She sighed, turning beneath him, offering herself up to his loving.

She was still magnificent, a little fuller, a little older, but still magnificent. With her, here like this, Cade was only eighteen years old again. Her passions were more sophisticated now, as were her practiced touch and her responses. If anything, she was better than she had been when they were younger. Tenderly, he pressed his lips to hers, the touch lingering, becoming more ardent, more urgent.

The afternoon sun filtered through the draperies into the room, lighting his hair to gold. Irene raised her hand, running her fingers into the wealth at the nape of his neck, feeling the strength of him, the muscular length of him, as he covered her body with his. His lovemaking was slow, languorous, titillating her senses, filling her with an unquenchable need for him.

He teased her, taunted her with his light touches, grazing her skin with his fingertips, awakening her responses. Every nerve in her body cried out for him, ached for him, damned him for playing with her this way, loving him for it. He watched her, his eyes burning where they touched her flesh. A smile played about his mouth, his beautiful mouth, his mouth that was doing such indescribably lovely things to her. He loved seeing her this way, she knew. Watching her tense, arch herself toward him, begging for more, always more.

She reveled under his gaze, knowing the picture she created: lips parted with passion, hair tumbled, skin flushed. She watched as his eyes followed the path of his hand, watched his fingers play against her flesh. The lowering sun ignited the downy hair on her belly to gilt, and further down, where it became darker and delineated her firm thighs, his fingers strayed.

The first touch sent a quiver of pulsating throbs through her. Then, as the novelty became familiar, her body moved of its own accord beneath his hand. She raised her eyes, locking them with his, and saw that his pleasure was in pleasuring her.

Wanting him, needing him, she clasped him to her, driving herself beneath the weight of his body, her hips stating her demands, her cries voicing them.

He drove into her with fury, locking her legs over his shoulders, taking his pleasure in her, giving pleasure. Together they spiraled the heights of carnality, each enhancing the other's sensuality, each feeding the other's lusts.

Breathless, shaken, Irene lay in Cader's arms, her head on his chest, making it wet with her tears. When she was calm enough to speak, she said softly, "I don't know if I'll ever be able to forgive you for robbing me of this for all these years."

Beth Thomas tied the bright sash of her sun dress into a neat bow as she squirmed and struggled before her mother's pier glass. "How do I look, Mama?" she asked, her eyes unnaturally bright.

Irene frowned slightly at her child's intensity as she watched her yank at the side of the mirror to get a better view of the bow at the back of her dress. "You look sweet and lovely, Beth," she answered honestly. "You just look like my sweet little girl."

"What's that supposed to mean, Mama?" Beth said, whipping around and challenging Irene with her eyes.

"Why, darlin', it just means that you look nice and pretty. Just like my little girl. . . . Whatever are you takin' on about?"

"How old do I look?" Beth demanded irritably.

"Old? I never thought about it, but now that you

mention it, you look right this minute like a little girl going to her first party. Remember? You were twelve years old and you wore a sun dress almost like that one?"

"Twelve years old! Sweet!" Beth cried in outrage. "Oh, Mama, how could you say such a thing? I hate this dress!" she shouted as she pulled and tugged at the bow. "Why do you buy me such ridiculous clothes? If I had worn this to the party, my first real party, they would have laughed at me. How could you, Mama?"

"Beth, honey, calm down. You look like a little lady, like a Hayden should," Irene said defensively.

"A lady!" Beth screamed at the top of her lungs. "Mama! Well, I'm not wearing thi-this . . . baby dress," she snapped as she pulled it over her head and tossed it on Irene's bed.

"Beth Thomas, where is your brassiere? I don't believe I'm seeing what I'm seeing," Irene exclaimed.

"It's in the drawer. Nobody wears a bra. I have to find something to wear!"

"You're not 'nobody'! Now you put it on this minute. Don't you dare walk down the hall to your room in just your bloomers. I forbid it!" Irene ranted. "What if your brother should see you, or, God forbid, your father? Young lady, I don't know what's got into you. Maybe your father was right and you're too young to go to this party. You're not leaving this house without a brassiere, Beth Thomas, and that is my final word!" Irene scolded, following her daughter at a near run down the long hallway.

Once inside the girl's room, she sank into a bright

scarlet beanbag chair. She watched in horror as Beth pulled a tube top from her drawer and pulled it over her head. More frantic searching in the closet and she had a short denim skirt in her hands.

"You look like a trollop," Irene gasped in a hushed voice as though afraid someone would hear. "I only agreed to buy you that ridiculous outfit so you could wear it over your bathing suit. You look scandalous! Now, take it off!"

"Mama, do you want the other kids to mock me out? I'm wearing this. All the girls dress like this. I can't imagine how I let you talk me into wearing that babyish sun dress. Ask Kevin; he'll tell you all the kids wear these outfits."

Irene threw up her hands in despair. "It's just that you've grown up before my very own eyes."

"Oh, thank you, Mama." Beth smiled, her eyes narrow and keen. "I knew you would see it my way. Don't worry about me; I'll stay with Kevin every single minute."

"Darlin', I know that Luther is such a nice boy. You'll probably be the most envied girl at the party with Kevin and Luther to watch over you. Why, I can well believe that the boys will be standin' in line to fill your card," Irene doted.

Beth sighed. "Mama, when you boogie, you don't use cards, and this is not a formal dance. It's just a get-together." Beth squinted at her image in the mirror and fluffed her long, red-gold hair. "Can I use some of your perfume?"

"Just use a little. Perfume can drive men to dangerous lengths," Irene said knowledgeably.

"Just a dab," Beth said brightly as she skipped alongside her mother. "Come on, Kev," Beth squealed, "it's time to go. You did say we were picking up Boomer and Judy, so let's hurry. I told Boomer we would be on time."

Kevin frowned but said nothing when he noted Beth's skimpy outfit. If Mother thought it was all right, who was he to stick his nose in and get it bitten off? Besides, he didn't like the look in Beth's eyes. They were almost feverishly bright and there was a noticeably tight line around her mouth. He didn't say anything when she hopped in the front seat of the car and sat down next to him. Instead, he clenched his teeth and jabbed the key in the ignition.

"Are you picking up Boomer or Judy first?"

"Boomer, and then you can move in back with him," Kevin answered curtly.

"In the back! Only niggers ride in the back, Kev. I'll sit up here with you, and Judy and Boomer can have the back seat," she said slyly, watching him out of the corner of her eye.

"It doesn't work that way. If you think you're old enough to date Boomer, then you're old enough to follow the rules. You and Boomer go in the back seat, and I'm telling you now, watch him, he's got seventeen hands."

"You just want to be with Judy by yourself. You don't want me around anymore; all you want is Judy. She's no good, Kev; everyone talks about her. She has a bad reputation," Beth cried wretchedly.

"Well, I happen to like her, so lay off, Beth. You're going to have all you can do to handle Boomer."

"Are you going to kiss her?" Beth asked in a childish voice.

Kevin's face flamed. "I might and I might not. Don't you go making out with that stupid Boomer, hear?"

"If you kiss Judy, I can kiss Boomer," she continued in her childish vein.

Kevin seethed. He knew every trick she was pulling on him. What should have been a fun evening was going to be a nightmare, he could feel it in his bones. So what if he kissed Judy? And, maybe, he grinned to himself, a little something else if things went all right. He would have to keep his eye on that stupid Boomer every minute or Beth would be going home without her skimpy little tube top, and without a few other things too. Damn it, how did he allow himself to get trapped into this? He was tired of playing mother hen. He wanted to be a rooster for a while, cock of the walk, like Cader Harris.

Kevin steered Arthur's Lincoln into the driveway and gave a light tap on the horn. Boomer came racing through the garage and sprinted to a stop, his eyes taking in Beth and her outfit. "Oh man," he said, his eyes lighting up as he climbed in the back seat. With a firm shove from Kevin Beth opened the door and slid in next to Boomer. Boomer leered. "I like that thing you're wearing."

"This old thing! Why, Boomer, I didn't even think you'd notice."

"Are you kidding? I love it when girls don't wear bras," he whispered in Beth's ear, ogling her small, nubile breasts through the clinging, skimpy jersey top. "Kev, are you a leg or tit man?"

Kevin almost choked as he backed the Lincoln from the driveway. He knew he had to give some kind of answer or by tomorrow it would be all over town that he was a fag. "A little of both," he said nonchalantly.

"Yeah. You ever been over to Aunt Cledie's, Kev?"

"Not lately," Kevin lied, pretending firsthand knowledge of Hayden's infamous cat house. Beth was certainly getting an education. Well, she asked for it.

Boomer, not used to sitting with his hands idle, made a grab for Beth and pulled her against him and whispered in her ear. "Remember, Bethy, you said you would do *anything*. Those were your exact words, *anything!*" His whisper became softer, huskier. "I want your panties for a souvenir," he groaned as Kevin pulled the car to a stop outside Judy's door.

"Be right back," Kevin said warningly as he climbed out of the car. "Watch it, Boomer, that's my sister. Any funny stuff and I put you through a wall."

"She's as safe with me as she is with you," Boomer grimaced, waiting for Kevin to approach Judy's door. "Come on, Beth," he said urgently, making a wild lunge for her, his hands groping with her tube top.

"Stop it! Get your hands off me! Stop it, Luther, or I'll scream!"

Luther retreated sulkily. "Is it so goddamned much to ask from a girl who said she would do 'anything' if I took her to this party? I didn't bring you for your looks, you know."

"Just leave me alone!" Beth pouted, her eyes intent on Kevin's back as he waited for someone to answer the door.

"You're nothing but a cock teaser," Boomer shouted. "You said you'd do anything, and this is anything. Go to the party yourself. I'm leaving," he said, opening the door.

Beth paled. If Boomer walked out on her, Kevin would take her home and go to the party alone with Judy. She couldn't let him take Judy, not without her. "Wait a minute, Boomer. What I meant was here comes Kevin and Judy. Later, after . . . when it gets dark, we'll go outside and . . . I'll do what you want!" she almost shouted hysterically.

"You mean it, Bethy? You'll do it?"

Beth gagged but managed a sickly smile. "Come on, Boomer, get back in the car; here they are. Don't say anything to Kevin . . . he's a . . . a turkey."

"Yeah, I know," Boomer said, getting back into the car. "He's never been to Aunt Cledie's, I know. I asked."

Judy settled herself beside Kevin and turned around to smile at Boomer and spoke to Beth. "This is your first party, isn't it . . . honey?"

Ill at ease and out of her depth with Boomer breathing heavily next to her, she answered coolly, "Yes, and I plan to have a really good time. Don't you worry about me; Boomer is going to take care of me and make sure I enjoy myself." Her defiant eyes met Kevin's in the rearview mirror.

"You and Boomer are staying with me and Judy," Kevin said quietly.

"That's so . . . big brotherly of you, Kev. If that's what you want, then I'll do what you say, won't we, Boomer? By the way," she babbled, "don't you think Boomer looks just like Nick Nolte? He's so handsome, Nick I mean. Don't you just adore him?"

"Yeah, just adore him," Boomer grumbled. "Just remember what you promised, little cock teaser," he hissed to Beth beneath the sound of the car stereo blaring the latest rock tune.

Beth giggled nervously. With Kevin in close range Boomer could make all the threats he wanted, but Kev would take care of her. And Judy could have Boomer. They were two of a kind as far as she was concerned.

"Guess what I heard at the tennis court today," Boomer said excitedly. "Sally Davis and Jack Matthews have the clap. Sally gave it to him, Jack said, and to Sam and Will. Jack gave it to Andrea and her old lady found out and now everyone in town is having a fit."

No one said anything and Beth sat back against the seat warily. Why should everyone be having a fit? What was the clap? She made a mental note to ask Kevin later.

"I'm surprised you don't have a dose of it yourself. I heard you've been hanging around Aunt Cledie's. All of her girls have it. Mom said they're always in the office for treatment." Judy watched in malicious satisfaction as Boomer's face paled and then flushed.

"You putting me on, Judy? Whores are supposed to be the cleanest women going; they take care of themselves. That's what it says in *Hustler* magazine."

Judy smirked. "Listen, if you don't believe me, ask Janice Harper. She works in the drugstore and she sees how many prescriptions they get, and my mother will tell you the same thing. I bet you got it, Boomer." She laughed.

"Just shut the hell up, Judy."

"What are you going to do, Boomer?" Judy taunted.

"I'm not going to do anything because I don't have to do anything. Do you think I'm so green I wouldn't have used protection?" he said glibly.

Judy wouldn't let up. "You just walk in that place and you got it, turkey; those germs are all over." She laughed. "Maybe you better put him out of the car and take Beth home, Kevin. She might get contaminated."

"I'm warning you, Judy, shut your mouth. I don't have anything. Guys like me watch out for themselves. You can just knock it off or I'll give you a sample right now."

"Kevin wouldn't let you hurt me, would you, Kevin?"

Before he could answer Beth spoke up, not wanting to hear her brother commit himself to Judy over anything. "Why don't you drop us off right here, Kev, and park the car. The driveway looks full. We can wait out by the pool with the kids. I think you passed a parking space back there near Hibiscus Drive."

"Sure thing." Kevin nodded.

"I'll stay with you," Judy said, smiling, "and you won't have to walk by yourself." It was too late for Beth to change her mind; Boomer was yanking her by the arm and dragging her out of the car.

As twilight descended, Beth found herself hard pressed to find excuses to keep herself out of Boomer's clutches. Kevin was always within close range, Judy hanging all over him. Beth's lips tightened and a muscle twitched in her cheek as she watched one of the boys place a new record on the turntable.

"This is great, isn't it, Bethy?" Boomer whispered in her ear. "Come on, let's dance, I want to feel you against me. Pretty soon it will be dark and then, yeah man. I found a good place down at the end of the garden. I staked it out in our name," he said, leering down at her.

Beth's stomach lurched and she was almost nauseated. Or was it Boomer who was making her feel like this? No, it was Judy draped all over Kevin by the pool. Just wait till she told Mama he was so busy with Judy that stupid Boomer could have dragged her into the bushes and he'd never have known the difference.

A low, throaty laugh from Judy wafted toward her. Kevin must have said something funny to her, or something. . . . Her hand went to her mouth and she swallowed hard.

"Boomer," she said, turning and placing her hand on his arm, "let's make it the next dance. I want to go to the powder room and comb my hair," she muttered distractedly.

"Yeah? You better not be teasing me, Bethy. I hurt," he said lecherously, "and you, Bethy, are the only thing that will make the hurt go away."

Beth skirted around Boomer, pretending to head for the house. Glancing over her shoulder and seeing Luther dancing with Sue Ellen, she backtracked and took off on a dead run for the pool. Her small face puckered into a look of hate as Kevin moved closer to Judy on the chaise longue. They were whispering and, oh, God, he was going to kiss her. Kevin was going to kiss Judy. He couldn't kiss Judy; he just couldn't. If he kissed Judy that meant. . . . It was dark out. People kissed in the dark and it meant . . . it meant other things. . . . He couldn't kiss Judy. She, Beth, wouldn't let him.

"Kevin, Kevin, where are you?" she shouted. "Kevin, I don't feel well and I want to go home. Kevin, can you hear me? I feel sick; I want to go home."

Kevin was off the chaise and on his feet when Beth skidded to a stop at the edge of the pool. "What's wrong? Is Boomer putting the arm on you? You were fine when we got here." Ignoring Judy, he walked over to Beth and put his arm around her shoulder. "I tried to warn you; you aren't ready for the likes of Boomer. You have a lot of growing up to do yet, Beth, before you can handle something like this."

"And I suppose you're grown up!" Beth challenged. "I saw you!" she hissed. "I saw you, Kevin. You were going to kiss Judy."

Anger shot up Kevin's spine. He was humiliated that Judy was witnessing Beth's tantrum and chagrined that Beth caught him in what Irene would have called a compromising situation. "Why don't you ask Sue Ellen for some aspirin, and then if you don't feel better, I'll call Dad to come and get you."

"Sure! Take two aspirin! And while I'm doing that you'll be making out with Judy, right Kevin? You brought me and you're going to take me home. Now!" she shouted.

"Oh, grow up, Beth." Judy laughed. "Why must you spoil everything? Kevin's right. You're not ready for this kind of party. Why don't you just go call your father to come and get you. Don't spoil Kevin's good time."

Beth sneered, her face drawn into an ugly mask. "And I suppose you're going to show Kev that good time. Right? There's a name for girls like you. . . ."

"Shut up, Beth," Kevin threatened, seizing her by the elbow and shaking her violently.

"Let her go, Kevin," Judy soothed. "Boomer is putting on the squeeze and she can't handle it, right Beth?"

"Make her stop talking to me like that, Kevin!" Beth wailed. "Slap her! Hit her, Kevin! Make her stop!"

Kevin threw his hands up in disgust. "Fight it out between yourselves," he said coldly as he headed for the area where couples were dancing. "Okay, Boomer, I get the next dance with Sue Ellen," he called.

"You stupid, whiny, bawlbaby." Judy turned furiously on Beth. "Now look what you've done! Grow up or drop dead."

Tears streaming down her cheeks, sobs tearing at her throat, Beth clenched and unclenched her fists. She wanted to smash Judy's face till it was no more than a bleeding pulp. Judy was taking Kevin away from her! And Kevin was letting her do it! Judy was going to kiss Kevin and make him forget all about everything except making out with her.

"Beth! Beth!" she heard Boomer call. Mindlessly, she turned and ran, darting through the bushes, careful to stay in the shadows until she made her way into the house and stumbled to the powder room. Once inside, she locked the door and sat down on the toilet, a thick terry towel pressed to her mouth to stifle her sobs of self-pity.

After what seemed like hours, she stood and went to the sink to splash cold water on her face. She looked terrible and she felt terrible. A rapping on the door and a muffled, "How long you gonna be in there?" broke her attention away from her reflection.

"Just . . . I'll be awhile yet. Can't you use the powder room upstairs?" she managed to reply, fresh tears threatening to choke off her voice.

"No problem. Just didn't want to hike upstairs," the voice answered. Beth waited expectantly for another sound from behind the door. She relaxed when she realized whoever it was had gone away. She wanted to be left alone. She didn't want anyone to see her this way. She couldn't face herself in the mirror, so how could she face Judy or Boomer? Worst of all, she didn't want to face Kevin and see his indifference.

Damn that Judy! God, how she hated her! Why couldn't Kevin see Judy for what she was? A conniving bitch! Beth lowered her head onto her arms, pressing against the cool, ceramic sink. What was happening between Kevin and herself? Why was she behaving this way? She couldn't blame Kevin for hating her, not after the way she'd been treating him. But she couldn't help herself somehow. It was just that she was so scared of losing him. Without Kevin she wouldn't have anyone. Bad enough he was going away to college in a few weeks; now Judy was stealing whatever precious time they had left together.

And just now, when she'd asked Kevin to take her home, he had acted as though he didn't care what happened to her as long as it didn't interfere with his making out with Judy. Judy, Judy! Always Judy! What would it take for Kevin to see how much his own sister needed him?

Everything had changed since Mr. Harris came back to town and hired Kevin to work in his store. Kevin was away from home so much of the time now, she didn't have anybody to talk to, no one to rely on. It wasn't even as if they had parents like other kids. It didn't take a genius to see that there was something wrong between Mama and Daddy. It had always been just the two of them, Kevin and Beth. Hadn't they always been close? Closer than any other brother and sister because they only had each other? Now, Cader Harris and Judy were wrecking everything, taking Kevin away from her. Well, she wouldn't let them. No matter what she had to do, Kevin was hers; he would always belong to her.

"Come on, Bethy, you've monopolized the bathroom long enough." Judy's voice held a note of contempt. "You're hiding out, aren't you? Come on, I have to use the bathroom and I'm not going upstairs."

Beth riveted her attention on the closed door, the only barrier between Judy's contempt and her own inadequacy.

She wished she could strike Judy Evans dead, right through the wooden panel. Hatred grew in her, matching her panic. Kevin. She couldn't lose Kevin. She had to make him see that she needed him. Her panic became almost tangible and drums sounded in her head. Home. She wanted to go home. Home with Kevin. She had to get him away from Judy, whatever the cost!

Judy's voice called again, her words indistinguishable through Beth's desperation. The eyes that looked back at Beth in the vanity mirror were wide and frightened, glaring out of her whitened features, staring back at her until all perspective was lost and she could only perceive the hollow, empty eyes of the skull on a bottle of iodine. Only one of them could have Kevin, she realized that now. Only one of them—either Beth or Judy.

Her throat was dry, parched, closed against a choking knot of despair. Her hand trembled as she reached for the bathroom glass and turned the cold water faucet as far as it would go. She held the glass beneath the full rush of water, watching it fill and overflow.

"Did you hear me, Beth? When are you coming out of there?" Judy insisted.

"Never," Beth muttered beneath the sound of rushing water. "I'm never going to come out of here. I'm going to die in here and then Kevin will be sorry."

"Beth Thomas!" Judy called again, her tone barely concealing her contempt. "Answer me! I know you're in there, Bethy." Suddenly her tone changed. "Beth, are you all right?" she questioned, concern edging her words now.

"Answer me, won't you? Bethy?" After a breath or two, her concern changed to impatience. "Bethy Thomas, open this door. Do I have to pry the lock? I can do it, you know. I only have to turn this little thingamajig with my fingernail. Beth!"

Beth's attention was centered on the doorknob. Hysteria mingled with resentment as she watched the circular insert in the knob slowly turn. Every nerve in her body tightened. Her fingers closed over the slippery glass, crushing it into lethal shards. Blood mixed with running water, turning it pink before it churned and whirlpooled down the drain. Shocked by what she had done, Beth happened to catch sight of her reflection in the mirror. A reflection of a sly creature peering out from behind her own eyes.

The bathroom door swung open. "Bethy?" Judy's harsh intake of breath. "Bethy! What have you done to yourself?"

Beth fixed her eyes on her upraised hand which still clutched the fragments of glass, the crimson of her blood running down her arm. Her fingers opened. The shards of glass fell into the sink.

"Oh, my God! Are you crazy? What'd you do that for?" Judy cried, reaching for the towel and rushing toward Beth.

"Don't touch me!" Beth screamed. "Don't you dare touch me!"

"The bleeding . . ."

"Don't touch me!"

Judy proceeded toward her with the towel; the blood

was now running freely, dripping onto the white tiled floor. The shock of seeing what Beth had done was evident in her whitened features and her look of horror. She was barely keeping herself under control in the face of so much blood.

Just as Judy was about to wrap her hand in the towel, Beth screamed at the top of her voice, "No! Don't touch me! Don't ever touch me!"

"You're covered with blood. . . ." The words were cut off in Judy's throat. Beth's eyes had become pinpoints of madness and her movements were frantic as she rubbed her bloodied hand over her left arm and across her neck. Splinters of glass scratched her skin and pricked painfully and then went unnoticed.

"Kevin! Kevin!" Beth screamed, only slightly aware that the hum of conversation and celebration in the next room had suddenly ceased. She pushed her way past a dumbstruck Judy and stumbled through the doorway. "Kevin!" Her face contorted into a mask of frenzy as she ran from the room screaming. "Kevin! Kevin!" The sound burst from her lungs and echoed shrilly above the blare of the stereo. She moved toward the doors leading to the swimming pool, her bloodied arms extended like a sleepwalker's, her eyes glazed with panic and madness. "Kevin, help me!" she wailed pitifully between sobs rising from her throat.

Beth hardly noticed the horror and confusion in the faces of the others as they made a path for her between their ranks. The only sound was the melodic rhythm of

"Hotel California" and the sound of her own pleadings. "Kevin! Help me! I'm bleeding!"

Suddenly, she saw him, standing alone and she began to run to him, frantically waving her arms. "Kevin! Kevin!"

Kevin's face was wild with horror. Boomer leaned against the wall muttering over and over, "Oh shit, oh shit!"

"What happened?" Kevin demanded, trying to force her arms from around his neck to quiet her down.

"I'm bleeding! I didn't mean to do it! I'm bleeding! Take me home, Kev, please take me out of here!" Her words ended in a chattering shudder that frightened him.

"We have to stop that bleeding. . . . Judy . . . where's Judy?" His eyes frantically scanned the crowd gathering around them. "For Crissakes, get me a towel or something. . . ."

Beth pulled herself away from him, leaving a trail of crimson across his shoulders. Judy . . . always Judy! Here she was, bleeding to death, and all he could think about was Judy! "I want to go home, Kev," she wailed weakly. "I want Mama!"

Kevin grasped her by the shoulders. "We gotta stop that bleeding! We gotta make sure you didn't cut an artery or something. . . ."

"No!" Beth shrilled. "I want Mama! Mama! Take me home to Mama!" But Kevin wasn't even hearing her. He was looking at Judy, who had brought him the towel from the bathroom.

Beth broke away from Kevin and pushed her way

through the gathering crowd. "Mama!" she continued to scream as she raced across the patio and around the front of the house.

As Kevin raced after her, the last thing he heard as he rounded the side of the house was Boomer shouting at the top of his lungs, "Oh shit! Oh shit! She tried to kill herself!"

Chapter Twelve

Irene Thomas powdered her slim body and felt satisfied. Tonight was going to be Arthur's night. She was no fool; she could read him like he read his undertaking manuals. Carefully, she pressed the thin material of the prim-looking nightgown over her hips and smiled at her reflection.

"I've been a good wife, Arthur," she mouthed silently. "It's just that sometimes I . . . sometimes I remember another time and another place. I'm thirty-six years old and women . . . *I* start thinking about that other time and that other place. I *have* been a good wife and mother. I'm not a selfish person. Didn't I give you Beth? Didn't I give you a daughter who looks like you? I did that for you, Arthur. If I wasn't a good person, I would never have wanted to have a child with you. You'll never know that Kevin isn't your son. I atoned for that by giving you Beth. I don't feel guilty." *If you don't feel guilty, then why are you defending yourself?*

a small, niggling voice asked the reflection in the mirror. Irene straightened and moved back from the square mirror. "Because . . . because I know that I still love Cader Harris. I gave you Beth as your own. My obligation to you has been paid and now I can do what I want. You have a beautiful home, lovely children, your rightful place in the community and a devoted wife. I am devoted . . . in my own way," she said grimly. "All these years, all the unsatisfied, sleepless nights. It's my inalienable right. You never knew about Kevin, and there's no reason for you to know anything about this. I'll protect you, Arthur," she whispered to the mirror.

A dab of perfume on each ear lobe and a quick splash between her breasts, and she was ready. She opened the door a crack and stood for a moment watching Arthur turn the pages of one of his pathology textbooks. She opened the door wider and leaned languidly against the frame, her eyes moist and warm as she stared at her husband. "Artie," she called softly.

Arthur's head jerked up and his eyes widened. She hadn't called him Artie since the first time she let him seduce her. Sweet Jesus! Before he could say another word she was on top of him, her breathing out of control, her hands caressing his naked chest as her lips clung to his. He'd been reading too many of his own magazines. He must be dead and on his way to heaven. Was this Irene Hayden doing all these delicious things to him? "Sweet Jesus," he moaned as he felt her tongue begin to work its special magic. He knew, he just knew, that this was going to be one of those once-in-a-lifetime fucks. "Oh, Jesus," he moaned over and over as he straddled his panting, heaving wife. "Oooooh, oooooh . . ."

What seemed like hours later, Arthur spoke. "God, Irene, it took you eighteen years, but you finally did it. I'll never forget this night, ever," he said as he patted his limp penis.

Irene was still gasping like a fish out of water as she listened to Arthur's words. She wanted it again and she knew she was capable, right this minute, right this second. It was Cader Harris. All she had to do was substitute Cader's face and cock for Arthur's and she could get it off. If it worked once, it would work again.

She rolled over, her eyes closed tightly as she slid beneath the covers, her hands and mouth searching desperately for Arthur's penis that he clasped protectively in both hands. "I want it," she moaned hoarsely. "Now. I want it now!"

"Oh, God. Oh, God. Oooooh. Oh, God. Oh, God. Oooooooooh."

Arthur's last thought as he drifted off to sleep was that he hoped no one would die during the night. If they did, they were on their own, and he couldn't give a good roaring fuck.

Cader Harris gave the Venetian blind on the front door of the shop a vicious tug and was stunned to see Beth Thomas racing down the street screaming, "Mama! Help me! Do something; I'm bleeding!" Her brother was in hot pursuit. Now, what in hell was that all about? He walked outside, hands on hips, staring after the running twosome.

Everybody was screwed up, why should those two be any different, he thought philosophically. He had other things on his mind, important things. Things that wouldn't go away by thinking about something else. The phone would ring shortly. "What the hell," he muttered as he walked back into the shop and slammed the door. Another hour to piss away before the phone call. An hour that could be spent making time at Aunt Cledie's.

Irene Thomas woke, fear clutching her throat. "What . . . what is it?" she called in a shaking voice. "Beth, stop the screaming and answer me! What's wrong?" Quickly, she scrambled into her robe before Beth could burst into the room and catch her nude from the lovemaking.

"Arthur, wake up!" She poked the sleeping form beside her. "Arthur!"

"Oooooh," he groaned, rolling over and burying his head under the pillow, trying to drive Irene's screams of passion from his ears. Why was she bleeding to death and what did Kevin have to do with it? . . . Kevin!

"Mama! Make it stop! Make it go away!" Beth cried hysterically. "I'm going to die," she bellowed, "and Kevin didn't do anything to help me! I ran all the way home by myself! Mama!"

Irene's mouth dropped open as she was confronted with the sight of her daughter smeared with dried blood.

Kevin burst through the front door and bounded up the stairs. He was breathless and his face was white with shock. "Bethy!"

Beth extended her hand for Irene to examine. The bleeding had slowed considerably, and it was difficult for Irene to imagine how Beth had managed to cover herself with blood. One glance at Kevin and his bloodied shirt and Irene felt dizzy. "Oh, my God, you've had an accident with the car!"

"No, we didn't . . ." Kevin rushed to explain before Irene interrupted.

"Arthur! Arthur! Get yourself up and come out here! Hurry! Kevin's had an accident with the car and Beth is bleeding to death!" she called as she put her arm around Beth and half dragged, half carried her to the bathroom.

"We didn't have an accident with the car! Beth cut herself somehow! Christ! The kids are saying she tried to kill herself!" Kevin ran his hand through his hair, a deep, vertical crease forming between his brows.

Irene paused for a moment before she grabbed Beth's right hand and brought it up for examination. "Arthur! For God's sake, get yourself out here and call Marc Baldwin. Tell him we need him right away! Now, Arthur!"

Arthur Thomas staggered out of the bedroom. His pajama bottoms kept slipping around his waist, and he had to keep hitching them up so he wouldn't trip on them. In his haste to put something on he had screwed up the string ties. His robe flapped open and his hands kept groping for the elusive belt.

"Look, Dad, I don't know what happened to Beth. She came running out of the bathroom, screaming she was bleeding to death. She was covered with blood. When I tried to do something to stop the bleeding and see what was wrong with her, she ran away from me. I ran after her, but she had a good head start on me, and I still don't know what's wrong with her. I left your car at the party. I'm sorry, Dad. All I could think of was to run after her. God only knows what she's gone and done to herself. Now the kids are saying she tried to kill herself."

"Take it easy, Kevin. I know that whatever it is, it's not your fault. Beth's always been high-strung. It must be the Hayden blood in her. Go and change your shirt. Beth's got you covered with her blood."

As Kevin changed, he could hear Arthur talking quietly to Dr. Baldwin. He heard Arthur lower his voice as he said, "Irene wanted you to come over here. Look, Marc, if Beth did try to do something to herself . . . well, things get around this town as it is. If we took her to the hospital, there would be no stopping the rumors and people would just make it out to be worse than it is. It can't be serious. The only blood I saw on her was already dry. . . ." Kevin listened as Arthur said his thanks to Marc Baldwin.

Low tones, then Irene's voice penetrated the silence in the house. "But, Beth, I don't understand. If you cut yourself on the bathroom glass, how did all this blood get all over you?" Irene pried Beth's hand open and looked at the wounds. "That's pretty nasty; there's imbedded glass. Not to worry, Marc will get it all out," Irene soothed.

"Where's Kevin?" Beth asked, wincing slightly.

"He's out in the hall, dear. You gave him quite a scare." Irene looked at Beth and for an instant she got the impression of some sly creature peering out of her daughter's eyes.

"I just don't want him to be angry with me, that's all," Beth explained. "I just ruined his night, I know I did. But I couldn't help it, Mama! I got so scared! And Kevin was no help at all! He just wanted to wrap a towel around it! And I wouldn't let him." *Just like I wouldn't let him stay and mess around with Judy*, Beth thought exultantly.

"I just can't understand all this blood!" Irene complained as she worked feverishly with a soapy washcloth and towel while Beth stood quietly, only wincing occasionally when her mother plucked a sliver of glass out of her palm. "What could you have been thinking of to be so careless with a glass, of all things? And did you hear what Kevin said? They . . . they think you tried to commit . . . Oh, God! It's too horrible! Think of the rumors! I won't be able to hold my head up in this town! And neither will you, Beth Thomas. What in the world did you do to yourself?"

Arthur knocked on the closed bathroom door. "Beth? How are you? Irene, what's going on in there?"

"It's open, Arthur. Beth just cut her hand on a bathroom glass. Isn't that right, honey?" Irene said with false brightness. "All it needs is some cleaning up. Did you call Marc?"

"I got that poor man out of bed to come and clean a few cuts? We could have taken her over to the emergency clinic!" Arthur complained.

"No, we couldn't. Imagine, this town would be rife with rumor of terrible things about Beth and . . . and her mental condition." She eyed Arthur frantically so that he would shut up and let her handle it.

"Where's Kevin?"

Arthur ignored Beth. "What do you mean, 'her mental condition'?"

"Daddy! Where's Kevin?" Beth whined.

"You know as well as I do," Irene said hotly. "You heard what Kevin said. Some of the children are saying that Beth tried to . . . Oh, never mind!"

"Daddy! Where's Kevin?" Beth demanded.

"Out! I told him to go and get the car," Arthur answered impatiently.

"Now, Arthur, go downstairs and wait for Marc. I'll help Beth get into bed. Laws! Did you ever see . . ."

"Daddy! Are you saying Kevin went back to the party?" Beth directed her gaze on her father.

"No, I didn't say that. I said he went to get the car. But I wouldn't blame him if he did go back to the party. If only to make up for all the unpleasantness you've caused tonight."

"Arthur, this isn't the time for that." Irene shook her head warningly. "Kevin must be very upset. Are you certain he'll be all right to drive?"

"Mama," Beth whined, "here I am, bleeding like a stuck pig, and all you could think about is Kevin! It's always Kevin. Kevin this and Kevin that. You've always loved him more than me!"

Disgusted, Arthur turned and left the room.

Insensitive as always to her husband's feelings, Irene complained to Beth, "Honestly, now what's gotten into him? Here, now let me wrap this towel around your hand. We'll get you all nice and cozy in your bed. Now, how does that sound . . . ?"

"Shut up, Mama," Beth said flatly. Beth's eyes were glaring, her mouth was set in a tight thin line as she thought of Kevin returning to the party. And to Judy.

Cader Harris hunched over his desk, his face cast in shadows by the downward tilt of the gooseneck lamp near his left hand. The phone receiver was pressed to his ear. His expression betrayed his misery while his voice strained to exude confidence. "Well, what if it is taking longer than we planned?" He braved a chuckle. "The results will be the same. Look, I've been meeting with the town's merchants and they're on our side. Even the Board of Education sees the advantages to having Delta Oil come into town. They know the value of a buck."

Cader listened, his face grim, while the voice grumbled discontentedly on the other end of the line.

"I've made a friend here in town, a very influential friend. She's promised me her support, and she's making good on her word. Who do you think got me in to see the Board of Ed?" He listened again to the voice at the other end of the line.

"You've got to make certain, Cader, that you keep to the deadline. We at Delta Oil are getting edgy, I don't have to tell you that. The only reason we haven't stepped in before now is because we don't want any reverberations a year or two from now. That's why we sent you as our emissary.

We don't want some loudmouth blabbing about a payoff. But I'm warning you, Harris, at the price we're paying we can't afford to make mistakes. If we have to bypass you and handle things ourselves, we will. Then you'll be out in the cold, and you won't get your percentage."

"You're not telling me something I don't already know," Cader said bitterly. "I don't mind telling you I don't trust you bastards as far as I can throw one of your oil tankers." A fine beading of perspiration stood out starkly on his brow. "Just keep your cool; things are working out fine. Just leave it up to me; I'll handle it."

Kevin walked the deserted street, putting one foot in front of the other. He'd wait until later to get the car. Much later. After the scene Beth had made he didn't want to face anyone. He raised his head from between hunched shoulders and noticed he was rounding the corner near the sporting goods store. A dim light glowed from within. He tested the door and found it open. Curious, he moved inside. The light was coming from Mr. Harris's office, and Kevin could hear the faint murmur of conversation coming from behind the closed door.

Cader had just hung up the phone when he noticed the doorknob on his office door turn. *What the hell?* He stood and rocked back on his heel, a paperweight gripped tightly in his hand as he stared at the door in fascination.

"Yo! What have we here?" He grinned as Kevin entered the room.

"Mr. Harris, I found the front door open and thought

I'd take a look around. I didn't realize you were in here," Kevin mumbled, shuffling his feet.

"Damn white of you, boy. But what are you doing around town at one in the morning?" Cader reconsidered his last statement. "Listen, kid, you don't owe me any explanations. Your business is your business and my business is mine. If you want to talk about it, that's something else." The boy looked as though something was bugging the hell out of him. He could spare a few minutes for wise and sincere counsel, Cader told himself. Aunt Cledie's girls never slept. There sure as hell was a lot to say for twenty-four-hour service. Kevin's problem must have something to do with his whacked-out little sister.

"It's not important, Mr. Harris. Just a little family hooray. I was just out walking."

"I can think of better things to do to work it off. Listen, Kevin, you ever been to Aunt Cledie's?" At Kevin's negative nod, Cade continued. "How would you like to come with me? I'll fix you up with some poontang and a little white lightning, the likes of which you'll never get anywhere else."

Cader waited for Kevin's response and smiled to himself. Arthur Thomas may have raised Kevin at his own knee and influenced the boy's upbringing, but he, Cader Harris, would see to his own son's sex education. Let Arthur Thomas handle the insignificant matters; Cader would handle the important ones.

Shit, out of the frying pan and into the fire, Kevin thought wildly. If Judy was right about what she told Boomer, the last thing he needed right now was a dose of the clap. Or was Judy just putting Boomer on? "No, I've never been there. The guys say all the girls have the clap." His face flushed; Kevin backed off a step and watched Cader Harris to see his reaction.

"Yo, is that what they're saying? Cledie spreads those rumors herself so she doesn't get all those unseasoned highschool kids. Cledie's girls are so clean they squeak. Do you think I'd risk a dose of the clap? Come on, kid, take my word for it. You haven't lived till you've had poontang. What do you say?"

Kevin's misery weighed against him, pressing down on his shoulders. He'd sell his soul to be like Cader Harris, who seemed to have no problems in hanging it all together. If a little poontang could straighten out Mr. Harris's head, maybe it would do the same for him.

"You got it, Mr. Harris. You're right, that's exactly what I need."

"If we're going to get poontang together, you can stop calling me Mr. Harris. Make it Cader. And as a special favor to you, I'm going to personally handpick your girl. You want one or two?" he asked as an afterthought.

Kevin blinked. *Why the hell not?* "Two sounds good to me."

"Not that it's any of my business, but have you ever . . ." Cade grinned at the wretched look on Kevin's face.

"Oh, kid, is Aunt Cledie gonna love you. When she gets a virgin, she rolls out the red carpet. Cledie keeps a sort of track record of her 'virgins.' Reads like *Who's Who*. You get a plaque after ten years. See what you got to look forward to? Any time you're ready, kid. The sooner we get there, the sooner we get what we want. Look at it this way, in one month you got two diplomas, one for school and one for life. Yo, I would have made one hell of a good teacher!"

Cader drove his rental car down the deep rutted road with its low-hanging trees. "Jesus, this is the only thing I hate about this place. One of these days Cledie has got to get some kind of light around here. A man could kill himself on this fucking road. Kid, it's worth it." He grinned in the darkness. "To your left, see those lights. That's going to be your home away from home from now on. Night or day, you'll always find a welcome here."

Kevin laughed nervously as he watched Cader maneuver the car between a dilapidated pickup and a long, pearl-gray Lincoln that looked like Destry's status symbol.

"Take a good look, kid. Once you go through those hallowed doors, you ain't never gonna be the same."

Kevin risked a quick glance around the junk-filled yard and at a stray chicken scratching near the rickety steps that led to a sagging front porch. "I thought chickens slept at night," he said inanely.

"Boy, there ain't anyone that sleeps at Cledie's! Okay, this is it, kid; smile. Always smile, makes the girls think they're getting something special. It's when *they* smile and show too many teeth that you have to worry."

Kevin fixed a smile on his face and followed Cader into the room which seemed to be overflowing with overstuffed burgundy furniture and people. He squinted into the dimness and wished that Aunt Cledie used something brighter than a fifteen-watt bulb. Inside, the air was stifling; not a breeze blew in through the windows where light, lacy curtains were knotted to allow any stray breath of air free passage. As his eyes became adjusted to the yellowish light, he could see several women, some of them young, some not so young, lounging around on sofas and chairs, their bare legs exposed by scanty, bright satin robes. Kevin got the impression of glistening brown skin and white teeth.

Several black men were sitting near a makeshift bar constructed of wooden planks and a barrel. One of them was Destry, his father's associate. When Destry's dark glance flicked over Kevin, the boy felt like running, afraid to be seen here, afraid Arthur would find out. But the way Destry turned his back on him, Kevin knew that his secret would be safe.

Several women smiled at him. There seemed to be more teeth in this one room than all of the Osmonds' put together. His stomach lurched slightly as he noticed a buxom, dark-skinned woman bearing down on Cader. She was dressed in a ruby-red wrapper and her bare feet were pushed into silver sandals. Her breasts were huge and swayed with each step she took, and her plump hand brushed at her frizzy hair, wiping the perspiration which trickled down her face.

"Lordy, lordy, twice in one week! Ah jus' don' believe it! Mah gals are shoah ta go up in smoke! What's this youah bringin' me, honey?" She grinned at Cader, showing bright gold caps for front teeth.

"Jus' what you like best, Aunt Cledie. An eighteen-year-old virgin. Treat him just the way you would me, you hear?" Cader said piously.

Cledie's eyes swallowed Kevin whole and spit him back for the other girls in the room to devour. "Honey, we've all been jus' sittin' here pinin' for somethin' lak this. Pretty baby," she crooned, patting Kevin's head, "Auntie Cledie is jus' gonna make a man outa you. If'n you live ta be a hundred, you ain' never gonna get an edjucayshun lak you're gonna get t'night." She laughed, a deep, husky laugh that made Kevin want to shrink into the farthest corner.

"Stop lookin' like you're ready to crawl up your own asshole!" Cader whispered fiercely. He then turned to Aunt Cledie who was already speculating which of her girls would have the treat of breaking this youngster in. "Don't rush with him, Cledie. We don't have to leave until around sunup."

"Honey, edjucaytin' a man's not somethin' we do in a hurry. This pretty baby is gonna learn and he's gonna learn Aunt Cledie's way. Y' can settle up when you leave. I jus' might throw this one in for free. Too soon to promise, though. You take it easy on my gals, you heah, Cader Harris? I got a whole passel of young studs comin' up from N'awleans, but theah ain' a virgin in the bunch," she said disgustedly. "Ah specialize in virgins, in case you haven't heard," she said as she fixed Kevin with a scorching look.

"Don't just talk about it, Cledie. Show him before he wets his pants. I'll just take Charlene upstairs with me. She's just a little too frisky for our young man here. See ya 'round, kid." Cader grinned. "Don't thank me, just enjoy yourself."

Aunt Cledie snapped her fingers. "Viola, chile, c'mon over heah. There's somebody ah wants you ta meet."

The girl Aunt Cledie called Viola stood up from an oversized chair in the corner. Kevin gasped when he saw her. He remembered her from school, only Viola had dropped out in ninth grade. Kevin gulped. How was he going to get it on with somebody he knew? He thought everybody here would be a stranger, not some girl he'd gone to kindergarten with! Kevin's eyes were fastened on Viola as she picked her way across the room. She was tall, almost as tall as he was, and the scanty slip she was wearing clung to her full, round breasts and almost boyishly slim hips. He could see that she wore nothing beneath the slip, and the slight protuberance of her belly was sharply indented near the center where her navel was, almost as though someone had punched his thumb into soft dough.

Kevin suddenly felt wet under the arms, and he became aware of a buzzing in his ears as he gulped and swallowed. Viola looked at him with shining dark eyes, her finely defined lips parting over strong white teeth. "C'mon, honey," she said huskily, a knowing smile on her face, "we ain't got all night." She moved closer to him and he could smell the slightly musky femaleness of her, he could almost feel the warmth of her body radiating across the space between them.

"G'wan, chile." Aunt Cledie laughed throatily, "an' when y'all come down them stairs, yo ain' gonna be a chile no moah." This seemed to strike the other occupants of the room as funny, and a titter of laughter danced through the room. A tremor ran down Kevin's legs and sparked between his toes, feet ready to run. Viola reached out her slim arm and touched him lightly, calming his apprehensions.

"Y'all jus' follow me, honey. Viola's gonna take real good care of you." She led him toward the stairs. As she mounted the steps, Kevin in her wake, he focused on the exaggerated swing of her narrow hips and the remarkable length of her legs, shown off to perfection in her rundown high-heeled slippers.

Just when he thought he couldn't take another step, when he felt the irrepressible urge to turn around and slink down the stairs out into the safety of the dark night, something happened. Viola turned and looked down at him, a radiant smile lighting her pretty face, and in her shining eyes was a look that said, "I like you, Kevin Thomas; I've always liked you, and thank you for letting me be your first."

Kevin returned her smile and jogged up two steps to catch up with her. They mounted the remaining stairs together, arms around each other, and when she pressed her warm body close against his, Kevin laughed out loud. If he had anything to do with it, Viola was going to come away learning a few lessons herself!

Chapter Thirteen

Destry suppressed a grin as he watched Arthur Thomas make an ineffectual swipe at the stainless steel table. His chocolate eyes noted the almost silly expression on his associate's face and the haphazard way he had been doing things all morning. The suppressed grin blossomed when Destry remembered that it had been Kevin at Aunt Cledie's the night before, and not Arthur. There wasn't another thing in the entire world that could make a man look like Arthur Thomas looked except a trip to Cledie's and a good roll in the sack. This just might be the right time to talk to Arthur, when he was in this expansive mood and agreeable to what looked like almost anything. Son of a bitch, hadn't he offered to let him, Destry, embalm a white man? That alone set some sort of precedent. After lunch, he told himself as he watched the last of the embalming fluid drain through the tube. Done. And another white man has bit the dust.

Arthur matched his silly grin and said, "You just finish up in here, Destry. I'm going into my office and . . . and finish that Anaïs Nin book. Carry on, Destry," Arthur said airily as he flounced from the room.

"I'll be a ring-tailed son of a bitch." Destry laughed aloud as he watched Arthur's retreating back. It just might pay to find out where the white man had spent his night.

In his office with the door closed and locked, Arthur Thomas sat back in his comfortable swivel chair and propped his legs on the corner of the sleek mahogany desk. The hell with Anaïs Nin. Nothing could top last night. It had been so long since Irene got it off, he'd been thinking her twat was as dry as good ol' Aunt Matilda's meat loaf. Was Irene experiencing her second awakening? Jesus! Even though he wasn't a Catholic, he crossed himself reverently and prayed that last night was a preview of things to come. Jesus! The phone shrilled on his desk.

"It's Sunny, Arthur. I was wondering if it would be all right to stop by around four-thirty."

"Sunny, good to hear from you. Why don't you stop by now? If you're not busy, that is. Destry is . . . Destry is busy and we'll . . . Look, why don't you come over now? I'd like it if you could stop by," he said firmly as his hand found its way to his crotch.

Arthur smiled to himself and continued to talk in what he thought was his sexiest voice, "I'm just going to close my eyes and keep them closed until you get here. I'm going to sit here and think of all the beautiful things you're going to do to me when you do get here."

Sunny bit into her lower lip as she hung up the receiver. Arthur had it all wrong, and she was too much of a dummy to tell him over the phone. He thought she was coming over for a little nooky and her hundred-dollar tip. Nothing could be further from the truth. What she wanted to see Arthur about was his wife, Irene.

Late yesterday afternoon Cader had come to her apartment. She was delighted to see him, but there was something strange about him. To quote the poets, one could say he almost had "stars in his eyes." After an unabashed drilling, he admitted to her that he had renewed his relationship with Irene Thomas.

Cader's revelation had stunned her. She feigned a lightheartedness she couldn't feel. It was happening again, after all these years; she was losing Cader Harris to Irene Hayden all over again.

After Cader left, Sunday Waters agonized for the remainder of the day and long into the early morning hours. She came to the conclusion that she wouldn't lose Cader to Irene twice, not without a fight. She would nip this little romance in the bud, doing anything she must. Sunday figured she had nothing to lose. If she did nothing, Irene would win, just as she had the last time when Sunday waited for Cader to come back to her. She knew she risked losing Cader if he ever discovered she went to Arthur with the information, but she had to take her chances.

During the short ride to the funeral home, Sunny rehearsed what she would say to Arthur. She hated doing this to him; he was one of Irene's victims, just as she was.

She didn't place any blame on Cader, he was an innocent who had never grown up and was still trying to cross the tracks by making love to Princess Irene.

Arthur was waiting for her just as he had promised. His face was wreathed in a smile of genuine affection. Arthur was always happy to see her, and not only on these quiet afternoons. Arthur was a friend, and whatever else existed between them was for their mutual benefit.

With a sinking feeling, as if someone was churning her insides with a red-hot poker, Sunday realized she could no more break this man's heart by squealing on Irene and Cader than she could whip a sick puppy. Arthur Thomas was probably the only real down-to-earth, hundred-percent human being in this whole eff'n town. Sunny told herself she might be a lot of things, but a fink wasn't one of them.

It wasn't so much the expectant look on Arthur's face, it was the more than noticeable bulge in his trousers that prompted Sunny to say "Just sit there, Arthur," she whispered, opening the buttons of her blouse and clicking the lock on the door behind her. "I'll do all the rest."

Later that night, sitting alone in the living room, Arthur reflected on the rebirth of Irene's sex life. Ever since he'd returned from the funeral home that evening she'd been casting him sidelong glances that promised him "everything." Arthur shifted in his chair, pulling the center seam of his pajama bottom away from his crotch. The head of his penis was sore and red. But it was happy! One good ol' happy cock expertly serviced by Irene and Sunny!

Arthur Thomas closed his magazine and walked into the hallway when he heard Kevin's key in the lock. The boy looked happy, happier than he had seen him in a long while. "Have a good time, son?" Arthur asked as he slipped his arm around the boy's shoulder.

"Yes, sir, I did. The movie was great and then we walked on the beach for a while. Judy had to be home at ten-thirty or we'd still be there. We just talked, Dad."

"I know that son. But where'd you go after that? It's nearly one A.M." Arthur pierced Kevin with a curious glance. He had picked up the slightly sour odor of beer and whiskey almost the moment Kevin had walked in the door.

Kevin hung his head and couldn't meet Arthur's eyes. "Well, some of the guys got together and we had a couple of six-packs. I met them on my way back from Judy's house," Kevin lied. He couldn't tell Arthur that he'd run into Cader Harris and had spent the last few hours talking man-talk and drinking boiler-makers.

Arthur sighed. "Well, I suppose boys'll be boys. You didn't have too much, I hope." He bent his head to look up into Kevin's guilty expression. Hell, he shouldn't make it hard on the boy. After all, he would be going off to college in a few weeks. From his own experience Arthur knew about the "beer brawls" that were a part of campus life. It was better that Kevin had his first taste here, close to home, rather than among strangers miles away where he could really get into trouble. Let the kid learn to handle the stuff while he had some kind of supervision. He could see Kevin was very uncomfortable under his scrutiny and he tried to calm him. "Look, son, you don't have to explain anything to me. I'm glad you feel you can be open with me."

"I don't mind telling you about what I do, Dad. All I had was a few beers. As for Judy, I like her a lot. I'm taking her to the clambake."

"That's good, son. Listen, are you hungry? Beer can do that to a guy. D'you want a sandwich? A glass of milk, maybe?"

"No thanks, Dad. We had a hamburger and a Coke at the stand in town. I'll sit with you if you want something, though."

"I don't need it, Kev." Arthur patted his belly. "It's late and we both have a busy day tomorrow. Get a good night's sleep. I'll see you in the morning."

In his room Kevin peeled his clothes off. *A cold shower should do it*, he thought as he stripped down. Cader Harris said it was the best thing for what ailed you when things got temporarily postponed.

As he shucked out of his jeans, a dull thunk caught his attention. Christ! The flask Cader had given him. He must have had more to drink than he thought to forget that and leave it where Mom might find it. He fished through the pocket and extracted a slim, shiny flask. He shook it and realized it was still half full. He considered dumping it down the sink and then rinsing it out, but instead put the flask to his lips and downed it. He choked as the liquid rushed down his throat and began to warm his insides. Still coughing, he went into his bathroom and rinsed the flask under the cold water tap. Before he left to tuck the cylinder into his drawer, he turned on his shower.

He suddenly felt the need for the bracing water for more than a general feeling of horniness. That last drink had packed a wallop all its own. The moment the needle-sharp spray touched his body he felt better. Cader was right again. He was always right. Tonight, after his early date with Judy, Kevin had gone to see Cader hoping he would suggest a trip out to Aunt Cledie's. Instead, they had gotten into a heavy discussion about sex and drinking. Cader sure knew what it was all about, Kevin nodded to himself. Just like he told him about cold showers. He'd also told him not to jerk off, that only kids did that. He said there was enough free ass around so that a guy didn't ever have to waste himself on his own hands. Kevin supposed Cader was right, but it sure would be a welcome relief along about now. At least he had the clambake to look forward to. Judy wouldn't have her period then and she had all but promised they would "get together," if he knew what she meant. He believed her. He liked her and was glad she would be going to Tulane with him. He was suddenly glad his life was changing and he owed it all to Cader Harris. Without him he would still be dragging his little sister around behind him. Not that he didn't like Beth, he told himself, but a guy had a right to do his own thing. Kevin crawled beneath the thin sheet, not bothering with his pajamas. Men like Cader Harris and Kevin slept in the raw.

Beth lay for a long time after the sound of the shower in Kevin's room stopped. She knew why Kevin was showering so long. To wash off the smell and feel of Judy Evans. He would have to shower for hours, she told herself, to get rid of Judy Evans. He must be in bed now. What was he thinking about? Was he thinking about Judy?

Beth's eyes circled the dimness in her room and came to rest on a bevy of stuffed animals Kevin had won for her at various state fairs. She loved each and every one of them because Kevin had given them to her. She loved them almost as much as she hated Judy Evans. Hate, hate, hate!

She couldn't sleep. Was Kevin sleeping? Crawling from her bed, she walked over to the open window and looked out into the still, quiet night. *Starlight, star bright, first star I see tonight. Wish I may, wish I might, have the wish I wish tonight. I wish Judy Evans would drop dead. Dead, dead, dead!*

Her stomach churned and she fought back the tears that burned her eyes. It was so hot, so hot she couldn't breathe. Quickly, she pulled off her thin nightgown and stood before the window. She shivered. It wasn't hot, it was cold. Reaching down, she grabbed at the terry robe and gratefully snuggled into its warmth. Something was wrong with her. Her head felt fuzzy and her mouth was dry. Her breasts felt funny. Funny and good at the same time. It must have something to do with periods, she thought as she sat down on the edge of the bed. Now she was hot again. Maybe she should wake Mama and see if she had a fever. Kevin. Kevin would know what to do. Kevin always knew what to do. She would wake him and ask him.

Quietly, she tiptoed down the hall to Kevin's room and

carefully opened the door. He was asleep. She could hear his regular breathing above the hum of his air conditioner. Dropping her robe to the floor, she turned back the sheet and slipped in beside him. Immediately, she detected the sour smell of stale whiskey on his breath. As her hand slid over his chest, he mumbled something. It sounded like a name . . . Viola.

Chapter Fourteen

Damion Conway checked off each name on the clipboard as the band members climbed aboard the bus that would take them to Disney World. He wished he felt like they did, carefree and happy. No worries except to have a good time. He glanced around. Looked like the whole town was out to see the kids off.

He knew she was there before he turned his head. He could feel her presence. His eyes narrowed slightly beneath the polarized lens. She was so still, so quiet, as she stared at the laughing, chattering youngsters. Her eyes met his and locked. Time stood still. The desire to reach out, to run through the crowd of milling people, was almost unbearable. He wanted to touch her, say something to her. Words, any kind of words, just to speak to her. Just to say her name. Keli. Keli.

"And what do we have here?" Cader Harris mocked as

he slapped Damion on the back. "Surely, we don't have a case of unrequited love, or do we? Doesn't one of the Commandments say, 'Thou shall not covet another man's wife'? For shame, Damion."

"You bastard!" Damion hissed through clenched teeth. "What the hell do you know about the Commandments? Watch it, Cade, or I'll knock every one of those pearly whites right down your lying throat."

"Here? Before the pillars of the community?" Cade taunted. "You have a look in your eye and a bulge in your pants that says you lie. Now, just what the hell kind of parson does that make you? Makes me downright sick to think these people come to you for spiritual guidance. I bet you have a thing going, like that dentist back in New York who got his jollies with his patients when they were gassed up. Makes me downright sick. And profanity . . . I'm appalled!" Cade clicked his tongue to show his disapproval and moved slightly so that he was out of Damion's reach, just in case he decided to throw a wild punch. There was no way he wanted all of his porcelain scattered around the town of Hayden. "As to those Commandments," Cader continued in a mocking tone, "I made up the eleventh one. It's called 'Harris Eleven.' Want to hear it, Parson?"

"I don't want to hear anything from you. You're disgusting, Cader. Now, why the hell don't you buzz off and leave me alone?"

"Now is that any way for you to talk to an old friend?" Cader goaded, knowing Damion's temper was at the boiling point. He didn't like himself for the way he always needled Damion, but he was beyond helping himself. Grudges died hard and he supposed he never forgot the way Conway refused to let bygones be bygones over that stupid debate in senior year. "From those moonstruck looks I saw you giving Keli, I think you got a good thing going. But," he wagged a playful finger, "she don't want to play, right? Hell, I'd give that situation a wide berth myself. That crazy colonel she's married to would just about cut off your balls if he caught you with his wife. Either way you could lose. I read somewhere that those Orientals are some kind of nuts. An eye for an eye, that kind of thing. What is she? A Filipino? A Jap? Yeah, I read it in *East Wind Rain*. They just cut a man's cock right off if he gets caught messing with someone's wife. The colonel probably learned it from her. Watch it, Damion."

"You son of a bitch, I'll kill you yet," Damion grated, his fists clenched and knuckles itching to pound Harris's face to a bloody pulp. Glancing around at the children, he forced himself to regain control.

"There's nothing worse than a cockless man unless it's a man with *no* balls and *no* cock." Cader grinned as he feinted to the left out of Damion's arm's reach. "See you around, ol' buddy. Hey, Damion!" he added as an afterthought. "I've had a few Chinks in my time, and take my word for it, they ain't what they're cracked up to be. They're nonmovers. Shit, man! You could masturbate and get the same effect. But," he grinned, "they do say, 'Thank you,' when it's over." Cader laughed all the way back to his car.

* * *

Cader felt a deep anger gnawing away at his insides. Words kept surfacing in his brain. No matter how he tried to put them out of his way, they refused to budge. It was true he had old scores to settle and he was going to do it before he left Hayden. It was a piss-ass world and he didn't like it one bit. Who the hell did these people think they were? His hand was on the doorknob of the shop when he saw the reflection of the long black Lincoln going by. Foster Doyle Hayden. Now, there was an old score and one he had every intention of settling. And soon.

The sporting goods store was cool and dim after the direct glare of the sunlight. For some reason that angered Cader. He likened it to the time the old man had come to the shack he called home. It had been cool and dim that day too, beneath the tarpaper roof of the shanty.

Cader's hands toyed with the empty coffee cup on his desk as he let his mind swirl back in time to that hateful day when he had sold his soul to the devil: Foster Doyle Hayden.

"Mr. Hayden, what brings you way over here?" Cade had asked nervously, debating whether he should invite the impeccably dressed man into the shabby two-room shack. The decision was made for him when Hayden shouldered him aside and marched into the room. His eyes took in the peeling paint, the sagging furniture and the linoleum-covered floor in one swift, appraising glance. Cader's back stiffened as he moved three days' worth of newspapers from the one good chair so the older man could sit down. Hayden peered at the chair and remained standing.

"I'll get right to the point, Harris. I'm here to do you the biggest favor of your life. But first, I want you to understand something. I am aware that you've been seeing my daughter, and, as of this minute, it must cease! Don't deny that you've both been sneaking behind my back. If there's one thing I won't tolerate it's a lie at this stage of the game."

Cader bristled at the old man's tone. Just who the hell did he think he was coming to his house and looking down his nose at him? "Did you tell Irene you were coming here?" Cader asked brazenly, all the while quaking in his shoes.

Foster Doyle Hayden ignored Cader's question and continued. "I said I was here to do you the biggest favor of your life and I mean it. How would you like to go to Tulane University, all expenses paid?"

Cader was dumbfounded. "What do I have to do? Are you talking about a football scholarship?"

"I'm talking about me paying for your education, four years of it along with off-campus housing, a car and a five-hundred-dollar-a-month allowance."

"Just like that?" Cader asked quietly, his nimble brain running over the numbers. "Why? Why me?"

Foster Doyle Hayden pulled a cigar from his breast pocket and bit off the end. He didn't bother to look around to see if anyone was watching; he just spit the tip of the cigar on the floor. "I feel like being generous. You have great athletic potential and I feel that it can be developed at Tulane. I personally guarantee that you'll be All

American the first year out. This is your chance, Harris, to get away from here," he said, a sneer in his voice as he looked around the shabby room. "Here," he said, handing Cader a slim, white folder. "A one-way ticket to a prep school where you'll obtain the credits you need to enter Tulane in the fall."

There was more to this than a generous man offering to help a kid from the wrong side of the tracks and Cader knew it. "I don't know. I'll have to think about it, talk it over with my father."

"There's nothing to talk over. I'm giving you the opportunity of your life to shake this . . . squalor and move among decent people. Take it or leave it. Now!"

Cader stood up. "No. I said I'd think about it. I might be a dumb kid from the wrong side of the tracks, but I know you want me out of here for a reason. If you tell me what the real reason is, maybe I might give you the answer you're looking for now."

The old man's face was mottled and his hand, holding the unlit cigar, held a slight tremor. "Very well, there are strings, certain promises I want you to make. The minute those promises are broken, all aid ceases. Do we understand each other?"

"Spell it out, Mr. Hayden," he said curtly.

"As I said, you are not to see Irene anymore. Nor are you to get in touch with her, ever again. I want you to leave tomorrow. A friend of mine will meet you and take you to your apartment where your new car will be waiting along with your first month's check in the amount of five hundred dollars. You'll receive your monthly stipend on the first of each month. I don't much care what you do with it."

"As long as I keep my mouth shut and do what you say?" Cader said arrogantly.

"Exactly."

"You're sending me away just so I won't see Irene anymore?"

"More or less," the old man hedged.

Cader was suddenly aware of the older man's acute discomfort each time he brought up Irene's name. His eyes narrowed. At that moment he became a gambler. "I don't think so, Mr. Hayden. I like it here, and if I work summers and weekends, I can make it through junior college. If I'm lucky, I might get a scholarship. Thanks for the offer though. It was nice of you to think of me. Tell Irene I said hello when you see her."

"You stupid fool!"

Cader's gambling instincts rose to the fore. "Tell me why? Tell me why you're buying me. Tell me why I'm selling myself. I want to hear it. If I'm selling out, I want to know why."

Foster Doyle Hayden lowered himself into the lopsided arm chair and lit his cigar. "Very well. You leave me no other choice. You've impregnated Irene, and there's no way I plan to welcome you into the family. The matter will be taken care of."

"Is that the same as Irene being pregnant?" Cader asked stupidly, knowing full well what the old man meant. He had to stall for time while he digested the words. Irene was pregnant. Jesus. No wonder the old geezer was upset. He was going to take care of it, he said. The word "abortion" rattled around in Cader's brain. He was too young to be a father. A baby! Jesus. Cool, he had to be cool, pretend he knew all about it. Just like Irene to let him be the last to know. The old man was right, if he cut and ran now, he was selling out. Selling out for the chance to shake this place and move among all the straight arrows out there. Tulane! An apartment of his own! A car of his own! Five hundred bucks a month! Jesus. All he had to do was walk away and never see Irene again, and let Foster Doyle Hayden "take care of things."

"What kind of car?" Cader asked craftily, already knowing he was going to accept the offer.

"The best."

"You want me to leave tomorrow?"

"Yes."

"And you'll pay me five hundred dollars a month for four years along with all my expenses?"

"Yes."

"In turn, all I have to do is walk away from Hayden and keep my nose clean?"

"Yes."

"One last question. How are you going to explain all of this to Irene?"

"I don't have to explain anything to anyone," Foster Doyle said huffily.

"That's what you said when you came in here and look

at you now." Cader laughed, enjoying the old man's annoyance.

"I'll handle matters. For now, I want your word that you're accepting the terms I've offered, and from this moment on, my daughter is off-limits. That means you don't see her, speak to her or write to her. Is it a deal?"

"It's a deal, but if it's all the same to you, Mr. Hayden, I'd rather not shake hands with you."

Hayden was surprised at the remark. "And why not?" he asked harshly.

"Because it goes against my grain to see a father sell his daughter for fifteen thousand bucks plus expenses."

Foster Doyle Hayden's face turned ashen at Cader's words. "I don't ever want to see you back in Hayden again. Be sure you understand that, Harris. I'll keep my part of the bargain as long as you keep yours. The moment you back water, I'll squash you like this," he said, and tossed the smoldering cigar onto the worn linoleum and ground it beneath his heel.

The screen door slapped against the frame and was still. Cader bent down to pick up the warm cigar. He stared at the frayed tobacco leaves and grimaced. He bunched the leaves in his fist and tossed them across the room. Wiseass old bastard buying and selling people like they were cattle.

The remains of the coffee in the cardboard container dribbled down Cader's arm as he realized he was crushing the cup like he had crushed those tobacco leaves so long ago. "Well, you wise-ass old bastard, your days of buying and selling people are over," Cader snarled to the quiet office. "You may not know it, but they're over, old man."

Judy Evans settled herself some little distance from Kevin and slowly unwrapped her sandwich. She wriggled experimentally to get herself more comfortable and stretched out her legs. "Ah, that's better," she sighed. "I wish Mr. Harris would get some chairs in here. I don't mind sitting on the floor to watch TV, but I hate to eat my lunch in the storeroom while I'm on the floor. Yuk," she grimaced, "I hate egg salad."

"Trade you," Kevin said quietly. "I've had ham and cheese every day this week." He leaned over and changed his position slightly so that he was nearer the packing crate Judy was leaning against. He liked the look of her long suntanned legs. They looked so silky and shiny, almost like the girls at Aunt Cledie's, and she didn't have half as many teeth when she smiled.

A light flush crept up his neck as his hand touched hers. "I like egg salad." He grinned. Cader said you always had to grin. Anyway, he told himself, he felt like grinning. Every time he saw Judy Evans, he felt like grinning.

As they ate in silence, Judy repeatedly glanced over at Kevin who was quietly munching at his sandwich instead of wolfing it down the way he usually did. He had seemed unusually quiet all day, now that she thought about it. "What's the matter, Kevin? You got something on your mind?"

"Huh? Oh, no." He grinned again to show her everything was fine. Only the smile didn't quite reach his eyes.

"I just thought there might be something wrong. You're pretty quiet today. You're not mad, are you? That I had to be home by ten-thirty last night? Did you go right home after you dropped me off?"

"Nope. I'm not mad, that is. Nothing like that. I just guess I'm tired today. On my way home last night I ran into Mr. Harris and we killed a couple of six-packs between us." He didn't confide in Judy about the boiler-makers they were drinking or the slim flask that Cader had given him as a gift. There was no sense in arousing Judy's curiosity about the relationship that he'd developed between himself and Cader Harris.

"Well, it doesn't look as though beer agrees with you, Kevin. You've been so out of it all day." Judy went back to nibbling at her sandwich. She didn't want Kevin to see that she was annoyed that he hadn't gone directly home after leaving her. She absolutely didn't want to start nagging at him the way Beth did.

Kevin swallowed the last of his container of milk. His stomach still felt queasy from the drinks he had consumed the night before, and his head still throbbed, but he'd die before he'd admit it to Judy. He didn't want her to think he was such a hick he couldn't handle his booze. But that was the last time he'd ever drink like that, he swore to himself. Kripes! He didn't even remember getting out of the shower last night or how he got to bed. The last he really remembered was taking the last hit out of the flask and the bracing feel of the needle-sharp spray of icy water.

And dream! He'd had wet dreams before, but never like that! He'd dreamed he was screwing Viola, then Judy, then Charlie's Angels, all three of them. Actually, he hadn't even remembered his dream. Not even when Dad had had to come into his room and shake him awake so he wouldn't be late for work. It wasn't until he'd gotten down to the breakfast table and saw Beth that he'd remembered. It was something about the way she looked at him, almost as though she knew what he dreamed in his sleep.

"Did Mr. Harris say where he was going or what time he would be back?" Judy asked, biting into the ham and cheese sandwich.

"Just that he wouldn't be back till after three and to tell you to work the register. He also said you should set up a display of the Spalding balls."

"That's so boring. I would rather stay out here with you; at least we can talk. If there aren't any customers, I just doodle on a pad. It's boring," she repeated.

"I'll yell at you from time to time so you won't get lonely," Kevin grinned. "You *are* going to the clambake with me, aren't you?"

"If that's an invitation, sure," Judy said, flexing her long legs. "Ah, Kevin, is . . . what I mean is . . . you aren't . . ."

"No, I'm not bringing Beth if that's what you're trying to say."

"That's what I was trying to say. It's not that I don't like her, it's just that . . . well, what she does is . . . she clutches at you. I don't like to hear the kids mock you out over your sister. It's not right. She should have her own friends, Kevin."

Kevin swallowed hard. He should say something in defense of Beth but the words wouldn't come. All he could think of was Cader Harris's words, "Grin, kid! Makes 'em think you know something they don't. You have to set women up. They expect it. Hell, they want it, and I've known a few that begged for it. But," he had warned, "it goes two ways. Women, if you don't watch them, can set you up and *bam*! They get you right in the balls, which was their intention all the time. I knew this one broad that I swear to Christ had the balls of a Saint Bernard. When I tell you she set me up, she set me up. I fixed her ass, though. I knocked her up and took off like greased lightning. And for Crissakes, kid, remember to grin. You got good teeth; show them."

Kevin grinned.

"What's wrong with you, Kev, you look like you have a toothache. You know, you have nice teeth. Not as nice as Donny Osmond, but nice. I go for nice teeth."

Kevin grinned again. "You want to go to a movie tonight?"

"I'd love to go to a movie with you, Kevin. First show or second?"

"Let's make the first show and then we can take a walk along the beach."

Judy thought about it for a moment. She leaned forward slightly and rubbed her hands over her thighs. "I like to sit on the beach. Will you bring the blanket or should I?"

"I'll bring it. I think there's one in the trunk of Dad's car. I like to sit on the beach, too." He grinned again. Maybe, just maybe . . .

"Ooops, there's a customer. Thanks for the trade, Kev. I'll look forward to tonight," Judy said, getting up and smoothing her short skirt.

"I'll pick you up at quarter to seven." He grinned again.

"Kevin, are you sure you don't have a toothache?" Judy asked, concern in her voice. How could he neck with someone on the beach if he had a toothache?

Kevin continued to grin, only this time it wasn't a practiced grin. "I have an ache, but it isn't in my tooth."

Judy laughed. "I'll just bet you do. If you get bored out here, come into the store and we'll set up the balls together."

"You got it," Kevin called after her as he hefted a carton of football helmets onto his broad shoulder. *Boy, I hope you know what to do with it when I give it to you.* He shrugged philosophically. Now that he was experienced, he could teach her if she didn't know. He laughed to himself. Cader Harris called it higher education of the first order. And just think, if it weren't for Cader Harris coming back to Hayden, this might have been just another dull summer.

Keli McDermott busied herself at the stove, stirring the spaghetti sauce Gene had taught her to make. From time to time she glanced out the window into the backyard where her garden grew. The tomato plants were nearly as tall as she was and the bright, gleaming purple of the eggplants peeked through the luscious green leaves which protected them from the sun. If the weather kept up this way, the children would have a good time at their clambake. They would be returning from Disney World, Florida, in triumph as they did every year, looking forward to the annual clambake with anticipation and a little sadness. Summer was almost over.

Everything looked so bright and clean outside. The light rain during the night had made everything smell fresh and clean and somehow honest. Almost like a new beginning. If Keli wanted, today could be the first day of the rest of her life. She had read that somewhere and liked it. Today is the first day of the rest of your life.

She heard a light step on the back porch and raised her eyes. The screen door squeaked as Marsha opened it and stepped into Keli's colorful brick and copper kitchen. "I have to talk to you, Keli," she said in a strangled voice. "You haven't been answering your phone or returning my calls."

Keli nodded, her eyes wary and watchful. "May I offer you a cup of coffee, Marsha?"

"Yes. Yes, I'd like that. Thank you." She watched her friend Keli go about her kitchen duties as though there were nothing more pressing on her mind than measuring the correct amount of coffee.

Softly, the words almost a whisper, Keli said, "It will have to be instant."

"That will be fine." Marsha's eyes followed Keli as she busied herself with cups and boiling water. The gleaming copper pots against the dull old brick with its vivid hanging baskets of ferns made no impression on her. Her mind boiled with the words she had come to say. "Keli, I have

to talk to you. I have to know what you're going to do."
Impulsively, she reached her hand across the table to grasp
Keli's and winced as though she had been struck when
Keli pointedly withdrew her hand and placed it on her lap.
"I read your file, Keli. I know I had no right to do that, but
I had to know. Do you understand?"

This could be the first day of the rest of her life, if she
wanted. Sorrowfully, she said, "I wish you had not done
that, Marsha."

"Keli. For God's sake! They have excellent surgeons in
New Orleans. I've heard about the doctor Marc wants you
to see. He's magnificent. If . . . if it's serious, they say he's
the best for reconstructive surgery. Keli, you can't wait!
Oh, my God! Why can't I make you understand? You hear
me but you aren't listening. Damn you, Keli," Marsha
shrilled, "you could die! You're the best friend I ever had; I
won't let you do this to yourself."

Before Keli could frame a response to Marsha's statement a shadow fell across the table.

"Gene!"

"What are you trying to do to Keli, Marsha?" Gene demanded as he braced his hands on the table top, his heavy
body threatening.

"Trying to talk some sense into her, since *you* don't
seem to want to do anything," Marsha shot back, not in the
least intimidated by his menacing manner.

"Keli's no concern of yours and never will be. I'm going
to pretend I didn't hear what you just said, and Keli is
going to pretend she never heard it. I want you to leave this

house, and I don't want you to ever come back. Do you understand? You're an interfering busybody, a crepe hanger; you're sick!" he spat vehemently. "Now, get your tail out of here before I throw you out like the garbage you are."

"Sick!" Marsha hissed. "How would you know? If anyone is sick, it's you! What kind of maniac are you that you won't allow Keli to have a lifesaving operation? You'd let her die, wouldn't you? And you call me sick? I want her to live. I read the file in Marc's office. I saw her chart. If you don't allow her to have that operation, I'll tell everyone in town that you wouldn't 'permit' it. They'll run you out on a rail, Gene McDermott!"

"It's Keli's decision, not mine. You ever spread a rumor like that and I'll kill you!"

Frantically, Marsha turned to Keli who was sitting at the table, eyes lowered, head hung low. "Is that the truth, Keli? Is he allowing you to decide for yourself? Or are you going to let him have his way. Don't you see what he's doing? He'd rather have you dead than alive. If you're dead, he would have had you all to himself. He'd never have to worry that someone else would love you. He's a madman, Keli. Don't, I beg you, don't sacrifice yourself to his insanity!"

Keli stood up from the table and looked first at Gene and then at Marsha with utter calm. "I will be the one to make the decision. I have already called the surgeon in New Orleans and made an appointment. It is my body, my life. I made the decision for myself, not for you, Gene, nor for you, Marsha. For myself. I want to live and I want to love," she said softly, looking into Gene's eyes.

"Now, see what you've gone and made her do?" Gene turned viciously on Marsha.

Keli was almost to the doorway when she turned and said quietly, "Today is the first day of the rest of my life. I made my decision today, and, whatever happens, I'll live with it. It is my life."

Cader Harris mounted the stairs behind the Monde Boutique two at a time. This news was too good to keep to himself, and he only had Sunny to share it with. *Hurry up!* he thought. *Christ! This is too good to keep to myself; I've got to tell somebody about it!* He glanced down to the alley where she parked her car. It was there. She had to be home. "Sunny! For Crissakes, open up! I wanna talk to you!"

A fumbling sound and the door swung open. "Cader? What time is it? I was sound asleep."

"Yeah, I know," he muttered as he shoved past her into the dimness of her apartment. "Listen, I had to talk to you. I've got the greatest news! I did it! I did it!" he crowed. "Get a couple of glasses; this deserves a toast!"

"Sure, sure." She smiled, catching his excitement, shuffling out to the kitchen on bare feet and groping in the cabinets for two clean glasses. "Okay, shoot!" she said as she presented the glasses and watched Cader struggle with the wire on a bottle of sparkling Burgundy.

"I did it, baby! Ole Cader Harris pulled it off!" To her questioning look, he explained. "Delta Oil! I did it! There's a town council meeting right now, and the vote is expected to come in a definite 'yes.' I have it on the best source."

Sunny's blue eyes lit and the smile touched her lips. She loved to see him this way. Victorious. And her joy was complete with the knowledge that he'd come to share his victory with her and not Irene Thomas. "I knew you could do it, Cader, I just knew it."

"Yeah! Well, here's to me and Delta Oil!" He clinked his glass against hers and downed the burnished liquid. He refilled his glass and offered another toast. "And here's to me getting out of this stinking town. The Peyton Place of the South. Screw it!" He drained his glass again.

A frown developed between Sunny's brows. She didn't like to hear Cader talk that way about Hayden. After all, she was a part of the town, too, and she always took it personally. She forced herself to be honest and admit that if Cader had said "we" were going to get out of this stinking town, it wouldn't have bothered her a bit. She always waited for him to say something about taking her away with him when he left, but he never did. Leaving her half-finished drink on the counter, she moved toward the stove to put on a pot of coffee. "Tell me about it!" she coaxed above the sound of rushing water from the sink. "How do you know this thing with Delta Oil is going to go through?"

"Friends, baby," Cader chortled. "The right friends in the right places."

"So tell me who your friends are. Don't leave me out in the cold." She struggled with the manual can opener on an unopened can of Maxwell House. "Shit!" She dropped the can opener and studied the thumb of her right hand. "I broke another nail."

"Yeah. I told you to get yourself one of those electric openers," Cader said disinterestedly.

Sunny glanced up at him quickly. "I don't like to be dragged down by owning too many things. I like to travel light. Know what I mean?"

She begged him to understand her, to know that she was talking about him and that she'd be ready to leave with him anytime he said the word.

"I know what you mean, baby. Sure do. Anyway, about my friend in a high place, you'll never guess who it is."

Sunny slammed the coffeepot onto the stove. There were times Cader Harris's skull was as thick as a hog's. What did she have to do? Spell it out for him? "Who's your friend, Cade?" she asked in a monotone, hoping he'd see her annoyance and ask her about it.

"*The* Irene Hayden Thomas! Would you believe it? Right now, she's down at the Town Hall fighting her little heart out for Delta Oil and me."

Sunny raised her eyebrows. "Does Irene know your stake in it?"

"Yes and no. All little Irene wants is for me to stay here in Hayden, and I told her in order for that to happen this town's gotta boom. Hence, Delta Oil. We've already got Mayor Guthrie on our side, the greedy little man. And you know about the town's merchants and the Board of Education. It's gonna go, Sunny! It's gonna go! With Irene Thomas at the helm, it's gonna go! And then I'm gonna go! And this time when I leave this town it'll be for good. And in my pocket will be a nice fat check!"

"I hope so, Cader, for your sake."

"What d'you mean, you 'hope so'? It's a sure thing, honey, a winner," he cackled as he poured another glass of the sparkling Burgundy. "What could go wrong now?"

Sunny hesitated. The sound of assurance and confidence in his voice reverberated through her head. He wasn't going to like what she had to tell him, and she only wished it didn't have to come from her. "If you'd come by last night the way you'd promised, I could have told you then."

"Told me what?"

"Two men came into the Lemon Drop last night. Strangers. They were staying at the motel in the back. I know because they asked me to reserve a room for them. When they finished their dinner and drinks, they paid their check and left. I cleaned off their table and I found this." Sunday fished in her handbag and withdrew a slim, silver, executive ballpoint pen. She pushed it across the Formica counter top toward Cader who stared at it in disbelief. He picked it up as though he were touching cat shit or something equally disagreeable. On the side of the pen was engraved, DELTA OIL.

Suddenly, the fizz of the sparkling Burgundy became flat on his tongue.

Chapter Fifteen

Irene Thomas busied herself in the kitchen, hoping that activity would calm her nerves. It wouldn't be long now before Foster Doyle discovered how she had gone before the Board of Education with her plea to admit Delta Oil into Hayden. She had gone well-armed, with the support of the Junior Women's League and the League of Women Voters. And, because she was Foster Doyle's daughter, he would have to forgive her campaigning against him. Hence, everyone else who opposed Hayden must be forgiven right along with her.

"It's a perfect evening for the clambake, Beth, don't you think?" Irene asked Beth, a look of concern on her face. "Is something wrong, dear? You haven't been yourself lately. Beth, if you're dwelling on what happened to you at Jackie's party . . . well, you just can't. I'm certain every-one's forgotten about it by now, and you're just going to have a grand time at your first clambake. Is Luther picking you up or are you going with Kevin?" As she spoke, Irene began whipping egg whites with a wire whisk in the gleaming stainless and white confines of her practical kitchen.

"I'm not even sure I want to go!" Beth retorted hotly. "Luther is taking Sue Ellen and Kevin is going with Judy."

"Not go to your first clambake? Whatever are you thinking of, Beth Thomas? If you don't go, then for certain everyone in town will start talking *again*! You've looked forward to this all year. It's your special time, and I can't imagine why you would even contemplate not going. You're not the only one without a date. And to think that this minute your father and Destry are working on the barbecue pit so everything will be nice for you young people." Irene adjusted the gay scarf she wore on her head to protect her hair. It always struck Beth as funny that her mother wore the scarf like the tignons that old nigger women wore.

Beth listened to her mother's ramblings and knew she had intended to go to the clambake all along. In fact, there wasn't anything in this whole world that could keep her away from the beach tonight. Not anything. She had to talk to Kevin; she had to get him alone, some place where he couldn't turn his back on her. Everything was wrong. How could Kevin treat her this way? As if she didn't even exist. He should be treating Judy Evans the way he was treating her. A deep flush stained her cheeks and clashed with her red-gold hair. Irene droned on and on about how she was only young once. Ever since that night when she had been feeling sick and she had gone in to Kevin for help and he had done that to her, just the thought of the special secret she had to share with him could make her feel all jumpy inside. It was a secret, her secret. But soon, tonight, it would be their secret. Beth's and Kevin's. She hugged the thought to her. Kevin would be so happy to know that she really loved him. Then he could stop pretending to like Judy and things would be the same again, just like when they were little kids. When there were just the two of them. Only now they were grown up and it would be better than it ever was. Kevin was going to be so happy when she told him what he had done to her in bed that night.

"You can wear your new halter sun dress, the one I bought you last week. I know how you young people love to show off your suntans. You're going to look just perfect, and Luther will be sorry he invited Sue Ellen. Why, Sue Ellen's mother told me herself that Sue Ellen was going to wear those tacky blue jeans she's glued to. And the child needs a wave to her hair. I can't believe her mother allows her to go out in public dressed that way. Now you, Beth, are a perfect lady. You have to admit that no one would ever say you look tacky." Irene played with the meringue she was heaping on top of the lemon custard pie. "It's a shame the river has changed so much since your daddy and I were your age. Then, it was our only place to swim. I suppose it was dangerous then too, but we just didn't realize. I have cautioned that no one should go swimming at the clambake. It's one thing during the daytime, but at night . . ." Irene shuddered. She continued to chatter. "Thank God, there haven't been any drownings there this year, but wasn't it only just last summer that nice nigra boy, Johnson was his name, I think, drowned."

Beth nibbled on a piece of pie crust and listened patiently. "Ummm."

"I suppose it's because most people have swimming pools, and the children don't use the river for swimming as much as they did in my day. But, Beth, that river is treacherous! I was the one who brought that up at the town council meeting yesterday. You know, the one concerning Delta Oil taking over the beachfront for those tanks. People have very short memories, but not we Haydens. *I* reminded them of the lives that river has claimed. Yes, indeed. As for boating, well, most everybody who's into that sort of thing uses the marina further downriver anyway." Irene patted her apron and adjusted the scarf on her head. "It's the foolish mother who allows her child to swim in that river!"

"Have you seen Kevin, Mama?"

"Not since lunch. Today was only half a day at the sporting goods shop. Did you forget?" Irene hummed tunelessly as she placed the pie in the oven. Suddenly, she turned and looked inquisitively at her daughter. "Beth, do you know what's bothering your brother? He's acting so strangely. So withdrawn and remote. Why, he's barely civil to me, and I'm his very own lovin' mother."

Beth shrugged, her mind questioning Kevin's whereabouts. Irene continued to babble as she covertly watched Beth out of the corner of her eye. Beth noticed her mother's glance and began toying with the sticky utensils on the counter top. "He's probably out somewhere with that Judy Evans."

She watched her mother's reaction. It came right on cue.

"I spoke to Daddy about Kevin, but, as usual, your father's no help at all. He refuses to listen to me and says Kevin is old enough for a girlfriend and old enough to choose his own friends. What troubles me the most is the way Kevin is behaving toward you, his own sister." Irene sniffed as she stacked the dishwasher. "Kevin's behavior is cold and cruel and there are actually times when he behaves as though we're his *enemy* or something! It must be that Evans girl who's making him behave this way." Irene admitted to herself that she didn't like Kevin's attachment to Judy Evans one bit. But what bothered her the most was that she was losing her hold on him. He was coming into his own too soon, too fast.

"Yes, Mama," Beth answered idly. "It is Judy's influence. He acts as though he doesn't even have a family who loves him. But I know how Kevin feels deep down, Mama, and he doesn't really think I'm his enemy. Kevin loves me, Mama. He's loved me from the time we were little. He'll get over this, I just know he will. You'll see, Mama. Why, it could happen tomorrow! Kevin will open his eyes and see how much I mean to him." Beth cuddled her secret closer to her. She was going to tell Kevin about her secret tonight. She had to. It was her duty. Look how Mama was worried about him! She owed it to her family, didn't she, to make Kevin see how much he loved his little sister?

"You're right, of course, honey. I suppose it's just a stage boys go through, to rebel against their families." Irene began to hum tunelessly again as she wiped the counter. It occurred to Beth to wonder if Irene had a secret too. Mama had been all glowing lately, humming around the house and singing all those old love songs from years ago. And just look at the pounds she had taken off since the beginning of the summer and all those long visits to the hairdresser. Not to mention a complete renovation of her wardrobe. Beth looked at her mother again, questions rising in her green eyes. Whatever secret Mama had, it couldn't be as wonderful as her own secret.

Beth left Irene humming in the kitchen and went upstairs. On her way to her room she stopped outside Kevin's door and knocked softly. "Kevin, let me in. I want to talk to you. Mama is looking for you and I said I didn't know where you were," she lied. "I know you're in there, Kev," she whispered, her mouth pressed close against the door. Silence. "If you don't open the door, I'll tell Mama you've been in there all along and then she'll punish you and not let you go to the clambake. You know how she is, Kev, about us telling her where we are at all times. She'll say you gave her four new gray hairs today. Open the door, Kevin!"

Beth stepped back in shock at the expression on Kevin's face. His eyes looked like one of Daddy's customers. Where was the color in his face? He looked worse than one of Destry's best efforts. "Go away, Beth. I don't want to talk to you and I don't want to see you." His voice was cold, embalmed, without life.

"Kevin, don't act this way with me. I'm your sister and I love you the way you love me. You're just being mean and I don't like it!"

For answer, Kevin closed the door softly. The click sounded so final, like when Daddy closed the lid on one of his boxes for the last time. Those boxes he put all those dead people in were so final. You were dead when you were in one of those boxes. Kevin wasn't dead; she wasn't dead. That meant she still had a chance. Kevin still had a chance. She would get to him at the clambake tonight and it would all come out right.

The beach was crowded with people. The pit for the clams was smoldering. The oversized grill for the franks and hamburgers was red hot and ready for the first slap of cold meat. Two big tents stood ready to be opened for the dancing on the makeshift wooden floors. Musical instruments were being tuned up and everywhere there was the sound of laughter and happiness.

Beth stood in the shadows and watched as Kevin raced after a Frisbee, his long, muscular body glowing in the orange torchlight that bathed the beach in its eerie glow. How could he be having such a good time? How could he be so happy when she was so miserable? Her eyes narrowed as she watched Kevin race after another Frisbee only to collide with Judy. They both went down in the sand, laughing and rolling over and over each other. Kevin helped Judy to her feet and put his arm around her as they walked away down the beach out of sight of the orange light and the other happy frolickers. Where were they going? What were they going to do? Hot, searing jealousy ripped through her as she stepped from her secluded spot and headed away from the narrow strip of beach and the bright, smoking torches.

She knew the kids were staring at her, but she didn't care as she raced along the sandy beach. She had to hurry and get out of the light. If Kevin and Judy were in darkness, then so would she be.

If she hadn't heard Judy's giggle, she would have passed them. She stopped, hardly daring to breathe. They were right above her on the shelf of sand. She lay down and stretched out, straining to hear words she didn't want to hear. She had to hear them. There were no words only soft moans. She had heard those moans before. Kevin wouldn't do that with Judy. He knew Judy was nothing but a tramp. He might kiss her, but that was all he would do, wasn't it? It was too quiet. It must be a long kiss she decided. Judy was like that. She would clutch and hang onto him and never let him go. Quietly, she slithered closer to the high shelf of sand and drew in her breath as her hands closed around something soft and silky. Her eyes widened in the darkness as she clutched the minuscule piece of nylon. Boomer said that when a guy got a girl for the first time, he tossed her panties over his left shoulder. A tradition, he said. Boomer should know. Boomer knew everything when it came to girls. Only instead of her panties, Judy lost the bottom of her bikini swimsuit.

Shaking with rage, she slid backward. Quietly, she got to her feet, the bikini bottom still clutched in her hands. Her knees were like rubber as she walked back up the beach to the gala festival. She got a plate of clams and a Coke and sat down next to a girl she barely knew and began to eat. The food was like sawdust in her mouth and she washed it down with Coke. It was important that no one should see something was wrong. She waited, her eyes riveted to the dark stretch of sand beyond the torchlight. She set her empty Coke can down next to her and felt her hand go to the big patch pocket of her sun dress. When someone lost something and someone else found it then that someone was responsible for returning it. That's what Mama always said.

Beth walked down the beach, out of the light and into the dark, back toward the secluded spot where she had left Kevin with Judy. As she approached the place, she could hear voices, now hushed whispers actually.

"Where is it, Kevin? I can't find it anywhere! God! I can't walk around in this short dress without anything covering my behind! C'mon, Kevin! Help me look, we've got to find it!" Judy's whisper held a note of panic.

Beth patted the large pocket of her sun dress and smiled in the darkness. *Now, I wonder what they could be looking for? It just wouldn't be Christian to bother Judy with the fact that she had her old bikini bottom right here in her pocket, would it? Not when Judy was so busy looking for something.*

"I am looking, Judy," Kevin said. "I know they've got to be here somewhere!"

"Hi!" Beth said brightly as she stepped within range. "What are you two doing way down here? The party's going full blast now, music and everything. Can't you hear it?"

"Beth. What the hell are you doing here?" Kevin asked bitterly. "Jesus H. Christ! Can't a guy have any privacy?"

"Kevin Thomas! If you keep swearing like that, I'll have to tell Mama. Maybe she can have Reverend Conway have a talk with you. I just was taking a walk. I didn't know you were here," she lied. "Looks like you lost something, Judy. Can I help? What was it?"

". . . er . . . my rings!" Judy said hastily, her nervousness making her voice shaky.

"Rings! You'll never find them with all this sand and in the dark!" Beth said smugly, her hand covering her pocket. "You sure you lost your rings?"

"Yes . . . it . . . it was my rings." Judy answered, smoothing the short skirt of her sun dress down over her thighs.

"Where'd you lose them?" Beth asked stubbornly, relishing Judy's discomfort. She almost pulled the bikini bottom out of her pocket, wanting to see Judy's face as she dangled them in front of her. But something held her back. After all, wasn't it only proper that Judy should tell her the truth? When somebody lost money or something, didn't they have to tell how much it was or identify it somehow?

"Will you get out of here, Beth?" Kevin growled. "Can't you see we're busy?"

"I want to talk to you, Kevin," Beth said sweetly. "It's important."

"Not now, for Crissakes!"

"Yes, now, Kevin. I have to talk to you. Alone!" She pierced Judy with a hateful stare.

"You . . . you stay here and talk to Beth," Judy said, squirming, wanting only to get out from under Beth's knowing glare. "I have to go to the little girls' room anyway.

I'll see you back at the clambake." Judy moved away from the duo, back toward the lights. After she'd gone a couple of yards, she turned and ran, holding her short, flaring skirt tight against her legs.

Kevin looked after Judy, a concerned look on his face. Beth watched Kevin, her jealousy growing by the second.

"What d'you want to talk to me about, Beth? I think I've heard everything you have to say." Kevin's tone was cold and aloof, just as it had been since the night of Jackie's party. But what she had to tell him would change all that. She could make him happier than that trampy Judy Evans could. Once she told him, he'd remember that night, and then he'd know that he didn't need Judy. He'd have her, Beth, and that was all he needed.

"C'mon, Beth. I'm waiting to hear what you have to say. I want to get back to the party."

"You don't want to get back to the party; you want to get back to Judy! But what I'm going to tell you will change all that, Kevin. After you hear me out, you'll never want to see Judy again."

"Cut it out, will ya, Beth? I don't want to listen to any more gossip about Judy that you've dreamed up in that sick little head of yours. Judy's a good kid and I like her, a lot. Nothing you could say could change that. When I get to college and get into a fraternity, I'm going to give her my pin. So just cut the crap and leave me and Judy alone."

Stunned, Beth persisted, "How can you give her your pin?"

Kevin interrupted, not allowing her to complete her

thought. "Not too many people know this, but Judy's going with me to Tulane. She was accepted a few weeks ago. That's how I'm going to give her my pin. She's going to be right there with me." For an instant Kevin gloated to see the shock on Beth's face. Now, maybe she'd leave him alone. Maybe she'd realize he had his own life to live. Maybe she'd stop trying to eat him alive.

Beth almost staggered beneath the weight of what she'd just heard. Judy Evans going to Tulane with Kevin! Judy Evans getting her claws into Kevin. Making Kevin like her, making Kevin kiss her, touch her, make love to her. It couldn't be! She wouldn't allow it! Kevin was hers; he belonged to her! It had been that way ever since she could remember. Kevin and Beth. Beth and Kevin. Tears welled in her eyes; her voice was a choked, strangling sound. "How could you do this to me? How could you leave me behind and take up with that whore? After what we've been to one another. After what you did to me."

"Take it easy, Beth. We haven't been anything to one another. We're brother and sister. What more could there be? And I didn't *do* anything to you. You've got your own life to live, Beth, and I've got mine."

"You're hateful, Kevin Thomas! But I'll forgive you; I always forgive you. I . . . I love you so much, Kevin. So much. I even proved it to you."

"I don't want to listen to you anymore, Beth. I'm going after Judy." Kevin pushed Beth aside and stepped past her.

"You better listen to me, Kevin Thomas. What I have to say will make a difference in all your high and mighty plans. You love me, Kevin, I know you love me. . . ." Her words were cut off by the sight of his back, tall and straight, walking away from her.

Suddenly, he turned, his eyes burning into her. "I'd like to love you, Bethy. I'd like you to be the little sister I always cared about. But you've changed. You won't let me live my own life. You hang around my neck like the albatross. Right now, this minute, I wonder that I ever cared anything about you at all."

"You do love me, Kevin, I can prove it. I know!" Beth was so overwrought with emotion that her teeth chattered. "Remember the other night? The night when you came home late? I heard you talking to Dad downstairs. You said something about drinking. Then I heard you come upstairs and get into the shower."

Kevin stood stock still. He knew she was going to tell him something he didn't want to hear and yet he was powerless to stop her, to stop himself from listening. He'd had bad vibes about that night. And now, the answer was there on her face, waiting to be read.

"I . . . I didn't feel well. I . . . I was sick. I went into your room, Kevin, and . . . I got into bed with you. It was only to keep warm. But you liked it, Kevin, I know you did. I could tell by the way you touched me. . . ."

Kevin's face went white. His fists doubled and clenched. He knew if he hit her, he would kill her. If she were telling the truth, it was what he had been afraid of, what he had refused to remember. Lightning flashes of memory charged through his mind and the gorge rose to his throat.

The defenses to maintain his sanity rose to the fore. She was lying! She *had* to be lying!

"Why are you looking at me that way, Kevin? It wasn't so terrible. It was nice. I liked it. Please don't look that way, Kevin. I didn't mean to make it sound as though it was all your idea, as though you'd done something terrible to me. I *love* you, Kevin, and you love me! I know you do. It was almost like when we were kids and we used to go into Mother's room and look at Daddy's magazines." Her hand reached out to touch him, wanting him to draw her near, to comfort her, to tell her that he loved her and that everything was going to be all right again. Only better. That they'd have each other, and no one, not Judy, not anyone, would ever come between them again. She waited for Kevin to tell her that he wouldn't see Judy anymore, that he'd wait for her to go to college and be with him.

Kevin's face crumpled before her eyes. Revulsion twisted his handsome features into a mask of agony. "Get away from me, Beth!" he menaced hoarsely. "Get away from me and don't ever come near me again!"

He backed away from her. One step, two. Then he broke into a run, his breath coming in gasps that she could hear across the widening distance he put between them. "Kevin, wait! Kevin, don't go! Don't leave me like this! Kevin! Don't leave me alooooone!"

She watched, long after he disappeared into the darkness, heading back toward the lights, toward the party, toward Judy. Judy. Nasty, dirty, whoring Judy.

Chapter Sixteen

Kevin stood outside the tent where the five-piece band played their rendition of Neil Sedaka's "Bad Blood" and tried to regain some sense of normalcy. He felt a light touch on his shoulder and turned to see Reverend Conway.

"You probably won't believe this, but I used to stand where you're standing, right here, and listen to the band, wishing I had the nerve to ask someone to dance. I was young once, you know. I just saw Judy. She's your date, isn't she?"

Kevin flushed and nodded.

"I just saw Beth awhile ago, too. Who'd she come with?"

"I guess she came alone. Where'd you say you saw Judy?"

Damion pointed in the direction of the restrooms on the far end of the sandy strip. "Girls haven't changed much since my day. Always having to comb their hair and join in a little gossip in the john."

"Then I guess I'd better wait for her here," Kevin murmured.

"Want a little company? Say, I can get us a couple of Cokes. Rank has its privileges, you know. No waiting in line for me. Wait here."

Within moments, Damion was back carrying two cans, a Coke and a beer. Kevin sank down onto the sand, legs crossed. He accepted the Coke from Damion and, after popping the tab, leaned back on his elbows.

"Might as well relax," Damion said with a chuckle. "That's a pretty long line outside the john." He looked off in the direction of the portable toilets and saw Judy standing in line, shifting her weight from one foot to the other. "Judy's a pretty girl. She has her mother's good looks."

Kevin only nodded, seeming to be lost in his own thoughts. He took another swallow of Coke and leaned back again, staring off into the distance. Something was troubling the boy, Damion would bet his boots on it, but the annual clambake was hardly the place to question him about it.

A group of kids passed by on their way into the tent, and, when they saw the Reverend, carefully picked up their feet so they wouldn't kick sand. One of the girls hanging on Boomer's arm called out to Kevin, "If you're looking for Judy, she's over there in line for the john."

Kevin merely nodded, lost in his own thoughts as he pushed the empty Coke can deep into the sand. He wished he could bury himself the same way he did the bright aluminum. Deep, beneath the soft, loose sand. So deep that it would cover his ears and eyes and hide him from himself. And from Beth.

Beth stood just beyond the edge of light, looking across to the tents, seeing Kevin sitting there with Reverend Conway. Her relief that Kevin was not with Judy came to a swift end and was replaced with a pang of fear that Kevin could be confiding in the Reverend about what had happened between them. She quickly rejected the idea. Kevin would never tell. Never.

Beth's eyes surveyed the crowd, looking for Judy. She was somewhere, but where? Her attention fell on the long, snaking line of giggling girls, waiting to use the john. She saw Judy, standing sullenly amid the others, her hands still protecting her skirt against a wayward wind that might reveal her bare behind. Beth was pleased by the discomfort she had caused her.

Crouching low, working her way through the scrub pines that lined the slight ridge just behind where the portable toilets had been set up, Beth maneuvered till she was just a few feet away from Judy. If she stood far enough back into the scrub, the light wouldn't touch her. She would make Judy come to her. Judy was dumb. Everybody knew that except Kevin.

The door to the portable john was set facing the ridge, away from the beach, to afford the greatest possible privacy. Just one more girl to come out of the john and then it would be Judy's turn.

The area near where Beth waited lighted momentarily as the door swung open. The girl inside stepped around the front of the john, signaling that it was ready for the next occupant. Judy's turn.

Beth waited, holding her breath. Judy rounded behind the building. "Oooh, Judy, is that you? Can you come over here a minute? I think I have something that's yours."

"Beth? Is that you?" Judy's spine stiffened at the friendliness in Beth's tone. And what was she doing hiding just beyond the light behind the toilet? The meaning of Beth's words suddenly struck Judy. Could she possibly . . . ? No. It wasn't possible! Beth couldn't have the bottom of her bikini, could she? That would mean she knew about her and Kevin and just how she had lost the bottom to her bathing suit.

"Judy? Come over here," Beth called again in a hushed whisper. "I have something I know you're looking for."

One backward glance toward the toilet. Should she go tell the next girl in line to go ahead of her? Deciding against it, Judy walked into the scrub, out of the light, toward Beth.

"I think these are yours." Beth held the bikini bottom aloft. "At least I think they are because they have a tape in them with your name on it. Don't you think you're old enough not to have your mama sew your name into your clothes?"

"Give me those!" Judy rasped, reaching for the bikini. Beth snatched them away with a lightning movement of her arm. "Beth Thomas, give me those!" she hissed, glancing behind her to see that no one could hear.

"Not until you tell me why your mama sewed your

name into them," Beth teased wickedly, hiding the bikini behind her, out of Judy's grasp.

"So when I go to the swim club I know which is mine in the locker room. Now, give me those!"

"No! Not right now at least. First, you have to promise me something."

"Stop being a baby. Now, hand them over."

"No. First you have to promise."

Exasperated, Judy grumbled. "All right. What do you want me to promise?"

"That you stay away from Kevin."

"Stop being stupid. I can't promise that. Now, will you give me those before I . . ."

"Before you what? I've made you angry, haven't I? I didn't mean to. I'm just trying to do what's right. You know that, don't you? I only want to save Kevin from you. Now, will you promise to stay away from Kevin, or should I go and tell my mother how I found your bikini bottom?" she taunted, enjoying the misery on Judy's face and the power she held over her.

"Cut it out, Beth. Now, give me those!" She reached again and grabbed Beth's shoulders, struggling with her for the bikini.

"You don't seem to understand," Beth said levelly. "I want you to stay away from Kevin. I'll *make* you stay away from him. I'll do anything I have to do to make you stay away from him. You're bad for him, Judy. You make him forget about his family and everybody. You make him forget he even has a sister who loves him a lot."

"Grow up, huh? Give me that bikini!" Judy said forcefully, muscling Beth aside, groping for the silky bottom.

"Nothing will stop you, will it, Judy? You don't care if my mother knows you've been screwing around with Kevin. You don't care if anybody knows it, do you? All you care about is getting your pants back on so you can go back down the beach and be with Kevin. You're bad, Judy, and somebody should stop you before you hurt Kevin. Before you take him away from the people who really love him!"

Judy stared in amazement at Beth whose voice was becoming strident with hysteria. *This kid is off the wall*, Judy thought. *Right off the wall!* She sensed that Beth was becoming desperate to hear her say she would stay away from Kevin. There was a strange look in Beth's eyes, a glittering, menacing look that was visible even in the darkness as though a sly and clever creature were peering out at her from behind Beth's eyes. And the way she was talking through clenched teeth, spitting really, sounded dangerous. Deciding she'd never get her bikini back by arguing, she began to humor Beth. "All right, Bethy, anything you say, only give me back the bikini. I can't very well up and take off for home without them, can I?"

"Then you promise? I don't want to tell my mama about you and Kevin. I don't want to get him into trouble, but I will if it means saving him from you."

"I said you win, Beth. I won't go near Kevin again. Now, give me that bikini." Judy was shaking with barely controlled panic. She'd never seen anyone act like Beth before and didn't know how to handle it. Kevin would have to know that his sister was getting drugs from Boomer. That had to be it. Normal people just didn't behave like this!

Beth brought the silky bottom around in front of her, tentatively handing them out to Judy. Judy made a quick grab to snatch the bikini away, but not before Beth caught the smug look that flashed over her features. Too late. Judy had the swimsuit.

"You . . . you tricked me! You aren't ever going to leave Kevin alone, are you? You bitch!" Judy was bending down to step into the bikini before Beth could tear them away from her.

Taking advantage of Judy's precarious balance as she stood on one foot, Beth knocked her to the ground and struggled to retrieve the bikini. But Judy was bigger and outweighed her. Beth had to stop her. She couldn't let her win. Judy would have the bikini and Kevin too.

Her hand touched a rock in the sparse grass beneath the trees. Forcefully, she brought it down on the side of Judy's head with a crack. Instantly, Judy fell limp, the bikini still clutched in her hands.

Beth scrambled to her feet and stood looking down at the still form. Swiftly, as though still fighting for their possession, she snatched the bikini out of Judy's unprotesting fingers and stuffed them once again in the pocket of her sun dress.

A sound behind her brought her to full alert. "When are you coming out of there? Didn't fall in, did you?" the voice called. Beth realized it must be the next girl in line for the john. "Hey! There's nobody in here! Whoever it was must have gone out around the other side. I've been waiting all this time for an empty toilet!" Beth stood motionless in the cover of the shadows and watched the girl step into the cubicle and close the door behind her.

She knew she couldn't stay here. She couldn't be found. What if the girl saw her when she stepped out of the portable john, when she was facing in the direction of the trees? Beth bent over and grasped Judy beneath the arms and tugged, pulling until they were both hidden deeper in the shadows. A tiny, whining sound escaped from Judy's throat as Beth moved her. It reminded Beth of the sick kitten she and Kevin had found when they were little. She couldn't stay here, and she couldn't leave Judy here either. Someone might see them and Judy would tell what she had done.

Back through the scrub pines Beth pulled Judy. It would be easier out on the sand down toward the river. Through the shadows, across the darkened sand, away from the party, away from Kevin, Beth dragged Judy. Little by little. Carefully, stopping every few seconds to listen for sounds of activity. Pulling, pulling, until she thought her arms would break. It was easier on the sand. Down the rise, toward the river, she almost lost hold of her burden. Against the sky, the dark tree limbs lining the shallow rise became apprehending wraiths reaching out for her, to hold her, to tell what she had done. Moonlight lit oblique patterns on the sand, lighting the way for what she had to do. For Kevin.

She was tired, so tired. *How much further? Don't look,*

she told herself. *Just do it! Do it for Kevin. For Kevin.* Judy was struggling back to consciousness, but she was too stunned, too weak to do more than moan a barely audible protest. *Quickly, quickly,* Beth told herself. *Hurry! Don't give up. For Kevin. For Kevin.* She dragged Judy's semiconscious form almost to the place where she had found her with Kevin. The party was a safe distance away, around the bend, further up the river. So far, no one had seen her, not even the sea birds which sometimes traveled this far into the Delta to escape a storm.

Beth stopped. Something was wrong. Something didn't fit. The dress. Judy's dress. She wouldn't go in swimming with her dress on. Or her shoes. Hurriedly, carefully, so as not to tear the material, she removed the sun dress. After pulling the strapped sandals off Judy's sandy feet, Beth looked down at her too-still form. She marveled at her own strength in managing to pull the heavier girl across the sands. Judy's legs and hips were full-fleshed. Unlike her own too-thin, narrow hips and thighs. And Judy had so much hair down there. She would too, someday, she promised herself. Quickly, before she could think a second time, she ran back toward the overhanging shelf of sand and rock and deposited the dress and shoes and ran back to Judy.

Panting with exertion, Beth brought her burden to the water's edge. Just a bit more. A little bit more. Her own feet were in the water, feeling the soft clay bottom oozing between her toes. Soon. Soon. For Kevin.

Judy struggled to consciousness. Felt her legs being

dragged across the small stones at the water's edge and into the soft clay. The water was cold, icy cold. Something held her around the chest and under the arms. It was strong and tight and she found it hard to breathe. Her legs were getting wet. Now her hips. She moaned. Awareness shot into her brain like a flare. It was Beth's arms around her chest, holding her, dragging her, pulling her into the water. She felt herself become buoyant. Her legs sought the bottom, struggling for footing.

She had no breath to scream. Her head hurt; her eyes wouldn't focus. She realized her arms were free, but they felt useless and leaden. With mighty effort, her hands groped, fingers clawing, reaching behind her, reaching for Beth.

Judy's hand broke the water's surface for an instant, and she caught a glimpse of Beth's face. Beth's lips were compressed into a grim line; the cords in her neck bulged with the exertion of pushing Judy back under the surface of the inky black water. But her eyes, her eyes! Slitted, cold, dead, yet behind them was that sly creature again. Sly and evil and deadly.

The night was still, with only distant sounds of music playing somewhere. Stupidly, amid her struggles, incongruously, she recognized the tune as "Help Me Make It Through the Night." Water lapped around her, she realized her struggles were useless. The force holding her was strong, becoming stronger. Her head was plunged beneath the water. With a last desperate strength from her trapped body, Judy fought. Her head surfaced. She couldn't touch bottom. She had been dragged into the current where she knew the shelf of mud and river bottom dropped off to a depth of over fifteen feet. Still, the force held her. Beth. Beth was the force.

Wet loops of hair covered her eyes, twisting around her neck. Gulping for air, she took in water. It seemed as though she were inhaling the whole river. Writhing, struggling, fighting with the last of her diminished strength, she managed to twist around to face her killer. Under, under, water pouring into her mouth and nose, filling her ear cavities, blurring her wide-eyed stare. She felt the fabric of Beth's sun dress in her hands and clutched at it frantically. Then the black waters of the river crashed through the last of her defenses. The slim cord of her life was strained, stretched taut into a black vortex of oblivion.

The last sound she heard was Beth's voice hissing, "I hope you go to hell, Judy Evans. I hope you go straight to hell!"

Kevin had wandered away from Reverend Conway and went to look for Judy. Several girls told him that Judy had been on line for the john, but she wasn't there now. He knew she hadn't come down to where the band was playing; he had just come from there.

He wondered if she had gone off in search of her bikini bottom and headed off in that direction along the beach.

A thousand thoughts tormented him as he pushed his feet through the sand, and he didn't see the discarded dress and shoes until he nearly tripped over them. Recognizing the articles immediately, he frowned and scanned the surface of the water.

All reason left him as he ran to the river, stumbling and rolling down the incline from the ridge, his eyes never leaving the two shadowy struggling figures in the water. He splashed toward them, silent prayers forming on his lips. His legs felt heavy, leaden, refusing to work in coordination with each other. He felt the clay bottom slope downward, the water rise to the height of his hips. The sky was black, the water blacker. The now solitary figure reflected the thin, wavering moonlight. Beth!

He swam with long, powerful strokes to reach his objective. Reaching it, he dove beneath the water and groped blindly, his fingers brushing against cold flesh and tangling in long hair. Fighting the need for air, he seized the form and heaved it to the surface.

Beth pounded on his back. "No! Let her die! Kill her, Kevin! Kill her!"

Kevin pulled Judy's inert form back toward shore, his feet searching for bottom. *God, don't let her die; please, don't let her die.*

"Kevin! Didn't you hear me?" Beth wailed. "Let her die, let her die!" She swam toward him, pulling at his arms, trying to push Judy's head under the surface.

"Don't touch her," Kevin growled. "Don't ever touch her again."

Beth backed away, a madness in her eyes. "I did it for you, Kevin, because I love you," she sobbed. "I love you. . . ."

"Your kind of love is sick, Beth. Get away from me. Get away from Judy and me."

For an instant he thought she would strike him, fight

him for possession of Judy. His muscles tensed, ready for her onslaught. Instead, she backed away from him, then turned and pushed for shore. As he was struggling with Judy's weight, pulling and dragging her onto the beach, he saw Beth scrambling over the ridge.

He worked feverishly over Judy, tears and river water blurring his vision. Judy's head rolled as she spit and gagged. She was alive.

Kevin's stomach was churning so wildly he could barely carry Judy. He had to get her home, safe, away from Beth, away from everyone. He had hastily dressed her in the discarded sun dress and shoes that Beth stripped off her. He couldn't think about Beth, he didn't want to think about Beth. He had to take care of Judy and get her home safe and sound. Thank God no one had seen what happened, and thank God he had come looking for Judy. A cold chill washed over him. Another minute and he would have been too late. Another five minutes and Judy would have been dead and his sister would have been a murderer.

"Kev," Judy whimpered, "take me home, please. I want my mother," she said, burrowing her head against his chest.

"It's okay, it's okay," Kevin soothed. "Beth is gone and I'm taking you home. It's all right now, you're safe. Beth is gone."

"I can walk, Kev. Put me down. I want to walk, really I do."

Gently, Kevin set Judy on her feet and protectively put his arm around her to steady her. "What's your mother going to say and do?" Kevin worried aloud.

"Let's sit down a minute," Judy said shakily. "We have to talk about this. My mother will . . . she'll . . . what she'll do . . . she'll go off the deep end. She's just getting it together for herself, and I don't think she could handle this. I'll just say I don't feel well. I can carry it off. It's you who has the problem, Kev. What are you going to do? Are you going to tell?" she asked fearfully.

Kevin's arm tightened around Judy's shoulders. "Oh, God, I don't know what to do," Kevin groaned. "How can I let Mom know that Beth . . ."

"Kev," Judy shivered against him, "Beth isn't . . . she's . . . crazy!"

"Are you okay now? Do you think you can make it?"

"Sure," Judy said, forcing a weak grin.

"Are you sure you don't want your mother to know?"

"I'm sure. I'm okay now, but there's no way I'll ever get within a hundred feet of your sister, ever again. There's no point in upsetting Mom. You do whatever you think you have to do. If you decide we should tell, then I'll do it. It's up to you, Kevin, after all, Beth is your sister."

Kevin wanted to throw up. Here Judy was, walking alongside him after his sister almost killed her, telling him to handle it, placing her trust in him. If her mother, who was a grown, sensible, reasonable adult, couldn't handle it, why did Judy think he was going to fare any better? Judy smiled up at him, and he knew that he could handle it. He fought down the bile rising in his throat and tightened his hold on her shoulders. He could handle it.

A dim orange light glowed from the Evanses' front

porch and an even dimmer light glowed from within. "Mom's in bed, but not asleep. That's the night light she left on for me. If we're quiet, we can just walk through the door."

Kevin gathered Judy in his arms in the shadows of the gnarled oak tree. They said nothing, did nothing, but reveled in the comfort each gave the other. It was Judy who broke away and gazed up at Kevin. "Everything is going to be all right, Kevin. I can feel it and so can you. It's going to be all right," she reassured.

"Judy, you mean so much to me, I can't leave you. I don't want to stay here in Hayden, I want to go away to college and never come back. I can't wait, Judy. . . ."

"Ssh . . ." She silenced him by touching her fingertips to his lips. "We're going away together. You're going to Tulane and I'll be right there with you. We'll be together, Kevin, and we'll put this behind us."

"It's late; you better go in," Kevin said softly. Judy squeezed his hand and smiled. Kevin watched her run up the steps, stop at the top and wave at him. His heart started its wild thumping. Jesus God Almighty, if he had been one minute later, he wouldn't be standing here watching Judy go through the front door. In the quietness he could hear the soft snick of the bolt. His shoulders slumped as he turned and headed for home.

Kevin scuffed his feet as he moped along, dragging one foot after the other. He had always loved the sound of the crickets late at night, but tonight he paid them no heed, his mind on only one thing. If he had only one wish in the world, he would wish he was at Tulane, never to return, never to set his eyes on Beth again. He stopped short under the yellow glow of the street lamp and stared at the car swerving into the driveway behind the sporting goods store. Cader was going into the store. Vaguely, he wondered why, since he himself had set the burglar alarm. He shrugged; maybe Cader forgot something. Before he realized what he was doing, he was running after the car and shouting, "Hey, Cader, can I talk to you a minute?"

Cader Harris climbed from the car and frowned. *Now, what in the living hell . . . ?* "Kind of late for you to be prowling the streets, isn't it?" he said sternly.

"If there's one thing I don't need right now, it's my boss sounding like my father." Cader felt the blood leave his face. "Can I talk to you about something? I wouldn't ask, but it really is important."

"Must be the night air and all these damn crickets, makes me go off the deep end sometimes," Cader said gruffly. "Come on in. I have a couple of beers in the cooler. That's why I stopped by as a matter of fact; there isn't any in my apartment. Don't just stand there; you said it was important."

A bottle of Heineken in his hand, Kevin gulped and stared at the man sitting across from him. Cader Harris was a guy who had been around. If anyone knew what to do, it would be Cader. But first, he had to get the words out. Jesus, this was almost as hard as going to Aunt Cledie's that first time.

Harris's eyes narrowed. Whatever was about to pop from

the boy's mouth wasn't going to be good, he could feel it in his gut. "Help me," he mouthed silently to a God he had never called on before.

"Remember the night we sat here talking?" Kevin asked. Cader nodded and waited. "Well, I had more to drink than I should have, and I was a little drunk. I took a shower but it didn't help much. I guess I passed out and I was dreaming that Viola was in bed with me and we were . . . you know. I thought I was dreaming, but I wasn't. I wasn't dreaming at all. It was Beth in bed with me. We . . . I think . . . she said . . . I don't know what I did." Kevin took a swallow of beer as he watched Cader's frozen face. He didn't look shocked. "Tonight, Beth tried to drown Judy Evans. I got there just in time. A few more minutes and I would have been too late. I can't handle this, Cader. I don't know what to do. Judy doesn't want to tell her mother and she's trusting me to take care of . . . of . . . Beth."

A wild, alien surge of parental protectiveness shot through Cader Harris. He wanted to grab Kevin and hold him, to stroke his hair the way a mother would do and then thump him on the back the way a father would do. He raised his eyes upward. There was no bolt of lightning, no roll of thunder to help him. He was on his own. He had to tell his son what to do. He swallowed hard, forcing himself to remain in his nonchalant position in the swivel chair.

"Kevin, the dream, the actuality, isn't important. Whatever it was, it's over and you can't do anything about it.

The problem now is something else. My best advice and my only advice to you is to go home, wake your . . . your father and talk to him. He's got to be a good man if he has a son like you. He'll know what you should do. I think you've known all along that is what you should do. You saw me coming here at just the right moment, and you needed to talk at that moment. You need your old man, kid, not me." He made his voice purposely gruff as he spoke. He didn't want Kevin ever to regret coming to him. "This is between you and me; it won't ever go any further."

"I know that, Cader; that's why I wanted to talk to you. You're an okay guy. I'd like to keep in touch with you after I get to Tulane if you don't mind. My dad is an okay guy, too. I love my dad, Cader, and I'm not ashamed to tell you that. That part about the dream, that was one thing, but I didn't want to hurt Dad by telling him about Beth. I was all mixed up there for a while. Thanks," Kevin said, sticking out his hand. Cader pretended not to see it as he got up from the swivel chair. If he touched the boy now, it would be all over. He wanted to put his arms around Kevin, to put in a claim for his son. He loved the boy, enough not to succumb to his own needs, but to think of Kevin. The boy was too close to the brink; the last thing he needed was something to confuse him even further.

"I didn't do anything, Kevin. Look, do you want a ride home? It's late."

"No, I think I'll walk. You won't forget, will you . . . about keeping in touch?"

Now, what in the goddamn hell was that lump in

his throat? Cader nodded as he held the door open for Kevin and then carefully locked it. "I'd like that. I really would . . . son."

"See you tomorrow," Kevin said, loping off down the street. He could handle it if Cader said he could.

Arthur and Irene Thomas sat in the dark, paneled study and listened to Kevin's tortured words. Only once did their eyes meet and then both carefully looked away. Arthur laid a paternal hand on Kevin's shoulder. "Your mother and I will take care of this. We're both proud of you that you didn't take the easy way out and say nothing. I know what it must have cost you to come to us like this. Trust us, Kevin, to do the right thing. Tonight there are no answers. Tomorrow is something else. Try to get some sleep."

Kevin looked at his parents, loving his father and respecting his mother. He did as he was told and left the room. His hands and arms seemed to have a mind of their own as he found himself wedging the desk chair beneath the doorknob. He knew he wasn't going to sleep, but he felt better with the door secured. He'd never feel safe in this house again.

Chapter Seventeen

Irene Thomas laid the hair brush down on the dresser and walked to the window. Foster Doyle Hayden was climbing from the sleek car, his face a murderous mask of fury. It was time. By now, Foster Doyle would have gotten wind of her traitorous plea to the Board of Education the day before.

"Irene!" the furious voice bellowed.

"Just a moment, Father," Irene called down the stairs. She took her time, glancing in the mirror and then straightening her dress. Deftly, she rubbed her index finger over her lips and then reached for a tissue. Her movements were slow, unhurried as she descended the stairs. She was numb. As numb as she had been the night before in Arthur's study when Kevin had spelled out the sordid truth about Beth and she had to face Arthur's stony silence.

"I want to speak with you, Irene. Now!"

"Why don't we go into the study, Father? Beth is having

her breakfast in the kitchen. You go along and I'll bring some coffee," Irene said firmly, heading for the kitchen.

"Mama," Beth whined, "this milk is sour." Irene ignored her daughter and started fixing a tray. "Mama, did you hear me?" Irene continued her fluid movements, completely ignoring her daughter. Later, after her father left, she would acknowledge the child, unless she could think of another way to get through the day pretending she wasn't there.

"I'm sorry, Mama. Look at me and tell me you aren't angry with me. Mamaaaa," she shrilled. Irene picked up the laden tray and moved the door with her shoulder. Beth watched her, her eyes narrowed and her bottom lip trembling.

"Here, Father. Black, no sugar, right?" Irene said, pouring the fragrant brew into a delicate china cup. She poured herself a cup and held it lightly in her hand, her eyes fixed on her father. "What did you want to talk to me about?" she asked quietly. "If you raise your voice, I'll leave the room," she said warningly.

Foster Doyle took a deep breath, aware of the rattle of the cup against the saucer. "How dare you defy me the way you did at the Board of Education meeting? How dare you go against me? What possessed you to endorse Delta Oil? Good God, Irene, have you lost your senses?"

"No, Father, I haven't lost my senses. I think I just came to my senses, as a matter of fact. I really don't want to discuss it. It's done; I've taken my stand and that's the beginning and the end of it."

"Cader Harris put you up to it, don't deny it," Foster

Doyle thundered. "You never used your brain before he came here, admit it. All of a sudden Harris shows up on the scene, and he had you eating right out of his hand. You're his puppet, Irene. He told you what to do and you did it."

"And what if I did?" she asked defiantly. "I love him and he loves me. He's got a secure future with Delta Oil and will be able to take care of me. It's not like before when we were younger. Now, he has something to offer me and I intend to take him and his offer."

Foster Doyle's face turned ashen and then purple. His clawlike hand reached out to grasp the back of a chair. His breathing was labored and he looked like he was going to drop to the floor. Irene watched her father without emotion. He was old; he had lived his life. "And you think because Cader Harris has money that it's going to be all right?" the old man gasped. "Well, he had money once before and he didn't take you with him. He sold out. To me. I bought him off. That's why he went away. Is it your intention to leave or stay here? Are you going to flaunt your affair in front of me? What do you have to say to that?"

"Not much." She couldn't, she wouldn't, give him the satisfaction of knowing what the spoken words were doing to her. "Tell me," she said, setting the fragile cup down on a cherry wood table. "How much did I go for?" she asked softly.

"Too much," the old man gasped as his knees began to buckle. Only with supreme effort did he manage to stay on his feet. "He didn't care that you were pregnant with his child. The only thing that interested him was money and a chance to leave this town. Don't you understand, Irene? He didn't care about you then and he doesn't care about you now. He knows Kevin is his son. If he does say he wants you, it's because of Kevin." This time Foster Doyle's knees did give out and his flimsy hold on the back of the wing chair gave way.

Irene picked up the phone and dialed a number, then spoke softly. "Father, if you can hear me, the ambulance is on the way." There was a detached, vague look on Irene's face as she picked up her coffee cup and sipped the cool liquid. Her eyes met Beth's as the child backed off one step and then two, finally swiveling and running out the front door. "I think you've had a stroke, Father," Irene said, peering down at the inert man. "Don't worry about anything. I'm more than capable of running your affairs. I'll see that you receive the best care available."

The shrill whine of the siren heralding the arrival of the ambulance made one of Foster Doyle's legs twitch.

Irene stood aside as the ambulance attendants entered the room, pushing the stretcher. Quietly, she stood near the fireplace and watched as the men checked her father's vital signs. Their faces revealed nothing as they lifted his body onto the stretcher and then covered him. "Do you want to ride to the hospital with us, ma'am?" one of the men asked.

"No, thank you." The attendants looked at one another and picked up the stretcher.

From her new position at the window Irene watched the

scene at the rear of the ambulance. She frowned when the rear doors were closed and locked. It sounded so terminal.

Beth's eyes were hate-filled as she ran through the room and out the door. She hated them all. She ran, looking neither to the left nor to the right, her thin legs pumping rhythmically. She'd show them all. When she reached the mortuary, she slowed to regain her breath. Her knuckles were white on the heavy doorknob as she thrust open the door. Daddy would be in the office. She made her way through the meadow of thick carpet and marched into Arthur Thomas's private office. He was alone. She stared at him as she kicked the door shut. "I know Kevin told you what happened at the clambake. She deserved it, Daddy," Beth said with vitriolic vehemence. "She's a slut; even Mama said so."

"And because of that you decided you had the right to kill her, an innocent person," Arthur said coldly.

"I knew you would be on Kevin's side. You don't care about me; all you care about is Kevin. Kevin isn't even your son. He's Cader Harris's son. I heard Grandpa tell Mama this morning. I heard them talking. I think Mama is going off with Mr. Harris. I bet they take Kevin with them. And you think they're all so wonderful. What do you think now? How do you like it that Cader Harris is Kevin's father?"

"Do you think I care?" Arthur said, sitting down behind the desk. "I love Kevin and he's my son. I'm *your* father and look how you turned out."

"I always knew you and Mama loved Kevin best. He's not even my real brother. But I only wanted to protect Kevin from Judy Evans. I was helping!"

Arthur Thomas's voice was deadly when he spoke. "Go home, Beth."

"You're hateful, Daddy. You're just hateful. I don't care if you die like Grandpa. The ambulance came for him. You didn't know that, did you?" she said, running from the mortuary.

"And another pillar of the community bites the dust," Arthur said through clenched teeth.

Somehow, he had known all along that Kevin wasn't his son. He had never wanted to face the truth behind Irene's eager submission and hasty, panicked phone call. He smiled. It made no difference. He loved Kevin as much as he loved life. Kevin was his son by the right of love.

By the time Beth reached the sporting goods store her eyes were wild like those of a trapped animal. She raced up the loading dock steps and into the stock room. Frantically, she searched the area for some sign of Cader Harris. A hiss of sound escaped her parted lips as she saw him near a display of football helmets. "You're Kevin's father," she shrilled. "I heard my grandfather and mother talking this morning. My grandpa told my mother that you took money from him and went away because you didn't want Kevin. That was a disgusting thing to do. And it was disgusting of my grandfather to give you money; you're nothing but white trash. I heard my mother ask how much you took, but Grandpa wouldn't tell her. You want Kevin, don't you? Everyone wants Kevin. I told Daddy you were Kevin's father."

Cader Harris, stunned for the moment, could only stare at the wild-eyed girl in front of him. "You what?" he shouted, grabbing her by the arm.

"You heard me. I told Daddy you were Kevin's father, and do you know what he said? He said he didn't care. He said he loved Kevin. Everybody loves Kevin. Even Grandpa loves Kevin best, and now he's in the hospital. The ambulance took him a little while ago. And it's all because of you. Everything went wrong when you came back here. You don't belong here with the rest of us. You're nothing but trash," Beth said spitefully.

"You know something, kid? You're absolutely right. I don't belong here. I never did. But there's one thing you're wrong about. It's not me who's trash, it's you. They should lock you up and then throw away the key."

Long after Beth was gone, Cader Harris sat thinking. How could he have ever thought he loved Irene? She was just like Beth. In her own clutching way she would destroy Kevin just as Beth had tried to do. He shouldn't have talked to the girl that way; there was no excuse for it. He was an adult and she was a sick child. Jesus! And Arthur. Should he go to see him, say something? What the hell was there to say? Kevin was with the only father he knew. He wasn't that much of a bastard. A bastard, yes, but he would never do anything to hurt Kevin or Arthur. They had something special and he was fortunate to have been permitted to know them both even for a short while.

He hadn't lost a thing. If anything, he was a better person for this experience. He wasn't so tough after all. He hadn't lost a thing. He hadn't lost Irene because he never really had her. He hadn't lost Kevin; he had found Kevin. So he would leave, neither losing nor winning.

Arthur Thomas drove slowly down Jatha Hayden Boulevard. A deep crease of concern formed between his heavy brows. Christ! What a day! He still hadn't recovered from what Kevin had told him the night before about Beth trying to kill Judy Evans. But he didn't doubt his son's word for a minute. His son. Cader Harris's son. No, his son. All the years of love and companionship had to count for something. His feeling hadn't changed for the boy just because he had learned the truth. Nothing could stop him from loving Kevin.

Arthur's direction took him past Harris's sporting goods store. He frowned again when he noticed Irene's black Continental parked in the lot. His heart sank and his stomach churned. She was probably in there with Cader, breaking the wonderful news that he, not Arthur, was Kevin's father.

Making an illegal turn on the boulevard, he pulled into the lot beside Irene's car. As he parked, he pictured the scene he would have with Irene. She had been behaving strangely lately and now he knew why: Cader Harris.

Arthur glanced at the left rear tire of Irene's car. It looked like it could use air. He kicked at it to test it and suddenly wished he were kicking Irene. He realized in that split second that he had never liked her. Never had and never would. All that lovely Southern charm and grace had never done him one bit of good. It never had and never would.

Everything was going wrong. The whole town was off its axis. Ever since the beginning of the summer, after the high-school graduation. Ever since Cader Harris had come to town.

The town had already changed, and now that Delta Oil was a shoo-in to get that beach front, it would never be the same again. He was beginning to hate the town of Hayden and he was beginning to hate Irene. He leaned against the fender of her Continental and waited.

Irene stood facing Cader in the office of his shop. She ignored the cold light she saw in his eyes. She had come to tell him about Kevin, but she didn't know how to approach it. It wasn't something you could just blurt out.

Earlier that day, Beth had come running into the house. Her eyes were red with crying, and although Irene had determined to ignore the girl, Beth stood in front of her and screamed, "I did it! I went and told Daddy and I told Cader Harris what you and Grandpa were talking about this morning. And do you know what, Mama? They don't care! They don't care!" she shrieked on a higher note. "They don't care about anything except Kevin. They don't care about you any more than they care about me."

So, the cat was out of the bag at last. There was no going back, there was only the beautiful future to look forward to. Foster Doyle was struggling for his life in the hospital, but they said he would never be the same. That meant that she could finally take over where Foster Doyle left off. *She* would be the most important person in town. It was *her* decision that would count. And Cader, too, would profit from this new importance.

"Cader," she said, trying to get his attention. "I have the most wonderful news to tell you."

"Spit it out, Irene; I don't have time for games."

"It's about Delta Oil and you have me to thank for it," she hedged, pushing back the issue of their son, Kevin. She was still frightened that Cader would bolt and run. He might see Kevin as a responsibility, and she knew from experience that that was one fact of life Cader Harris couldn't handle. "The deal was closed a few minutes ago. I just came from the Town Hall."

Cader staggered under the news. Joy lit his face. He could almost feel the weight of the payoff from Delta in his pocket. "When? How?" he asked, temporarily forgetting about Kevin.

"Actually, it's still top secret. Two men from Delta Oil came into town a few days ago and clinched the deal with the town council this morning. Of course, everything is very hush hush. Delta is going to build a municipal swimming pool for the young people in place of the beach they'll be taking over. Also, they've promised to help with the school budget. No more sewing new gold braid on old band uniforms. Isn't it wonderful?"

Cader managed a smile through his confusion. Why

hadn't he been told? Suddenly, he realized why he hadn't heard from Delta Oil in two days. Just about the time the reps from Delta had come to town. Just when Sunny had told him about the two strangers and finding the executive ball pen with DELTA OIL inscribed on its side. Through his confusion, his smile brightened. What did it matter if they told him or not? They had to know it was due to his efforts that the deal was pushed through. Now he could leave with a quarter of a million bucks in his pocket as well as a contract as public relations man for their commercials. Irene was still babbling. He focused his attention on her and listened.

"And by the way, Cader," she said happily, "you'll be pleased to know that your reputation as our town celebrity has preceded you. One of Delta's men asked if I knew you, and, of course, I said yes. Anyway, he had a message for you. Some kind of football tactic, but it sounded so funny at the time that I laughed."

"What was it, Irene?"

"He told me to ask you if you'd ever heard of a kiss-off."

Cader's face fell. His stomach churned. Disbelief registered on his features and his fist tightened. Through fuzzy vision he could see Irene smiling up at him, pleased with herself. What had she said? He had her to thank? He got the message all right, and he knew what a kiss-off was. It was a big foot right up your ass.

Irene was puzzled by Cader's silence. He seemed to be thrown off balance. "Cade, there's something else, something I've got to tell you. . . ."

"If you're going to tell me that Kevin is my son, Irene, I know all about it."

"I know you do. Beth told me she came to see you. . . ."

"You don't understand, Irene. I didn't need Beth to tell me Kevin is my son. I've known all these years. Ever since I saw the announcement of his birth in the paper and I counted back on my fingers."

Irene was stunned by this announcement. Wildly, her mind raced, putting together the pieces of the puzzle. "You . . . you knew? And you never came back? For Kevin . . . for me?" she asked weakly.

"And if I had it to do all over again, Irene, I still wouldn't come back. Not for Kevin and especially not for you. I'm not Kevin's father, I only sired him. Arthur is the boy's father."

Irene snapped her gaping mouth shut. She refused to believe what she was hearing. "How much did my father pay you, Cader? What did I go for? What price did you put on your own child and me?"

"Around five thousand a year, tuition at Tulane and a Mercedes-Benz. Four years, Irene, and a new car every year."

"I see. I came cheap, didn't I?" Slowly, as though she were being dragged down into the depths of hell, she turned to him, a world of pleading in her eyes. "It doesn't matter. That was then; this is now. I love you, Cader; nothing can change that. And you love me, I know you do." She extended her hand, reaching to touch him.

Cader stepped backward, avoiding her touch, but his eyes held hers. "The same way you love Kevin?" he asked, his voice harsh. At her questioning look, he continued. "Kevin came here last night. He told me about Beth. I told him to go to his father. Now, I'm asking you, Irene, what are you going to do about it?"

"Do? What do you mean 'do'?"

"Yes," Cader smiled bitterly, "I can see why that question would be beyond your understanding. Beth tried to kill someone last night and she almost succeeded. She's a very sick girl and she's destroying Kevin. She crept into his bed, took advantage of the fact that he was blind drunk . . ." Exasperated, he demanded, "I'm asking you what you're going to do about it!"

Irene bristled. "What should I do? Expose the whole nasty business? Throw myself on the town's mercy? That little tramp Judy isn't going to say anything. . . ."

"You'd sacrifice Kevin so you could maintain your standing in the community," he said flatly. "I'm not concerned with you, Irene. What about Kevin?"

"He'll live with it and some day even forget it. . . ."

"That's not good enough and you know it!" he shouted. "You would destroy that kid; you'd throw him together with Beth until it happened again and again, until there's nothing left of him. Between you and your daughter, you'd eat him alive!" Sudden realization dawned on Harris. "Yes, you'd like that, wouldn't you? He's too strong for you now, but soon, after Beth bites away everything he believes in, everything he stands for, Kevin would be yours. He would never leave you. He'd be broken and as sick as Beth. And you would have won."

Irene shook her head in denial. "No, you're wrong. . . ."

"Kevin is the only decent part of your life, Irene. And I'm counting on Arthur to save him from you. Get out of here, Irene. I can't stand the sight of you. And I'm warning you, if Arthur doesn't make the right moves to protect Kevin from you, I'll have to take things into my own hands. And that you won't like, Irene, I promise you."

Irene lunged toward him, locking her arms around his neck. Her voice was shrill with desperation and her words came in a rush. "No, don't leave me. I'll do anything you say, only don't leave me. I love you, Cader. I don't want Beth; I don't need Kevin. . . ."

Cader wrestled her arms from their frantic clutch. "Arthur can save Kevin from your grip, Irene. But if I stayed with you, who would save me?" His words fell like stones. "Get out of here, Irene, you disgust me."

Slowly, in a moment that seemed like an eternity, Irene shrank away from him. He turned away from her, expecting to feel her claws rake his back. Instead, he heard the back door open and close.

When Irene Hayden Thomas walked out of the dim coolness of the sporting goods store and into the heat of the parking lot, she was startled to see Arthur leaning against her car. With an enormous amount of willpower, she managed to regain a semblance of composure. As she approached, she fidgeted with the sleeves of her blouse and flushed guiltily.

"What are you doing here, Arthur?" she managed to ask, choking back the tears she knew she would shed in private.

"Waiting for you, Irene." His voice was toneless, his eyes unreadable. "How nice to see you speechless for once," he added snidely. "I suppose you're expecting me to create a scene. Well, I won't. You're not worth it, Irene. I suppose I waited here to tell you I was leaving."

"Arthur! You can't! What about the children? And your business? You just can't leave. Where will you go?"

"I'm leaving, Irene. I think I would have eventually left even if I hadn't found out about you and Cader Harris."

"Arthur, what about me?" she whined in a shaky voice.

"What about you, Irene?"

"What will the children and I do without you? We need you, Arthur."

"You only need me to look respectable, Irene. You don't need me, Arthur Thomas, the man. You never did. I'll be by the house after dinner to pick up what I need. I'd appreciate it if you weren't home when I arrive. And I won't embarrass you by remaining in town. Kevin will be leaving with me."

Irene stared after him as he climbed into his car and started the engine. Her mind couldn't grasp what was happening to her. Yesterday she had so much and today she was left with nothing. Her eyes flicked back to the loading dock and the door into the store.

As Arthur backed his car out of its parking place, Irene waved frantically, mouthing something he couldn't hear over the whir of the air conditioner. He stopped and rolled down the window, leaning out to her.

Breathlessly, she ran over to him, her eyes wide and

questioning. "Arthur . . . I have to know . . . is this a kiss-off?"

Arthur expelled air from his lungs. He wouldn't ever understand her, not if he lived to be a hundred. With great patience he nodded and said, "Yes, Irene, this is a kiss-off." He gunned the motor and left her standing alone in the parking lot. It was one of the few times he had ever seen genuine comprehension in his wife's eyes.

Chapter Eighteen

Keli McDermott sat on the edge of her bed, her suitcase open but empty. What should she take with her? What did one take to the hospital to have one's breast removed? There was no doubt whatsoever in her mind that she would return less than whole. But she would return, and she would be alive, even if it was just for a little while.

Toothbrush, comb and brush, slippers, robe, nightgown. Those few things didn't fill the yawning suitcase. Different clothes to come home in? Was this home? Could it ever be home again?

As she packed, she could hear the furious sounds of Gene's typewriter. He had said he was nearing the completion of his book. He wanted the world to know that Colonel Gene McDermott, USAF, Ret., had done his bit.

The click-click of the typewriter followed Keli down the hall. She heard it stop for a moment as she passed the open door of Gene's study with her suitcase in hand. She took the luggage out to the car, and, when she returned, the rhythm of the electric machine had altered slightly. Almost as though it was drawing to a close. She could always tell when Gene was winding down. Did that mean the book was finally finished? Would he come out of that room now? He had closeted himself in there ever since the afternoon Marsha had come over begging her to keep her appointment in New Orleans. The afternoon Keli had told both Gene and Marsha that she had already decided to go and do whatever was necessary to save her own life.

After Marsha had left, pursued from the house by an irate, enraged Gene, he hadn't said a word to Keli. He had just looked at her as though she were a stranger to him. Then he had gone into his study, and his typewriter had clacked almost ceaselessly until now. No words, no explanations, nothing. It was almost as though she had simply ceased to exist.

She could tell him she was leaving. She could risk his trying to stop her. Or she could simply drive into New Orleans tomorrow and sign herself into the hospital. Later. She would decide later.

As Keli stood at her open bedroom window, she thought what a beautiful night it was. The crickets sounded joyous. She smiled. The world would be such a beautiful place if everyone could be happy.

Keli needed support and comforting; something she could never find behind the locked study door where Gene worked on his book. More, she needed these things from Damion. Desperately. Something inside her told her that Damion needed her too. Damion.

Keli had no second thoughts. There was no fear or daring in her as she picked up her car keys from the dresser. Damion told her she had a choice. Choice. Damion *was* her choice.

Through the door and down the stairs, out the door and down the porch and across the lawn to her car. Damion was her choice. She needed; she wanted.

Out of her car, across the parking lot, up the parsonage steps. She blinked and stood back as the sound of the door chimes rang in her ears. Soft yellow light from the porch lantern cloaked her in its aura.

Damion Conway opened the door and smiled down at his visitor. Keli didn't move but stood gazing up at him, her face quiet and serene. "I've decided to go to New Orleans tomorrow. I'll check into the hospital and see the surgeon Marc Baldwin told me about. My bag is in the car. It is my choice. Mine alone."

So many words, Damion thought. So many words from Keli. She seemed to need to tell someone, to talk until her words were exhausted. She needed someone to listen to her. Just listen. Silently, he stood aside, motioning her to enter.

A veil dropped over Keli's eyes and her resistance became a reality. Damion sighed forlornly. The need to talk, to be understood, was there, but his finely honed instincts concerning Keli told him she hadn't been able to muster the courage she needed to confide her feelings.

Looking into his eyes with a silent plea he could not

answer, Keli turned and walked away, her back straight and unyielding.

"Keli," he called softly after her, "I'm here when you need me. I want you to need me, Keli. Not to make decisions for you, but to support you in your own decisions. Don't do this to yourself, Keli. Don't do this to us."

Feeling as though he were locked in a vacuum, he watched her continue down the walk. No sound came to his ears but the slight click of her heels against the flagstones; no sight filled his senses except the vision of her slight frame, dark hair swinging around her hips as she turned away from him.

Head held high, tears blinding her vision, Keli returned to her car in the parking lot next to the church. She had made her decision, but, God help her, she was afraid. Afraid of being mutilated, afraid of dying, afraid of being alone. Afraid that she would never know what it was to reach out to someone who loved her, someone that she loved.

She imagined she heard Damion close the door as she walked down the path. A lonely sound, a sound that shut her out. She had shut herself out. Away from Damion.

She stood there in the half-light for what seemed an eternity. Thoughts whirled around in her head, questions beat at her, and always she knew her answers would be found with Damion.

Shoulders squared, chin lifted high, eyes bright with triumph, Keli walked determinedly back to the parsonage. As she took the last few steps she felt as though her feet weren't touching the ground. Thrusting the door open, she called for him.

The first floor was deserted, and, as she mounted the stairs, she heard the running shower. She followed the sound, noticing the cigarette burning away in the large ashtray on Damion's nightstand and the trail of discarded clothing leading to the bathroom.

Not allowing herself a second thought, she pulled off her clothes, kicked her shoes beside Damion's near the bed, and stalked into the steamy, tiled bathroom. Seeming to have a will of its own, her hand flung back the shower curtain and she stepped in.

Surprise marked Damion's face. A warm, welcoming expression lighted his dark eyes as he smiled and gathered her to him under the warm, needle spray.

As Keli felt the imprint of his eyes on her water-beaded body, she experienced a thrill tingling the insides of her thighs. She pressed closer to him as she raised her open lips to his, and he kissed her as though he were sipping the sweetest wine.

His hands possessed her tenderly, bringing her closer, always closer.

Damion gazed down at her with such love and tenderness that Keli began to tremble. With an answering look from her, he lifted her into his arms and carried her out of the shower stall and into the bedroom. He settled her down on the bed and lay beside her, encircling her in his arms and breathing in the delicious scent of her.

Keli pulled away from him, rising up from his arms and

turning to face him. "Not yet, Damion," she protested, "I want to tell you something first." Her soft doe eyes locked with his and her intensity moved him. "Tonight, I am a whole woman. By tomorrow, I may not be. I want you to make love to me, Damion. To me, Keli, the whole person. Tonight. Now. I want to know what it is to lie beside the man I love while I'm still whole. I've never been with a man, Damion. I'm a virgin. I want to know, to remember, while I still can."

Damion looked deeply into her eyes and found peace there. His love shone upon her as he said gently, "Keli, you will always be a whole woman. A whole person. Surgery won't change you, or what's inside here," he touched a finger to her breast over her heart.

"Do you want me?"

"God only knows how I want you. I love you, Keli. You're the most beautiful creature I've ever seen. I've loved you from the moment I first saw you. It's something that's been growing inside me ever since time began to have any meaning for me. You have to know that it's you I love, Keli, not your physical perfection. I love the woman you are, not the woman's body. When I make love to you, it will be as a man who loves a woman. You must understand that, Keli, and know it with your heart. Because it won't be just for tonight, but forever. And when you leave for New Orleans tomorrow, you won't be alone. I'll be with you."

Keli looked down into his beloved face, tears welling in her eyes. Tears of happiness. It would have to be forever. He wouldn't be used. Not even because he loved her. "I understand, Damion. And the woman you make love to will love you as a woman loves a man," she told him, her eyes shining brightly as she fell into his arms and whispered, "Show me how you love me, Damion. Show me."

Gene McDermott typed the last word of his manuscript just as Keli closed the car door. It was finished. Carefully, his movements sure and precise, he stacked the pages of his book and placed them inside his desk drawer. He covered the typewriter, but not until after he had pulled the plug and wrapped the cord around the carriage knobs.

When the engine of Keli's car sprang to life, he walked over to the table and withdrew his service revolver. There was no point to looking to see if the bullet was in the chamber. Only fools kept empty guns as a threat.

He clicked back the hammer and stood in front of the full-length mirror on the closet door. The moment he heard the car pull away from the curb, he placed the gun to his temple and pulled the trigger.

Chapter Nineteen

Damion opened the door for Keli and then climbed behind the wheel of his car. "Are you certain, Keli, that you don't want to stop at your house before we leave?" he asked quietly.

"There's no reason for me to stop. My bag is in the trunk. It is my choice, my decision. I will not return. I told you last night when we talked. I'm so glad you're going with me, Damion."

Damion's voice was gentle, loving, when he spoke. "I'll always be with you, honey."

Keli smiled. No matter what happened, no matter what the outcome of her appointment in New Orleans, all was right with her world.

"I called the Bishop early this morning, and he's sending a new minister on the afternoon plane." Keli touched his arm, her hand gentle, her eyes understanding. "It's just as well that we're leaving. Hayden will never be the same again. It will grow and prosper with Delta Oil calling the shots."

"What happened, Damion?" Keli asked hesitantly.

"I wish I knew. I've tried to think it through and analyze it, and the only thing I can come up with is Cader Harris. As soon as he arrived, he brought out the worst and the best in all of us. He's a catalyst; he makes things happen. No matter where Cader Harris goes, he takes trouble with him, and if he fails in that, then he stirs it up. I suppose he'll be leaving soon, too."

Damion pulled the car over to the side of the road and turned to Keli. "Look back if you want to; we're leaving Hayden. Once we get on the interstate, Hayden will be part of the past, nothing more than a memory."

"I don't need memories, Damion. I have the one I want, and he's sitting here beside me."

Arthur rummaged through the assorted litter that had accumulated in the rear storage closet for the past eighteen years. Deciding he had chosen those things he wanted to keep, he tied the large cardboard carton with rope, looping the knot tightly.

He walked to the back of the mortuary and called through the door of the preparation room. "Destry, can you come out here a minute?"

Destry stood in the doorway, his spotless white smock fitting him as though it were tailor made. Arthur sighed.

He had rented his smocks from the same laundry, and his whites never fitted him that way. Destry looked down at the heavy, bulging carton.

"This is the last of it, Destry. You're on your own now." His tone, instead of sounding melancholy as Destry would have expected, seeing that Arthur had run the business for eighteen years, sounded relieved. As though a two-ton weight had been lifted from his squat shoulders.

Arthur extended his hand and Destry shook it warmly. "Good luck to you, Mr. Thomas."

"The same to you, Destry. I know you'll make a go of it. You know the business inside and out. I guess this is good-bye."

Destry watched him until he was out of sight. He had never seen such an unhappy man. Yet, there was something in Arthur Thomas's eyes that sparkled with hope. Destry shrugged. With a proprietorial eye, he cast his glance around the office. This was his now, all his. Who would have ever thought it? He hadn't believed Arthur when he approached him yesterday afternoon about buying out the business. As if a black man could ever have that much money. But Arthur had been serious, so serious he had dragged Destry off to the bank to make the necessary arrangements. Monthly payments and terms stating a percentage of the profits to be paid at the end of each fiscal year, after taxes. It was an opportunity not to be refused.

Destry carried himself with new authority as he sashayed through what now belonged to him. His long brown fingers possessively touched the furniture and the

ight fixtures. This was his, all his. He became reflective
and wondered if Mr. Thomas were telling the truth when
he said he was going back to medical school to become a
medical examiner. Destry smiled. Arthur intended to give
Quincy, that TV M.E., a run for his money.

Destry leaned back against an ornate bronze coffin in
the display room and pondered his next move. He would
have to hire a white mortician. Black men weren't supposed to embalm white folks. Not in the heart of Dixie,
anyway. He laughed. Wait till he told Aunt Cledie he was
taking over the business. Destry laughed, a great roaring,
booming sound as he slapped the cold metal coffin. Aunt
Cledie would piss her drawers.

Arthur parked the car at the curb near the sporting goods
store and motioned for Kevin to remain seated while he
went inside. Kevin was puzzled, but nodded. Arthur opened
the door and walked over to Cader Harris. "Mr. Harris, I'm
Arthur Thomas," he said, holding out his hand. "I'm sorry
we haven't had a chance to meet before this. I wanted to
stop by before leaving Hayden to tell you I appreciate what
you've done for Kevin. I know that he came here first the
other night and that you sent him home to me."

"Mr. Thomas, the boy would have gone to you on his
own. He just happened to see me first. I gave him the best
advice a friend could give. I hope you understand that."
Arthur's eyes smiled at the word "friend." Cader continued. "If it's all right with you, I would like to keep in touch
with Kevin, but only if you agree."

"The boy needs both of us, Mr. Harris. I want you to know that I'll always do the best I can for Kevin."

"What more could I ask?" Cader grinned, sticking out his hand. That damnable lump was back in his throat and from the looks of Arthur Thomas he had the same in his own throat.

"Kevin's in the car. He wanted to come in, but I asked him to wait outside. I'd like it if you'd come out and say goodbye."

"I'm sorry we didn't meet under other circumstances," Cader said honestly.

"I am too. Good luck with the store."

Cader laughed. "You aren't the only one leaving. I'm closing up shop and leaving here . . . alone."

Arthur Thomas watched Cader as he stuck his head in the window and talked with Kevin. Arthur should hate Cader, hate him, and Irene too, but he didn't. Kevin was the only one who was important. Arthur understood that and Cader Harris understood.

Cader Harris stood back from the curb and watched the car drive off. Jesus, he felt good. And it had nothing to do with his cock. Goddamn, he felt good. Yo!

Cader Harris hefted the duffel bag over his shoulder and grimaced. He was leaving Hayden almost the same way he had left it the first time. With all his worldly possessions stuffed in an army surplus duffel bag. Only this time he didn't have the prospect of college or a burgeoning career on the gridiron. So he bombed out. It happened to the best of men. At least he had his Beechcraft in the hangar at the airport. When he ran out of cash for fuel, he supposed he could sell it.

Cader wasn't sorry to leave Hayden. Christ! He couldn't wait to shed the stink of the place. "This has got to be the hellhole of the universe," he muttered, "and that's being kind."

He couldn't let it get to him; if he did, he was finished. It was New York and the rounds of seeing the ad boys. All those long-distance phone calls he had charged to Delta Oil would certainly bear some kind of fruit. He had four nibbles for commercials. He was photogenic; he couldn't miss. Just flash the old ivories. What the hell, a buck was a buck.

"And where do you think you're going?" Sunday Waters demanded as she closed the door of the shop.

"New York and commercials. That's all that's left, baby. I blew the deal, and I can't wait to wash the stink of this town off me."

"I'm coming with you. My bags are on the way to the airfield. You're not getting away from me again. See this?" She waved an oblong strip of green paper under his nose. She danced away as he made a grab for the paper. "No strings, no ties, just this little piece of paper. If either of us wants to walk, no explanations are necessary," she teased, still waving the slip. "A yes or a no, Cade."

"It would help if I knew what you've got there."

"It's the same thing as a marriage license, Cader. You want this, you've got to marry me." She held out her hand, offering him the strip.

Cader Harris stared in amazement at the narrow slip. A check for one hundred and fifty thousand dollars, compliments of Delta Oil, made out to Sunday and Cader Harris. Cader's mind raced. "Look, Sunny . . ." he stammered, "you can believe this or not. But I was going to stop by to ask you if you wanted to see the big city. I've been looking for someone to wash my socks for a long time." He grinned sheepishly. "Besides, you're the best piece of ass I've ever had."

Sunday laughed. "You're a first-class fuck, Cader Harris. Every time you tell a lie, you grin and show all forty-two teeth. But face it, I've got you by the short hairs . . . and every time you stray, I'm gonna reel you back in."

He knew he should ask her how she managed to wrangle the check out of Delta, but it didn't seem important right now. All that mattered was that it was here in his hand and it was already beginning to burn his fingers. He looked at Sunny and could see she expected him to ask questions. She was ready to bust with the answers. "So, okay," he grinned, creasing the check and stuffing it in his pocket, "tell me how you got it."

"It's simple. For once in your life you told the truth. You told me about your deal with Delta. When it looked like they were going to leave you out in the cold, I went to see those two guys staying in the motel behind the Lemon Drop. I told them what I knew. That it wouldn't be just your word against theirs, and how, together, we could make it pretty sticky for them here in Hayden. That's our payoff. You've noticed how it's made out, of course. For some reason they assumed I was already your wife. Any other questions?"

Never one to look a gift horse in the mouth, Cader showed all forty-two teeth again and said, "Wanna get married? They'll cash the check, no trouble, in Las Vegas."

"I thought you'd never ask." Sunny laughed.

The air was balmy, more like an Indian summer day than a day in late August. Irene Thomas sat in the breakfast nook and lit her ninth cigarette of the morning. She drew the smoke deeply into her lungs and then exhaled it forcefully. If she had been a gambling woman, she would have known how to lose gracefully, but since she wasn't, she felt at a loss. Arthur was gone, Kevin was lost to her, and Cader, her wild love, was gone. And all because of Beth. How was she to fill her days? What was she going to do with herself in the long winter evenings to come? Busywork bothered her and she hated it. Committee meetings were usually over by nine P.M. and then she would have to return home to an empty house. No, it would only be empty if she made a decision to send Beth away. As long as Beth was around, the house wouldn't be empty.

Irene crushed out the cigarette and glanced at the kitchen clock. It was after ten and she should be doing something, anything, but not sitting here thinking morbid thoughts. She had the day to get through. She could start by planning the dinner menu. Meat loaf could now be served without any complaints. Beth loved meat loaf, and she herself could eat it when there was nothing else available. She would make a note for Dulcie and leave it on the kitchen counter. A trip to the hospital to see her father. How depressing. She didn't want or need that feeling, and she hated all the young nurses in their tight uniforms. Foster Doyle hated it when she went to the hospital and sat in the dark brown chair, staring at him. His eyes killed her over and over as she returned his unblinking gaze. He should have died three days ago, but he was still lingering on and the doctors just shrugged and said it was a miracle that he was hanging on like he was. Those doctors could think that all they wanted. Foster Doyle Hayden would hang on until he saw her blink. Life did go on. She would go and sit in the sterile room for three hours, pat him on the hand and stare at him. She smiled slightly. What she was doing was called "the right of divine retribution." That was two decisions she had made in only the space of a few minutes. Now, she would check on Arthur's daughter and see how she was doing.

Beth sat in the window seat and watched a fat blue jay drag a worm into his nest. Her eyes went to the double-edged razor blade she had partially unwrapped. If Kevin didn't call by tonight, she would use it on her wrists. Carefully, she closed the thin paper over the blade and laid it back on the dresser. The blue jay struggled and managed to get the bulging pink worm over the side of the nest. If he didn't call tonight, she would give him till noon tomorrow. Then she would use the razor blade. Perhaps that was too soon. He had to sign in and get all settled. Tomorrow night. He should call by tomorrow night.

The blue jay was out of sight, now content with his breakfast. Friday or Saturday might be soon enough. She picked up the razor blade and put it under the blotter of her desk. It would be there when she needed it.

"Beth, I'm going to go to the hospital to see your grand-father. Do you want to come along?" Irene called from the hallway.

"No, Mama, I'm waiting for Kevin to call."

Catch up with love...
Catch up with passion...
Catch up with danger....

Catch a bestseller from Pocket Books!